THE REUNION

THE REUNION

Tim Nichols

iUniverse, Inc.
New York Lincoln Shanghai

The Reunion

Copyright © 2005 by Timothy R. Nichols

iUniverse books may be ordered through booksellers or by contacting:

iUniverse
2021 Pine Lake Road, Suite 100
Lincoln, NE 68512
www.iuniverse.com
1-800-Authors (1-800-288-4677)

ISBN-13: 978-0-595-34948-7 (pbk)
ISBN-13: 978-0-595-79661-8 (ebk)
ISBN-10: 0-595-34948-X (pbk)
ISBN-10: 0-595-79661-3 (ebk)

Printed in the United States of America

CHAPTER I

ONE NEVER KNOWS

John McMorrow's clean white shirt, black bow tie, and neat black coat without a speck of lint spoke of the professor's ordinary ways, but crimson splotches of blood on his white cuffs protruding beyond his coat sleeves said that things had changed for the moment. John straddled the big student sprawled on the floor. The professor's hands restrained the student's wrists against the polished wooden planks.

The student clutched a Bowie knife in his right fist. The blade slashed John's sleeve, cutting away a gold button that clinked when it landed to the side.

"Git off me! I ain't finished with 'im yet." The student, dressed in the same white shirt, bow tie, and black coat worn by all his classmates in this small college in Clarksburg, Virginia, spit out the words with a gurgle. Blood ran from his nose into his mouth and down both sides of his face, but he seemed not to notice. The front of his shirt was speckled with red. Drops of the student's blood dripped from John's nose too. The louder the student shouted his demands, the higher the sporadic blasts of blood shot onto John McMorrow's face and into his dark hair and beard.

"Drop the knife! It's over, man, it's over."

The flashing blade jabbed and probed the air as far as the pinned fist could stab it. The student's whole body bucked. Knees kicked at John's back, landing soft blows that were not about to dislodge the professor.

John looked up at the circle of young men, the mob that only moments before had been an orderly body of students sitting at desks in neat rows. Now the desks cluttered the edges of the room while students elbowed for positions with a view.

"Somebody go for the sheriff. Get the knife! I can't hold him all day."

"It won't matter," sputtered the student on the floor. "I'll get him sooner or later."

"This isn't Kansas," the professor said. "You're in Virginia now."

A booted foot came out of the crowd and kicked at the knife. The man on the floor, still clutching the handle, tilted his head back, glaring at the owner of the boot.

"None of you get it. Only one way to silence an abolitionist," said the student pinned to the floor.

Someone threw a greasy cloth, that had been hanging on a nail beside the stove, over the young man's bloody face. Then the boot stomped the fist. The knife clanked onto the boards.

The sheriff came and took the student away in handcuffs.

John McMorrow stood, looked around at gaping eyes, and felt the responsibility to put back the pieces of the shattered decorum of his classroom. He started to brush his coat with his right hand, but stopped when he remembered the blood. After a deep breath he said, "I'd be grateful if you gentlemen would put the desks in order while I go wash up a bit."

As he walked out the door John felt a sense of temporary accomplishment as the sound of scooting desks echoed from the walls. Down the hall, now filled with miscellaneous students and teachers with gawking eyes and questioning expressions, he went out the door. Pain shot through his knuckles when he cranked the pump handle. The cold water magnified the throbbing ache as he washed, but it felt glorious as he rinsed another's blood and his own sweat from his face.

Returning to the classroom, he found the desks lined up in their neat rows and students sitting in their appointed places. Above the hubbub of students sorting out and recounting what had happened, he said, "Now then, where were we?"

The students responded with silence

"Let me remind the class that this is a course of study in philosophy. We talk about ideas here. Logic. That's what it's about. Reasoning our way to rational conclusions. If your ideas differ from those of another, that's good. Contradictory ideas give us material with which to work. Debate is a healthy thing. Come now, where were we?"

No one spoke.

"Listen to me," the professor shouted. "The incident we've just witnessed proves the value of this very point! Persuasion is born of ideas. True convictions rest upon careful thought. A man who lets himself be bullied into nodding his head in agreement with the position of another has not been persuaded. He's been coerced! Gentlemen engage in honorable debate. All matters of disagreement can be settled that way. To allow petty thugs to close our mouths by the use of knives and guns is to turn the world over to them. Debate is better than bloodshed. Violence ends debate. Coercion chokes off logic."

John paused again, waiting for someone to move the discussion forward. Still, no one spoke. He reached for a newspaper that had been rumpled in the fray just moments before. Someone had returned it to his desk. He picked it up and waved it before the class.

"There's more than one point of view on every subject. For every voice that favors an idea there's another to say it's very wrong. It's not about counting noses. It's about reasoning your way through what folks are saying until you're satisfied you've found the truth. It's not a matter of letting the man who yells loudest to have his way."

The professor slammed the newspaper onto his desk for effect. He saw the side facing up, the side he had been waving before the students. It was splattered with blood.

"Now then," he said, looking at the student in the third row who had last spoken before the outburst. "You were saying that you favor laws that would abolish slavery once and for all. No shame in that. It's clear that not everyone agrees with your point of view." His eyes swept the room. "I assume that there might yet be others in this very room who disagree with you. I trust they're not hiding knives or guns beneath their coats, but I hope they'll speak their mind, offer their reasons. This is just one of thousands of subjects that we'll need to examine using the tools I'm trying to give you. Gather the facts. Think about them. Let them take you wherever they naturally lead."

Finally, a student sitting near the window raised a hand. John acknowledged it.

"What kinds of facts settle the slavery question?" the student asked.

"Examine what you already hold to be true for a start. The Bible. The golden rule. Do these bear on the question? The Constitution. If you consider it the final arbiter in disputes involving civil affairs, then maybe the Constitution would be the place to start. History."

John raised his eyes above the students. A likeness of George Washington hung on the back wall.

"Some of our founders who drafted the Constitution owned slaves. Maybe that's a fact to remember." He cringed at his own words that might seem to argue against his own conviction that slavery was a great evil, contrary to the golden rule. Then he congratulated himself for the unbiased mention of the facts that came to mind.

The professor pulled his watch from his pocket, saw that it was passed time to end, and dismissed the students.

Young men shuffled out. John felt bewildered about what he had accomplished. Apart from the pro-slavery ruffian from Kansas, none seemed offended by anything he had said or done. He was sure that the turmoil they had all experienced would be the talk of the town for awhile. It pleased John to notice one fellow moving toward him rather than the door. He cherished the thought that this student might want to dig deep into the big questions of the day.

"Mr. McMorrow," the young man started.

"Yes?"

"Will there be much on the examination from that last part of today's lecture? I had trouble following it."

With a sigh of relief—and anguish—-John McMorrow replied, "One never knows. One never knows."

The young man went out.

$$*\quad*\quad*\quad*$$

SHE WOULD MARRY SOMEONE

Anna Lee sat on the porch swing with her lap desk, alternating between reading a book and writing in her journal as serious thoughts came to her. She had finished feeding the chickens, weeding the bean patch, and gathering the roasting ears her mother had asked her to fetch. The corn husks, turned inside out, lay at her feet. She would get to them after supper when the barren cobs could be added to the pile and disposed of at the same time. The water would be boiling soon and she would help her mother prepare supper. Katie, Anna Lee's older sister, sat on the steps and read a book of her own. This happy, settled family was content in its snug little hollow in the hills just west of Grafton, Virginia.

Anna Lee had slowly grown to awareness that she was unusually intelligent. Her modesty would not allow her to speak of it, but she had the vague sense of it. As a child it had confused her. When others seemed not to understand things that were obvious to her, she sometimes assumed that she was the one not catching what others were seeing, yet the facts often demanded what Anna Lee could not easily dismiss in deference to others. When she attended the little school in town, she grasped ideas quickly and advanced rapidly in the grades. She had thrilled to read great literature and to live for brief periods of time in far away places involved in dramatic events. She saw the green grass in books, felt the breezes, and smelled the salt of the sea. Anna Lee saw the colors of exotic plants, and touched the textures of garments portrayed by ink on paper. Mathematics stimulated her. Others judged it a barren and useless chore. The relations between numbers and quantities and the calculations that could be made of things seemed almost magical. School taught her that consensus does not define truth. There was room for self-trust regarding verifiable things. Regarding all other matters, she had concluded that divergent opinions held by others were tolerable as long as they were not forcefully pressed. Her self-awareness pulled Anna Lee into herself. Girls were not supposed to have the capacity or the interest that had become involuntarily evident to Anna Lee in herself. She would search for ways to be useful with a deliberate measure of restraint in revealing her abilities to others. She determined to become neither an ostentatious freak nor a passive bootlicker. Anna Lee would wait to marry until she had found a man who would be prepared to appreciate and benefit from her abilities without competing with them or stifling them because they threatened him. She would marry someone who was secure enough to stand on his own two feet without her, but who could stand taller and stronger with her help.

Her father worked the farm and sometimes did odd jobs in the area. Her mother labored to maintain the kitchen garden. The home place nestled between the hills stayed clean and tidy because of the joint efforts of all four. Everyone fit. Mr. Stone struggled with the business end of things, but Mother had a knack for keeping the books and accounts up-to-date and clear. Anna Lee had assumed, in her early years, that this was the way of all families. When she saw other men faltering, who seemed as equally skilled and hardworking as her father, she wondered why their wives did not make things work. Now she understood that families organized themselves differently. She saw how her parents complemented one another. She wondered how well her father might have done without her mother. In the bad years when the crops failed Anna Lee had seen her father's face in his hands and her mother's hand on his shoulder, assuring him that they had enough stored away to get by the winter and into the spring. She had heard her parents discussing how to overcome one problem after another and she took note that her mother had often gently nudged them to sound decisions without making demands or insisting upon any particular course of action. It dawned on Anna Lee, now that she was nearing her nineteenth year, that her father had earned his reputation as an honest and industrious man with the help—and even guidance—of her soft-spoken mother, who had kept out of sight most of the time. Had her father married another, things might have been different.

The future was now a matter of focused interest for Anna Lee. A fellow over in town was earnestly courting Katie and folks teased about wedding bells, babies, and changes. This unsettled Anna Lee. Her pleasant, settled world was changing. Katie's suitor seemed a good man, but he was not one of *us*. *Can our circle expand to include him?* When this suitor tried to tell a story that made no sense to anyone in the family, Anna Lee was uncomfortable with the perplexed look on her father's face. She was relieved when her mother rescued everyone from puzzled silence by saying simply, "Well, that's a new one for me." Mother seemed often to know the simplest way to untie a tangled knot. Katie seemed disposed to accept some proposal of marriage, but no one spoke about it openly. Their father expressed no disapproval, but he had not said much in the way of approval either. The family held its collective breath without mentioning the woozy feeling produced by the lack of oxygen.

These developments touched Anna Lee, not only because they had to do with the sister she loved and the family she cherished, but also because they had to do with her own future. She wanted to observe the process and give thought to her own manner of dealing with these mystifying transactions when it came her turn. No one had noticed the looks that had passed between Anna Lee and Micah Johnson. The brief lingering moments under the apple tree after services had not provoked comment. Anna Lee was not sure what to make of them herself. She had found herself sitting beside him at the church picnic a few weeks before. Sitting on the porch, she relived the rare excitement. When their elbows had brushed together, she noticed that he took more than the customary time to pull his away. Hers stayed put. This happened more than a few times that day. Micah was passionate when he spoke of what goes into making a first-class rifle and mentioned that he was getting close to mastering the art. Micah had a faraway look in his eyes, scanning the mountaintop, when he said with obvious exhilaration, "And I'll be getting my own set of tools." She was impressed, not with gun-making itself and all the intricate details about the boring tool and the rifling machine, but with the joy he expressed in learning and growing in a productive way that brought him pleasure. This set Micah Johnson apart from other men. He was driven to use his hands to develop his skills in much the same way that Anna Lee wanted to increase her knowledge of things beyond the farm and the town. In quiet, analytic fashion she calculated how she might help Micah in ways that paralleled her mother's shared life with her father. These fleeting thoughts came to Anna Lee as she thought about her sister and the suitor.

Anna Lee was aware of her beauty. She would not speak of it aloud, but she was sensible to the reality. Folks turned heads when Anna Lee entered the room. This had not always been true. As a child Anna Lee had been quite homely. Overnight she blossomed. Her father had always told her that she was "the prettiest girl" he had ever seen. He said that about Katie too. Her mother agreed but then added, "Pretty is as pretty does" or "There's more to life than being pretty." Anna Lee's family kept it an issue of small importance. Her mother emphasized inner qualities. At the same time, her mother was perfectly willing to help Anna Lee and Katie fix their hair and order their clothing to advantage. She beamed when they looked their best, but to Anna Lee it was more akin to playing with dolls at home than it was preparation for public display. It was like her father's habit of caring for the animals as though he intended to exhibit them at the county fair, even when he had no plan to show them to anyone at all.

Anna Lee had determined not to use her appearance to unfair advantage. She would wait for the right man to show her attention for more than just the pleasure of seeing and touching her beauty. She longed to give him that pleasure and yearned to share in it, but she would not knowingly use it as bait to catch a man who could not also love her for whom she was apart from her striking looks. She kept this in the solitude of her mind and discussed it with no one. She underlined Proverbs 31:30 in her Bible: "Favour is deceitful, and beauty is vain: but a woman that feareth the Lord, she shall be praised." She took her mother's words to heart and sought those virtues in life that surpass mere physical beauty in importance.

"I wonder if I might have some help in the kitchen?" a quiet voice asked from the door that neither daughter had heard opening. Anna Lee quickly put away her things and followed close at Katie's heels as they raced to help Mrs. Stone.

*   *   *   *

I COULD NEVER CAST THE BRASS

Micah Johnson ran his rough hand along the milled stock of curly maple. It was the next of many that he had made without supervision. With some smoothing off and generous applications of boiled linseed oil it would be ready to fit onto the barrel that Micah had manufactured without a soul looking over his shoulder. He was only days away from presenting it to the fellow who had ordered it. *What will be his reaction?* Micah wondered. *It will have no visible flaws.* He knew that it would pass inspection with the man who had spent so much time training him in the vanishing art. Rifles were produced in the north and in Europe at a much faster rate using methods of mass production, but those, to Micah, were not works of art. He was proud of the accuracy, careful craftsmanship, and beauty of his rifles. This one was the finest he had made with his own hands.

It was time to close up shop but Micah could not find a stopping place. He imagined how the powerful, promising grain would be drawn out by the oil and made to look like a cross between tiger stripes and Anna Lee's curled hair. *After I've worked in the oil, it will shine.* The engraving would bear the markings of the man he had served so long in apprenticeship, but it was Micah's own product.

Micah wondered if the buyer would appreciate its unique qualities. A rifle this nice, with this grain, really ought to be fitted with all the showy brass fittings. *I wonder if the buyer would consider adding them? If he doesn't want to pay for them, maybe I could just do it anyway, with his permission.* And then he remembered what his master teacher had warned: "You can't give away your services, son. You have to let folks decide what they're willing to pay for and give them that much and no more. If looking at our examples of how the brass furniture looks is not enough to convince them to pay for it, you just have to let them go off with what looks to you like an unfinished rifle." It made sense to Micah—from a business point of view. But Micah had become an artist. What he sculpted in wood and steel was more than a product to sell. All of his rifles would shoot straight and true. Many a deer and wild turkey would be in the stew pot not long after these muzzles roared. He could pick up any one of these rifles and knock the eyeball out a chipmunk—the perennial standard—at 200 yards with a rest. He could drop a deer at 300 yards with relative ease—and he knew men who had claimed to do so at much greater distances—although he wondered if their measurements were made by pacing off or by sounding off to their friends. Distance can stretch a bit with the retelling. His own measurements were exact. He told of them to inform patrons of the capacity of the rifle rather than to impress them with his skill. If anything, Micah was more inclined to shave off a bit of the distance so as to be sure not to misinform.

From all indications, Micah would soon be given leave to set up his own shop. Micah Johnson had stuck it out and paid his dues. He knew it. His teacher knew it. It had been a hard row to hoe. At the beginning he had felt humiliated at the flaws pointed out to him in his workmanship. He had silently resented what often seemed like nit-picking criticism. Micah's teacher had told him that he tried to work too fast and then he had been asked to account for the time he had taken to accomplish his work. The master craftsman who taught Micah had been impatient with Micah's progress at first—and slow to see improvement. Incrementally, however, Micah had grown from novice to expert. He now recognized that he had been treated appropriately—if not always kindly—along the way.

He reckoned that he would open his own shop some distance from Grafton. This was not entirely out of deference to his teacher, although it was partly out of that. The young artisan knew that competition with his teacher would be stiff if he remained too near and that rivalry would hinder them both. Maybe in a few years, after his teacher retired, he would come back.

Micah could continue to work in his present arrangement for years to come if he chose. His readiness to strike out on his own, experiment with his own designs, build an independent reputation, have his own name on the rifles, and other such hungers combined to nudge him out. He might compete with other gunsmiths, but not with his old teacher. He cast his thoughts about in search of a location at which to build a life.

Ruminations about his future naturally opened a place for a wife—and then children. Micah had given only passing thought to these until recently. He always had appreciated the beauty of certain ladies. His fantasies involved more than he knew to be morally right. He felt a passing sense of shame. Now Micah anticipated the day he would marry, carry his lovely bride across the threshold at his new home—wherever that would be—and then slowly open the gift that had been waiting for him as a glorious present under the Christmas tree and then taste the delights that would be found there. These were misty visions of a hazy future. He dressed the faceless woman in a wedding gown to make his visions more acceptable to his moral leanings, but he still fought with the rules and knew he ought to rein in his thoughts.

Passionate images did not always intrude against Micah's will. Sometimes he slowly and deliberately invited them—pursued them—and enjoyed them. Guilt and pleasure, repentance and ecstasy, were partners—and enemies—in his exploration of the edges of the permissible and probes into the territory of things hoped for. He thought of the danger of putting gunpowder too near to flame, or even near what might make a spark. He would keep the flame where it belonged, he believed, and be as fully aware of the explosive powder as his moral nature insisted.

Sparks had recently erupted. Anna Lee had held her gaze longer than average in church for the past few weeks. Micah had held his, too. She was the prettiest woman he had ever laid eyes on. Everyone thought so. Her dark brown hair framed a soft, sweet face like none he had ever seen. *Were her brown eyes pretty because of their color—or shape—or...what was it? They were pretty because of...because of the light that seemed to be behind them.* That was it. She was an uncommon woman in every way he knew how to compare her with others. Micah allowed himself to think that maybe Anna Lee could see fit to have him if he kept up what seemed to have started between them. Then he dismissed the thought. *She's made for finer things than I'll ever have. She has the kind of grain and shine and texture that call for all the brass that can be fitted out for her. I could never cast the brass to fit her or find the oil to bring out what's in her.*

Micah relived the moments talking with her and rubbing elbows with her at the picnic. *I wish I knew if that's common or if she didn't even notice that I'd bumped against her.* He relished the memory but felt that he had stolen a touch that she might not have offered. He settled on the notion that *she was probably used to having men touch her arm and act like it didn't happen.* Maybe she was just looking back at him at church out of boredom or jest? *Or maybe…No, she's not the sort who could be interested in a plain gunsmith. Not for long.*

He ran his fingers across the stock of the unfinished rifle.

*   *   *   *

NO LONGER MERELY ACADEMIC

Professor John McMorrow lifted the collar and buttoned the top button on his wool coat as he moved deliberately down Main Street in Clarksburg on the frigid 23rd of December 1860. His boots beat a confident, steady rhythm on the board sidewalk. Others drummed a louder and less regular sound. John caught a glimpse of his own reflection in one of the many store windows decorated for the Christmas season. The professor thought how like the window he was. Dressed for the occasion. He wore a black suit, a clean white shirt, and black bow tie. His black leather shoes were polished to a perfect shine. A year before, he had put away the top hat and studded cane that he had used only a few times after his father presented them as gifts. John McMorrow despised ostentation. He only grudgingly accepted the imprecise rule that men in his profession needed to dress like gentlemen. A circus clown could not feel more conspicuous than John had felt wearing the top hat. Had he violated some principle by compromising to wear such things? John had not decided yet. But he determined that he would keep only the minimum required wardrobe for a man in his position. Even at that, the reflection in the glass seemed to be that of another. The very idea of aristocracy had eroded from the minds of many in western Virginia. John did not aspire to it.

His widowed father, for whom John was shopping for a last minute gift, worked the farm and sometimes hired out as a carpenter. John felt a stab of pain in recalling that he had once felt embarrassed as a child when his father had walked into a fine store dressed in tattered homespun. John had kept out of sight, hoping that none of his friends would associate him with the unkempt man— knowing that everyone knew anyway. Now, it struck him as a certainty that he would be prepared to thrash any man who would dare cast aspersions on his father's dress. Beneath John's fancy coat lurked the disposition and ability to do it, at least with most men. His six-foot frame was still solid. Farm work had built a body now inhabited by a gentleman—according to appearances—but John felt more like a farmer in disguise.

When among old friends John wanted to rip off the disguise, but they would not allow it. None had risen with him—intellectually—and they forced him apart socially. Friendly, they were, but distant. Some admired and respected him from a distance. They yielded to him in the street and in casual discussion. But John was ready to trade all admirers for a few good friends if he could only make the exchange without pretending. Few of his colleagues,"men of his station in life," as such men described their class, were from Clarksburg. Those who were seemed to play up to those who were not. Those who were not seemed "uppity," as his father would say. Like the bubble in his father's level, John McMorrow looked for his center.

In his twenty-third year of life and his second year at his teaching post at the college, John was aware of his good fortune to be where he was and doing what he was doing at such a young age. *Good fortune*, he mused, *is not the word for it.* Tracing his past to his present he thought, *If it had not been for the encouragement of my teachers here at the school, the hard work of my dear father, the nudges from those who made the contacts to get me into Bethany (who had themselves been nudged by my father while he was selling them grain, building their outbuildings, or hanging their cabinets), the patience and prodding of my professors, and who knows what other forces—I'd still be a farmer and a carpenter content to roam these hills with my squirrel rifle as my only diversion from work. No, I would not have loved the work. I suppose I'd have loved the identity, but not the time and attention taken from matters of the mind. As much as I admire hard physical work and skilled hands, I would not have felt content to make that my life. The world of ideas would have pulled me away when books landed in my hands. Or maybe I'd have felt trapped in another's world. 'Good fortune' has not deposited me here. Providence, people, kindness, and— maybe—chance have carved out a spot and fitted me to it. At least I'm trying to fit.*

The reflection in the glass looks like another man. Not exactly what my father raised his boys to be.

Thoughts of those who had lifted him led John to think of their stark contrast with those few who had exerted a downward pull on his life. The most notable was Samuel Hawkins. From their early years Samuel had been John's severest critic and relentless adversary. John had been forced by repeated encounters to measure Hawkins from a distance—and John kept that distance as great as possible.

Hawkins had been in constant competition with him and John could not avoid the game without withdrawing from life itself. It was as though Hawkins never diverted his attention from what John was doing and had no other goal in life than to prove himself John's better. When John excelled in examinations, Samuel whispered of cheating. When John did well in simple games Hawkins would almost certainly suggest that some rule had been broken. John's every success was Hawkins' failure. Lips that praised John, by that same action somehow insulted Hawkins.

When John had taken his turn doing simple tasks around the school house, Hawkins felt compelled to carp of how they ought to have been accomplished otherwise and better. It was Samuel's self-appointed business to inspect the chalk boards after John had washed them and the area around the stove after John had carried coal and stoked the fire. Chalk dust or small chunks of coal or excessive smoke from a damper that had not been closed in the right way never escaped the close inspections that Hawkins made—whether the faults were real or imagined. A schoolmaster once spoke to John about the "obvious personality problem" between the two of them. John tried to explain that he was not a party to rivalry but an unwilling victim of some problem on the part of Hawkins alone. John had walked away feeling the sting of injustice. He garnered blame for a hardship he could not escape.

The substance of the issue perplexed John. Samuel Hawkins was not an ignoramus. He had native intelligence and strengths in areas where John had weaknesses. *If Hawkins could only strip away his excessive pride and his unyielding ambition for attention,* John thought, *he could make his own contributions to the world.* Hawkins was physically stronger and John sensed no need to challenge that truth with words or actions. John hoped that Hawkins' relative strengths would somehow relieve the pressure that seemed to fill Hawkins with a yearning to surpass John in all things. John had decided early that he was perfectly willing to be bested in order to remove the constant threat; but he could not bring himself deliberately to do less than his best out of a sense of intimidation.

As they grew older, John watched Hawkins develop into a self-absorbed ogre who craved attention. He thought he understood something about how this bully had been shaped by his family. Hawkins' father insisted upon perfection. He was demanding and overbearing with his son but protective of him when anyone outside of his family challenged him. When there was trouble at school Samuel Hawkins was never to be blamed and his father supported him to outrageous lengths. The bluff and bluster of the father cowed teachers into accepting his explanations without holding Samuel accountable for misbehavior. To John it was an amazing thing to overhear Mr. Hawkins talking to folks in the general store about how other children tended to pick on his son "because of his superior abilities."

Samuel Hawkins loathed all who failed to express open adoration and praise for him. Grasping for distinction, he spoke with great authority of things about which he knew nothing at all. His native and true abilities disguised his ignorance. Weak boys who innocently counted themselves beneath him became his followers. Hawkins drew disciples by his appearance of strength and wisdom. He praised sycophants who posed no threat, and made them feel powerful by their associations with him.

After John left to begin his studies at Bethany, he felt relief for having escaped Hawkins. On his first visit home, however, he learned that new challenges had arisen. Hawkins had spread the word that John had left town abruptly after having been discovered in bed with a young girl—whose name Hawkins supplied— who was only 15 years old and not an entirely willing participant. Hawkins' father had given less specific detail, but he had spread word through the rumor mill that "John McMorrow has done some horrible things that we must not speak about openly."

By the time John finally learned of the rumor, it had done its work and could not be undone. The fact that folks did not speak openly of such things worked against John's efforts at correction. He wanted to find the most public way possible to clear his soiled name while protecting the timid and innocent young girl, barely known to him, who had been equally slandered by Hawkins.

John confronted Hawkins, who would not deny that he had said such things, reveal his sources, or issue some statement that he had not said such things. This refusal to deal with John cost Hawkins some followers who had confidently said, "It happened. And Samuel Hawkins has the full details!" When Hawkins tightened his loose lips—after John challenged the rumor—he left those who had trusted him out on a limb. In the end, the young girl found the courage to be quite emphatic in saying that no such thing had ever happened. Her father, who had to be restrained from physically harming Hawkins, was grateful that John had taken steps to put the thing to rest.

Such damage, however, is seldom fully undone. Samuel's father, incredibly, spread the word that John McMorrow had caused his innocent son to suffer a nervous breakdown by confronting him. A prominent friend of the Hawkins family inflicted further damage by vouching for them in veiled terms: "I know them well. Samuel Hawkins is a fine and intelligent young man and would not lie. The truth is always found somewhere between the extremes. If young Hawkins has said some things that have troubled this young McMorrow, surely there is some grain of truth to it. Otherwise, why would it trouble a young man who is completely innocent?"

After the facts had been well established and it was clear to all involved that Samuel Hawkins had been caught in a bold and malicious lie, his father declared that he, himself, had never said that John had done "horrible" things. Instead, he had only meant to compliment the young man by saying that he had done many "wonderful" things. "Someone," he demanded, "simply misunderstood. As for my son, I'm quite ashamed of his conduct and will deal with the matter at home." John found that attitude sickening—to see the father leaving the son out on a shattered limb, who in turn had left his friends in the lurch with unverifiable rumors—and to see everyone abandoning accountability while blaming others and counting themselves victims. Some of John's most trusted friends had been caught in the web and had joined the circle of fools, fearing prominent men who might further them in some way. John nearly lost his faith in humanity before it was over.

John returned to Bethany with a new touchstone that would help to shape the rest of his life: Reputation is not a worthy aim in a world of small and dishonest men. Character is more important. Few benefits came to John from his efforts to deal with the slanderous lie other than the satisfaction of having done it—for his own sake and for the sake of the young girl—and a new sense of freedom from Hawkins. After the confrontation, Hawkins sulked in the background and said nothing at all to John McMorrow. John would not see Hawkins again for many years.

As the professor rounded the corner he saw a group of men gathered around the large glass window of the newspaper office. They were focused on some item posted from the inside. They were animated. Some closest to the window were gesturing wildly and talking loudly. Recent arrivals at the place stood behind those in front, just staring. Two men walking away, farther down the hill, were arguing, evidently ready to come to blows.

As Professor John McMorrow neared the group, the crowd seemed to open up to allow him to move close to the posting. He felt ashamed to think that they might have done so because of his imposing appearance but that thought faded as he read the words on the poster that was now framed by his chest in the reflection of his broad frame in the glass: "EXTRA: SOUTH CAROLINA HAS LEFT THE UNION…." The question was no longer merely academic.

✳   ✳   ✳   ✳

COME TO CALL ON ANNA LEE

"Pass the salt—if you please." Mr. Stone smiled as he reached to take the shaker from Katie's graceful hand. The dinner table teasing went on about as it normally did in this close-knit family.

"You're not supposed to wear your hair like that." Her father was looking at Anna Lee who had put her hair in a bun atop her head with just a few dainty curls dangling on the sides. His face had a mock seriousness to it that all thought they could read. He was setting them up for a jest but they could not trace it to its end. Trying to keep her face in the sober mode, but failing, Anna Lee asked, "And why not, my dear, wise father?"

She supposed, as did the others, that one question would not pull out the full answer. He would keep fishing, dangling the baited hook, as he often did. "I don't rightly know exactly why," he continued as he forked green beans toward his mouth and looked at his plate, "it's in the Bible somewhere." Starting to question whether or not this really was a playful—but real—admonition to alter her hair style, she held her hand to her head and asked, a bit more in earnest, "Do you think that this is so extreme as to be immodest?" Anna Lee's father seldom made jokes about the Bible and she grew genuinely concerned that she might have crossed a line by having Katie help arrange her hair as the ladies in town did theirs. The others around the table began to think that they too had misinterpreted this as a joke. Katie had helped and encouraged the thing. Mrs. Stone had given it her unqualified approval, saying that she had never seen a more beautiful and elegant lady in all her life. They all knew there would be no harsh consequence if he really did disapprove, not these days, but no one in the foursome wanted to see needless contention develop between them.

Mr. Stone tasted the growing apprehension and held his sober face. "It's not about modesty, as far as I can tell." All three of the ladies ran Scripture references through their minds—and many were there—but none found a solution. They each thought of, and then silently dismissed, the reference in First Peter in which women are admonished not to let their beauty be "that outward adorning of plaiting the hair," but to "let it be the hidden man of the heart." The women were prepared to point out that the same passage that he might have in mind also puts the "wearing of gold" and the "putting on of apparel" in the same category as "plaiting the hair." They had discussed this in Bible class. Mrs. Stone looked at the gold band that Mr. Stone himself had placed upon her finger so many years before. Anna Lee thought to say that she would have to both undo her hair and run naked if the passage were to be taken in the way that some take it and followed to its reasonable conclusion. But Anna Lee and Mrs. Stone remained silent on that point. He had just said that it had nothing to do with modesty. Katie recalled aloud that the virtuous woman of Proverbs 31 made herself garments of tapestry and clothing of silk and purple. "Unrelated," was all that Mr. Stone responded as a slight, involuntary smirk—visible only to Anna Lee who could detect it when others could not—materialized.

All were silent as Mr. Stone mashed his potatoes with his fork. He would wait for another question—and he could usually wait longer than anyone else—before pulling in his catch. He knew he had already set the hook pretty well. He liked the tension. It made for a stronger yank on the line.

Anna Lee kept her insight to herself. *No sense spoiling his fun.* Maybe she would ask the next question if no one else would take a genuine bite. *Sometimes he needs a little help. In the end, we all want it to come off right*, she thought as she looked toward the front door with other thoughts intruding.

"'Somewhere in the Bible' is a big section of Scripture to cover all at once." Mrs. Stone was reaching for the big, black volume on the dry sink. Handing the revered book to Mr. Stone she continued, "I wonder if you could narrow it down to something more specific?" Mrs. Stone was still not sure whether this was a jest or a lesson, but she wanted to know the conclusion.

Retrieving reading glasses from his shirt pocket and opening the book, he turned immediately to Matthew 24 and slid the book to Katie with his finger pointing to verse 17. She read aloud, "Let him which is on the housetop not come down to take anything out of his house." Now, they all knew that this was a play on words, but none had yet grasped the point. "There it is." proclaimed Mr. Stone. "That's it."

"What is it?" asked Anna Lee, hoping to get him to go ahead and finish.

"Right there. Plain as day. 'Top knot come down!'" This evoked an authentic chuckle from Anna Lee who enjoyed her father more than his joke—which would not have seemed funny to her at all if it had been printed in a book—and two groans. Mr. Stone crunched a carrot as he winked at Anna Lee.

As the girls cleared plates from the table, footsteps thumped on the front porch. Anna Lee wiped her hands on the apron and pulled it off in one fluid motion as she hurried to her room. "Anyone expecting company?" Mr. Stone asked as he headed for the front door, which he reached at the same instant that the soft knock sounded. He opened the door and there stood Micah Johnson, dressed as if he were on his way to church, and groomed even better. "Good evening, sir. With your permission, I've come...," he swallowed hard and his Adam's apple plunged beneath his collar and floated back up like a cork bobber, "I've come to call on Anna Lee."

CHAPTER 2

A YOUNG LADY IN THE BALCONY

"It is as though two men had made a contract. One of the two parties fails to live up to the terms. The relationship changes—as all will agree." John McMorrow listened intently. The debate was one of many in recent months. John preferred the debate format to the one-sided harangues presented by stump speakers on either side of the issues. Straw men were easily torn to shreds and he had seen many of them trounced.

John had travelled all the way to Grafton to hear a debate. The speaker was doing a good job of presenting his case—and this grated on John. *No*, he reflected, *It's not so much that he's doing a good job. It's that his opponent was doing such a sorry job.* That is what had the blood rushing to John's face and made him want to stand up and take the podium from the local fellow who was soon to respond to this speech. There is nothing more unnerving than to sit silently listening to poor arguments in defense of a right position. John had been unnerved all evening. The polished speaker from out of town had been forceful, clear, and courteous. The local fire eater produced a lot of thunder but no rain. His local reputation had grown more from his shouting about things already agreed upon by those who had pressed him to take up the debate than from careful reasoning.

"Suppose that my neighbor agrees to deliver to my farm a particular cow— one we've agreed upon with special identifying marks. In exchange for the cow I agree to pay a particular sum. These events, by our mutual agreement, are to happen on some specific day and time. Suppose that on the appointed day and hour I wait at the appointed place ready to pay the agreed-upon sum. The money is in my hand. Let's say that my neighbor shows up with another cow, judged by me to be inferior but claimed by him to be of equal value. Will you demand that I must pay him the sum in my hand and accept what he is now offering? Suppose that he brings a pig instead of a cow. What then? You would all immediately take my side and demand that I am free to hold onto the sum in my hand if I choose—or to enter into a new contract for the fresh offer! That he retains the duty to deliver the original cow and to accept my money as agreed upon is, like-wise, not a matter of doubt! For him, on the contrary, to arrive on the scene with something else and demand my acceptance of new terms—on the spot—is so unreasonable as to be laughable."

Heads nodded here and there. John's was still. He knew where this was going. He wanted to stand up and shout: "Illustrations prove nothing. First prove the truth of your assertions and then illustrate them with clever stories."—but he remained in the order prescribed by the occasion.

"The neighboring farmer is the government in Washington. His contract with the sovereign states is called the Constitution. The states have kept their end of the bargain. They have conducted their affairs in compliance with it. The states are not to be blamed for the contentions of the past few years. The government in Washington, contrary to the original agreement under which the several states came into this union, has presumed to have the power to direct the affairs of the states. This is agreeable only to those in the North—where their way of life is not threatened and where their institutions are unharmed. They will see the day when they too will regret allowing their contract to be voided and replaced by a new one. Those in the South, who see their time-honored institutions threatened by the powers in Washington, wish honorably and kindly to decline to accept the new offer. They have used themselves up in efforts to press the government in Washington to honor its original agreement. These states now stand ready to make new agreements among themselves. Some have entered into a pact of honor to form a different government. Not only does duty call upon us to consent to let them go—but reason cries out from every marketplace and mountaintop for us to join hands with them!"

The crowd met this with foot-stomping, hooting, and a few muted "amens!" The moderator called the crowd to order and reminded them that the rules of debate called for no audible approval or disapproval from the audience. Within a few minutes the hearers settled into grudging compliance.

John McMorrow scanned the audience during the lull. Were any of his students here? Would this material make good fodder for the next lecture?

He had grown bolder in expressing his own views in the classroom on the current distress. After his first attempt at setting the table, on which he had hoped they would come to feast, he had been discouraged to learn that virtually all of his students had considered his comments to be the whole meal. Some went home reporting that their professor had argued in favor of those who were for preserving the union. Others were equally sure that he had defended states rights and slavery. These reports filtered back in the form of a few direct questions from those who knew him well—or thought they did—and in the form of brightened eyes and firmer handshakes from those who believed that he had championed their cause, and downcast eyes from those who believed that he favored the other side. He tried to force the impressions left by handshakes, eyes, and body language out of his mind. These were not reliable measures. They brought back memories of his reception upon returning from Bethany when neighbors received him as an escaped rapist returning to the scene of his crime.

John found no students in the audience. As he was about to turn to endure another harangue from the fire eater who was moving into position to speak, his eye fell upon a young lady in the balcony. Her dark brown hair was in a bun atop her head. Curls dangled from the sides. Her beauty riveted him. Her posture and expression pulled him. While the ladies around her fanned themselves and looked around to see who was looking at them, this one looked intently at the podium— oblivious to the social affair taking place between the floor and balcony.

When the evening's debating ended, John quietly left the auditorium and headed for the front door. Others spoke rapidly to those seated near them. In the foyer he met a man from Clarksburg, known to him only casually. John could not recall the man's name, and this pained him a bit. It would be rude not to speak. So he spoke.

"It seems to me that the core questions have not yet come to the fore in this debate."

"How so, Mr. McMorrow?"

It pained him again that he could not pull up the name.

"The question of whether or not the Constitution has been cast aside by Washington was only touched on by one suggesting that such a thing would justify rebellion." John used the term *rebellion* deliberately. He hoped that it had effect. "The government has not yet acted in the ways that these men suppose it will act. They are arguing from the supposition that the government will switch cows at some point in the future." The man did not entirely follow this, but he was not willing to say so. "Well said. Let's hope that cooler heads will prevail." The man, whatever his name, walked away.

As John started out he felt a hand on the back of his arm. "Excuse me, sir." He turned. It was the young lady from the balcony. "I couldn't help but overhear what you were saying to the gentleman just now. I'm sorry. I hope I'm not rude to ask for a moment of your time."

As he looked into her eyes he saw what he had rarely seen in his finest students at their best. Honesty. Genuineness. Inquiry. As he took in the whole of her he could not imagine that she could say anything to him that could be described as rude. The tension generated by what he had endured in the auditorium drained away, replaced by a new, pleasant, tension. He tried to find acceptable words to tell her that he would be more than happy to give her more than a moment's attention. "That's perfectly all right," he started. "How might I be of service?"

Anna Lee Stone spoke earnestly. "It's about the pivotal questions being left out. I thought the same thing when they were talking. The one seemed to make no differences between what the government has done and what the government might do. The other just let him get away with it. Folks around here think that he knows what he's doing—and he's a good man and all—but it seemed like someone should have seen the gap and filled it in."

John was not sure how to respond. Here was a gentle woman whose mind soared. He had heard only a few words from her soft lips, but these were enough to take the measure. He had always marveled at how often two people could experience the same events and see them in such different ways. It was a rarity to find anyone of either gender who would size up a thing in just the same way as he had and then express it in words that he might have used. He wanted to tell her of this pleasure even more than he wanted to proceed with the actual subject. "I'm glad to hear you say that." He was still casting about for the best words. "The lack was missed by most of the audience. At least I fear that such is the case."

The discussion progressed. John agreed to share some relevant books. Mr. and Mrs. Stone along with Katie, who had been standing nearby all along, came to stand beside Anna Lee. It at last dawned on John that they were together. Social custom dictated that Anna Lee must now introduce her new acquaintance. She knew this and so did John. The two had not yet exchanged names. John extended his hand to Mr. Stone and said, "Good evening, sir, I'm John McMorrow from Clarksburg." Mr. Stone took charge from there. He introduced his family. When he came to Anna Lee—when he pronounced the name Anna Lee—John knew that he would not soon forget it. The group parted after John received directions so he could deliver the promised books"soon," and John found his way to his horse in the stable. He would make the trip to Clarksburg tonight, but he would return earlier than planned on Monday to hear the conclusion of the debate.

Moments before he had decided that he had heard enough of it. Now, he would not miss it for anything.

✳   ✳   ✳   ✳

"THE MOMENTOUS ISSUE OF CIVIL WAR"

To threaten secession was petty—childish. Most in western Virginia assumed that politicians would deal with such foolish factional maneuvers with some sort of compromise. Even those who did not see the Southern cause as foolish figured that tensions would resolve without actual division. It all made for interesting news, but it was not yet a crisis. Of course the Union would hold together. If the Southern cause in western Virginia drew out the sympathy of some—even if it drew the passionate blessing of some who rallied around the brave men of the South who dared to shake a collective fist in the face of government—it was still an internal problem that would be settled in the usual ways. Or so they believed.

To presume to carve away a section of the United States to form another country was unprecedented and dangerous. The formation of the Confederate States of America inspired some and infuriated others, but it unsettled all who paid attention. It unsettled western Virginia. Mild opinions crystallized into firm convictions. Irritating differences slid down the scale in the direction of intense bitterness. Disputes, good natured at first, became earnest fights. Few remained neutral. Talk of war spread across the country. Abraham Lincoln, an unknown entity generally thought to be weak and ineffectual, had just taken his place at the helm of government. The fellow who had just left office had not plotted a course. James Buchanan had been friendly with the South—even meeting with Confederate representatives as though they were ambassadors from another recognized country. The table had not been set to Lincoln's tastes.

In his inaugural address on the steps of the incomplete Capitol building, the new President made it clear that he did not intend to meddle with slavery, but that he could not recognize the South as a separate nation. He pronounced the Union "unbroken" and directly addressed those who had presumed to have left it: "In your hands, my dissatisfied fellow-countrymen, and not in mine, is the momentous issue of civil war. The government will not assail you. You can have no conflict without being yourselves the aggressors. You have no oath registered in Heaven to destroy the government, while I shall have the most solemn one to 'preserve, protect and defend' it."

Few believed that war would come. Few favored it. Few were indifferent about the issues and most favored one cause or the other. Tensions grew. War seemed at least a threatening possibility. Abe Lincoln called for volunteers to put down what appeared to be a growing rebellion without giving the country a clear sense of how the troops would be put to use. Seventy-five thousand men were called for three-months service, to include Virginian troops and to march across Virginian soil. This call added to the growing and already unstoppable momentum. Virginia called this an act of war, joined hands with South Carolina, and left the union. Arkansas, Tennessee, and North Carolina left the union and joined the Confederacy.

To don gray uniforms and to attack a flag-flying military installation of the United States of America was altogether intolerable. Treachery. Infidelity. Hostile action against the flag for which their forefathers had fought and died could not be ignored. Unprovoked belligerent shots blasted in anger at Americans by Americans was suffocating for many in the North and for a good many in western Virginia. Provocative images of Rebels—or patriots to some—ripping down the Stars and Stripes from over Fort Sumter roused men. Bands played. The aggressors had been duly warned and "the momentous issue of civil war" had been decided at Fort Sumter on the coast of South Carolina at 4:30 in the morning on April 12 when a flash of light, an arc of fire, and a numbing explosion shook Fort Sumter—and the North American continent.

A trickle of sons from western Virginia answered President Lincoln's call for volunteers to put down the rebellion. John McMorrow's two older brothers were among them. It was no longer a question of whether or not to oppose secession or those who pressed for it. It was now a matter of defending the United States against aggression. This, many were sure, could be done within a few months.

A few fathers and sons went south to join the Confederate army in preparation for the coming invasion. Why would Abe Lincoln call for warriors without plans to make war? Virginia had thrown in with the Confederacy. How could loyal Virginians do anything other than defend the honor of Virginia?

All participants were patriots. All were traitors. All were loyal—to something. All were hostile—toward something. All were spoiling for a fight. The magnetism and romance of going off to fight glorious battles while sisters, daughters, wives, and lovers prayed at home attracted men with few political opinions. These put on both blue and gray. A bully fight made a man look bigger than he could be made to look behind a plow.

Micah Johnson was in his shop when he heard about the fall of Fort Sumter. The news struck him like a hammer. How could a rabble mob force a fort belonging to the United States to surrender? How could Lincoln let it happen? Micah would be no part of any Confederacy that would dare defile the sacred flag, even if the defenders of that flag at Sumter were not up to their work. He could not fathom the idea that Virginia was in on such doings.

Micah was relieved to note that Anna Lee and her family were firmly for the Union. She had made him promise to sell no rifles to Confederates—at least none known to be Rebels. She looked him in the eye and reminded him that principles are more important than money and that she would have nothing to do with any man who would sell the nation for thirty pieces of silver—or any amount. It pleased him that she felt as she did and that she was willing to say so. He saw the implication that she would have something to do with a man who would not sell arms to Rebels. He would gladly fit that bill.

John McMorrow was torn by the news of Sumter. Until then he held onto the hope—the expectation really—that matters would be settled without bloodshed. His own father favored the Confederate cause. "John," he had said, "niggers have always been happy to serve the white man. It's only the d-—abolitionists who've stirred up the manure pile that would be smellin' sweet now if it'd been left alone to just crust over. Slavery has been a blessing to the slaves. They'd still be livin' in the jungle without knowing the Gospel if white men had not rescued them and made them useful. Since God cussed Cain it has been their place to be slaves. It was all goin' along like it's planned until the government in Washington decided it was up to them to fix a thing that ain't broke. If the Confederacy wants to keep things the way they've been all along and the government in Washington thinks they ought to change—then it's the government in Washington that's causin' the commotion."

John had not known, in his childhood, that his father held these convictions. They had never had any slaves. There had never been any talk of having any. None of their neighbors had had any. John had known no blacks in the area during his childhood. His own convictions had grown out of what he had been taught in Sunday School, what his mother had taught him, from his teacher's comments at the regular school house, and from his trust in his own ability to reason. His first encounter with slaves had been at Bethany. He had been aware of disagreement among his neighbors, but he had assumed that his father had agreed with his mother. His father was a good man, an honest man, but not a man to talk about consequential things with his young son. Beyond squirrel hunting, carpentry, and farming there had never been much in the way of talk about principles and ideas. The hickory switch had taught John to comply with his father's rules. John was vaguely grateful for that. Their minds had seldom met on higher ground than the ground they worked on the farm. It struck John that his father was proud of him—of his education—of his accomplishments, but ashamed of John's convictions; embarrassed when John spoke of them in town. John sensed his father's regret for having failed to school him about slavery—and his father's eagerness to make up for lost time. It pained him to tell his father that his sentiments were so very different from his own.

The contrast between the two families, John's and Anna Lee's, was glaring. He had been finding excuses to drop by the Stone farm for weeks. What began as a book exchange had evolved into a regular literary symposium. The whole family took part. They were not blank slates waiting for him to impress them. They shared ideas. Serious talk about serious things—sprinkled with double entendres from Mr. Stone who also contributed deep and useful points of view. Original thoughts from Anna Lee. All grasped ideas more quickly than most of John's students. All questioned the group, or any member of it, without insult. All agreed that the Union must be preserved and all knew their various reasons for this shared sentiment. Katie was slowest to follow lines of thought, but she was a welcomed participant who gave opportunity for the others to patiently simplify and review the ground they covered.

John saw how this family had produced Anna Lee: confident, informed, independent, strong, genuine—real. Had they noticed that Anna Lee had captured his heart and soul? Was Anna Lee remotely aware of it? Did she know that he thought of her so often and with such power that her beauty and essence poured into his mind whenever his concentration was not focused on something else, and danced around the edges when it was? With all his education and knowledge of other things—John felt clumsy in the presence of Anna Lee. He yearned to make the transition from visiting friend of the family to Anna Lee's suitor, but he lacked the courage to risk the loss of what they all shared together. He most feared Anna Lee's rejection—even if kindly expressed as he knew it would be if it were to come. He was certain that he loved her. He knew that he was welcomed in her home and admired by her family. He hoped that time would help the rest. He yearned for Anna to be the first to speak of what he felt—hoped—was a mutual love. She was braver, more confident.

*   *   *   *

AND NOW THEY ARE SOLDIERS

Lincoln was wrong. What had seemed a resounding call for seventy-five thousand troops for three-months service now seemed more like a feeble whisper. Those who had predicted peace within sixty days were now seen as dense. Money, men, and equipment poured into the effort to suppress the rebellion. Committed souls on both sides would now dole out the last dollar and send the last man to end the matter. There was no longer the sense that time would cool passion or that a few musket blasts would send the other side home and end it.

The Union defeat at Bull Run on July 21, 1861, degenerated into a catastrophe for the Union army. It energized the South. It imparted hope and strength. Like an uncertain colt trying out its legs for the first time and discovering that it can run, the South reacted to its success at Bull Run with visions of ultimate victory. The Confederacy was on its feet.

The catastrophe energized the North too. Bull Run compelled it to stiffen its upper lip, get back on its feet, look at the South with tough, steely eyes, and reconsider, like a strong man knocked off his feet for the first time, what had to be done to recover and win against this stony giant who had looked so small. In the North, Bull Run stripped off the kid gloves and put on the brass knuckles. The strong man took a long second look at his foe.

General George McClellan won plaudits at the time as a great leader of men. He inspired soldiers and civilians alike. Folks wrote songs about what he would do with the "Grand Army of the Potomac." One popular song spoke of the great general who had "just sprung up, who'll show the foe no quarter." The government raised five hundred thousand more volunteers to put down the rebellion. These citizen-soldiers were ready to fight to end the dispute between North and South. If his men were primed to get in the next lick after having been knocked down, McClellan was reluctant to swing without full assurance that his next blow would topple the strong man. Such certainties seldom come. He would not send his army as a fist toward the Rebel jaw. Other Union troops made progress in Tennessee and other points westward, but McClellan waited for his grand opportunity. It did not materialize.

The North held its breath. The South continued to shake its fist, and gained courage from the relative inaction of the North. When McClellan boasted of plans to take Richmond and those plans remained on hold—in spite of his greater numbers ready to march and awaiting orders—the South saw bluff and bluster. They discerned clouds, thunder, and lightning—without rain. Threats without force. Grand promises unfulfilled demoralize more than no promises with a little action. The North was ready to punch. The fist, McClellan, remained limp. Mind and body were not in partnership. Like a paralyzed limb unresponsive to ardent will, the Army of the Potomac drilled and paraded on safe ground while Rebels stood by and jeered.

On July 1, 1862, "Father Abraham" sent out the call for six hundred thousand more volunteers. The 12th Virginia (Union) Infantry Regiment of Volunteers was organized and mustered into service later that summer, accepting the invitation to hold and press the line against Rebels. These were mainly patriots, native Virginians by birth who joined at a time when victory was uncertain, in order to press for victory. These were mountain-bred, self-reliant men—used to fresh air and hard work on the rugged farms of western Virginia. Many had friends, even brothers, fighting in the Confederate army. Companies of the 12th Virginia came from Marshall, Ohio, Harrison, Marion, Taylor, Hancock, and Brooke counties. Its colonel was John B. Klunk, from Grafton.

First Lieutenant John McMorrow felt the world had turned upside down as he tried to make sense of his new station in life. He accepted his commission as a matter of duty. He felt, once again, like a circus clown with gold braid and brass buttons replacing the top hat and studded cane. Now John was to command volunteers and to teach them to soldier. He believed that he could learn to give orders once he figured out what they ought to be and to whom he ought to give them. He felt confident that he could oversee the work of teaching men to fire their muskets by the numbers just as soon as he could learn it himself. He knew no more about soldiering than those he was to lead. His company commander, James Moffatt—from Shinnston—had only then gotten his copy of the manual, and he promised to loan it to John soon. But the 12th Virginia Infantry of Volunteers was now an entity. Fresh. New. Raw. Clean men wearing loose-fitting uniforms that drew laughs from both wearers and observers. Spotless off-white haversacks. Bedrolls. Smiling, eager faces. Boys. Shiny new muskets. Camp Willey was a beehive of activity as the regiment mustered into the service of the United States of America. A few words. Some papers drawn up. And now they are soldiers. Ready to go into action, according to any of them.

John McMorrow did not feel that he had abandoned his post at the college. The few students who would enroll in a few weeks for the fall semester would be taught by the skeleton crew not occupied by the war, unless the doors were closed for lack of students. His greatest concern about leaving involved Anna Lee. He had not made the transition to suitor, at least not openly. He could not be sure that he would see Anna Lee again. The war dropped into the middle of life and redirected its stream. What had been moving forward was now piling up and looking for new direction.

His father was settled and able to care for himself with the help of good neighbors. His older brothers had all enlisted as privates in the Union army when the first call for volunteers had come. He sensed safety in learning that Samuel Hawkins had gone off to fight for the South. At least his father would not have to deal with whatever menacing and ridiculous slurs Hawkins might cook up locally with John away.

His only unfinished business at home was Anna Lee. Was he selfish for wishing that he had left with a clearer sense of where they were with each other? When the whole Stone family had bid him the emotional farewell, and when he hugged each of them, did his long, lingering embrace with Anna Lee mean something to both of them? When he had tasted her breath without touching her lips and stroked her hair with his eyes and drank in her unique smell and stashed them in his soul, had she taken in some portion of him? Would it have been fair to Anna Lee if he had begged her hand in marriage and then marched off to war? No. It was better as it was. At least under the current crisis it was best—reasonable—to leave her a free woman, his dearest friend.

"Let's get these men to their quarters," Captain Moffatt said. "We're to have them at the train station first thing in the morning."

✳   ✳   ✳   ✳

HIS AWKWARD RETREAT

Mr. Stone was just putting the last of a load of corn in the crib when he glimpsed the figure on horseback approaching down the lane. He had become more watchful in recent months with all the talk of Rebel activity. He had not seen them, but he had heard they might be around at any time. His rifle was loaded—except for the percussion cap in his pocket—and leaning against the wagon. Some of his neighbors were secesh, possibly ready to point out Union sympathizers if it came down to it. He had been clear and public about his convictions from the beginning. He had kept himself from speaking of his worries in front of the family, but they had seen him bolt the door at night. When he took the rifle into the fields he mentioned the abundance of squirrels this season.

In the twilight he saw the dark figure dismount at the gate and tie up to the white picket fence. His right hand was on the rifle, tense. His left felt for the percussion cap. The man on horseback turned and looked at him. A hand flew into the air that startled him. "Hello, Mr. Stone." It was Micah Johnson. With a casual wave he returned the greeting. "Hello, Micah. It's good to see you." With labored breath he went on, "I'll be right in. Anna should be in there somewhere." Striding toward Mr. Stone with easier steps than ever, and with a surer voice, Micah said, "No, sir. Let me help you with that corn first and then we'll both go find your lovely daughter."

They loaded the corn together. "Have you noticed all the squirrels this year?" Mr. Stone asked, reaching for his rifle. "They're thick this year and their hides are tougher than usual."

Micah played the game. "That's a sure sign of a cold winter."

As they reached the front porch Katie came to the door, drying her hands on her apron. When they entered, Anna Lee came from the kitchen. Her apron was still on. Her father noticed. He leaned his rifle in the corner behind the door and said, once again, "Squirrels are everywhere this year."

As Anna Lee and Micah moved toward the parlor, Micah turned to Mr. Stone. "Speakin' of rifles…I mean really, on a whole 'nother subject…. I've had some new developments about my rifles." He was trying to be casual, but it was clear, at least to Anna Lee, that something really big was behind his affected indifference. Micah explained that he had just signed a contract with the government to produce rifles for the Union. Not the regular kind that were being cranked out in factories, but sharpshooter rifles. The rifles regular soldiers carried were inferior. Some still used smooth bore muskets that, according to Micah, "Could not hit the broad side of a barn, except by luck." His enthusiasm showed. Micah forgot that he was trying to be casual. He explained that the government would supply the rough barrels—good steel, wooden stocks, and some tools. He would turn these into some of the most accurate rifles ever made. Using his own ideas he figured that he could turn out at least two of these each week. "I can stay right here in Grafton. There's more work than I ever figured to have in my life. And the pay is good." With undisguised pride he added, "And I'll be putting my own markings on the barrel."

This was impressive. All agreed. Micah had been torn by the war. He had fully planned to enlist with other young men, but men who seemed to know more about it told him to stay with his work, to help the Union cause that way. Now he could do his part. He could do it without going too far from Anna Lee. He could use his ideas. He could earn a good living. His stamp would be on the best rifles in the army.

The evening passed without Micah and Anna Lee spending time alone—until it came time for Micah to leave. Anna Lee walked with him to the gate. The family stayed inside. The moon was full. Micah could see well enough to get home. The horse knew the way anyway. "I'm proud of you, Micah. If your things aren't exactly going as you planned, it looks like they're coming out in a good way." He fumbled with the reins, put his foot in the stirrup, took it back out again, turned and looked Anna Lee full in the eyes. "Anna Lee,…I…I…I love you."

She was stunned. She knew that she was fond of Micah. She felt something for him, but she did not know that she was yet ready to call it…love. The power of the moment, the anticipation in Micah's eyes, the lingering sense of John McMorrow's vague affections for her—and her's for him—the commitment, or lack of it, that would be conveyed by her response: all of these pressed her. She paused. Tears welled in her eyes. Taking his hand in hers and squeezing tightly she said, softly, "And I am very fond of you, Micah. I'm proud of you." They embraced. He cuddled her while she rubbed and patted his back.

Anna Lee returned to the house while Micah made his awkward retreat. From the window she watched him dissolve in the moonlight.

*   *   *   *

"BUT AIN'T HE SECESH?"

The 12th Virginia Infantry boarded trains at Wheeling en route for Clarksburg. *Of all places*, Lieutenant McMorrow thought. Confederates under General Albert G. Jenkins were raiding "West Virginia"—as some were now calling it since the 50 western counties had united to form "The Restored Government of Virginia." They had petitioned Congress for re-admittance to the Union.

"If Jenkins and his Rebels want to try to teach us a lesson, then I figure school will soon be in session. But we will see who will be schoolmaster." John was working on communicating with his men in ways they could understand. Those gathered around him on the train were not college students. Their inspiration would not come from reason. It would come from bravado and bluster according to other young officers who fancied themselves born leaders. John knew better than to count himself ready to lead. He felt that he was now the student and that he would have to experiment a bit before claiming to know the formula. He knew how to convince rational minds, but he knew nothing of the art of inspiring passionate souls.

John rode the train with the enlisted men. No one had told him where he ought to ride, so he placed himself with his men, where he supposed he belonged. The men seemed to reckon otherwise. Most in his immediate vicinity stared uncomfortably forward. No one took up his parable of the schoolmaster and none seemed to hear it. On the other side of the car men spoke freely. Those around John were not being rude, at least not by any measurable standard. He had not addressed anyone in particular so no ones silence specifically rebuffed him. He wanted to tear away the gold braid and wear the uniform of a private, at least long enough to connect with these men. He paused for several long minutes.

The soldier to his right was uncommonly big. A giant really. Strong. His hands showed the effects of hard work. John had seen him around Clarksburg, as he had many of the others, but he could not place him or identify him. Taking a silent, deep breath he turned to the man and said, "I'm John—Lieutenant—McMorrow, from Clarksburg." He hated going by something other than his name. "Looks like we're both headed home for a time." He extended his hand—and held it there for what seemed an unnatural stretch of time. The big private looked down at him, took the hand, shook it, and said, "Edmund Jasper Smith, sir. Most folks call me Jap." Before turning as if to look at something out the window—and there was nothing there but a blur of vegetation on the bank—the big man said, "I guess we'll just go where you tell us."

It occurred to John that this fellow saw in him the full authority of the government and the Union army. He saw himself as much a chess piece—a pawn on a checkered board waiting for other hands to move him—as the private. He wanted to explain this...*but...but maybe it would be best to let that sense of things stay as it is—at least for now. At least until I learn my way.*

"What sort of work have you done—up until now?" John cringed at his own question. His goal at the moment was to make conversation. The effect of his question might be to cause the man to feel judged. He tried to frame a new one to cancel out the first one when the reply to the first one eased his tension. Turning from the window the private spoke, "Mostly farmin'—and lately lumberin'—I've sold a good bit of lumber to your daddy. I loaded his wagon with a good pile of oak boards a few weeks ago."

Common ground. John had found it with one question. "My father's quite a carpenter. Still stays pretty busy."

With an innocent, honest, confused look, Jap looked his first lieutenant in the eye and asked, "But ain't he secesh?"

John's face drained of all color. He had hoped, and believed, that his father had kept his views at home. Who had heard Jap say it? Who else knew? How long before his whole company knew? What would be the consequences? Looking at the floor, as though the plain planks held something worth looking at, John mumbled: "He is a good carpenter. He's an able farmer. He's been a good father. But he sometimes talks before he thinks…and sometimes he doesn't think too well."

Jap went back to examining the blur of vegetation. John looked at the floor. The train clanked on.

CHAPTER 3

SOME IDENTIFIABLE LANDMARK

The regiment spent little time in Clarksburg after it arrived there on September 2, 1862. The 12th had been posted to protect the railroads from Rebel forces under Jenkins. These fighting men of the 12th Virginia, scrapping for a fight, spent their first days in service riding on a train and then picking blackberries—which were plentiful that fall around Clarksburg—before dividing into two detachments and going to other locations in that part of the state. They would soon settle into the dreary routine. Army life was not mainly battles and blood. It was hurry up and wait, drill and practice…and drill…and practice. Army life was marching to camp, setting up tents, and more drill. It was picket duty. It was blackberry picking. Military existence was talk around the campfire. It was hardtack and coffee on the march. It was drill. It was boyish pranks, letters to and from home, and taking down tents. It was drill. Marching. Songs around the campfire. Packages from home. The officers and enlisted men of the 12th Virginia were beginning their lessons in army life together. If battles and blood—glory and honor—were out there in front somewhere, the path was strewn with tedium, routine training, drill, and time.

Lieutenant Colonel Robert S. Northcott led a detachment of four companies to Beverly, about sixty miles southeast of Clarksburg. They marched to the western base of Cheat Mountain in the Tygart Valley where they arrived on September 5. From Beverly, they were ordered to Webster—forty-two miles away—on September 13. They arrived there on September 15.

A few fugitive slaves joined the march to Webster. To men not accustomed to contact with blacks, the "coloreds" were a curiosity. It unsettled some to see that some were much lighter in color than others. The blacks stuck with Company I along the march and inclined to stay with it at Webster. Captain R. H. Brown wanted to shed the burden and distraction caused by the runaways. Entrusting them to the care of two men going into Grafton, he told them to lose the the blacks before returning to camp. At Grafton they found a train of Ohio soldiers ready to depart for Wheeling. The colonel of the Ohio boys refused to consider taking on the slaves. Their story did not move him at all. His business did not include transporting runaways to freedom.

When that plan failed, the men and their charges passed to the rear of the train where they found some enlisted soldiers prepared to bargain. "What'll you pay us to take the darks?" At least one of the Ohio boys had a conscience for sale. After haggling and the payment of a few greenbacks, the former slaves climbed aboard. Like passive cargo they took their allotted space on the floor. The train left. No one from the 12th Virginia ever heard from them again.

While this was going on, John McMorrow remained with that part of the regiment ordered to Buckhannon, twenty-eight miles or so from Clarksburg. The divided regiment reunited on September 22 when both detachments marched back to Clarksburg. The reunion generated a great deal of excitement. A band played stirring martial airs. These first weeks began a settling-in process for the boys of the 12th Virginia.

The first marches began with enthusiasm. Rebels might be lurking anywhere and the thought created excitement. Jokes passed between the men in loud voices. Needless motion distinguished the forming up for these early marches from later ones—after anticipation of what was about to happen led men to conserve energy. The loud clanking of expendable equipment—soon to be lost, used, or discarded—played ditties that would not be heard after experience taught them. Nervous laughter and loud talk launched these first marches.

The long marches were drudgery. The hot sun baked heads full of notions that they were tough men prepared to do the deadly work of hardened soldiers. Hours of putting one foot in front of the other under the weight of packs and muskets, while dust stung recently bright eyes and hindered labored breathing, gave them time to reflect. The experiences gave them material for reflection. Innocent fantasies that had kindled passion for glory did not include endless hours of back-breaking toil that earned nothing more than another spot of rocky ground beneath the trees and the opportunity to repeat the struggle at dawn. Men who had been cocksure that they could endure any battle and defeat any foe now wondered if they could just continue to march.

The marches taught the troops new pleasures. A cool drink of water from some spring or stream became a treasure. Crisp green grass in the cool shade of some oak along the march was Eden. Dark clouds that would have *threatened* rain before, gave *promise* of cleansing relief while on the march in the heat of late summer in western Virginia.

John McMorrow felt secretly gratified when men stepped out of the moving ranks and staggered to the side of the road, either to straggle a bit and catch up or be picked up by the ambulance and carried forward to the evening's camp. It was not that John wished them any harm or shame. He did not. It was only that it gave him a measure of his own progress. He was not proud of himself for staying on his feet until the end of each march, at least not in the sense of feeling superior to those who did not. It was more a sense of relief, and surprise, that he did it. This mingled with genuine empathy for those who did not.

Senior officers rode on horseback. Some junior officers did too. Some of John's own rank rode in the ambulance for copious stretches of time—"to check on the men riding there." John had ceased wiping the sweat from his eyes, a waste of energy. There was nothing to look at for long anyway, at least nothing that differed much from what he had seen in the miles of dusty road behind him. He looked up long enough to pick out some new goal, some identifiable landmark to which he believed he could walk without falling down. He continued to put one foot in front of the other until reaching the goal. Then he reckoned that he could make it to the next bend in the road up yonder—or clump of trees or outcropping of rock. Between these goal points John did not allow himself to consider the question of whether or not he could put his next foot forward. He could make it to the designated place. Then he would let himself question.

John's method freed him to ponder other matters while burning, aching feet pounded soil and raised choking dust to add to the regimental cloud. Surrounded by hundreds of men, John McMorrow was alone and elsewhere much of the time on the march.

The young lieutenant recalled his earliest memories: The warmth of his mother's lap. The pleasure of cool, sweet watermelon on a summer's day. His shock upon seeing his first locomotive. Its size. Its power. His father's hand on his shoulder...and the approving pat when he barked his first squirrel. His first day at the schoolhouse. Carrying coal for the teacher. The privilege of ringing the bell. Reading his first words on the first page of the primer. Writing his name and the pride of having done it. Gifts on his birthdays. Christmas. Carrying wood for the fireplace. Milking cows. Plowing fields. Planting corn. Putting up hay. Hiding in hay from his brothers. Feeding hay to livestock. Bethany College. Learning. Questioning. Stretching. Standing. Teaching.

John catalogued smells: Fresh *cut hay. Curing hay. Put up hay—same smell but weaker. Manure. Fresh. Old. Cow. Hog. Chicken. Leaves. Newly fallen. Rotting. Soil, just turned. Skunk. Damp deer hide just stripped from the carcass. Dead animals left to rot—all the same. Husked corn. Fresh cut pine. Black walnut. Walnut husks green with black spots. Wood smoke. Musty books. Coal smoke. His mother's roses. His mother. Frying bacon. Fresh bread right out of the oven. Clothes right off the line. Clean. Anna Lee.*

John pondered the future while marching. The transition from past to future reminded him that he was now in the army. It shocked him for an instant. He pushed past the present drudgery to try to envision the future. War. *How long? What will it be—for me? Marching? Drilling? Fighting? Death? Pain? Suffering? Victory? Defeat? Glory? Prison? Honor? Shame? Will I make it through?*

And after the war? His imagination was dim on that future leg of the journey but he explored possibilities. He had to look up long enough to find some new landmark positioned in that time in the future toward which he could step off the distance between now and then. Marriage? *Children? Back to teaching? Something else? Anna Lee?—Anna Lee.*

He would live for the day when Anna Lee would become Mrs. John McMorrow. The rest could stay fuzzy. This would remain clear. Whatever happened during the war, he could endure as long as Anna Lee was there. *I'll write her and declare my love as openly and clearly as words will permit. I'll secure a promise from her. She'll wait for me. We'll marry. We'll have children. I'll love those children. Teach them. Make their lives a pleasure. I'll discipline them with love. I love them now, as though they were already here. Anna Lee'll love them and put herself into them. The human race will raise a notch when Anna Lee bears my children and puts her stamp on them through years of daily association. I'll teach…or go into law…or something. Every night I'll pillow my head in the arms of Anna Lee and awaken to each new day with Anna Lee by my side.*

The contrast between John's spirit and body was stark. He neared the clump of trees he had picked as his last goal. He raised his right arm to wipe the dusty sweet from his forehead. He wiped his right thumb on his already wet shirt. He cleared his stinging eyes with his thumb, one at a time. With the flesh side of the end of his right thumb he pressed on his right nostril and blew the dusty mucus from his left nostril. He used the thumbnail side and repeated the process, blowing the right nostril clear. He cleared his throat and spit the grainy slime on the ground, just missing the heel of the boot ahead. He took a deep breath. His burning feet cried out for relief and his exhausted body demanded a pause the instant he allowed himself to hear them again. He looked ahead. *I can make it to that level spot in the turn up yonder before I fall. I can get there.*

✳   ✳   ✳   ✳

CENTERED ON ANNA LEE'S HEART

Micah's contract with the government gave him more than business. It provided training. Previously guarded trade secrets flowed his way and he freely used patented ideas. Some came to him from the government. Others he used without interference from Washington. Diagrams, charts, tools, advice and other such things that he could not have found or discovered months before now found their way into Micah's shop. He was now subcontracting the work of finishing rough stocks. Locks—the mechanical, moving parts of his rifles—trigger guards, telescopic sights, and such things now arrived at his shop from other places.

Micah concentrated on the barrels. The barrels were the key. When all the parts were assembled, the small blast from the percussion cap would reliably set off the powder in the barrel and propel the newfangled "Minie ball" through the rifled barrel. The deadly bullet would spin as a lead gyro to the target. The barrel determined the accuracy of the round. Sharpshooters would load the powder and ram the conical lead into position. This was out of Micah's hands. The shooter would rest the barrel on some immovable stone, log, or carcass—horse or human—and pull the trigger. Other hands would adjust the new telescopic sights and drive holes through men hundreds of yards in front of them. Some victims would not hear the blasts that took their lives. Those who lived might hear the gunshot only after they were on the ground. Micah bored and rifled the barrels, assembled the parts, fit the stocks to the men who would use them, and sent sharpshooters on their way. Micah was in awe of what his hands created.

Anna Lee was another growing wonder. She came to his shop often now. That Micah had less time to call at the farm was no offense to her. She understood. She said that she admired the cause of it. This did not surprise Micah.

What surprised Micah was the mind of this beautiful woman. She grasped concepts faster than he himself had taken them in during his long training at his craft. If Anna Lee's tender hands could not do what his could do, her keen mind could comprehend it. Only her questions had drawn it out of him. When he explained with the proud air of mastery how the boring machine tunneled down the center of the rough steel and how the rifling machine worked like an internal lathe to cut the twisting groves that would cause the Minie balls to spin, she did not ask why this was done. Instead she asked if changing the threads on the screw that sent the cutting tool into the barrel might alter the rate of spiral to some advantage. When he showed her how the Minie ball was hollow at the base to allow the powder blast to expand it to make contact with the rifling and increase accuracy, she understood and added, "I suppose it would have been hard to ram one in there that tight every time you shoot."

Micah's purposes shifted. He no longer thought he might impress Anna Lee with his knowledge—of anything. She had always been able to memorize Bible verses at church and connect them with other verses faster and more to the approval of Sunday School teachers and preachers than anyone else. Now she showed that this extended far beyond Bible class. He could not—and would not try—to compete with her. He was amazed that she—this beautiful, intelligent, fun-loving, desirable woman—who could have the attention of any man with eyes—would condescend to give him attention, friendship, and *was it love?* It was affection, at least in some measure. It was attraction of some sort. *Was it love?* Could it lead to marriage? She was willing to come into his world and marvel with him at the work he was now doing. She was ready to help with the books and to fill in gaps that he failed to think about. She was not impressed with his brawn—which was considerable. She did not tell him that she thought him handsome, although he thought her eyes said so. She expressed approval, but not awe, of his skills. She said that she admired his dedication to his work, and to the Union.

Over time, Micah's purpose moved from that of impressing her to that of letting her into his world, allowing her to help. To the extent that Micah could perceive anything about Anna Lee's intentions he vaguely sensed that she wanted to help. Anna Lee filled in the gaps. She was useful. She met needs and shared goals.

The gunsmith was not blind to his own deficits. Micah saw the gaps in his abilities beyond the making of guns. When his goal had been to impress her, he had tried to hide these from Anna Lee. Now that his intention was to allow her into his world, without actually admitting the flaws openly, he allowed her to see them. He asked for her help with the books. She had offered. He listened to her thoughts about rifle building. They were good. He slowly grew to expect help, to need help, and to depend upon Anna Lee for help. He paid her for valuable work. His boyish infatuation matured into settled love. Love ripened into respect. It was still infatuation and love, but it came to have the deeper qualities of connection, admiration, and friendship.

Micah could build a rifle that could pierce a man's heart from hundreds of yards away, but he felt helpless when it came to touching the heart of the woman so close. He would have to wait and see what she would choose to do, or to see what would happen to her against her will, to move her to requite his love. As he bent over and looked through the telescopic sight that he had just fitted to a perfect barrel, he imagined the cross-hairs centered on Anna Lee's heart and the barrel ready to deliver cupid's arrow—or maybe some love potion packed into a Minne ball—or maybe just a sense of how much he loved her. He would have to find words to do that. Micah's heart raced as it had when he took aim at his first big buck as a child. He reached for the trigger. Its place was vacant. The parts, all laying on the bench, had not yet been assembled.

✳   ✳   ✳   ✳

SMALL, INSIGNIFICANT ANTS

Anna Lee's mind wandered as she sat on the porch with her lap desk. The heat of the sun beat on the swing and Anna Lee. The air was still. She moved to the shade at the side of the porch and dangled her legs off the edge. A small piece of leaf, pale green against the sandy soil beside the porch, moved to the left, paused, moved to the right, paused, and then moved to the left once again. She bent closer. Two tiny ants—much smaller than the leaf—were playing tug-o-war. Others were lined up like soldiers in near-perfect files going to and from some unseen camp over in the grass.

Why? Why would two creatures sharing the same goal place themselves at odds with one another? Colonies of ants are supposed to share a common mind and work in concert. What forces placed these two on opposite sides of a chunk of leaf expending precious energy, each trying to wrest it from the other? Is it possible that each sees only the leaf and that neither is even aware of the other? Their world must be quite small and the leaf must be huge—in that world. If they came upon the prize from two different sides at the same time…maybe each thinks the leaf itself is offering resistance. If they could see it from my point of view—from up here on the porch—maybe something could be worked out. The leaf can be divided in two. Both can drag from the same side. One can take it while the other makes himself useful by hauling another. Both can let go and some other can take it to the camp for the common good of all.

Why does it matter? Ants. Small, insignificant ants. There must be—what?—a thousand colonies just like this one in an acre of ground. Millions of individual ants. I can't measure the toil, struggle,—effort. All for…what?

How many die every day? Predators eat them. Wagon wheels and horses' hooves smash them. Human feet squash them. Plows slice them. Rains drown them. No one knows or cares. No one mourns the loss. Each death means the colony has one less mouth to feed. The soil is scarcely enriched by a negligible speck of humus. And these two continue the struggle for a piece of leaf while the yard is littered with leaves—some closer to the little ant encampment over there in the grass somewhere. The neat files march on as though they have great purpose and their toil has meaning.

Shaking her head, slowly, and leaning against the edge of the clean, painted, white poplar siding where the house and porch met, she unfolded the letter in her hand. She had read it many times in the days since she had received it. She was not really reading it again.

Anna Lee was reviewing parts that now pulled at her. The first reading, days ago, had taken her breath away. Each review provoked new sensations. Hope. Profound love. The comfort of feeling completely enveloped, embraced, in another's affection. Fear. Uncertainty. Pain. Indecision. A longing for a thundering voice to shout from heaven to give specific and clear direction. A sense that life had carried her to a crossroads, or that she was nearing a fork in the road, and that something needed to be settled—and by her.

Her eyes went straight to the words penned by John McMorrow while her soul drank.

If words could absolutely convey all that is within me, then these would leave this page and gently hold you in their arms. They would breathe indefinable sentiments into your ear that would fill the most obscure reaches of your soul with the absolute certainty, intensity, and immensity of my love for you. They would banish every possible vestige of doubt. They would caress your hand. You would feel the touch, and that touch would radiate into your heart what I intend when I send it to you. They would look into your eyes and pour into them a true and pure sense of my yearning and you would grasp it entirely. They would assure you of the sheer sincerity of my intentions and possibly unsettle you with their obscurities regarding the future as they spoke of undefined hope. They would, because they are honest, give a sense of my own vagueness concerning the wisdom of speaking them while the future is so uncertain. War is unpredictable. It is because words are so weak that I labor so to wring from them their last drop of usefulness. But even after I've used them to their fullest, I feel that I've transferred only a drop from the ocean that is within me to your comprehension. No dictionary, thesaurus, encyclopedia, song, or book of poetry can help me to empower them to send what is in my heart. Even if they were spoken in person and the words had the aid of eyes, inflections, arms, hands, and gestures they would be impotent. No forbidden sensual act would give them any more strength—and the attempt to express my heart to you in that way, under our circumstances, would likely turn this love into something dark and loathsome in your eyes. I think that this will restrain me nearly as much as the knowledge of God's eyes. So my words, if truly faithful and strong, would convey a sense of safety.

Anna Lee felt she was reading a novel rather than a letter to herself. Her father had always frowned upon reading fiction. He felt that such things confuse people and get them to dreaming of things that cannot be. She had read only a few such things and had been caught up in stories that had set her to dreaming. Now, these words were real, written to her from flesh and bones and the heart and soul of the man who wrote them. If she had before sensed the possibility that John McMorrow had a growing fondness for her before leaving for the army, she had not allowed herself to believe that it had grown this strong. She had not prepared for it. So much had been bottled up inside him and this letter poured it all out at once, like a flood. A few drops before the deluge would have helped her get ready. A simple "I love you, Anna Lee" would have at least begun to open the flood-gate before the whole dam broke over her.

Anna Lee loved—felt affection, strong attraction, connection, deep devotion for—John McMorrow, and Micah Johnson. She had openly declared her love for neither. Both had expressed, in words, their love for her. *Love—what is bundled in that word? What does it mean and what do I mean by it?*

Micah's had begun as a spark of physical attraction, grown into a flame, and developed into an expectant, understanding friendship and partnership. The fire was there and so was a deeper sense of compatibility. It had begun to translate in practical terms into her ability to fit into his world and help him to make progress in his work. She felt needed, almost essential, in Micah's world.

John's relationship had begun as friendship, with an almost mystical connecting of minds. That had evolved into mutual affection. And now it was love. At least in all the ways Anna Lee knew how to attach meaning to the term.

Each of these two men was much like the other. Both were handsome, at least now. Micah had been handsome at first sight and John had grown to become so. Both were men of principle. Good men. Moral. Honorable men. Both had goals and dreams. Beneath the thin social veneer that separated them, the clothes forced on them by work and station, they seemed nearly like one man.

They were so much alike in so many ways that it seemed they were one man in two bodies pursuing the same goals in different ways. One was the intellect, the other the skilled hand. Both were intelligent and both had practical skills but each specialized in one of the two areas. Both loved her and said so freely. One was capable of taking care of himself with less help. One seemed to need the tender help that she had always expected to give to her husband, as her mother had with her father. One could carry her farther and stretch her mind further. One could benefit from her mind and be carried and stretched by what she had to offer. Either would make a good husband in all of the practical ways that she knew to measure. Either would make a good father and provider.

As she thought upon their striking similarities she found herself thinking of how she could pour her love on *him*—and then corrected herself—*them*—and then corrected herself once again—*one of them*—for life. She returned to their differences. *Even if those differences are subtle—even if I can form only vague impressions of them—these will be the foundation of my choice. Will I help the one who most needs me? Will I move on at the side of one who is able to go on without me—but who might enrich me with what he can show me? Is this a selfish measure? Is it arrogant to think that I could make a positive difference in the contributions that I might make to either? Is it fair to John to make anything like a final decision while Micah is near and John is far away fighting for a cause that we all hold dear?*

It struck Anna Lee that neither had proposed marriage. *Might it be that one is—or both are—toying with me in some way that I cannot detect? Which one? Am I naive to think that both are really in earnest in their declarations of love? Will time and other women solve the riddle? Will indecision send both away and leave me with no one?*

Does either even know of the other? Are they like the two ants—each pulling furiously at a side of the leaf fragment and unaware that the other is on the other side? Will either let go if he learns of the other?

Are we all like the ants, thinking that our movements and choices really matter in the greater scheme of things? Will the bigger world be changed in the least by what we do? Even if the choices we make—I make—were to produce a difference in this world, at this time, will they matter in a hundred years? Is the earth just a speck of dust in the universe? Are we just trivial bits of life with no significance when all is taken in?

No. Her eyes traced the lines of ants marching to and from their hidden camp. The struggle for the leaf was still in progress. *No. Man is created in the image of God and humans are not ants. Ants find meaning in going on. I will see my place on this earth as worthy of consideration. The stars and planets out there do not even know they exist. Ants do not care if they live or die. I am a woman. A daughter of Eve. A daughter of Adam—a child of the dust into whose nostrils God breathed the breath of life. What I do now matters.*

Anna Lee entered some thoughts in her journal about confusion and uncertainty, but nothing about indifference. She composed a letter to John McMorrow which began: "Dear John: Thank you for your welcomed letter. I am overwhelmed by your words. I am amazed at your ability to use them. They are not weak, as you suggest. They touched me deeply. Of course you know that I am also quite fond of you."

She wanted to tell him of her love for him. She wanted to tell Micah too. She wondered how long she could forestall the pain. First to herself, and then to one of two men she loved equally and deeply.

And why can't the Confederacy just let go of the leaf so John can come home?

*   *   *   *

PROXIMITY BREEDS KINSHIP

"I say, Major, that is a capital line." The drill-master worked the men at Buckhannon incessantly. They were exhausted. Drilling became the life of soldiers in the 12th Virginia Infantry. Loading the musket by the numbers, responding to commands on command, moving as a unit—left flank, right flank, to the rear—march. These filled most of their days and intruded into their dreams at night. "Weary of training," "tired of drilling," and other such phrases found their way into nearly every letter home.

Beneath the complaints blossomed a growing satisfaction. To hear the drill-master compliment their alignment to their major after so many failed attempts to form a straight line was about as pleasant a thing as any could hope to hear. They were soldiers and now they were acting like soldiers. They were accustomed to hard work, but the sustained work of drilling and marching hardened them even more than farms had done. Strong men became powerful men. Sluggish movements of slack companies became ordered and efficient performances of tight units responding with celerity to orders., at least much of the time. It was not uncommon to find that men were out of original order after moving by different flanks and to the rear and then back again. But no one in the ranks was prepared to mention it and the drill-master rarely noticed, so it could be ignored.

On October 19, 1862, the 12th Virginia marched to Beverly. Few men fell out of ranks. All had learned to lighten their loads, pace themselves, and make it. The regiment was nearly full. Bullets had not yet decimated its numbers. Sickness had not thinned the ranks. About 800 strong men made the march to Beverly.

No force on earth could stop us. John McMorrow was on foot again with his men. As he surveyed the body of men all around him he sensed viscerally how formidable it had become. He tried to calculate the number of comparable regiments then in service and envision that horde massed for battle. *Hundreds?* John did not know, but for the sake of his calculations he settled on an indefinite *hundreds*. He pictured that number marching as one unit, all trained to fire their muskets and move into the ordered positions as needed. He could not fathom how any band of Rebels could withstand such a force. In time he would learn that more than a thousand regiments comparable to his own would be put into service before the Union army would put down the rebellion.

On the march to Beverly the regiment passed through the battlefield of Rich Mountain. It was the regiment's first taste of war, merely an aftertaste. They paused where saplings had splintered and where thick trunks of large trees were badly torn by shot. Graves dotted the landscape. Union forces had driven Johnny Rebs from the place. Inscriptions said that sixty or so Rebels were buried in a trench at the side of the road. While the Rebels had held that ground they dug the trench and put up a sign that read: "TO HOLD DEAD YANKEES." John McMorrow thought of the possibility that the hand that had inscribed those words might well be rotting now in the trench beneath the soil. In a nearby garden, graves bore the names of boys from Indiana and Ohio regiments.

"Men died here." John spoke to anyone within earshot willing to listen.

Exhausted and sober faces looked at him, pondering his words. *This might be one of those teachable moments,* but John's lesson plans were not in order. "All of our training…the marching…the drills…have been to keep as many of us out of trenches like this as possible. I figure we'll feel like running when we face the enemy. I don't guess there's any shame in that. But the art of war has been studied—worked over by men who know more about it than we do. They tell us that we're safer if we work together—do what we are ordered to do and have been trained to do—as a unit. If we come apart, then the Rebels can pick us off easily. Now, I don't know when we're going to get our chance at 'em. When we do, remember that our nerves—and training—can push us to drive them into confusion—and to put them in these trenches. Down South they boast about one Rebel being able to take on ten Yankees. That's just talk. It isn't…it ain't so. Does anyone here believe that the Rebels have it right?"

No one answered verbally. A few shook their heads from side to side. "I'm not sure I'm ready to go into battle beside a bunch of men who don't seem to think we can do it." "Okay. Let's do it this way. If you think they can whip us just stay quiet. If you think we can whip them, then speak up. Can we whip the Rebels?"

Several spoke up. "Yes, sir."

He gave it another try. "Can we take the Rebels?"

"Yes, sir." The cry was much louder this time. The momentum carried it from there.

"Can we whip them?"

"YES, sir!"

The men of John's company rose to their feet. Muskets in strong hands leaped into the air. One musket towered above the others. It belonged to Jap Smith, who stood head and shoulders above the rest. Color returned to faces that had been white with exhaustion and with dread at the sight of the trench. Sober expressions gave way to smiles. As the 12th Virginia formed up to continue the march to Beverly, it sang.

At Beverly the 12th camped near the 9th Virginia and the 87th Pennsylvania. They were just north of town on the bank of the Tygart River. The commander of the 87th Pennsylvania, Colonel George Hay, drilled the 12th Virginia along with his own. A friendship developed between the two units that lasted for the duration of the war.

Proximity bred kinship. While it might have been more natural for the boys of the 12th to take up with boys of the 9th, both western Virginia regiments with home ties in common, the seemingly random placement of troops on the banks of the Tygart forged a bond between the 12th Virginia and the 87th Pennsylvania. As he gazed at the campfire flames licking the locust logs, John McMorrow tried to form some broader principle that would account for a development that had transpired the previous night.

Some soldiers from the 9th Virginia had been on guard duty with orders not to permit any soldier to enter the town without a pass. Some restless souls from the 87th Pennsylvania, just wanting to have some fun, tried to slip past the guards. This was not uncommon. Volunteers felt entitled to a little time to themselves, spent in whatever way they chose to use it. They would do their duty when the time came, but they would risk being caught sneaking into town when they had no specific duties to perform. It was a game.

But the night before one of the boys on guard duty—according to orders—fired a shot that struck one of the boys from the 87th Pennsylvania. Pandemonium broke out in the camps as the story disseminated. Some said the boy from the 87th Pennsylvania was dead. Others said he was wounded. According to conflicting shouts and excited explanations from those who claimed to know, all over the camps, it was at close range and after the fellow had raised his hands in surrender; it was a deliberate retribution for some insult; it was from a distance and a ricochet from a rock; the fellow who had been hit fired first; the other guards held the prisoner in place while the picket ran a bayonet through him. All the wild reports made the facts impossible to determine from any distance.

Impulsive young men from the 87th Pennsylvania ran to their tents, loaded their muskets, fixed bayonets, and prepared to avenge their fallen comrade. Scrapping for a fight, they had found an enemy. Cooler heads prevailed. The officers of the 87th Pennsylvania got their troops under control, promised a careful investigation, and assured the aggrieved that all would be put right.

John was most struck by the way that a good number from the 12th Virginia had loaded their own muskets, fixed bayonets, and stood by as if in reserve. These had immediately taken up for the 87th Pennsylvania, against the 9th Virginia Regiment, and few in the 12th Virginia tried to stop them. The 12th Virginia men accepted accounts of the incident that favored the Pennsylvania troops.

John McMorrow took note and formed the tentative principle: *Proximity breeds kinship*. He searched his memory for past instances of this. The mountains between eastern and western Virginia, and the proximity of western Virginia to Ohio, seemed to fit. Whole towns and counties seemed to, as a general rule, have united views in favor of either the Union or the Confederacy, instead of having individuals sprinkled all through the population with differing views. That seemed to fit.

John considered how he might use the principle to advantage. He would put himself among his men and share in their campfire songs and tales, at least as far as permissible and practicable. He would put himself in the company of other officers too, at least some of the time.

Anna Lee. John was powerless, in this forced circumstance, to be physically near her. The realization bit him hard. *Other men are near her.* The fact took hold of him like a cold vise. He groped for loopholes to the law he had just discovered. *Humans are creatures of choice. They are not driven by circumstances or accidents— not always. Anna Lee is an uncommon woman.*

If these adjustments in his thoughts loosened the grip of the vise that held him, they did not free him from it.

CHAPTER 4

THE MUTTON WAS GOOD

Keeping livestock anywhere near an encampment during the War of the Rebellion was every farmer's challenge. When hungry troops were not foraging under official orders they were scrounging to supplement their army diets without them. The rules—on paper and as announced to the men—were clear enough while the 12th Virginia was at Beverly: Leave the property of citizens alone. The rules governing actual conduct were not on paper, but in stomachs and whispered in the camps. Combining restless men with time on their hands with growling stomachs resulted in a thinning of the flocks and herds around Beverly.

Jake McCormick of Company K, conspired with comrades to arrange a steak dinner. Down by the river they found a herd of cattle. Jake put a musket ball in the head of a huge bull. With his friends he stripped the hide, quartered the meat, and hauled it back to camp. Willing knives divided the feast. The aroma of roasting beef drew hungry men from every direction.

John McMorrow held the stick that held his bayonet that held the fresh, sizzling beef over the coals. His mouth watered. His stomach rumbled. John knew this meal had not come through the quartermaster. He asked no questions for conscience's sake. He drew his skewer back and sprinkled a little salt on the meat as he turned it around. He poked it with his knife and watched juices ooze out. He sprinkled pepper, returning the meat to the roasting zone above the coals. John wondered if he could discipline himself to wait until the beef was properly cooked before tasting it. He put a chunk of hardtack in his mouth and let it soak up the saliva—and swell. Within minutes the hardtack softened and doubled in size. He folded his tongue, jostled the flavorlessness mass from side to side, and swallowed without chewing. Considering the nature of hardtack John counted this a feat worthy of retelling.

Then it was ready. At least ready enough. His knife uncovered a pink center. He held the piece before his eyes, smelled it, blew on it gently, and then—slowly—parted his lips above and below his gums and gnawed at the edge of the beef. It was tough. It was stringy. The flavor was perfect. He drew it away from his mouth and his tongue moved without orders to lap the juices from his lips, mustache, and new chin whiskers. The grit that mixed with the delicate juice was only a slight vexation. His next bite went deep and was more deliberate. His last undisciplined bite crowded his mouth. John was glad that its toughness required work with his teeth. It would last longer. He chewed and refrained from swallowing except when it became involuntary. Then it was gone.

More hardtack. Some strong, fresh coffee. *That was a meal worthy of the waiting.* As he leaned against the rough tree he supposed that it is best that some things come to us infrequently. *What is always with us is not precious. Fresh beef. Shade on a hot summer day. Cool water. A place and an opportunity to sleep. The shelter of a tent. Being deprived of a pleasure until it can be had again increases its value. This too can be reduced to an identifiable, stated principle that will hold true generally.*

The next day, in the middle of drill, Colonel Klunk called a number of officers to his quarters. John McMorrow reported there with the others. A nervous-looking civilian, maybe fifty years old, in well-worn clothing and with taut lips stood beside the colonel.

"Mr. Thompson has a farm down by the river. His prize bull is missing. He figures that some of our boys might be responsible. He's not saying that they are, he's just wanting payment if they are—and he'd like to have some assurance that no further troubles develop. I want you men to make a thorough search of our camp. Mr. Thompson will accompany you. Report back to me with whatever you find. There's no reason to think that our boys were party to any such doings, but we need to make the inspection and impress upon the minds of our men that such things cannot be tolerated against the loyal citizens of this region. Question the men. I'll reward the man who can identify the culprit if he is among us."

John and the other officers fanned out to search the camp. The farmer went with one of the others. John questioned the men. No one reported seeing any fresh meat in his sector of camp. Freshly dug earth was evident beside the rubber blanket—strangely spread in the middle of the day—in Jake McCormick's tent. As he tugged at the wool blanket to cover the disturbed soil, Private McCormick reported that he had not seen anything of cows or parts of cows in the camp. Jap

Smith, the huge private John had ridden with on the train, tossed a log on top of the cold ashes—covering what might have been charred bones—and declared that he had seen nothing that looked like fresh beef that whole day. John knew that it was not an issue of what had been in camp on that day. The events of the preceding day were at issue. But when private Smith started to elaborate, John cut him off in mid-sentence, thanked him for his cooperation, and went on.

With his part in the thorough inspection complete, John nervously made his way back to the headquarters tent. Would the colonel question him too closely? Would he ask if John had any information in addition to that obtained by the inspection? Would the other officers make reports that differed so greatly from his own that his would stand out like Jap Smith in formation?

He stood outside Colonel Klunk's tent while two officers ahead of him made their reports. Others lined up behind John. The farmer and his guide were still not in evidence.

The Colonel's voice boomed. "Can you testify that the bones you saw were certainly beef bones? You are absolutely certain that they were not from a large rabbit?"

A softer voice replied, "No, sir."

"Well then Lieutenant, thank you for your report. You're dismissed."

The next, Captain Amos Prichard, reported briefly: "No evidence of fresh beef, sir."

"Thank you, Captain, you're dismissed."

Lieutenant McMorrow was nearly as brief. "I would like to report, sir, that no evidence of fresh beef was uncovered in my search."

"Thank you, Lieutenant, you are dismissed."

As John stepped away from the tent, tension drained. He smiled. He passed Captain Hagar Tomlinson, of Company A, ashen-faced and headed for headquarters. John saluted and continued on his way. He heard nothing further of the incident. Someday, maybe after the war, he might get the boys to pitch in and pay for the bull. That vague intention calmed, slightly, a churning conscience.

If enlisted men of the 12th Virginia learned anything from the inspection of the camp, it was that officers can look the other way when it suits them. It was not a complete trust that officers would always ignore infractions, but it was a growing trust. Crimes against fellow-soldiers would not be ignored. This too became evident at Beverly.

John heard it from Lieutenant William Smiley of Company D. Smiley was troubled by the notion that one of his men, Private King, had been severely beaten by some "comrade" who could not be found. "John, I'll tell you what. We need to find the man who beat him and punish him. King came dragging into camp last night with two black eyes, half his pants torn away, no cap, and no coat! When I asked what had happened, he claimed he fell into that ravine over in the woods. He wouldn't report to the surgeon until I ordered him to. The surgeon says it's possible that he fell, but we both agree that someone has likely trounced him good. Why would he want to lie to protect such a bully? Do you figure he's afraid he'll get more rough treatment? I've heard some of the boys making fun of the way King stutters. It ain't…it isn't right. I'd like to get to the bottom of it—and put a stop to it right at the first. We can't have our boys fighting among themselves."

John happened upon "the bottom of it"—quite by accident—the next night. He was on his way down to check on the guards by the river. He had no need of a lantern as he knew the way and he could see well enough by the light of the full moon. He heard the boys talking.

"You shoulda seen ol' King the other night. It was a sight to see." The unseen speaker laughed and slapped his knee. "It was King's plan. He got a bunch of us together and he said, just like this, 'B-b-b-boys, I ha-have it. Me a-and T-Tegard will g-go d-down to th-the lower end o' the field and take d-down a part o' the fence. The r-rest of y-you drive the sheep through the g-gap. M-me an' Tegard w-will l-lay down and g-grab 'em when th-they c-c-c-come through.' Well, we drove 'em through alright. They was wild as deer."

John held still in the moon's pale shadows and listened.

"King grabbed the first two by the hind legs. One in each hand. They was big-guns. He would not let go. Just kept hangin' on while they drug him along the ground—rocks an' all. An' here's the best parta the whole show. The whole rest of the whole flock stomped right on top a King's back on their way through!" He slapped his knee again. "The mutton was good. Real good. But the show ol' King gave us was worth it all—even if we'd a had to eat quartermaster rations that night. King didn't think it all that funny, but I'd pay a few greenbacks—if I had any—to see it all again."

John quietly turned and slipped back to camp in the moonlight. The men were awake and at their post. That was all he needed to know.

*   *   *   *

THINGS ARE CHANGING HERE

Anna Lee sat with Mr. and Mrs. Stone as she joined her voice with theirs and the others assembled for worship. Her voice had a soft quality that blended beautifully with most of the sounds coming from the congregation at Grafton. The few who lagged in singing the hymn, and the few whose notes did not match those written in the hymnal, did not distress her. She supposed that they were all singing from the heart and she knew that God was more pleased with sincere worship than with pretty performances. Besides, her father's bass and her mother's alto muted the more grating sounds of the "squawkers"—as her father had called the ones who "could not carry a tune, but decided to carry something anyway."

The hymn touched her.

> From all thy silent griefs and secret pain,
> Thy profitless regrets and longings vain.
> Wisdom and love have ordered all the past,
> All shall be blessedness and light at last;
> Cast off the cares that have so long oppressed.

Had wisdom and love ordered all the past? Whose wisdom? God's? Her own? Had all of her choices been wise? She could not say. Had apparent accidents—chance meetings—been ordered by the unseen hand of God? Would future events be completely out of her hands? She thought not. *No. God has given us directions—a guide—in the scriptures; but so many choices seem to be ours to make. If God's providence nudges things in certain ways it can't be by planting thoughts and motives directly in our hearts. That would make us puppets. Commands would be meaningless to puppets without ability to choose to comply or rebel. If wisdom and love have ordered all the past, at least of human conduct, it can only be to the degree that choices conformed to scripture.*

"Silent griefs," "secret pain," "longings vain"—these felt like intrusions into her private world as the whole church sang the words. Were these so common that all could speak of them in one united voice, with the substance of each individual's meaning being different? Are all longings "vain"? *No. The longing for heaven is not the only exception if this can be called a rule. The longing to have a good husband and to rear good children cannot be for nothing. The longing to love and be loved must not be evil. If longing for wealth and fame would fit the rule then maybe we ought to sing it that way.*

Directly across the aisle, Micah was "squawking" out the same words. He did not think about them at all. He did not know that he was not in tune. He paid no attention to the fact that others were in tune or that some were lagging behind. He was still tasting the last glimpse he had dared to take, in church, of Anna Lee. She was, to him, the epitome of beauty. Her soft lips moved as she sang. The end of her nose wiggled slightly in concert with her lips. Her warm hand held the hymnal. Her dangling curls framed soft skin and caressed her neck. Her flowered dress wrapped the package that he yearned to one day unveil, on the night of their wedding.

When the preacher stood to preach, Micah continued his ruminations.

Anna Lee focused on the message, taken from the 15th chapter of the book of Acts.

"Just as the brotherhood in former days—as early as the apostles—joined their hands together to spread the word and work of the Lord, we find it to be the duty of the whole church to join our hands and to work as a body. Small churches can do small work. The whole church can accomplish great work. Evangelism depends upon our hands being joined to those of others to spread the gospel. He that 'knoweth to do good and doeth it not' is guilty of sin. May we rise to the task of taking the gospel to a lost and dying world in the most efficient manner possible." Mr. Stone stiffened.

After the last "amen" and while the members passed out the door, most of them kindly congratulated the preacher on another "fine lesson." Anna Lee was only slightly surprised to hear her father's remark to the preacher: "We must take care not to turn the disciples into just another religious denomination." She knew that her father was opposed to the church in Grafton getting tied up with the American Christian Missionary Society. He had said many times that "the church that has Jesus for its head does not have any organization higher than the local church. If the local churches cooperate with one another, it must be in a way that leaves the structure and doctrines of the church alone, the way it was in the first century. God did not ordain any body of men to speak on behalf of the churches." He put this point of view before the preacher on his way out the door.

"But the Society takes nothing out of the hands of local elders, "the preacher protested. "It exists only to encourage, to exhort, to comfort, and to put the resources of local churches to more efficient use."

"That doesn't square with the facts and you must know it." Anna Lee was uncomfortable with—but not ashamed of—her father's blunt retort. He spoke in such a way only when he was sure of his ground and counted it important. "Two years ago they passed resolutions in favor of the North and published them for all the world to see as if they were speaking for the whole church. That's beyond the bounds of reason."

"But you yourself are loyal to the Union. Everyone knows it. How can you object?"

"Because the point is not whether or not the Union is in the right. The issue is whether or not any council of men can meet and pass resolutions and presume to speak for all the disciples. Whether I agree with the content of what they publish is not the issue. Next thing you know we'll be calling our preacher's 'reverend' and putting ourselves out before the world like we were just another human denomination if we don't find some way to slow the horses on these movements. If we're going to be the church of the New Testament, then we need to learn the boundaries of it. I guess we'll be hearing talk of moving an organ into the worship if this continues."

Softly, the preacher asked, "Would an organ really be such a great matter? With all the problems of the rebellion and the human suffering and all?"

With that, Mr. Stone shook the preacher's hand once again, firmly, and said "Good day, sir." as he turned to walk toward the family wagon.

Sitting in the driver's seat and taking the reins in his hands, Mr. Stone stopped, looked at his wife and daughters, and said, "I'm sorry if I've made a scene and shamed you—or us. I really..."

Mrs. Stone interrupted: "We understand. We must accept the state of things the way they are. It's not your fault. Things are changing here. We've seen it coming. You're in the right. We need to make whatever adjustments we need to make to the changes—but it is not wrong to resist them when they are wrong."

"I admire you, Father," said Anna Lee.

Katie agreed.

Mrs. Stone put her hand on her husband's shoulder. "I'd nearly forgotten. We were going to see if Micah would like to join us for Sunday dinner. What do you think? Would it still be good idea?"

Looking at Mrs. Stone, then at Anna Lee, then at Micah who was slowly, tentatively, walking toward his horse, Mr. Stone paused and said, "Well, I reckon if that was in the plan we might as well see if he can come."

When Mrs. Stone and Anna Lee simultaneously shouted his name, Micah looked up at the fulfillment of his most immediate hope. He ran to the wagon.

*   *   *   *

ABOUT LIKE HE HAD HEARD IT

John McMorrow had a gnawing pang in his conscience like a round burr that pricks from all sides. He had participated in the bull-beef appropriation and the farce of an inspection. John had looked the other way when men of his regiment abducted sheep—even if the transaction had cost Private King a good deal. If the burr was blunted a little by his intention to some day try to repay the farmer who had lost his bull, it was not removed.

Unofficial foraging was growing to be more acceptable among the officers and enlisted men of the 12th Virginia. Some had come to be see it as a soldier's prerogative of to take from citizens what he needed, or merely desired. To John, it was a licentious—immoral—practice that he had passively condoned. He let himself consider for a brief second that he had been trapped by circumstances and that he had had no choice. Then, as if someone else were speaking to him he rebuked himself. *No. We are creatures of choice. Whenever we begin to let go of personal responsibility for what we do—or do not do—we become like the animals.*

On the march from Beverly to Monterey in early November, the regiment divided into two detachments and marched by different routes. Companies F, D, and I, under the command of Major Francis P. Peirpoint, scouted through Pocahontas and Bath counties—through Elkwater and Huntersville—to Monterey. The rest of the regiment, including Lieutenant McMorrow and his men, took a different route that put them through Pocahontas and Pendleton counties under Colonel Klunk. The men believed that the citizens along these lines of march were favorable to the Southern cause, and that this gave the men ever greater freedom to exploit them and to "teach them the beauties of secession."

John's company made the march under Colonel Klunk with no overt incidents of foraging reported, at least to John. If such things happened, and John supposed they did, they were whispered between the men. He could live with that as long as he could keep himself from being party to it.

When the whole regiment arrived at Monterey, however, the men from the three companies under Major Peirpoint spoke freely about their exploits along the route. Lieutenant McMorrow came upon men at their campfire laughing about a citizen they had forced to surrender his coonskin coat. Their voices did not soften when John approached.

Even the officers laughed uncontrollably as one of their own recounted what had happened while they were camped at Mingo Flats.

"Here's the way Sergeant Orr tells it." A young lieutenant rubbed his hands together in front of the fire as he began the tale. "When we went into camp at a place called Mingo Flats there wasn't room for all of us to fit in the woods where Major Pierpont had told us to make camp. He told some of us to go ahead and set up over in a field that wasn't far off."

John leaned to the left to avoid the smoke that stung his eyes.

"Anyways, the boys looked around at the stacks of hay and the fence rails and some of 'em got the notion to make comfortable quarters of the stuff. First one group of men built a square pen—four or five rails high—but left the side open toward the fire. Pretty soon all of 'em were making these little pens. Then they put some hay on the ground—to sleep on—and some rails and more hay across the top to make a roof. It was like a little village just popped up in the field there."

John got up and moved to the other side of the fire.

"Now, that much I'm tellin' you from what I saw. Here's the part that Sergeant Orr tells. If I don't get it exactly right, you oughta have him tell it to you. Anyways, Captain Prichard is against foraging and he's always trying to get it reined in. He was with the boys in the field—and he was right impressed with their little huts all over the place. Some of the other officers are always lookin' the other way when foraging is going on. At least I do that sometimes—but it bothers me some. But, anyways, we all thought the huts were smart pieces of work."

One of the other officers gave out an exaggerated sigh and said, "Okay. We're impressed with the huts! But don't you think we ought to just go get the good sergeant over here to tell us the part that he saw?"

"Okay, I'll get to the meat of it. The rest of it fits in with the end of it. Anyways, a private over in Company I—they call him 'Nosey'—I don't know his name. Nosey was looking around, after his hut was built. About ten or twelve boys could fit in one of the huts and they all worked together to make 'em. Nosey was looking around for something to scrounge up to eat when he saw some calves across the field. Sergeant Orr says, 'With Nosey, to think is to act.' Nosey had visions of fresh veal dancing through his brain. So he runs over and grabs one of the calves by the tail. The calf is stronger than Nosey figured and it takes off running. Nosey will not let go. He's just runnin' along behind that calf, pullin' an' tryin' to stay on his feet. He runs—the calf with Nosey holding on to its tail and tryin' to stay up and pullin' and tryin' to git the calf to stop—he runs right toward where Captain Prichard was. Captain Prichard is against foraging—unless it's called for. Captain Prichard hears the commotion and comes runnin' out of his tent with his big cheese knife while everyone else is cheerin' an' yellin' an' hootin' and hollerin'. When he—that's Captain Prichard who's against foraging—came out he saw Nosey and the calf runnin' right straight at him. So he steps to the side and yells, 'Hold on there. Hold on there!' He meant for Nosey to stop what he was doing. But Nosey yells back—as he's runnin' by holdin' the tail of that calf—Nosey is runnin' right past the Captain and yells back, 'I will! I will!'"

He paused while the others slapped their knees and laughed. John laughed with the others. The lieutenant who had told it laughed with them, satisfied that he had gotten it about like he had heard it from the sergeant.

"That's not the end of it. Just about that time—after he—Nosey not the calf—yelled, 'I will! I will!'—just about that time some boy from Company D picked up an ax and whacked the calf right in the head. And down he went—the calf not Nosey."

John was still curious about Captain Prichard's reaction. "What did the Captain do then?" he asked with a more serious tone.

"I don't know. The way Sergeant Orr finished the story was by saying—this is Sergeant Orr talking—'So we all had fresh veal for supper.'"

Other stories around the fires told of adventures between Beverly and Monterey.

At Huntersville the detachment had come upon some Johnny Rebs who had just a tad too much apple-jack. They took the Rebels prisoner. The acting quartermaster, Lieutenant Bradley of Company I, went chasing after some of horses grazing there. Most of them got away.

At various places along the line of march the men had appropriated milk, honey, apples, and other such things. Citizens had buried their apples in holes for winter storage. Around the fires at Monterey the men laughed openly about the way some of the men had their heads stuck down the holes with legs poking out as they tried to get their fair share of the buried apples.

Another tale circulated about two men going into a house in search of food. John heard the version that went like this: "The men folk were all away from the house. That's the way of it in Rebel lands when the Yanks are around. For all their big talk, the Confederate men ain't ever in sight when Billy Yank is in town. There was only two young Rebel ladies at the house and when they seen our boys they put up their hands and yelled, 'Take our money. Take whatever you want. Don't hurt us personally.' Then one of our boys looked at 'em and said, 'You personally be damned. Where's the corn bread?'"

This one was not in the least funny to John McMorrow. He involuntarily thought of Anna Lee, her sister, and their mother. Blood rushed to his face. He envisioned what it would be like for them in such a circumstance. He felt powerless to protect them from Rebels who might visit their farm. If *Mr. Stone had to be away on some business and a force of Rebels were to harass his family what would he do? What could he do? What could he do if he was at home and they came? What would Anna Lee and the other women do?* John hoped they would behave just as the two ladies behaved when our men bothered them. He prayed that Rebels who might happen there would be looking for nothing more than cornbread after catching sight of Anna Lee.

The stay at Monterey lasted only a day. It was more a brief pause for rest than a destination. On the 9th of November the regiment started back to where it had begun the expedition, going by way of Crab Bottom, Franklin, Circleville, and Hunting Ground Mountain. They made camp just five miles below Beverly. Most men, John McMorrow among them, grew stronger from the hard marching—but some showed signs of weakening.

The weather worsened. From their camp below Beverly they marched to Webster where they arrived on the 18th. Rain was no longer a blessing. Snow was no friend. In fourteen days they marched a total of 238 miles—fording swift frigid streams swollen by cold rain and melting snow, stepping, slogging—one foot at a time—through thick mud well above their ankles that robbed many a soldier of his boots. John selected landmarks as goals that were nearer together than on the first marches and he often wondered if he would be able to meet them. He did.

When the regiment arrived at Webster, a good many were candidates for the hospital. Measles and dysentery spread through the regiment. It was a wonder that as many completed the march as did.

The next day, after completing such a hard march and sensing that they had reached a resting place, the men were informed that they were to proceed to New Creek, eighty-nine miles away.

John was about to protest with others who groaned and cursed when Colonel Klunk continued, "We'll be traveling by rail, boys. New Creek is only a few steps away from where you stand right now. You'll load into the heated cars just down the street from here, sit for a few hours, sleep if you can, and then step off the train to make camp right there by the tracks." Sighs coursed through the thinned ranks.

"And the mail should catch up with us at New Creek."

Morale grew as weary soldiers trudged to the station.

*   *   *   *

I'VE THROWN THE YARDSTICK AWAY

New Creek provided a welcomed respite from hard marching. Hot rations were regular fare. Camp spread out in evenly spaced tents with areas like streets between the rows. It was cold. Winter approached, but at least they were not struggling to lift feet from freezing mud. Those who had lost boots had new, dry brogans. They settled in and began to feel cozy. They would not have called it that a year earlier, but cozy by the new standards.

Light drilling, some turns at guard duty, and a chance to poke around in the small town of New Creek were all pleasures. The fort on the hill served as a supply depot along the Baltimore and Ohio Railroad. Men found ways to get whatever they needed to make themselves as comfortable as men can be living in tents in November and December in western Virginia. What the quartermaster could not supply the sutler could provide for a price.

John sat on the stump beside the campfire with a six other junior officers of the regiment. Jokes and tales and news and small talk passed the evenings until lights out. His overcoat was warm enough. It seemed to work best to keep it opened in the front as long as he faced the fire and allowed the heat to radiate into it. Like the others, John raised his palms to the fire every few minutes.

These men, all of them, were becoming a band of brothers, even the privates whose names John could not recall. A year ago they had had little in common. Most of the enlisted men had been farmers. Among the junior officers some had been merchants, some teachers, accountants, budding politicians, college students, or lawyers. The war took them from their jobs, their families, and their plans. It interrupted their dreams without robbing them of hope. The army had thrown them together. Uncle Sam gave them new tasks, new titles, and new plans for the duration of the war. When they mingled with other regiments they laughed at the accents from New England—and Germany and Ireland and other far-off lands—but kinship was real.

Mulligan's regiment, the 23rd Illinois, was here at New Creek and made up of Irishmen. Their ways and their songs added color to the warp and woof of the army. They had joined hands for a cause they all generally—if sometimes vaguely—believed in.

Around the campfire few men spoke of patriotism and war. They spoke mainly of each other, of incidents along the line of march, and of clever things spoken by others among them. They talked about home. Those who had wives and children spoke of them and pulled pictures from protected pockets and showed them to those who would praise their handsome looks even though the light of the campfire did not allow for close inspection. They recollected things they had done as children, with brothers and sisters and mothers and fathers. Tales of childhood pranks, first deer kills, and all manner of adventures evoked more of the same from others who waited their turn. Friendships grew deep in the days when the greatest kindness a man could show to another was to listen, nod, smile, compliment an image in a frame, laugh at a joke, and wait his turn to speak.

John was on pins and needles to get to his tent to read, again, the letter from his father that had just arrived. He had only glanced at it earlier and it seemed to speak mainly about things at church and around town, without anything remarkable. But it was from his father and it needed a close reading.

It would be rude to break out of the circle around the fire and go to his tent in the course of fraternizing without some clear stopping point. All the stories overlapped and nothing seemed to provide his opportunity until a group of privates approached one of the officers and patiently waited for a pause. The pause came and the newcomers asked permission to go into town "for a spell."

John stood and said, "If you'll excuse me, gentlemen, I've a matter to attend to." They nodded, waiting for the social hour to resume. As John strolled toward his tent, buttoning his coat, he overheard one of the officers say to the departing privates, "Now remember, boys, one night with Venus—a lifetime with Mercury." He wondered what it might mean, but was not about to reenter the circle to find out. Not now.

Entering the tent John struck a match and lit the candle that was already resting in his improvised "candle-holder." This was just his bayonet with the blade stuck in the cold ground and the socket sticking up about a foot. The candle rested perfectly, as if by design, into the socket. He turned, closed the flap, and tied it. He removed his coat and sat. Propped against his rough trunk and settled on his improvised bed—really four feed sacks stuffed with straw and elevated a few inches above the ground on wooden pallets from the warehouse on the hill—he retrieved the letter from his coat pocket. He covered himself with the coat—put it on backwards and poked his arms through the sleeves—and turned to get the cleanest use of the light from the flickering candle.

He pulled the letter from its dirty white envelope, unfolded the two pages, and scanned the words. John had seldom seen his father's handwriting except on a few bills of sale and other such documents. It struck him as odd that he would not have been able to recognize the letters as having been formed by his father's hand if he had been asked to do it.

He began reading closely. Mainly news from Clarksburg. One of the cows had gotten sick after eating some wild cherry leaves, but it looked like she would pull through. The wind had snapped and blown a section of the tree over into the pasture. He would cut it for firewood but might wait until spring, after the sticky sap had mostly oozed out.

John was surprised that his father wrote in complete sentences and spelled the words correctly, and that the sentences held together and expressed his meaning. He had not thought of this before. He read on.

"John, I have been wanting to tell you that I am not ashamed of you for going with the Union army." The line was full of meaning for John. It washed over him and settled a question that had gnawed at him. "When I told you how I believed about slavery and the way things used to be I did not know that this thing was going to get so big. I don't know for sure if the South is right or the North. I do know that I am proud of you personally. I don't say much about the war these days except to say that I hope it's over soon and that you boys can all come home and get back to the way things were before."

There was a little horizontal line on the page before the letter continued. Maybe it was supposed to mean something. *Maybe it means that he had stopped there and then continued the letter later on. Or maybe it was his way of saying that a section had ended and that he was about to start a new one. That must be it.* The paragraphs were not indented.

"Things are fine at church. A lot of empty spots where boys are off in the army. Two or three new families have been coming over from Grafton. They aren't saying why, but it's said around that some sort of fuss is going on over there. I met one man who says he knows you. His name was Stone. When I told him my name he said that he figured I might be related to you. I was proud to tell him that I was. His wife and two daughters are coming with him. The girls were both pretty but the one is what I'd call extra pretty. Some other fellow was riding with them from Grafton. I think he was with the extra pretty one. Not much else is new at church."

What was this? Katie had married her man and he had gone off with some other regiment. Who was this stranger riding with them? He told himself—audibly but quietly—that there was no sense jumping to conclusions, but he was not listening. He did convince himself that there was no clear reason to give up his hope. He could continue marching toward it. It was something like picking out an outcropping of rocks in the distance on the march and then trudging down into a big dip in the road where he could not see it anymore but continuing to march toward it anyway. *Even if it is Anna Lee he's writing about and even if this fellow was "with" her, that does not have to mean that he's anything more than some friend of the family, or maybe even a cousin—or maybe just some fellow who rides with them because they're friendly enough to give him a ride and then he sits or stands or whatever by Anna Lee because he wants to without her being the one who wants him there.*

—Proximity might be against me. Maybe not. Maybe so.

John hurriedly finished reading the letter. He barely took in the news about the fall harvest. His eyes rushed over the remaining words.

In the distance, in every direction, men were playing banjoes, slapping sticks—or spoons—together and singing as John McMorrow gathered his materials to write a letter. A circle of soldiers was trying to sing some song about "Abraham's Daughter." Another was doing the same with the "Battle Cry of Freedom" and how it "swells upon the ear." He thought of Mr. Stone and how he would probably have something to say, if he were here, about their music swelling his ears.

With knees bent and the slab of wood from a hardtack crate laid across his inclined lap, John penciled a letter to Anna Lee.

Dearest Anna Lee,

We are encamped at New Creek Station over in Hampshire County. Many in the regiment took sick and were sent to the hospital after we got to Webster. We traveled to this place, New Creek by rail. Tell your father that we also traveled by rail part of the way to Webster but that we had to be careful to get off the rail every time a train was heard coming. I thought of him when I heard someone say this along the way. We are comfortable and I am well here at New Creek. There is a big fort named for General Kelley up on the hill where they keep military stores for the whole army to the east. There is another fort called Fort Piano on the hill across from Kelley. I have not seen inside it. I think it's there to support and defend the other.

There is no church of the disciples here at New Creek. The chaplain is a good man. He is from Moundsville. He knows nothing, however, of simple New Testament Christianity. Some of our brethren from Clarksburg are in this regiment. We meet on most every Lord's Day to have the Lord's Supper and read some from the Bible.

Some of the boys are singing and playing now even though it is cold. They don't sing as pretty as you all do. You could teach them if they can be taught. I well remember the way you played the piano one evening there in Grafton and we all sang—not hymns.

John paused and inserted a little horizontal line before continuing.

Anna Lee, no one strikes all of the strings of my heart as you do. Some can strike the "intellectual" chords, but you do it with confidence and clarity. The notes make perfect sense. Others can strike the "comic" chord, but you strike it with a soft touch that sounds just a pleasant note without the jarring of mindless knee-slapping. Others can strike the painful chords but you touch them honestly and gently and that touch is welcomed. Those notes are a part of the larger harmony and they belong in the truthful strain without dominating it. You strike other chords to which I cannot assign names right now. Other friendships, relationships, memories, situations, and truths strike some of these and with different intensities. Some one, and some another. Some harder, and some softer. But you somehow touch them all and in the best ways and you produce a symphony inside my heart.

You must know how much I love you. We have so much in common as far as our thoughts and such have been shared. I need know nothing more about you before I am prepared to say that I love you completely. I have thrown the yardstick away. I took the measure of you a long time ago. I know that there are more things to learn about you and that circumstances would bring out new colors and shapes—but there is nothing that you can say or do that could alter the measure I have already taken. You seem not to know how different you are from all others I've ever known. It's not just that you are pretty. You are that. You are more than that. When I am with you I feel like I am connected to what feels like another part of myself. It is like your heart comes out and wraps around mine and they beat together. When I say what I think, you understand it. When you say what you think, I feel like you have read my mind and that you're saying back to me what I either already think or something that is worth thinking about.

Anna Lee, this is not just a lonely volunteer writing to someone out of loneliness. I thought this way before I left and I cannot shake the thoughts. I wish I had said them before I left. Someday we will have time and opportunity to be together. I believe that you will then know what I know already. I cannot ask you to wait for me. I can only express the hope that you will consider where we are in relation to each other in any choices that you make while I am away. If your own heart does not compel you to wait, then I hope that my words will not press you to do what is contrary to your heart. Whatever your decisions may be, I will always love you. It is the most involuntary and compelling love or feeling that I have ever known. Nothing in the great literature of the world, in any language, poem, or song comes near to describing it. Words fail me once again to tell you of it. You stand alone in my mind as the epitome of all that is beautiful, kind, loving, and wonderful. It is my hope, but not my demand to you or to God, that we might one day share life together. This war is going to end someday.

With all my genuine love.

John McMorrow.

It was growing late and *Tattoo* had already faded from the drum. Even though the rules regarding lights out were not enforced among the officers, John meant to observe it for the sake of the men who had to. The camp was quiet except for other young officers who still swapped memories and hopes at the campfire. John hoped that the enlisted men of his company would notice that their lieutenant was not among them.

John extinguished the little candle. He would have liked to let it burn for the little heat it gave off, but he conserved it. He wrapped a corner of his wool blanket around his head, tucked the rest around his body as best he could, and kept the overcoat in reverse on his body. He closed his eyes and waited for sleep while visions of Anna Lee and some stranger without a face or name danced.

CHAPTER 5

PAINFUL WORDS FOR TWO MEN

"I am confused," Anna Lee wrote in her journal. The words did not capture her sentiments but they were the closest she could find. On her lap lay the opened letter from John McMorrow at New Creek. Winter had come. Ants no longer struggled above the frozen ground for pieces of vegetation. Whatever conflicts had set the ants at odds had been settled by the weather.

She sat on the floor near the fireplace. Dancing flames illuminated the pages. She held paper filled with John's heart, poured out with a crude pencil. She had read and reread the words many times in the past few days. The opened page of her journal was blank except for the date, December 8, 1862, and three words: "I am confused."

The pages from New Creek resonated with certainty—finality. John's professed love for her was fixed and immovable. His hopes and desires were clear. His intentions were obvious.

Anna Lee allowed herself to write words in response to John's letter, but she would not send them. She wrote as a private experiment to see what would come out if she were to speak the truth without restraint. "I love you, John. To feel myself the sole object of your fervent affection is ecstasy. I long to be in your arms, to feel your embrace, and to taste your sweet kisses. I want to be your wife and to bear our children and to go with you wherever you might choose to go. I hope that it will not be far from Clarksburg...."

Boards squeaked in the kitchen floor. Anna Lee tucked the experiment inside the journal as her mother entered.

"You look troubled, child," her mother spoke softly and with evident concern. "Is there anything I can do for you? Anything I can get for you?" "No, thank you, Mother. I'm fine. Really. Just thinking."

Mrs. Stone sat in the rocking chair across from her treasured daughter. She could have sat in the chair more to the side. That would have given her a view of the journal, but she chose the rocker. "Let me tell you something that I've never told you before. It's something I've not told anyone. I'd like to keep it just between the two of us." Anna Lee nodded and closed the journal using the envelope from John's letter as a bookmark.

"When I met your father there was another young man who had told me that he loved me. I thought that I loved him too, and I said so."

Anna Lee blushed. Her mother saw it.

"Don't be ashamed of how you feel, sweetheart. That might be beyond you. Only watch what you do about how you feel."

Managing a slight smile Anna Lee asked, "Mother, were you telling me something about you?"

"I loved your father. I thought I loved the other man too. I just had to decide which one I really loved."

"And how did you measure love?"

Mrs. Stone looked out the window at falling snow, searching for the answer. She started to say something about "just knowing," but that was just because that is what she was supposed to say. She looked across the years and to the truth because Anna Lee needed the truth more than she needed to think that her mother had always seen her father as the only possible love. She wanted to give both to Anna Lee, if she could give both without dishonesty.

Looking at Anna Lee, Mrs. Stone said: "The man I thought I loved was a good man. Ambitious. Smart. Good-looking—but not as handsome as your father. He was going off to college with plans to make something of himself. I have to say that I think I was afraid to think of going far from Grafton. Your grandparents would have been hurt. And I didn't know if I could do it." She paused and looked, again, out the window.

"Was that all of it, Mother? That he might take you away from here?"

"No. I've not tried to put this in words for anyone before but…but I don't think he needed me. He thought he did. He said he did. But I didn't see how I could add things to his life that he needed. I could love him. I did love him. I thought I did. But he seemed complete without me. He seemed to need the kind of wife who could be like a decoration for him but not one who could help him get through."

"Did Father need you?"

Mrs. Stone blushed. She looked at her lap and wiped her hands on the apron.

"Your father's a good man. A solid man. He would have been able to make it. I think…I suppose that maybe I've been able to work alongside him in ways that made me useful. Who can say what my life would have been if I'd gone the other way?" She looked straight at Anna Lee. "I made the right choice. You will too."

Anna Lee thought about her question before she asked it and she looked for a response in her mother's eyes as much as she listened for her words. "Mother, is there really any such thing as the right choice—with the other one being wrong—when the two men are good men?"

Mrs. Stone paused. "I don't know, Anna Lee. I just don't know. You can make the most of it with the one you choose to marry. You can create happiness around your own family circle with the one you marry. Once you've chosen, I suppose it is important to not look back. Make it work. Make it good. There is so much to learn as you go along. You just can't plan it all out in advance. Things will take you by surprise. Whoever you marry will have qualities you couldn't have seen—and sometimes you'll think that it would have been better if you'd married the other one. Sometimes you'll be sure of it." She paused again. When she spoke this time she spoke with confidence, "Yes. There is a right choice. It's the choice that you finally make."

When her mother went back into the kitchen Anna Lee returned to writing the speculative letter. She continued where she had left off.

> I hope it will not be far from Clarksburg because I know that I would miss Mother and Father. Before we could even speak of marriage I would want to know your intentions for the future. You're a capable man. You've made much of yourself at a young age and I admire you tremendously for it. How would I fit into your life? What might I be able to add to it? I could love you. I do love you. I am drawn to you. I love another who also loves me. I know that this might be painful for you to hear, but I feel I must be completely truthful. Could you possibly want to marry me knowing that I love another man as completely as I love you? Does that truth not tarnish the halo you've put about my head? He is so like you that I cannot easily explain my sense of it. In some ways, to love him is to love you and vice versa. You are both kind and good and principled men. You both profess love for me that seems so gen-uine. Your words are stronger than his, but his eyes speak as clearly and his touch is as warm. I have made no attempt to deceive either of you and yet I feel that I've failed somehow in my duty by not telling you of him—and him of you. Now that I've told you I feel it my duty to also tell him. If all is equal then both of you must know the state of things with me. I love you, John and I am tormented by this unplanned circumstance.

Anna Lee stopped there. The experiment had done whatever it was going to accomplish. She read it again and then tossed it into the flames. She had a fleeting fantasy about the smoke floating over to New Creek and having some effect.

Then she composed a letter to John McMorrow, one she would send. After putting down some recent news and little events in the Stone household, she got to what she knew would be the real message.

> John, I am flattered and humbled at your expressions of love. I do not think them the wild sentiments of a lonely soldier far from home. I take them as true expressions of your heart. You know, John, that I have long been very fond of you. Your mind seems to take in all that your eyes see and you seem to be able to grasp immediately what others might spend a lifetime trying to understand. I have long been in awe of your intelligence. I admire you in many other ways. I admire what you are doing for the country in her time of need. I admire your way with words. When your words are sincerely directed at me they nearly take my breath away. I must ask you to bear with me while I take time to digest them and to give you the kind of honest reply they deserve. I will not try to match their poetry, for I cannot do so. What I say to you however, when I am ready to say it, will be heartfelt and honest. I hesitate to tell you this, but I feel that I must. There is another man who tells me that he loves me. I have held myself back from responding much to it as yet. He is quite like you in many ways. I hope that this is not too painful a revelation. It is not a rejection of you and you must not view it so.

She finished by promising to remember him and the good men who were with him in her daily prayers.

Before putting the letter in the envelope she took out another sheet of paper and composed a letter to Micah. She could not speak the words that she would write without sacrificing the equality of the message with the one she had just prepared for John. In it she told Micah about John. All was parallel and equal. She would mail it rather than hand-deliver it. She knew that both letters held painful words for two men she loved. She felt a strange sense of release.

Hugging her father and then her mother, Anna Lee went to bed and slept more soundly than she had in some time.

*   *   *   *

A WINTER MARCH TEACHES PLEASURES

It was a wonder to John McMorrow how quickly a town could just vanish. On the morning of December 11, just three weeks after establishing the village of tents beside the iron rails at New Creek, the 12th Virginia Infantry received orders to break camp and march to Moorefield. Just after the order arrived, John was given a message to deliver inside Fort Kelley on top of the hill. As he neared the fort he looked back at the neat rows of tents with their blocks of neighborhoods and clearly defined streets.

He did not pause for long. Cold December wind buffeted his face when he faced to the north. Men moved briskly. Fires were going out and their steamy smoke obscured his view of Queen's Point—the big outcropping of rock just across the Potomac River in Maryland. He had hoped that New Creek would be home for a longer time—at least until spring. But winter quarters are sometimes temporary resting places and the army does not issue orders by the weather.

In the fifteen minutes or so that it took him to deliver the message and begin his return trip, the whole town of the 12th Virginia had disappeared. What had been neat rows of white canvas was now a dark, smoky, dismal-looking patch amidst the other little towns that remained. *Any small patch of real estate takes on the nature of home when occupied by men for any length of time.*

The men formed up and the march began. Stiffly at first—in the cold and after three weeks of light duty—they trudged to the south of New Creek, parallel with the stream by the same name off to the left. The wind was at their back. John thought of the Irish blessing he had heard along those lines from some of Mulligan's men: "May the wind be always at your back." A very few local ladies stood in front of Carskadon Mansion on the hill to the right as the regiment passed. Bundled ladies waved handkerchiefs and called the names of men who tried to shout something in return. The return messages did not make it from the ranks to the hill because of the hissing and hooting of the others whose names were not broadcast to the four winds. Officers did not try to settle the men. Marching would quiet them soon enough.

About two and one-half miles south of New Creek the column turned to the left and ascended a long pull of a hill that reminded the men that they were in the army. Exertion had advantages. Men who had recently left the warm fires of camp were numb with cold, chilled to the bone. The hill warmed them. Heat filled garments and put feeling back into boots.

A winter march teaches pleasures that differ from those learned in summer. Shade is not sought or desired. Barren trees are uninviting. Grass is not to be seen unless in the form of coarse standing hay poking up from frozen ground through snow. There are no hopes for cool water—only for unfrozen. Men do not hope for long rest breaks. Stopping only sucks out the accumulated heat of marching and pulls in the frigid air. No sense ceasing the march only to stand in one place and stomp the ground when the ground could be stomped with forward motion.

Continuing on the march, at a slower pace than that of summer, is the best. Keep going until we arrive where we can build fires and make coffee.

As they topped the hill and veered to the left and started down a grade equal to what they had just come up, John noticed that officers on horseback worked hardest to adjust clothing to keep warm. In the ranks, men were more comfortable. Visible wisps of steam rose from unfastened collars. Soldiers found ways to hold the butts of their muskets with barrels over shoulders while keeping hands in cozy pockets or wrapped in rags—not according to regulation—but they felt their feet and the pain along the outer edges of their exposed ears was better than the feeling of having neither feet nor ears. Frozen officers on horse flesh were at a disadvantage.

At the bottom of the steep grade they came to Ridgeville and passed an inn. The 2nd Potomac Home Brigade, from Maryland, was headquartered there. The fires all around looked inviting, but they did not stop to share the warmth. The march continued on to Burlington on the now-gentle downward slope.

The regiment turned to the right and headed south at Burlington along Patterson's Creek. The ground was level for some distance. Rare, level bottom land spread out between the road the creek to the right. Men were not yet weary from the march. John had not even begun to pick out landmarks to keep him moving before the regiment halted. Men immediately gathered fence rails for small fires to cook coffee and warm hands. In a matter of twenty minutes there were hundreds of fires in the broad field between the road and Patterson's Creek. Acrid smoke and the pleasant bitter odor of coffee filled the air. Men filled canteens from the creek. Clumps of brush were designated, without anyone directing that it be so, as places for the soldiers to relieve themselves. Steam rose from circles of men. A few took off boots and dried socks of the accumulated sweat of fifteen miles or so of winter marching. Some held boots with open ends to the fires to dry them. Tin cups and crude coffee pots rattled and clanged all over the field. Subdued laughter, calm talking, and crackling flames had a musical quality.

These combined with other sights and sounds to portray soldiers halted on the winter march in western Virginia. The band of brothers grew tighter as men shared a common life, unlike what any had known.

In little more than two hours they marched on, leaving behind smoldering mounds giving fading testimony of the halt. Stiff legs settled into the pace that would loosen them. Men adjusted loads and settled hands into heat-holding pockets and rags. A few officers now led horses. As they trudged on, John took note of the vast difference in temperature between areas exposed to the sun that had found the valley and areas yet shaded by hills and trees. He took note of another principle: *What is a great blessing in one season might be a great curse in another.* The shade he had craved in the summer was now a curse and the sun he had despised was now his greatest pleasure.

The regiment marched on. They rested, cooked coffee, and gnawed hardtack just a few miles north of Petersburg. They trudged through Petersburg and on to Moorefield, where they went straight to work setting up tents and building fires—big fires here. This would, according to the hopes of all the men, be home for a time. They ate hot rations and prepared bedrolls according to the individual designs that suited each man. Rubber blanket, wool blanket, various articles of clothing, haversack pillows, and such combined in many formulas to make beds. The men dried socks and boots by the warmth of the fires before retiring to tents. No one other than those whose duties required it was stirring when it came time to beat out *Tattoo*. Someone had to awaken the drummer to tap the soothing cadence for men who heard nothing.

✳   ✳   ✳   ✳

"SHOULD WE DEAL YOU IN?"

Upon arriving at Moorefield the 12th Virginia was assigned to General Gustave P. Cluseret's brigade of General Robet H. Milroy's division. Severe weather set in. Men improvised a wide variety of shelters by combining their resources and bunking together.

Some combinations of rubber blankets, fence rails—which grew scarce where armies camped—sticks, pine boughs, straw, hardtack crates, and whatever else the men could find allowed for small fires inside, beneath contrived chimneys of sticks, mud, and rock. Fire pits were generally in the center of the enclosures. Men arranged themselves around fire.

Others went in for "spooning." This involved getting a number of men together—sandwiched between as many layers of rubber and wool as could be gathered for the purpose—and having each man lay with his bent knees resting in the back of the pocket created by the bent knees of the fellow resting beside him, with his chest against the other fellow's back. Spooning provided warmth, but turning over could only be done in unison and by mutual consent. For these, enduring the combined odors of unwashed comrades and mixed flatulence was an acceptable exchange for shared heat.

These were not the semi-permanent winter quarters they hoped to construct if they were going to be staying long in Moorefield, but men made the best possible use of what they had on hand.

John shared a shelter with other junior officers. They dug the fire pit into the center and managed to stay comfortable enough under the circumstances.

Warming himself at one of the big fires outside one night, John overheard enlisted men complaining. From what he gathered, some fellow by the name of "Jonah" was causing trouble in more than one of the shelters. Jonah, apparently a private, went from place to place knocking over coffee pots, stepping on feet, and making a general nuisance of himself. John thought of what might be done to protect the men from Jonah if the problem could be clearly defined and some plan of correction worked out.

With frigid wind whipping the flames in one direction—where John could not stand without being pocked by flying sparks—and the wind producing a colder zone on the opposite side, John figured it was time to turn in.

He opened the flap. Those inside untied the knot that held it tight. John entered the warmth of shared quarters, sensing that he had made a social blunder by bringing cold wind into the space. He secured the flap and tied the knot. John felt this act of penance might be enough to evoke a measure of forgiveness. He squeezed between a brother officer and the fire. The heel of his left foot tapped his comrade's shin. "So sorry," he said as he made his way to the far end of the hovel. There was no response.

"Should we deal you in?" asked one of the officers who had just finished shuffling the deck. "No thanks, I'll just read a spell before I turn in." The truth was that John had no earthly idea how to play the game and was not about to reveal his ignorance. His mother had prohibited cards and John knew that brethren generally disapproved of them. Pretending to read, he tried to make sense of the game. They placed bets, tossing with dirty hands various quantities of hardtack into a common pile. John accounted that this might not be the same as gambling for money. There was always more hardtack—at least up until then—and John would be willing to give some of his to anyone who might ask anyway. He asked no questions, but John kept track of the process and the combinations of cards that won the pot in the end.

"That was something about Colonel Northcott. I figure the scout will be decorated and promoted for that one." John was talking to no one in particular. "Is it a fact that he broke his hand in the fight?" No one knew or claimed to know. They had learned that it was not safe to count camp rumors as facts and John was trying to open a subject that no one seemed ready to go over again.

Men said that Northcott had stopped off at a house along the march, stayed long enough to get behind the regiment, and got himself captured by a Rebel scout. A Union scout, according to accounts, followed the Rebel and his prisoner, ended up fighting the Rebel hand-to-hand until he came out with the colonel without capturing the Rebel scout. The details were fuzzy. John wanted to fill in the blanks. He had heard some other officer reprimand a private for saying something about officers not being immune the rule of Venus and Mercury. John hoped to learn more of this mysterious rule without directly asking.

"Does anyone know how long we'll be here?" one of the men asked, "Or where we're supposed to be going from here?" No one knew any more than the others. All knew they were not supposed to be settling in for a long stay.

"I think the boys'd do better if they knew more," someone said. "They're making do," said another, "but we—they—don't seem to know whether to settle in more or keep things like they are."

"Have you men heard of some private by the name of 'Jonah'?" John's question generated smiles all around.

"Are you serious?" one of them asked, "Or are you just teasin' us here?"

"No. I keep hearing complaints and I thought something might be done."

"You really are serious." They all laughed as if out of control.

"John. John. Professor. Brother officer. A 'Jonah' is anyone who messes up all the time. It's a term the men use to describe a whole class of soldier. How long have we been in the army now? Six months or so? Five? Let's work on our vocabulary lesson. A 'Jonah' does not mean any harm—he just causes it by accident wherever he goes. A 'beat' is the sort of soldier who is more deliberate in trying to get out of hard duty no matter what kind of scheme he needs to concoct to accomplish that end. A 'Jonah' is innocent as to intention but an irritation to the men in close quarters." The others continued laughing.

John felt himself the subject of the joke. He felt little shame and was actually glad to have advanced his education in military lingo. He was not about to venture a question, not just now, about the mysterious Venus to Mercury line he had now heard twice.

Hoping to redeem himself once again, John retrieved a large log from the pile and placed it on the coals in the pit. They had all agreed that the larger ones should be saved until all were about to turn in for the night. Used in that way they would often last nearly until morning. As he pulled the log from beneath, a smaller one from the top rolled off and knocked over an empty pot belonging to one of the others. The others enjoyed a good laugh. John's face went red. He arranged himself in his bed, closed his eyes, and dreamed of Clarksburg—his element, where he belonged. He dreamed of kindling light in young men's eyes.

∗   ∗   ∗   ∗

HIS HEART SANK

Why would Anna Lee want to mail a letter? Micah was immediately anxious when he saw it. Anna Lee had just been in the day before, helping with the books. She seemed a bit different, but Micah had not made much of it. Combining that now with the letter before him, he worried.

He read the letter. Although Anna Lee spelled it all out and clarified all of the fine distinctions between rejection and asking for time, Micah had prepared himself for the possibility that Anna Lee would eventually come around to the conclusion that he was not suited for her. He recalled standing right where he now stood and thinking of how he would never be able to cast the brass that would fit her out right. Iinsecurity led him to read rejection between the lines. The words spoke of "fondness" and even of "enduring affection" and she had continued to help him in the shop, but these were not enough to erase what he felt sure was a friendly farewell.

His heart sank. Who was this other fellow off in the army somewhere? John *McMorrow. An officer. A former professor over at the school in Clarksburg.* He thought of the irony—officers are called "brass." The brass had already been cast for Anna Lee and Micah was made of no material to compete with it. He pictured Anna Lee entertaining high-toned guests and flashing her beautiful smile beside some professor, officer sort of gentleman.

Micah had always heard that no man can understand what is in the heart of a woman. He had allowed himself to think that he had begun to understand Anna Lee. The mistake had cost him. His loss was as real as if Anna Lee had told him outright that she would just as soon kill herself as marry such a man as Micah Johnson.

He tried to form an image of this John McMorrow. He saw a vague image of a tall, handsome, well-dressed man, with studded cane and top hat. *How could Anna Lee let such trappings lure her into the arms of such a pretentious and hollow man? Or do I have it right? It's not fair to Anna Lee for me to judge him from such a distance. I do know Anna Lee—well enough to know that she's not so vain as to let appearance and prestige alone pull her into some empty existence and possibly away from home.*

Micah slowly let go of resentment and, even more slowly, of his intention to try to pull Anna Lee back to himself. The pendulum of intention swung far from that of winning her back to that of pushing her away and finally seesawed around center. *If she wants this man instead of me, I'll let her go. I can't do otherwise. I might cause her pain by the effort. I'd drive her far from me by trying to pull her back. No. If friendship is all that I'll have from Anna Lee then I'll hold onto what I have. There's my best chance. This McMorrow could die in battle or come down with one of the diseases that are killing more than bullets.* He felt ashamed for letting John's death be his thread of hope. Anyway, he would adjust to matters as they now stood, as best he could, and let Anna Lee have her officer if that was her intention.

Micah finished boring the barrel. He sat down to pen a letter to Anna Lee. If she wanted this business carried out by mail, so be it. He began by thanking her for the letter and for her honesty. His hand wanted to beg her to reconsider. His mind filled with words he now wished he had used before to tell her of the immensity of his love for her. Instead, he wrote that he "understood her position" and that he would "adjust himself" to her wishes.

To Micah, the short letter meant that he would cease speaking of love and that he would not return to her home or expect to ride with them to church in Clarksburg. It meant he would withdraw from the race he had not known he was in. The words meant he was conceding loss—running up the white flag—and giving Anna Lee over to this McMorrow.

Mail caught up with John in Moorefield on December 15. He read it in the company of those who shared his little hut while they asked questions about happenings in Clarksburg. He had some news, in the letter, but he wanted to get past it right away and to read that Anna Lee loved him as he loved her. He passed along the little items of news as he read them.

After a moment of silent pause and a heartsick change in his expression, the men stopped asking questions. They respectfully allowed him to read.

John McMorrow saw nothing between the lines. He missed some of what was there. He took in the situation, for the most part, as Anna Lee described it. He thought that he felt the pain that she felt as she wrote the letter. He understood. He understood her reluctance to speak freely of love. Anna Lee solved the mystery of the stranger in his father's letter. John felt no resentment; no sense of actual loss. Slight panic at the possibility of future loss, but this passed. Mainly, he experienced sympathy for Anna Lee and the pain of her struggle.

He tried to place himself in her position. He felt her confusion. *If this other fellow is a good man*—and John assumed that he must be or Anna Lee would not be in this conflict—*then he might be the one she ought to choose. The one off in the army might die and never return home. Why cut herself off from a good man close to home and safe?* John would give her time. He had to. There was no choice. Demands would not hold Anna Lee so he would make none. His conviction that their love was mutual and involuntary would remain the basis for his hope. She would wait. Anna Lee would know, when he got home, that there could be no other decision for her to make than to marry him and bear him children. She would have to come to this on her own. John would not attempt to force it. He knew that he could not force it. *Not upon Anna Lee.*

John would not let go of hope. He would keep marching toward it. *The war will end. This is not rejection. This is a request for time and space.* He would grant it without objection. It was just a postponement of the inevitable. *She will come to me by her own choice—after settling all doubts in this allotted time—when the war is over.*

He fished out paper and pencil and put the slab of wood across his lap. Being careful to keep what he would write out of sight of the others, he sacrificed light for privacy. John wrote on the shaded page.

He thanked Anna Lee for the letter and for honesty. He told her that he "completely understood" her position and that he would "adjust himself to things" as they now stood. To John this meant that nothing had changed, other than his awareness of the situation. He would honor her request by backing away from profuse statements of his love. John knew that both he and Anna Lee knew in their hearts that she would return his love in time.

Maybe she would even be drawn to him more than before if he allowed her time to take note that he had backed off? It would not hurt to give clear evidence that he understood and would comply with her wishes.

CHAPTER 6

HE DID NOT INQUIRE FURTHER

On December 17 General Cluseret led his men, now including the 12th Virginia, on an expedition to Strasburg, Virginia. The first day they marched twenty-six miles in bitter cold and then camped that night along the banks of Lost River, four miles from Wardensville.

There was no time to arrange comfortable quarters. Icy wind cut through every crevice of cold-stiffened canvas and ripped blankets from shivering bodies until men forsook tents and spent the frigid night hugging large fires. Even the burning specks of flying embers that blasted windward faces did not deter those standing there.

In spite of all their misery some laughed when Barney Wiles, a private in Company D, yelled out that the fire itself had frozen solid—and several turned to see if it was so.

They formed up, ready to move on before the sun came up. The wind died. Marching warmed men, eager to march.

The first to test the surface of Lost River sent word toward the rear that it was frozen solid. It would bear the weight of men. Horses with riders tested it. It would hold up under the weight of men on horseback, but artillery broke through. Horses and men finally pulled cannon through the frigid water and jagged ice and onto the other side. Those exposed to the icy water were especially ready to march on without delay.

They marched through Wardensville and continued on toward Capon Springs. The thick forest gave little evidence that they were approaching anything other than more of what they had seen for eighteen miles. The men in the front suddenly began talking excitedly, laughing, and cheering. John and those near him strained to see what was going on to the front. He could see only that the column turned to the right and disappeared.

Coming to the bend in the road, he saw what all the fuss was about. He was awed by the sight of a grand and imposing edifice—shrouded by a misty cloud— appearing in full proportions in the middle of dense forest as if by magic. Mountain House harbored 410 rooms. Dry. Windproof. Warm.

Eighteen miles would be far enough to march on December 18. Spirits soared as men learned the value of warm indoors, mattresses, and standing before contained heat in stone fireplaces. All had experienced such things before, but on this day they discovered their worth for the first time.

John McMorrow marveled at the warmth of the water in the springs. Steam arose from natural water in the middle of winter weather that had solidified running water not far away. John laughed when he saw it. He took note and modified his recently formulated principle. *The seasons do not alter some things that remain constant no matter what else transpires.*

The men of the 12th Virginia slept soundly that night.

The pounding on the door in the dark morning hours of December 19 was a jarring intrusion. In the twilight between the dreaming obliviousness of sleep and the alert responsibility of wakefulness, John started to protest. It took a quick review of history to realize that he was in the army—on the march—and camped for the night in a soft bed. For a fleeting instant this came as a dismal disappointment. When John was on his feet and dressing, along with the others who shared his quarters, he accepted the reality of it all. He agreed to wake the others in adjacent rooms.

Feeling like a criminal, John banged doors and confirmed that men were awake. He could not be sure if Surgeon Bryon was joking or in earnest when he protested—after a brief pause—against the very idea of getting up so early. "It's not the ideal thing, and I don't believe in it—this thing of getting up at midnight to stuff victuals and start out on a Rebel hunt."

The men stuffed victuals, formed up, and after a collective, yearning, backward glance they faced to the front and marched eighteen miles to Strasburg.

Few of them had ever seen the Shenandoah Valley. It was beautiful, even in its bleak winter condition. The land was wide and flat all the way over to the Blue Ridge Mountains in the distance—except for Massanutten Mountain dominating the valley's center to the south. Strasburg itself seemed an ancient town to the eyes of men whose own small towns on the other side of the Alleghenies had been established more recently.

The Rebel General William E. Jones was still in Strasburg with a small force that retired as the Union army approached.

General Cluseret dashed ahead of the main force of Union infantry with only a small detachment of guards, who skirmished with the rear guard of the retreating Confederate cavalry. He formed a gallant picture as he ran forward in his corduroy pantaloons with his sword to the front. It cheered the men to see it: Contact with the enemy, brave conduct, and a few prisoners taken.

With the perimeter secured, the brigade camped at Strasburg on the north bank of the North Fork of the Shenandoah River in certified Rebel territory.

Next day the command moved six miles to Middletown where they made camp. The weather made an unseasonably mild turn. Straw and rail huts made fine quarters once again. The brigade's equipment and food had been left behind at Moorefield except for what men could carry. Foraging details went to work. This was official foraging in Rebel lands. John had less difficulty than before with his still-troubled conscience as he supplemented hardtack with local beef, mutton, chicken, and other meals gathered from fields, smokehouses, and cellars.

On Christmas Eve they marched down the Valley to the north for Winchester. Along the way General Cluseret received reports suggesting that a band of Rebels commanded by General Jones was pursuing them. Cluseret moved his men, all but about 2,500 men in the brigade, to a ridge about a half mile in advance and out of sight. He then had them march around the ridge in plain view and then back around to their starting place. This was to give, from a distance, the impression that a large body of Union soldiers were being reinforced by another large force. Whether or not any Rebels saw the show, it worked up close. Some of the 12th Virginia themselves believed they were being reinforced.

At Winchester—an old town in their view—Cluseret's men commandeered winter quarters abandoned by Rebels and left in usable condition. These were rough little huts of logs and cedar brush that seemed to serve the purpose well while they waited for the supply wagons coming from Moorefield.

Although the Rebels had abandoned the huts, the shanties were not empty. The Confederates had left behind armies of tiny mercenaries. The regiment called these vermin, who infested the huts and attacked without political cause, "graybacks." Graybacks sought out the warmth and nutrition of human bodies. The insects crawled into warm crevices. Graybacks respected the rank of colonel as much as they respected that of private. Like bushwhacking partisans they wore no uniforms, were hard to find, irritating beyond description, impossible to eradicate, and they followed the regiment from then on wherever it went. Graybacks taught the value of bathing and of boiling clothes at every opportunity. Primitive sorts learned to live with this enemy and to harbor him in armpits, crotches, unwashed hair, and filthy clothing; giving him bases of operation from which to launch unending attacks.

On New Year's Day, 1863, the wagon train caught up with the regiment at Winchester. Those escorting it had repulsed a Rebel attack and brought the train safely through from Moorefield by way of Romney and Blue Gap in five days.

This was the day on which the President's Emancipation Proclamation went into effect. The blacks of Winchester, many of them nearly white, seemed either to ignore the matter or remain completely ignorant of it.

A majority in Winchester seemed disloyal to the Union and, especially at first, showed open disgust for Yankees. The ladies pulled veils over their faces when passing Union soldiers on the street. Citizens dumped chamber pots in areas frequented by soldiers.

Before the troops' three-month stay came to an end on March 27, however, proximity had melted some of the ice that the season of war had formed in the hearts of the citizens of Winchester. Ladies who had veiled their faces before, now delighted in singing Rebel songs to—or at—the soldiers. They would sing "The Bonny Blue Flag" or some such song—and then apologize and ask the men not to take offense. The ladies were still loyal Confederates. They yet said so whenever the matter came into doubt, but to the men of the 12th Virginia and to other Yanks in town, they were beautiful.

An elderly black woman did some washing and cooking for the Union soldiers. When she overheard talk about how beautiful the white ladies of Winchester were, she took exception. In a motherly way she expressed the opinion that the Winchester ladies might be pretty in appearance, and even in some of their actions toward the soldiers, but "honey," she said with eyes widening, "they could jes cut yo hearts out."

Citizens of Winchester learned to benefit in other ways from the army. Some came into camp with cakes and pies for sale. Some, like many in the regiment, were illiterate. Not all of those coming to the camp could cipher. The more resourceful soldiers took advantage of the lack of education among some of the visitors, who were no more dullards than many in the regiment. One soldier was able to pass off a label from a bottle of *Perry Davis's Pain-killer* as scrip in exchange for fresh pies. Others boasted of coming away from transactions with more money in change than they had given in payment.

One of the local ladies who had grown comfortable enough to inquire, asked John, "What are you all comin' down here to fight us for?"

He explained that the Union must be preserved and that the Confederacy had attacked the United States at Fort Sumter. He tried to explain inoffensively that slavery had recently become one of the reasons that some were fighting. Union soldiers had come to think that the war might end human bondage and preserve the old Union and have all under one flag once again.

The friendly Rebel woman of Winchester gave the impression that she had heard nothing of his explanation. She continued as if John had told her that the men were there to punish and get revenge rather than to settle things as he had just explained. "How long do you all intend to carry on the war against us?"

Still trying to be courteous, but sensing that he would have to be more direct if he were to be understood at all, John said, "It will surely go on until the people in the southern states submit to the authority of the United States and return to the Union."

Her eyes grew large—as if some new and frightening idea had just come to her for the first time. Throwing hands to her face and turning swiftly away she exclaimed, "Oh! Oh!"

As she walked away John wondered if this was the view held by all of the South. *Have they lost so quickly the deep devotion that all Americans had shared for the old flag? Have they no sense of how far we will go to stand by it? Can they see nothing of the future welfare of the whole nation that will be ours by coming back together? Do they all see us as vindictive and hateful instruments of vengeance?*

As he tried to take in the flavor of the lady's sentiments John supposed that her views must be shared by a great many of his southern counterparts. What else could hold them in the field and keep them fighting for what they now counted as another country? He concluded that they really must have some deep devotion for their own flag and that some final rejection of the old stars and stripes had fully taken hold in the South. Rebels were prepared to fight until the Union had punished them enough. They were not going to yield. They would fight until the Union had its fill of retribution. For a moment he wanted to go home and just let them have their Confederacy.

Fraternizing with locals was limited, of course. The men stayed busy with guard, picket, fatigue duty—working on the fortifications around Winchester—and drilling, target practice, and scouting about the area. Time passed, as at other encampments, with growling, card-playing, letter-writing, reading and rereading letters and papers from home, and arguing about the controversial Emancipation Proclamation.

Many in the regiment could neither read nor write. Some were now eager to learn. Letters from home and a desire to send regards to loved-ones back in Harrison County produced students for John McMorrow whenever they could find the time. Newspapers became textbooks. Letters home were writing assignments. With John's help, and much time and revision, these became more polished pieces than some letters sent by fellow officers, even if the penmanship was crude. The professor felt that he was making himself useful. As both a teacher and an officer he grew into his element, learning the way in new circumstances.

Other than a few encounters by the cavalry of other regiments in the brigade, up in the valley, not much action involving the enemy took place at Winchester. Three more regiments and a twelve-gun battery of regulars reinforced the brigade.

On March 17 all the western Virginia troops wanting to cast a vote regarding the adoption of the new Constitution for the new state of West Virginia—already recognized but not officially organized and accepted—marched to the nearest patch of West Virginia soil across the mountain to make their approval official.

On the 27th the whole brigade struck tents once again and marched about ten miles to Berryville. They moved on the road leading across the valley toward Harpers Ferry, near the main course of the Shenandoah River along the base of the Blue Ridge Mountains. Two days later the 6th Maryland and the 77th Pennsylvania Infantry Regiments joined the swelling ranks of the brigade.

From across the river, using the Blue Ridge for a shield and refuge, Confederate guerillas led by Captain Andrew T. Leopold harassed the brigade. The guerillas fired at the Union outposts. Then, under cover of darkness on April 8, Southerners boldly slipped across the river and captured two cavalry pickets and five horses. Something needed to be done.

Lieutenant David Powell of Company H, 12th Virginia Infantry, served as provost marshal of the command. A gnarled old black man came into camp asking permission to buy sugar and coffee from the sutler. Powell questioned him about where he had come from and what he knew of matters across the river.

"I jes come from over there," he said without any apparent sense that the news would seem incriminating.

"Then you've been sent to spy for Leopold."

"No sah. I isn't no spy. Jes come for sugar and coffee like ah sayed. I knows da Capn'—an' 'is men, but I ain't in cahoots wit' dem mens. Deys at massas house right now. Goin' be stayin' der all night t'night."

"If you can take me to where he is before mornin' I'll give you fifty dollars." Powell figured this was more money than this poor black had seen in his life. If he was a spy, and Powell still counted that a strong possibility, then this just might be the thing to turn him around and assure some measure of safety for the men who might try to capture the Rebel captain.

The eyes of the old black man looked at the canvas above his head. He was thinking, weighing the thing out.

"Make that eighty dollars!" General Milroy had been listening outside the tent. He made the pot sweeter as he came through the flap.

"It'll do it," the black man said with a great white smile splashing across his dark face. "I was s'posed to take dis coffee and sugar back to dem mens tonight."

About that time John McMorrow walked by the tent on his way to gather old newspapers for his latest eager student. Powell yelled out to him, "John., come on in here."

While John gathered men for the expedition, Powell worked out a plan with the slave who was now a Union undercover agent.

Two hours later, John McMorrow, Lieutenant Powell, and thirty-eight men who John could grab on such short notice, were hunkered down behind brush on the riverbank. Lieutenant Thomas H. Means, Private James W. Caldwell, Sergeant Emanuel Adams, Lieutenant Joseph Caldwell, Lieutenant Josiah M. Curtis, Private Andrew O. Apple, Private Joseph McCauslin, Private Joseph R. Logsdon, and Private George H. Bird, all eager for action, were from the 12th.

The slave had crossed about a half-hour before.

Across the water someone lit a match. Then another. Then a third. "That's it," Powell whispered to Lieutenant Jesse Wyckoff of the 1st New York Cavalry, who then slipped into the water and swam across.

"What's that?" John tapped Powell's shoulder, pointing to an upper window in a farmhouse just up the bank where lights flashed. "A signal?"

Powell took four men to find out, returning about twenty odd minutes later with the lingering aroma of roast chicken about him. He brought with him another local black man to serve as a guide.

Wyckoff returned from the other side of the river with an old rowboat. When the men were all across, all but two of them quietly pushed on afoot to where the old slave had told them to look for Leopold and his men. The two remaining were to take the boat to a landing three miles downriver, where they would pick up the men and their prisoners.

Their new guide led them to the wrong house, not more than four hundred yards from the true target. Luckily the noise of bursting open the door did not alert the guard at the other house, where the Rebels would soon be found.

"Are you sure this time?" Powell demanded.

"Yes suh. Dis is de place."

Half the men knocked in the door and poured through it while the others encircled the house. The door literally flew off its hinges and fell on men who begged for quarter as soldiers in blue stood over them with muskets. Only one, a Rebel around the corner in the stairwell, tried to make a run for it up the stairs. Two pursued him to the top and found him hiding behind a chubby young girl, just waking from sleep.

"Come outa there or I'll shoot you." The Rebel let the girl go.

"Should we capture her too?" One of the men asked Powell.

"No. Let's let her finish her morning nap and be on our way."

The Union raiders searched Captain Leopold and seven of his men, secured their weapons, and took them as official prisoners of the Union army back to the river. It was getting light now. The boat was waiting.

Marching his men with their trophies into camp and then to the jail at Berryville, Powell tried not to smile or strut.

John felt like letting out a whoop, as a few of the enlisted men in the squad were doing. It had been a glorious adventure. John was glad to have been pulled from his cozy classroom in Clarksburg for moments like this. It somehow evened out the hardships. There had not even been a fight. It was the risk; the anticipation of possibilities had keened John's senses and filled his life with meaning. Winning the prize and marching the prisoners home was small compared with the contest that brought it about. John made a fleeting comparison with his quest for Anna Lee and quickly dismissed it, thinking the end of the quest and having his prize would be far greater than the attempt to capture her heart.

The next day John wandered near the jail and stopped to check on his prisoner.

"I'll tell ya what," Leopold bargained, "you give me fifty yards with six or eight of yer men ready to shoot and I'll give you fifty greenbacks when the war's over."

"I don't think so," countered John. "These men from western Virginia—just about any one of them—can kill a running deer a hundred yards off. My father's not here to tell you, but if he were, he'd tell you that I could do it myself. You just hold onto your money and your life for now."

Leopold seemed like a likable fellow, about like men in the 12th Virginia. At least he was no different in any way that John could make out. John later winced when he read in the papers that Leopold had been hanged on May 25, 1863, after a proper trial by military court at Fort McHenry in Baltimore. He winced again when he learned, after that, that their old black informant was literally shot to pieces by Leopold's comrades after the capture. Neither canceled out the other.

From the night of the capture of Captain Leopold until the end of the war, men of the 12th volunteered for any detail when it was noised about that Lieutenant Powell would lead it.

On May 9, 1863, the regiment received orders to proceed to Clarksburg to protect that city from a possible attack by the Rebel General Jones who had been raiding in that part of the country.

Clarksburg. John thought of Anna Lee—and then of his father. *Home!*

They were to march to Harpers Ferry. From there they would travel by rail to the hometown of many of these men, and near to the homes of many others.

It was a dark midnight when the regiment passed through sleepy Harpers Ferry. The town was deserted and quiet except for the tramping of Union soldiers. Someone at the head of the column started singing. All soon joined: "John Brown's body lies moldering in the tomb…." Some eulogized a fallen hero and prophet at the scene of his greatest acts. John sang of the extraordinary criminal who had inflamed passionate hearts at a time when reasonable minds were most needed. He thought of how quickly history undergoes revision when men are dedicated to an idea and require that every act of every man on ones own side must be seen an act of heroism. "….but his soul goes marching on."

The tramping of thousands of boots on cobbles and the singing of half as many soldiers awakened the citizens of Harpers Ferry. Windows hoisted, shutters parted, and lights streamed into the streets. *Few of these men,* John mused, *would be willing to disturb sleeping civilians without cause if acting alone. None would stand in the street with no one beside him and raise such a racket. But men acting collectively feel no responsibility for what the mob does. Mobs have minds that do not belong to their members. A conscience shared by thousands leaves very small portions for the individuals who divide it among themselves.*

On Monday, May 11, the brigade traveled by rail to fewer than five miles from Clarksburg where Rebels had destroyed a bridge. The regiment disembarked, ate hot rations—supplied by men selected as cooks more for their inability to be useful otherwise than for their skill at turning raw meats, grains, and vegetables into palatable meals—and marched into Clarksburg on the same day.

It was late afternoon as they tramped to the outskirts of town. Here and there individuals waved along the side. John and other locals scanned for familiar faces. Surely word had spread that the regiment was coming. He turned when someone spoke out, "That's the purdiest girl I ever laid eyes on." She was pretty, but she was not Anna Lee.

Closer to town the regiments divided and went to different sectors to make camp. Now there were clusters of citizens waving and cheering. Marching men straightened their lines somewhat, without orders, and took on more of a parade air than a forced march except that all eyes were not to the front. Still no sign of Anna Lee.

These were the scenes of John's childhood. He saw trees he had climbed, homes he had visited, people he had known, the cemetery where relatives rested, buildings John had helped his father build, and other reminders of the past that connected him with this place.

As the regiment entered Clarksburg, citizens literally lined the streets. Handkerchiefs waved, names echoed, bands played, and the 12th Virginia Infantry Regiment held its collective head high. They had done no great or notable deeds, but they were in the army and coming home for a time.

The regiment laid out camp in tidy rows of dirty white canvas, not as straight and orderly as at New Creek, but stark against the green hillside assigned to the 12th Virginia. Fires soon blazed. The smell of coffee and smoke combined with the clanking sounds of men in camp to signal the recommencement of the settled transient life of soldiers. Banjoes played. Men sang. John finished his duties and spent the evening with his body stationed before a fire surrounded by comrades who spoke of nearby homes and friends, while his thoughts were of his father just down the road and of Anna Lee over near Grafton. Although *Tattoo* put him to bed at the time appointed for enlisted men, John McMorrow did not sleep well that night.

Before the sun's warming rays struck the canvas John was up and dressed and ready to challenge the obstacles that might stand between himself and a pass. He rehearsed lines and practiced facial expressions. This was not a matter of asking special favors. It was a reasonable request for a thing that every soldier got from time to time. It was not a demand. He would not beg or seem to plead. He would accept the response as a gentleman accepts his fate, whatever it might be.

Before morning formation John went to his captain's tent to see what duties might be assigned him for the day, if such had been decided. He nervously put his case forward, mentioning his father's proximity to the camp, and felt relief when the captain took out a pencil, moved its point across a page, scribbled something above the line and said: "You seem to have no specific duties assigned today, John. The men will be spending most of the day drilling."

Lieutenant Powell's tent was surrounded by enlisted men, local boys, just after formation. For the first time in his military career, at least for reasons of personal convenience, John exercised the prerogative of rank and went straight in. Powell did not outrank John, but his position as provost marshall put Powell in position to give or withhold passes, following guidelines from the colonel that were sometimes ambiguous. Powell's own judgement was not supposed to matter, but it sometimes did and the colonel was pleased to have it so. The colonel did not wish to be bothered with all of the possible exceptions that might arise and he could wink at a few personal favors.

"John, you're just the sort of man I'm looking for." Powell was shuffling papers. "I've been asked to detail an officer to go into town and visit our men at the hospital. You seem to always show up when I'm needing someone. And your name's been scratched from the duty roster." Both smiled.

Trying not to look too pleased, John saluted and said, "I'm your man. What do I need to do?"

"Just visit them on behalf of the commander, pat them on the shoulder, and tell them we hope they're up and about soon. You don't have to say if they're fit for duty. That's up to the surgeons. But the question could come up sometime. We have only two men there. Here are their names." Powell passed him a paper with the names of two privates. Then he filled in a few blanks on another printed page, signed his name, and handed John the coveted pass. John could save his rehearsed explanations for another day.

He felt liberated as he spurred the horse down the dusty road to town. John would finish this little business at the hospital and then go find his father and learn news of Anna Lee.

He found the hospital, actually a huge block of whitewashed brick that had recently been an inn, and went inside. Patients had been funneled here from various commands. Their conditions were such that regimental or brigade field hospitals could not care for them. Some convalesced here. Others waited to die.

He found a surgeon who turned him over to a nurse. She looked at the names and walked him through the wards in search of the first, who was recovering from measles. On one ward John saw bandaged stumps and sleeves pinned at the shoulder and pant legs folded and pinned below the groin. On another he saw an assortment of men with wrappings about the torso. On these wards some cried out and moaned while others, who seemed not to notice the pain of men nearby, played cards. John smelled urine—strong old urine—and whiskey and sweat and other powerful odors he could not place.

He approached the bedside of the first on his short list. The patient was sitting, chatting with the fellow beside him. "Hello." He patted the man's shoulder as the private tried to make out John's business. "I'm Lieutenant John McMorrow from the 12th Virginia. On behalf of the commander, I am here to express our deep concern for your welfare."

The patient took on the pitiful look of a sufferer as he laid back on the off-white sheets and softly said, "Thank you, sir. I'm afraid I'm to be out of commission fer a spell. Measles is killin' some of the men." Patting him again and keeping his face under perfect control, John said that he and his comrades hoped to have him back in camp and to see him fit as a fiddle before long. The patient nodded and John was on his way.

The second bedside was entirely different. When the nurse told him, almost in passing, that he was about to see an advanced case of syphilis, John supposed that perhaps this meant that the man had advanced through the stages leading to near recovery. He could not have formed a more erroneous impression. John was not ready for what he was about to see.

The smell of rotting flesh filled the ward. Patients were still and quiet as John and the nurse walked between them. Some sat upright, but pained looks gave the impression that much effort held them up. They came to the private from the 12th Virginia. John fought the urge to look away. Here was a skeleton of a man on his back, completely naked except for a dirty white cloth about his groin. The man was covered with swollen, festering boils that disfigured his face and made it hard to make distinctions between nose, cheek, face, eyes, chin, neck, and mouth. His right leg cocked as if to avoid contact with the left and with the sheets. The figure in the bed was silent and still. The face, or where the face ought to be, canted toward the wall.

John patted no shoulder. "I'm come on behalf of the commander of the 12th Virginia to express our deep concern for your well-being." The head rolled ever so slightly in his direction. The region on the face—where the mouth ought to be—moved. If a sound came out it was covered by a cough to John's rear. The eyes were expressionless, utterly vacant.

"I say, man, I am here to express on behalf of the 12th Virginia a deep concern for your welfare." John detected a hint of a whisper. He leaned his right ear as close to the face as he dared as he repeated the script. He looked beyond the hideous torso only inches in front of his face. This time he was able to make out a faint, labored, whisper of three syllables spit out one at a time, "Go-to-hell."

John straightened. Others watched. John looked at the man, paused, and then said, "Certainly, man. I shall be happy to write your mother and give your regards to your wife." He turned and walked out with the nurse.

As the nurse started to leave, John inquired, "What can be done for such men?"

"Well," she said, "some seem to come 'round and improve with regular doses of mercury. They have to keep taking it and they never really seem to be completely well. Your man brought this condition with him into the army. He certainly contracted the disease years ago. At this stage, morphine—as much as we can spare—is all we can give him. It helps the pain but cures nothing. I'm sorry there's nothing more to be done."

John remembered the mysterious remarks men had made in camp about spending a night with Venus and then spending a lifetime with Mercury. He now had a fuller sense of the meaning than any man in camp.

John thanked her and left—grateful for fresh air and clean sunshine.

With a pass in his breast pocket that felt like manumission papers, a good horse between his legs, and an afternoon without specific obligations to be anywhere in particular, John set out to his father's house.

It was the first time John could recall being embraced by the man, even from childhood. After brief minutes all was normal, as though John had not been away at all. They sat on the porch. The older McMorrow detailed all the recent local news. He told of small incidents around the farm and of carpentry projects in progress for neighbors. John's brothers had not written recently. The mail could be slow getting to and from soldiers in camp. Talk got around to church. John tried to steer it toward the Stone family without revealing any great or unusual interest.

"How're things going with the new families at church?"

"Fine. I think they'll make good members. Some sort of problems seem to be going on over at Grafton. Something about corrupting the worship with organs and joining up with a group that wants to make the disciples a denomination. Several of 'em just won't stand for it. I figure they ought to stay put and make things right if they can, but I guess they figure they can't do more than just go somewheres else. The Stones said they knew you and that you'd been by with some books and such. I think I told you that in the letter. Everything's fine with them. I think they'll make good members."

John came out just a little to see if he could pull out more details. "You know, I sort of had my eye on Anna Lee before I went off. I don't guess we had anything like a clear understanding or anything, but I had my eye on her."

"I don't blame you, son. If I were your age and didn't have a wife yet I figger I'd be havin' my eye on her too. Looks like her and that Micah might be getting to where they could end up married."

John's face showed the pain. His father saw it as John inquired: "Did they tell you that? I mean are they talkin' that way or are folks around talking that way?"

"They've not said anything about it. I guess it's just an impression you get from watchin' 'em. I did hear some of the ladies kiddin' her an' she just seemed embarrassed by it. Anyway, you should be able to put your eye back on her at church tomorrow night if you can get to prayer meeting. That Micah doesn't generally come on Wednesday. He's makin' guns for the army and must stay pretty busy with that. I can't tell you what's going on with 'em. Not for sure. He's a good man from all I can tell, and she's a fine young lady. She's not just pretty. She is that, but she's good—just like she wasn't so pretty—like she's been raised up good. If I could pick one for you I'd pick one just about like her."

Looking toward the shed and the unfinished pieces of work that looked like islands of wood in a sea of wood shavings and sawdust, John's father said, "I guess the war has changed a lot of things and folks just have to adjust to what comes along. Girls don't always wait when a man's gone. You'll have 'at sometimes."

John remembered hearing it before. "You'll have 'at." His father said it when the Hawkins boy told a terrible lie about him and turned people to thinking John had done some awful thing. He had said it when John fell from the tree and banged up his ankle, even before John's mother had finished looking it over and saying "bless your heart." John had heard it after just about every event that seemed catastrophic at first. When the weather caused a general crop failure and the well seemed about to dry up, his father said it. John had soaked in this simple philosophy of life and often found himself echoing the sentiment in adult life in the face of tough things. "You'll have 'at."

John was not prepared to "have 'at" with reference to Anna Lee. If his father was trying to prepare him for some expected tragedy, John could appreciate the effort to help. He would not accept the implication that he would soon have to accept such a loss. Anna Lee would sort it all out and they would be married and have children—after the war.

The visit revived John. They shared a pleasant meal. Life started in and went on where it had left off years before, even before John had gone to Bethany. Talk of the war was limited to where John had been and what the weather was like and how big the inn was back at Capon Springs and how warm the water had been in the middle of winter. John wanted to tell of the capture of Captain Leopold, but he could not find a way to wedge it in without boasting about his own part in it. He would leave that for other lips to tell someday.

John returned to camp just before dark. No one asked where he had been all afternoon. He was at his appointed place around the campfire and felt strangely comfortable about being in yet another accustomed place that went on as though it had not been interrupted, as if it would continue as it now was.

He spent the rest of the week drilling with the regiment. John was not able to arrange to get over to town for prayer meeting on Wednesday. He had been put on the roster as the officer in charge of the pickets. Any officer could have done it, but it was John's job and he would not ask to be relieved of it—at least not yet.

On Sunday morning John dressed, groomed his mustache and whiskers, combed his hair as best he could and made his way on foot to the old familiar church building. Others ambled in from the camps and shuffled to the various churches. Civilians and soldiers mingled on the streets.

John lingered around the front of the old building with two front doors. It had been built that way for the ladies to enter on one side and men to enter on the other, but no one honored the old custom anymore. Most sat with their families. John was waiting for his father—if anyone were to ask—as he greeted old friends, hugged elderly ladies, and patted children who were impressed to see their old acquaintance in military uniform. He enjoyed the attention in spite of the embarrassment.

"John!" It was Anna Lee. The family wagon had just pulled up and she saw him first.

Lifting her skirt and rushing ahead of the others, who were also walking at a fast pace, she met him as he came toward her and they shared a nice, public, respectable embrace for a few seconds. He held his palm flat against her back and moved it as though to soak up affection and to transmit what was in him. He raked his nose across Anna Lee's hair and caressed the rounded part of the top of her right ear in passing, imbibing every particle of Anna Lee he could carry away respectfully and with her blessing. He would later dissect that seconds-long embrace into differentiated sections of smells, sensations, and feelings that no observer could have suspected he had gathered so quickly. "It's so good to see you, John! We'd all hoped you'd be here. We've missed you."

The embrace had been too brief for John. The references to "we" left him wishing for a few purely personal sentiments, but what he got pleased and excited him. The family lined up for more warm greetings.

Behind the line, Micah Johnson looked to be in an awkward position. John met Micah's eyes.

Micah extended his hand first. "I'm Micah. Good to meet you."

"Nice to meet you too. I understand you're a gunsmith. That's a fine thing." John meant it as a compliment.

Micah suspected that it was John's way of drawing attention to his lack of a uniform. "Thanks. I'm doing what I can."

John felt a hand on his shoulder and turned to see his father's broad smile. "We'd best get in here before they start without us."

They filed in. Someone, it seemed, should invite someone to sit with some-one, but no one did. The Stone family turned to the right to occupy its usual pew and John's father turned left. Avoiding confusion, John shuffled in beside his father. He looked across the wide aisle. Micah left an empty space between him-self and Anna. Anna Lee scooted over to fill it. John saw evidence of surprise on Micah's face.

Worshipers filed out after the final prayer. Those exiting pews from the left and right mingled—*about like the shuffling of a deck of cards,* John thought. Micah fumbled with putting the song book in the rack long enough to leave a deliberate gap between himself and Anna Lee. John filled it. All pretended that this was just a random shuffling.

"Anna Lee, "John inquired, "my time is so limited and my opportunities to leave the camp are so few, but I wonder if I might come to call if an opportunity presents itself?"

"You know, John, that you're always welcome at our home."

"And for that I am most grateful. As much as I want to spend time with your good family, I've hoped that you and I might have chance to talk."

"I'd like that, John. Please come see soon."

As John and Anna Lee spoke they both hurried outside, giving only obligatory greetings to others before finding the shade of the oak out in the yard. For John, getting started was the first obstacle. Having time to get it to some conclusion in such a brief, public encounter in the church yard was an insurmountable chal-lenge. His prepared script had expressions of deep love and devotion of which he had decided not to speak until matters were clearer—and then he had decided to speak mainly of them as they reached the relative privacy of the shade.

John saw the pained look in Anna Lee's eyes. He lost his resolve. He fumbled for some new plan. "Anna Lee, you know how I feel about you so I'll say no more about it just now."

Anna Lee yearned to hear more of John's love for her, feeling guilt for wanting to receive what she was not yet prepared to give—in words.

"I understand," was all she said.

"I'm trying, Anna Lee, to back away long enough to give you space. To see you torn is worse than the thought of seeing you make a choice unfavorable to my hopes." As his mind edited the intentions of his heart the result was a garbled message that represented neither John's heart nor his mind. Like troops, the heart and mind do not always act together in ways that either would act alone.

Anna Lee felt the loss of John's poetic expressions of his love.

The encounter in the church yard turned out to be the only one during this visit to Clarksburg that even came close to getting at the heart of the issues that would influence the lives of John McMorrow and Anna Lee Stone so dramatically.

Twice John found cause to leave camp and travel to Grafton, at some risk because his official duties were not there. Both times found the Stones at home without Anna Lee. During the first visit the family welcomed him. He enjoyed the visit. They told him that Anna Lee had gone to help with Micah's work in Grafton. John would not go to her there. During the second visit Mr. Stone just said that Anna Lee was away and not expected home until about dark. John did not inquire further.

On Tuesday, June 2, the brigade took freight cars to Grafton. The men pocketed two months' pay. Next morning they boarded a train for Martinsburg.

John rode with the other junior officers of the brigade. The green grass on steep hillsides passed in a blur. Passing open fields, John saw farmers raking and stacking around upright poles the second cutting of hay for the season. Life went on as usual for the civilians of western Virginia.

John cursed himself for having just spent more than three weeks within a short distance of Anna Lee without advancing. He held to his hopes for the future, but the hopes combined with new possibilities. Fantasy is often so much better than soiled reality. Imagined hopes and expectant dreams are spotless. Reality involves unpleasant dimensions that can be discarded in the imagination. John McMorrow vaguely acknowledged these truths while holding onto hope.

CHAPTER 7

"MICAH, I LOVE YOU."

Anna Lee's journal had leaped beyond the word "confused" at the top of a page. Now there were columns with arrows pointing in two directions and plus signs and scribbled, cryptic symbols undecipherable by other eyes.

She filled a page with answers in two columns to her own question at the top: "How might I be useful?"

One page explored "qualities of a good father."

Another, with both underlined and crossed-out phrases in each of two columns, dealt with "how I feel when I'm near him."

Now she wrote, several pages beyond "confused," of "the danger of indecision."

Anna Lee drew a stick figure representing herself. To the left and right she added stick figures of equal size and qualities. Arrows went from each to her and from her to each. Beneath, above, and to the sides of the arrows were words like "strong," "genuine," "overpowering," "poetic," "good," "powerful," and "wonderful."

The page achieved symmetry.

Anna Lee drew a horizontal line from margin to margin and wrote, "After the letters."

Anna Lee drew the stick figures again and in the same proportions. This time she drew arrows from herself to each of the men. Considering it, she added more arrows from herself to both. Still symmetrical. To broaden the scope she scribbled more stick men representing other young men who had shown interest. She drew arrows from herself to each of these and put words and symbols with each arrow, words and phrases like "no," "unthinkable," "over father's dead body," and "not if he were the last man on earth." Some figures rated minus signs and down-turned frowns.

She drew new arrows from the figures representing John and Micah—"after the letters" that pointed to the margins, away from Anna Lee. The arrows were equal. The page attained balance.

In the space beneath she wrote, "Prolonged Indecision = Loss of Both."

Returning to the first figure—*before the letters*—representing herself she drew a smile on the circle of her face. She scribbled a wavy line—for confusion—beneath the smile.

On the second—*after the letters*—she inserted a frown on her own circle and on the circles representing the faces of John and Micah.

She drew another line from margin to margin and then turned it into an arrow pointing to the right. It was a time line. Just below it she wrote, "After the decision is made." She drew three stick figures and put a smile on two and a frown on one. Out from the one with the frown she put another arrow, representing the passing of time, pointing to yet another figure with a smile. On the arrow she wrote, "eventually." Then she added a faceless wife and two children to join the figure who would eventually wear a smile.

Next day, at the gun shop, a completely unprepared Micah fought tears when Anna Lee abruptly put her hand on his shoulder and said, "Micah, I love you."

✳   ✳   ✳   ✳

BULLETS THAT KILL

Getting off the train in Martinsburg after dark on June 2, the 12th Virginia received orders to march for Winchester the next morning. Two days later, just southwest of Winchester, orderly rows of white canvas transformed a farmer's field into the regiment's home.

Fresh, invigorating tension filled the air. It filtered down from senior officers to junior, to sergeants, and finally to privates. It floated back up the ranks. The order went out for the men to lay close in their quarters, to keep their muskets at arms length. The provost marshal issued no passes.

Morale was high. Talk around the fires was of "spoiling for a fight" and "watching the Rebels run" when the regiment would finally see action. The 12th Virginia had been in service for nearly ten months. The regiment had not yet been, as a whole, in an engagement with the enemy. The mildest of men were anxious to test themselves in battle.

Civilians would not understand the eagerness. The baker who bakes no bread, the carpenter who touches no hammer, saw, or boards, or the farmer who plows no field, would understand the restless feeling that he ought to be getting about his business. To call oneself a farmer and never turn soil would be a farce. To accept pay for bread without having baked would be nonsense. The soldier who trains and drills and marches in preparation for war expects to test his skill in the craft. The distinctions between abhorring war and yet wishing to be a part of it when dangers threaten mothers, fathers, and loved-ones at home are blurred to those who see soldiering from a distance. Up close it makes sense.

John McMorrow noted the shift when he watched three full companies—D, E, and I—marching out of camp to the Strasburg road to reinforce the picket. No one grumbled about going out on a dark Sunday night. Instead, they just griped about returning to camp the next morning without seeing action.

John had the same sense when Companies C, F, H, and I—under Colonel Northcott—went out two nights later to support a battery of artillery that had been put in place in preparation for an attack. These, too, were crushed by the unfulfilled promise of confrontation.

Outside of the army there were hints of progress. Major Pierpoint gave his farewell address to the 12th Virginia when he left to become adjutant general of West Virginia—which would officially become a new state on June 20, 1863.

The 87th Pennsylvania, still close brothers to the 12th Virginia, accompanied some cavalry and artillery on an excursion about five miles out the Stasburg road, where they ambushed a force of Confederate cavalry. They returned to camp with about forty Rebel prisoners—and with promising accounts of the action that raised the hopes of those in the 12th Virginia who were yet spoiling for a fight.

"We skunked 'em. Not a man in all the 87th Pennsylvania was lost. We must have killed or wounded at least a hunnerd of them Rebels. They run off like skeered rabbits."

The 12th Virginia was more than willing to be an admiring audience for those who had earned the right to brag. If they felt cheated of the honor of being in the fray, they now had reasons for thinking that their chances were coming. For most, the enemy just down the road was good news. The thought that some might soon die referred to someone else. The 12th gave ear to the 87th Pennsylvania, placing themselves vicariously in the shoes of the victorious heroes who had experienced such success without personal loss. The thought that "I" might suffer agony and pain only gnawed at the edges.

Four willing, eager, companies from the 12th Virginia went down the Strasburg road that night to support a battery of artillery. No action. They spent the night alert to every cracking twig and wandering deer. The next morning came with nothing to tell. They were tired. Their muscles ached. They started to relax amidst the safe surroundings of tinkling tin, crackling fire, and familiar canvas.

The bugle sounded *assembly*. The whole regiment went into line. Soldiers eagerly made for positions in formation while fires sizzled smoke from dousing and Jonahs tripped and officers shouted orders to "hurry it up" at running men. Men stood and waited. The pause made all the rushing into position seem for nothing.

Orders finally came to break ranks, fill canteens, collect a day's rations in haversacks, and reform. Now they could hurry with purpose. They were to move out. Heading down the Strasburg road they heard the roar of canon off to the left. Battle loomed.

"Take off your knapsacks and leave them here!" The order originated somewhere down the line. Officers and sergeants relayed it to the regiment that was halted in a long line in a patch of woods. The men complied and got back into line. They heard strange sounds. These mountain men knew the natural sounds of the woods as well as anyone alive. Any of them could tell the bark of a squirrel from the cry of a jay, and the sound of a squirrel skittering down the opposite side of a tree from a leaf bumping against bark on its random glide to the ground. Any could mark the sound a deer makes when it is walking unafraid and distinguish that from the stomp it makes when alerted to danger. They could differentiate between turkey scratching and chipmunk scavenging.

These uncommon sounds, however, were confusing and hard to classify. They heard a sort of whistling sound, then *spat*, then *crack*. Leaves and acorns dropped to the ground here and there.

"Them's jays droppin' aykerns."

"No. It's just a little wind blowin' in a little rain. That's what it is. Rain's comin'."

John McMorrow listened to the debate for a few seconds before he decided to put an end to it. "Boys, those are bullets just as sure as you live." The increasing frequency of the sounds settled the matter anyway.

The Rebel skirmish line advanced straight toward their front. Now the regiment saw the enemy coming. They opened up on them. Hearts raced. Men breathed fast and hard. Mouths went dry. Minie balls struck closer now. Bark flew, dirt showered the line as lead dug into soil. Smoke filled the air as roaring muskets belched fire to the front.

John felt useless as a soldier with nothing more in his hand than his sword and with no other weapon than the revolver in his belt. His job was to show courage and keep the men firing. Every instinct demanded that he hunker down behind some tree or rock, but his duty was to show fearlessness. John could not know the effect of his work, but his men continued to reload and fire in the direction of the advancing gray line in front.

Some loaded and pointed, forgetting to pull the triggers. Ramrods stuffed barrels with balls that would never touch Confederate flesh. Ramrods shot like wobbling arrows from other muzzles when men failed to remove them after ramming the lead. A few ramrods flew to the front, but John had no idea what they were—or time to learn. These mysteries would be sorted out later and prove the value of drill and practice before battle.

The Union line held the Confederate advance. Terrified and enlivened at the same time—experiencing these as one emotion—John settled into the business with greater clarity. Bizarre happenings take on the semblance of order when they last. The hour filled with events that John would later be able to recall with precision, even in his old age. No one year of time in civilian life would be as filled as was that hour.

"They're flanking our right." John supposed this came from some senior officer but he could not identify the voice or its location. Company A bolted out of line and rushed to the right flank to form a skirmish line against the advance from that side. The rest of the regiment fell back, as ordered, behind a small creek in their rear.

No. The thought exploded in John's head. The colonel had ordered the men to fall back behind the creek, which seemed reasonable, but he marched them to the rear by file. *This is insane. There must be a better way.* John tried to recall from the manual some better command. He could not. Even so, this movement did not seem reasonable. *The whole regiment could just turn around and walk straight back to the creek in line of battle. That would get them there quick and easy. Instead, we're all in this long, thin, line going off to the left and then back around on the other side of the creek so that only the men on the extreme left are out of immediate danger while the boys from the right have to march the whole distance to the left before moving an inch to the rear. All the while they're exposed to fire from the front and unable to return fire.*

He saw Jap Smith up ahead, head and shoulders above anyone in the regiment. "Keep your head down, Jap!"

As he shouted the warning he stumbled over something. He looked down into the lifeless face of Lieutenant Tom Bradley of Company I.

John would later admire the discipline of the men while executing this movement. Every man in the ranks must have been able to see the flaw in the plan, but no one—as far as John had seen—used his own better judgment and made for the rear by a better route. John himself had come close to doing that. When an enemy minie ball shot the hammer off Tommy Burke's rifle, Tommy carried it to the end of the line and turned to the left, still carrying the useless weapon.

The regiment stayed at the creek until dark, when it fell back to a stone wall on the outskirts of town. Driving rain poured and thoroughly soaked men and powder. The knapsacks left in the woods were never recovered, at least not by Union soldiers. At two in the morning of the 14th of June the 12th West Virginia marched into the fortifications at Winchester. There the troops remained—soaked, tired, and hungry—until they moved out to a stone wall between the Strasburg and Romney roads about a mile out of town, which they held until ordered back. Skirmishing continued sporadically, but the battle died down.

Rebels held a position behind a stone wall to the southwest about 900 yards. Only a few sharpshooters with special rifles made in Grafton had any hope of reaching that range with small arms. A few pinged at distant figures. Union artillery knocked holes in the wall and sent Johnny Rebs scattering here and there as the 12th West Virginia looked on. They were too worn out to enjoy the spectacle. Some fell asleep where they waited, overcome against their wills. A random shot from the Confederate lines struck and killed Lieutenant John T. Ben Gough of Company F in his sleep. Others slept in spite of spattering water and lead. John found a spot as sheltered as any from flying lead and instantly fell asleep.

Alternating between cold from the rain, hot from the circumstance, rested from fitful sleep, and exhausted from attempted vigilance, John was aroused to alert attention by general movement all around him at the stone wall. It was about 5:00 on Sunday afternoon. At about 5:30 the Confederates let go with artillery blasts on the main fortifications. General Milroy ordered all regiments to fall back into the fort. If anyone had cared to ask John McMorrow how he felt about the idea, he would have told them that the fort was the target of heavy artillery and not his preference of places to go. But no one asked.

The siege guns in the fort fired deafening blasts at the Rebel guns on the ridge to the southwest. The common infantry soldier, not manning artillery, was just part of the collective target and a spectator. Men were both inspired and perplexed when General Milroy climbed the flag pole to get a better view of Rebel batteries on the ridge and to see the effect of Union fire. All were wide awake now—and John McMorrow cheered with the rest. The day's fighting came to an end sometime after dark.

At about 1:00 in the morning General Milroy called a council of war with his senior officers. They agreed to evacuate the 10,000 troops from Winchester. Orders went out: "Destroy the guns. We're getting out." The retreating soldiers spiked artillery pieces, cut up harnesses, sawed and burned axles and wheels, and the whole command moved out at 2:00 in the morning. The men of the 12th Virginia filled their new haversacks with hardtack from boxes placed along the way, quickly broken apart with musket butts.

The Federal column wended its way up the road to Martinsburg. General Milroy rode along the route and pressed soldiers to push along. "Keep these men moving. Quickly now. Daybreak must find us far from here. No straggling!"

Exhausted men pushed on. About four miles out from the fort a Rebel force holding the road slowed the column. Although the 12th Virginia was not in position to return fire, it heard the heavy exchange. Muffled *cracks*—unmistakable now.

Finally, after another uncertain pause, the troops left the pike and made for North Mountain across open fields. They trudged on unmolested until they staggered to the base of the mountain. The sound of musketry boomed. Word rushed back through the ranks that Confederate cavalry had opened fire. Determination, exhaustion, desperation, anger—a combination of these—replaced fear. As one man they poured lead into the dark figures, seen through the smoke, blocking their way. *We're to die here anyway—if this doesn't work. We might as well blast a hole through Rebel cavalry first.* This was the unspoken consensus of desperate men. In the darkness at least some mistook cattle for Rebel cavalry. This part of Milroy's command poured through the open door, amazed. They had not expected the door to open. John saw nothing of cavalry.

Ascending North mountain, one grueling step at a time, John McMorrow knew that he must keep going. His life might depend upon it. The men needed to see him moving forward. There were no ambulances or supply wagons or horses to carry stragglers. These would end up in prison camps or be shot by bushwhackers where they stopped. John was hot, caked with crusty, dried mud, and drained of all strength except that with which he would take the next step. He neared the summit. Stinging eyes picked out the next landmark to which he hoped to walk. He had just passed the little shack of a house that had been his last goal.

A feminine voice spoke clearly, "I need to see yer colonel!" John turned to the right and saw the most incompatible sight he had ever seen. It was a young girl who apparently had just come out of the house. She approached the column of filthy soldiers in her bare feet with a cool confidence that surprised John. He judged her to be about fifteen years old, wearing a clean but well-worn summer dress. Blonde hair hung in curls to her shoulders and dangled over her high forehead. *She's pretty*, John thought, *in a rustic sort of way.* Her rapid speech showed intelligence and deliberate intention to convey some message.

"I need to see yer colonel please."

"How might I help you, ma'am?" John had not really thought about what he was saying. He just said what came out as he tried to make sense of this pretty little girl coming out of nowhere and asking to speak with the colonel. John, himself, would not be prepared to call for the colonel without good reason. He could not, in his muddled exhaustion, conceive of what this child could possibly need with the colonel.

"I have somethin' to tell him about the Rebels. Can you get him for me please?"

John called out for someone to fetch the colonel. Word passed up the line while John talked with this fearless child, whatever her mission, who filled him with admiration. He sat on the ground beside her as they waited. John could gather only that the girl had information about the Rebels that might be useful. He wanted to tell her that they were not on a Rebel hunt today; that today they were the hunted. He waited with this child for the colonel in the cloud of dust as weary men trudged on.

As the colonel's horse approached, John rose with difficulty to his feet, saluted and said, "Sir, this—"

The mountain maid interrupted him and said rapidly, "Colonel, sir, yer men don't want to take this road yer on because I've heard that the Rebels are up ahead where the road runs into the railroad tracks."

The colonel was as dumbfounded as the lieutenant had been at the first.

"And do you think you could direct us to some better road?" He was still making sense of it more than he was gathering intelligence.

"I reckon I could. I'll show you the way myself." She started walking before he had time to respond.

"Just one minute, young lady."

Without the slightest evidence of fear or anger the girl turned to see what more the colonel might want to say.

"How do I know you're not a Rebel who wants to mislead us and send us right into some Rebel camp?"

"Cause I'm not one." And walking on she said, "The path you need to take is right over this way. Come on and I'll show you."

Walking—sidestepping—beside her and talking as he did, the colonel continued. "If you lead us into danger, I'm afraid I'll have to send some men back here to burn down your house."

John wanted to protest, but he let the threat stand. There was nothing he could do anyway.

The girl just shrugged her dainty shoulders and said with calm, rapid speech, "I'm not a Rebel and if I was one then I reckon you ought to burn the house down but since I'm not one I'm not going to worry about it and I reckon you ought to be callin' yer men to stop so we can get started on the better way that is right over this way that I'm takin' you."

With that the colonel mounted his horse. He asked John to stay with the girl while he informed the men of the change in plans.

She led the regiment over a narrow path through the woods along the crest of the mountain. Weary men walked in single file behind a pretty young girl with bare feet. The colonel seemed to be second in command for the four miles or so before the path came to another road that she assured them would take them to the Potomac River on the Maryland border. She stood on the side and waved as soldiers trudged past. Officers dropped coins in the patch of green grass at her feet.

The battle of Winchester had been a Union disaster. The 12th was one of four regiments that came out of the fight still holding its organization together. Two hundred or so were taken prisoner by the Rebels. These had been separated from the regiment. A half-dozen men from the regiment had lost their lives and three dozen were wounded.

In the whole command Milroy lost thousands of men, all of his artillery, and some 400 wagons. The troops who made it out had only their muskets to make the retreat good.

Spoiling for a fight was no longer foremost on their minds. Surviving the rest of the war to tell of this fight would be good enough.

Camping in the mountains and still struggling to put as much distance between themselves and the Rebels in as little time as possible, the next afternoon the 12th crossed the Potomac River into Maryland at Millstone Point.

Five miles up the river at Hancock, they ate the first meal they had had in days—and the first extended rest. At Hancock, other regiments and fragments that had escaped Winchester soon joined the 12th West Virginia. The 119th Ohio came in on one road. Portions of the 1st New York and the 12th Pennsylvania Cavalry, and stragglers from other commands, united. The combined force prepared for an attack from Rebel cavalry, reportedly coming from somewhere in the direction of Martinsburg.

When the attack did not come they all marched, much of the way under cover of darkness, eighteen miles to Little New Orleans. They at first expected to take a train for Cumberland, but they learned through a dispatch from the 1st New York that Rebels held the city, so they camped in the woods on a hillside near Little New Orleans and cooked coffee, meat, and flour obtained from the town. The next morning they set out for Bloody Run, about thirty-five miles over in Pennsylvania.

Pennsylvania had the comfortable feel of Union territory, unlike the general sense in Maryland, where the loyalty of citizens could not be taken for granted. Here the stars and stripes of the United States of America waved freely and gave obvious pleasure to those who hoisted them. The good people of Pennsylvania cheered the men along the way, and offered food and comfort. Stragglers had no fear of bushwackers here—and the lack of fear invited more straggling.

At Bloody Run they rejoined General Milroy, learning for the first time that he had escaped Winchester. Their elation spiraled down when the "Old Gray Eagle," as they had come to call their commander, was relieved of duty because of the disaster at Winchester.

John McMorrow, like many of the other officers and a good many of the enlisted men felt that a great injustice had befallen Milroy. Bullets that kill and failure in battle are often random events. Those who fall do not always crumple because of lack of courage or wisdom.

CHAPTER 8

"CAPTAIN MCMORROW"

Glory had eluded weary men who had sought it in battle. Hope, where it remained at all, was dim.

In subdued tones the men about the fires at Bloody Run searched for purpose in what had transpired at Winchester.

"The General showed a lot of courage at Winchester. I guess the sight of him hugging that flag pole and tryin' to get a look through those field glasses at the guns on the ridge will always stay in my head."

"He was like the rest of us, only higher up. He was doin' what he'd been ordered to do."

John McMorrow listened to the talk. He remembered his own helplessness when the regiment had been ordered to fall back to the creek by file instead of, somehow, by line of battle. This order, he assumed, came from Colonel Klunk. It was one flaw that John had seen up close.

"What went wrong?" Someone was fishing for an explanation.

"What good did we do in the overall scheme of the thing?" Another was probing for justification. All had been pressed to the limits. A few had died.

Sergeant Henry Spear of Company D stood at the edge of the circle of young officers. He had just delivered some message to a young lieutenant. A few months before, Spear might not have ventured a word in this setting, but the band of brothers had grown tighter as their shared fund of time and experience together had swelled. If all were sorely disappointed with circumstances, and with decisions and outcomes beyond their reach but affecting their lives, they were not embittered with one another. The shared misfortunes of war form bonds. Beyond friendship, the attachment has qualities that differ from it. Civilians have "friends" whom they do not trust. Soldiers place absolute trust in men they do not call "friends." Civilians labor for one another and speak kind words to friends in the expectation of getting something in return, even if the anticipated reward is nothing more than kind words and civil treatment. Soldiers fire muskets and remain on the battle line to save themselves and comrades and to advance the cause for which all fight together. Soldiers expect little in the way of kind words from those who also carry the musket. They expect only that the other will share his duty when lead flies. Good men in civilian life work hard to earn what they might choose to share with others. Good men in uniform work to survive and the benefits of work shared by every other man who takes his place in the line. When civilians break contracts with civilians, friendships are broken. When soldiers break trust with soldiers men die, sometimes before a firing squad of former comrades. "Friendship" is not the word for what invariably develops between soldiers. Friends are few. Comrades fill the ranks.

Now, after Winchester, Sergeant Henry Spear of Company D and all of the young officers in the circle of searching men knew that Henry Spear had earned the right to speak.

"It was the hurry in the fort. To git out I mean. I came out with someone else's gun. Somebody picked up my musket an' I had to use one from the stack that I hadn't practiced with. When the Johnnies was shootin' at us over at the mountain I slipped out in front and saw a feller in gray hunkered down behind a tree. I took careful aim. Careful aim. I coulda got 'im if I'd a had my own gun. I hit bark and he run off before I could reload. I'm gonna find my own gun or get one I can hit with."

Everyone knew that Spear's complaint was such a small part of the whole that it was no part of the reason for the disaster. Someone said something about needing to find ways to fix things that went wrong before the next engagement—"assuming the government doesn't just give them their Confederacy and send us all home."

John thought of the "things that went wrong" and could not see a clear target for blame. The Rebels had more men and guns. The general had done his best with what he had, and now Milroy was relieved of command. Sergeant Spear lost his rifle. Someone ordered the whole regiment to move to the creek by file. The most intelligent explanation that John could find, after much effort, did not come from the great philosophers of the world whose works he had studied well. The most thorough and refined explanation came from his father: "You'll have 'at."

The men about the fire proposed theories regarding the value of the failed efforts at Winchester.

"We accomplished nothing. It was all for nothing," said a junior officer who did not bother to look around to see if enlisted men could hear.

"We delayed them. If we hadn't slowed 'em down at Winchester they'd have been able to join up with Lee's men and get into Washington. We kept 'em apart."

"We thinned our ranks of weaker men and the ones who made it through are stronger now. It's like Darwin says—" A general protest interrupted. They named the names of now-dead men, attesting to their strength. John thought, *the shirkers and Jonahs still alive and well in the regiment. No. Darwin's theory sheds no light on what happened at Winchester.*

Colonel Lewis B. Pierce of the 12th Pennsylvania Cavalry became senior officer, taking command of Milroy's men. Colonel Klunk of the 12th West Virginia took charge of all the infantry. On June 20, the day West Virginia gained official status as one of the United States of America, the command marched from Bloody Run to Bedford, Pennsylvania, where quartermasters issued new blankets and new uniforms—blue, bright, clean, and fresh.

After a brief rest at Bedford the 12th received orders to march, on July 3, toward a place called Gettysburg, where Rebels raiding into the North were causing some trouble. On Sunday, the 5th of July, they arrived at London by way of Connellsburg. Along the way, on the 4th of July, a newspaper circulated among the men telling of a great battle in progress at Gettysburg. Old news, even news aged only one day, was more frustrating than informative. The report did not say how the battle was going.

On July 5 most of the infantry went on to Mercersburg to take charge of men and materiel captured from the Rebels at Gettysburg: 110 wagons and ambulances filled with Rebel plunder taken from loyal homes in Pennsylvania; 600 or so Rebel prisoners—about half of them wounded—and quartermaster stores of all sorts.

Hospitals at Mercersburg cared for wounded Confederates who waited days before their wounds could be dressed.

The infantry returned to London with all of the captured and recaptured loot and about 300 unwounded prisoners. They turned the wagons and goods over to the quartermaster.

Soon word spread that the Battle of Gettysburg had ended with a clear Union victory. Rebels had met a bitter, crushing defeat on Northern soil. Lee and his army had retreated. A new wind blew through the ranks of the 12th West Virginia. Cheers, songs, laughter, smiles, heads held high, and other signs of recovery streamed through the ranks and enlivened the camp.

On July 13, at 3:00 in the morning, they were eager to obey orders to march for Hagerstown, Maryland. After a three-hour delay the regiment started on the route through Mercersburg and Greencastle that would take them to Hagerstown the next day. They made camp about two miles south of town in the middle of the afternoon. Lee had made it across the Potomac before they arrived in the place where more fighting might have erupted. The men thrilled to talk about "what might have happened if Meade had put us here sooner."

When the 1st Corps boys marched by the camp of the 12th West Virginia en route to Harpers Ferry, in their tattered and filthy uniforms after Gettysburg, they saw the 12th West Virginia in the new, clean uniforms and shouted slights about "new recruits" and "Sunday soldiers." Given their own recent exchange they enjoyed it as a great joke on the 1st Corps rather than the scorning it was intended to be, an insult playfully and commonly poked at raw recruits.

On July 16 the command marched the ten miles or so to Sharpsburg, Maryland, the scene of the Battle of Antietam, in which the Union had claimed victory. The reminder added to rising morale.

Captain William B. Curtis of Company D was promoted to major at Sharpsburg, the place of his birth. Although he had left Sharpsburg for western Virginia in 1827, he found loyal relatives who welcomed him. His new rank placed him in command of the 12th West Virginia Infantry. Rebels had taken Lieutenant Colonel Northcott prisoner at Winchester. Colonel Klunk had taken charge of the brigade's infantry.

On August 4 the regiment was ordered to Martinsburg, West Virginia, where it camped on a beautiful lawn, about five acres on the edge of town. The holding, about 800 acres, belonged to "the Honorable" Charles James Faulkner who had gone off to fight for the Confederacy. Mrs. Faulkner and her daughters lived in the fine mansion situated at one end of the clean lawn. She claimed complete loyalty to the Union saying, "I would not give a cent for a woman that did not have a mind of her own—would you?"

In the heat of August 1863, the soldiers were pleased to pitch their tents in the shade of well-tended trees belonging to a Rebel. The general impression was that Martinsburg was a fine old town filled with thousands loyal to the Union. There was an air of welcome. If men in blue questioned the motives of Mrs. Faulkner for her declarations of loyalty, they accepted the general sense of fidelity among the citizens.

The government accepted the resignation of Colonel Klunk, on the basis of sickness in his family, while at Martinsburg. This made Major Curtis the ranking officer of the regiment. The organization seemed constantly to change.

On the 25th the regiment left the shade trees on the neat lawn and made camp with other troops northwest of town. General Montgomery Meigs, quartermaster general of the army, inspected the troops. There was a grand parade and review of the troops. Loyal citizens presented a new flag to the 1st New York Cavalry. Colonel Andrew T. McReynolds made a short speech. Regiments passed through Martinsburg as they streamed south to join General U. S. Grant's army at Chattanooga. It looked like the tide was turning in ways favorable to the Union cause.

A good many of those captured by Rebels at Winchester rejoined the regiment at Martinsburg. A private slapped one of these on the shoulder and asked, incredulously, "What are you doing back here?"

"Got paroled."

"You wasn't exchanged? Just paroled? I figgered that meant you was out of the army."

"It does." Then correcting himself, "It did."

"Didn't they make you promise not to fight no more before they turned you loose?"

"Sure did. Some of the boys is still down in prison at Richmond on account of they wouldn't swear to stop fightin'. Some of 'em figger to escape."

"Then what're you doin' back here?"

"Don't rightly know. The best I kin figger the government decided that we should go back and fight anyway because that's what the Rebels is doin' with the ones we paroled. The way they told it to me that makes it an exchange even if they called it a parole. Nobody asked me what I thought about it. I was figgerin' on goin' home."

"What was it like? Prison, I mean?"

"Well, the fight around Winchester was bad, but that only lasted a little while. Prison wasn't as bad as that, but it goes on ever day. A long time. One of the boys told me he got hisself captured on purpose 'cause he couldn't get no furlough and he figgered to just git paroled anyway an' then git to go home."

"Who was that?"

"Ain't tellin'. Besides, he ain't goin' back to prison on purpose no more. We all'druther be home I reckon, but most times we'druther be with the regiment than in some Rebel prison any day."

For the 12th West Virginia, Martinsburg was mainly a time to lick emotional wounds while drilling, and training, and performing picket duty until October 18. On that day General John D. Imboden's men attacked the 9th Maryland Infantry at Charles Town. The 12th West Virginia was ordered to Harpers Ferry along with a battery of artillery, expecting an attack there too. On the way they camped for the night right on the sleepy streets of little Shepherdstown.

Pickets were out, but John felt the collective tension as he tried to make himself comfortable. The weather grew colder just when the men had begun to settle in at Martinsburg and just when they might have to live on the move for awhile. They had no tents. It was chilly—promising to get harshly cold—and they slept in the open.

Like others, John laid out soft canvas and cloth to make a bed and then put his new blanket on top of him as he stretched out. His lumpy haversack would serve as a pillow.

He had heard a private talking about leaving the stuff inside "so's nobody could steal it. And I've tied my tin cup to it real tight." It seemed like a good idea. It would be hard for some thief to yank a haversack from under his head without alerting him. Everything else of value was on his person or at least under the blanket with him.

Tattoo at first had little effect, but eventually things quieted down. All was still. John went to sleep.

John bolted upright and reached for his revolver, which he had in his hand in an instant, scanning darkness for a target at the source of the noise.

A whisper said, "Sorry, sir. I guess I kicked a rock or somethin'. I'm just goin' out to relieve the picket."

"That's fine, soldier. I hope I didn't scare you." John tried to go back to sleep but it fought him for a time as the little incident stirred thoughts of Rebels slipping past the pickets and cutting a few throats. *A real possibility*, he thought. *We should have made fires even in the middle of town.*

Finally John went to sleep.

This time the clatter was no picket. It could be the result of no accident. John was on his feet with his pistol drawn and he could hear—but not see in the darkness—men all around him grabbing clanking muskets and asking what to do. John had no orders from others or any to give because he had been caught as much off guard as anyone. "Stay put, men!" he shouted. "Someone report. What's going on here?"

Then he heard the squeal of a pig, then laughter, and then the private saying triumphantly, "I got it!"

"You got what?" Several voices asked in unison.

"My haversack, boys. A danged Rebel hog tried to make off with my rations but I got it back."

In spite of racing hearts the men shared a good laugh in the middle of the night. Muffled sounds of continued talking did not keep John from getting back to sleep. Men would be alert for the rest of the night.

The rain began before the troops were ready to resume the march in the morning. The mud sucked at their boots and reminded them of worse days, but they made it to Harpers Ferry, where they brigaded with the 34th Massachusetts.

The 34th was a strange unit to most of the West Virginians. Their commander, General Jeremiah C. Sullivan, was a strict disciplinarian who treated his volunteers as a more rigid officer in the regular army might handle men. A sentinel was stationed in front of every officer's tent and no private soldier could enter without first having permission and specific business. Sullivan allowed no fraternizing between officers and enlisted men. These boys from Massachusetts had not seen battle. They had guarded the railroads, but their heavy guns found no targets and they had not experienced hostile fire. Their uniforms were neat and clean, even more so than those of the 12th West Virginia. To the ears of these West Virginians, the boys from New England talked funny. The 12th West Virginia was surprised to hear rumors that they themselves were regarded by their northeastern comrades as crude mountaineers, backwoods hillbillies. Subtle evidences confirmed the rumors. Condescension. Sneers. Even attempts at kindness when the northeastern boys took long and used simple words to explain things, as if talking to children.

On the 9th of November, several units then at Harpers Ferry issued three days rations and forty rounds of ammunition to each soldier and prepared to begin an expedition toward Staunton. Early the next morning, under the command of Colonel George D. Wells, the 10th and 12th West Virginia Infantry, the 34th Massachusetts, and a detachment with four pieces of artillery from an Indiana battery, made a short march to a patch of ground between Charles Town and Berryville. There they camped for the night. The 34th Massachusetts was not accustomed to hard marching and their knapsacks carried more than those of experienced regiments.

When they set out the next morning, the 12th West Virginia took the lead. Spirits soared now. The men started off whistling "Yankee Doodle" and kept up a fast and lively pace. When they came to Opequon Creek on the other side of Berryville, Colonel Wells ordered a halt, waiting for the engineers to put up a temporary bridge. Somewhat contrary to orders, but not really against their spirit, the 12th West Virginia plunged into the water and waded across. As John saw the first companies splashing across, he removed his boots and rolled up his trouser legs in the hopes of having dry feet after getting to the other side. Major Curtis sat astride his horse on the near side of the stream to John's right. Just as he came along side, Colonel Wells reined in his horse and asked Curtis, "What kind of men have you? They don't seem to care about water or anything else." Major Curtis half-suppressed a smile as he turned and said, loud enough to be heard in the ranks, "They're used to that kind of work, sir." Wells changed the orders. The entire command waded the creek.

Still in the lead, the 12th West Virginia pressed on at rapid pace. Winded so as to make whistling a challenge, not a man complained.

After some miles of this, the wagon master galloped to the front. "Colonel Wells, sir. With all due respect, sir, might it be possible to slacken up, sir? The men of the 34th Massachusetts are giving out. They're tossing blankets and extra clothing in the dirt and we're havin' a time keepin' 'em off the wagons and artillery carriages where they're tryin' to ride."

The front ranks laughed and now, willingly, obeyed the order to slow the pace.

That night they camped about two miles outside of Winchester with plenty of daylight to spare. Examining the scene of their only real battle, and their first lesson in losing, had varying effects on the men. Memories of specific comrades—with names, faces, and histories, killed in specific places—pulled up feelings of defeat, intentions for revenge, hopelessness, and purpose for continuing the effort. Some experienced all of these contradictory emotions. Shallow Union graves dotted the area around the stone wall. Soldiers stood again where they had stood during the battle, looked out at a peaceful landscape, and saw fire and smoke and blood no longer there except in vivid, indelible memory. A powerful sight.

This was their third visit to Winchester.

The first had been pleasant, even if the citizens had been slow to warm up to Yankees. The stories circulated among the men about cheating gullible citizens with such things as labels for scrip had provoked John McMorrow to speak with the chaplain about the need to express disapproval of such things—even swindles against Rebel sympathizers.

The second visit had been altogether different. The citizens had cheered the Rebels who had killed their comrades and belched fire at a gallant general literally wrapped in the stars and stripes. The fine ladies—uncommonly beautiful—who had first playfully sung the songs of Rebellion and then apologized for any possible offense, had fulfilled the prophecy of the aged black woman who had warned them that these ladies would cut their hearts out.

On this third visit John McMorrow did not exactly want to punish the citizens of Winchester. But he was now willing to turn the other way if the men behaved in ways that might weaken the Confederacy. His conception had evolved so slowly and by so many incidents that John could not trace the changes. When he had first marched from Clarksburg he was out to preserve the Union. He had questioned the Emancipation Proclamation and doubted that destroying slavery was a cause that he could take up as a personal reason for the struggle. Although he had been opposed to the institution, he had been fighting to preserve the Union. Now he found that he could approve of virtually any measure that might frustrate the Southern cause. If palming off a bottle's label for scrip fell into that category then John would have no more suggestions for the chaplain. *The people of Winchester might be friendly when it suits them, but they are not our friends.*

The next day they marched on to Strasburg where they camped for four days. John spied a private from the regiment just outside of town squatted down on his haunches separating links connecting a chain of cheap, imitation gold dollars. John started to ask his intentions, but decided to hold onto ignorance. Sitting before the fire back in camp, he saw the same soldier walk by with a smile on his face, carrying two fresh pies.

On the 18th the command continued toward Harrisonburg, camping at about sixteen mile intervals. It arrived there on the 20th. That evening Major Curtis placed the regiment in line of battle, anticipating an attack from Confederate General Jubal A. Early. No attack came. After dark they retraced their steps and paused at New Market before dawn. If all of this easy marching could have been explained to the men in the ranks, John would have gladly shared what he had learned from the captain. But men were not complaining, so John was content to know that the command was merely trying to draw Rebel forces away from Richmond to relieve pressure for Union troops there.

After a five-hour rest at New Market, the march resumed until evening. Just after dark some Confederate bushwhackers from across the Shenandoah fired on the rear guard and Curtis called the men, again, into line of battle. Nothing more happened there.

Resuming in the morning, all seemed normal until 400 or so Rebel cavalry charged the rear guard not far from Woodstock. Union artillery moved into position and drove them back. The 12th West Virginia did not engage.

The next morning the march continued. The 12th West Virginia took the lead with orders to keep up a brisk pace. The column reached Harpers Ferry in two days—forty-eight miles or so—by hard marching in severe winter weather. With Confederates threatening the rear, there was good reason and strong motive for speed. Few complained. Massachusetts men had no great difficulty keeping up. Hurried steps at the front of the column were not to spite, but to save the strange-talking men in blue bringing up the rear. Proximity and shared danger began to forge and temper the link between disparate Yankees.

The units camped together on the high ground and spent days awaiting an attack from Early's men that never came.

On New Years day 1864, the mercury claimed twenty-three degrees below zero at Harpers Ferry. No one present for duty disputed the report. Commanders ordered the troops, once again, into line of battle on Bolivar Heights, just back from Harpers Ferry, expecting Early to attack. It took only moments for men to decide that they could not carry out the order to remain in line. Military discipline could not force men to hold still and freeze to death. No compassionate officer could enforce the deadly order. Manuals detailing how troops should be handled had apparently been written in some other season of the year. The regiment stacked arms, broke ranks, built fires, and ran in place to keep warm. They kept the high ground occupied. That was enough. More than one figured that any Rebel willing to fight at this temperature deserved to have his Confederacy. There was no attack.

Just before nightfall the men returned to quarters. Those quartered in houses built fires and relished the warmth. Scouts came in soon after day dawned reporting that Early had moved his men back up the valley, away from their position. Six teamsters from the 1st New York froze to death in the night.

On January 4, the 12th West Virginia Infantry boarded freight cars, packed in tight, for Cumberland, Maryland. General Benjamin Franklin Kelley had called for help in guarding the place against Early's forces who seemed to be threatening everywhere. The ominous threat kept the Union on edge.

At Cumberland, half of the regiment found quarters at Shriver Mill and the rest at a large hospital. General Kelley ordered the men to stay close to their muskets—to lie on their arms—to have forty rounds of ammunition and three days' rations, ready to move at any moment. With fires to warm them, food to fill them, unknown quantities of time available to them, and space about them in the big hospital, some of the boys practiced their skill at dancing. Others found banjoes to play, spoons to clack, and songs to sing. No attack came.

Cumberland remained home for the 12th West Virginia for the rest of the winter. They received two months' pay on January 23. Major Curtis, by formal vote of the officers, was recommended for and appointed to the rank of colonel with Colonel Northcott still a prisoner of war. Captain Brown was commissioned major, to fill the spot left by Curtis, on February 6. Lieutenant John McMorrow became Captain McMorrow on the 13th.

Mail was regular here. "Captain McMorrow" wrote his name that way for the first time in closing a letter to Anna Lee. John had gotten a few letters out to her and to his father over the preceding months, but none of them had been written as deliberately as he could now find time to write. The few he had received over those months seemed to mirror his own quickly-written notes, with little more than greetings, good-wishes, and idle news. John had bridled his pen. Anna Lee had not yet begun to speak of her love for him—although he read that message in her every repeated reference to "fondness."

At Cumberland the world slowed down. John's life caught up. His former life had not left him. It had only fallen behind. When John put ink to paper he wrote as he would have written months before if he had only had the time—and paper and energy and focus—and he imagined that he was writing to Anna Lee just as he had left her. She was much of that life that caught up with him in Cumberland. He wrote of his love for her without using the word. He told her that her beauty was beyond measure, that her heart was warm, that her very breath was sweet, and that he cherished the knowledge that she held a "fondness" in her heart. He wrote of his "fondness" and tried to give it dimensions that would equal the "love" that he stubbornly refused to voice until she would willingly return it.

John remained sure that Anna Lee would return it.

He told her that his "fondness" knew no bounds; that it was as vast as the sea, and more determined than the combined resolve of both armies in the present conflict. He wrote that it came without conditions and that without the aid of his will, but not contrary to it, his "regard" for her had "unconditionally surrendered" a long time ago.

John made no specific mention of his promotion. He just signed the letter, "With deep and genuine affection, Cpt. John McMorrow."

*   *   *   *

BEFORE I HEAD HOME TONIGHT

Anna Lee heard the clunking sound on the porch as her father knocked mud from his boots before coming through the front door. Peeling a potato beside a steaming kettle on the stove, she heard the door close and the thud of boots coming across the wood floor in the front room toward the kitchen. The cold air reached her after the door closed.

"Somethin' smells mighty good," he said as he took off his coat and hung it on the peg by the pantry. "Hey, Anna Lee, what do you think is the prettiest part of a potato?"

It seemed a strange question, at least if asked by anyone else. Anna Lee assumed it was another of his dangling-hook species of joke, but she would bite. "Well…. Let's see…. I'd have to say that the white middle is the prettiest part."

"Nope."

"Well what is it then?"

"First let's see if your mother knows." Suspense was at least as much a part of this routine as getting to the end of the matter with Mr. Stone.

As Mrs. Stone entered the room and Mr. Stone started to ask the question, there was a confident knock on the door. Micah Johnson walked in without waiting for anyone to come to the door.

"It's cold out there." Micah was quite comfortable and virtually at home in the now-familiar and warm house. "Something sure smells good."

Anna Lee cut up the potato and added the chunks to the meat and carrots in the kettle. "It'll be a few minutes." She helped her mother set four places at the table.

"Doesn't seem natural having Katie living over the hill and us living over here." Mrs. Stone was counting out the silverware and putting utensils beside the plates. No one carried her point a step further except to nod quiet agreement.

"We got payment for the rifles that went out last Friday," Micah told Anna Lee.

"I'll deposit it at the bank and put it in the books in the morning," replied Anna Lee as she came out of the kitchen wiping her hands on the apron. She put her arm around Micah and kissed him on the cheek without awkward shame.

"Any news from John—or of the 12th?" This was a common question from Micah and he asked it with a real sense of concern for John McMorrow, a good friend of the Stone family, and for the others from that part of the country who served in the unit. "Paper says they're still at Cumberland and that some have been promoted. He's a captain now."

"Got a letter just yesterday," Anna Lee put in. "We're proud of him, and all the boys."

After a sketchy outline of events that had transpired in the overall war effort in recent weeks, with each filling in a little here and there, Mrs. Stone suggested they had all better get washed up to eat before supper got cold.

Mr. Stone gave the blessing for the food and asked God's blessing upon the success of the Union army against its foe. The four passed food and enjoyed the meal as they often did now.

"Father, I wonder if anyone else around here knows the prettiest part of a potato?" Anna Lee was playing her usual role—keeping her face as sober as if she were talking about the war.

"Don't reckon I know," said Mr. Stone as he mashed his potato with his fork and scooted some green beans away from a chunk of steaming venison. He kept eating, acting disinterested. Someone would ask if he would just give them a little time. They always did.

"I'd guess the inside," said Micah.

"Nope," said Anna Lee, "I already tried that."

"That'd only leave the outside—or maybe one of the eyes," added Mrs. Stone. "Is it one of the eyes? Are you tellin' us the eyes are pretty? Because that's all I can think of."

"Nope. Not the eyes. Just the outside generally."

This part was always enough to draw out Anna Lee with the big question that would draw out the answer. "Why is the outside any prettier than any of the rest of it?"

"Don't know why," Mr. Stone said, looking at his plate and lifting food toward his mouth. "It just is. You can go ask the school teacher or just about any-body else and they'll tell you that the outside of a potato is appealing." He winked at Anna Lee as three sincere groans answered.

After supper Anna Lee seemed to start clearing the table almost prematurely. Although everyone had finished, the time would normally be spent visiting around the table before this cleanup phase. Anna Lee broke custom, and it appeared peculiar to both Mr. and Mrs. Stone.

"Why don't you men folk go in the front room and visit while Mother and I clean up in here." Anna Lee's gaze at Micah lingered for a split second before she took his plate.

Picking his napkin from his lap and putting it on the table, Mr. Stone stood and said, "I reckon we could poke another log on the fire and get out of your way while you fine ladies clean up." He patted Mrs. Stone on the shoulder as he passed and thought that Anna Lee really wanted a little time alone with her mother. Mrs. Stone suspected otherwise.

In the front room Micah reverted to his earlier—more timid and uncertain— ways. He picked up a log and put it atop the fire and stood to face Mr. Stone, who was still standing. "Sir. Mr. Stone." Micah's Adam's apple plunged once again like a cork bobber. "Mr. Stone. Anna Lee and I have been talkin' and—"

Mr. Stone put his hand on the mantle to steady himself for what he now saw coming.

"We've been talking about the future and, well, I'm making pretty good money now—not that I should brag about that or anything—but I could sup- port—I love Anna Lee—and she loves me—and I have a good house now— and—and we love each other for sure—and if I can have your blessing, I'd like to ask for the hand of you maughter in darriage—I'd like to bury your daugh—I'd like your permission to…" Micah paused and took a breath.

Mr. Stone laughed. His upper lip twitched.

Micah now spoke in slow and deliberate syllables. "I'd like to have your per- mission to ask Anna Lee to marry me."

Mr. Stone looked at the stones before the fireplace and saw a teardrop there, evaporating before he realized it was his. A knot gripped his throat. Mr. Stone seemed to Micah to be someone other than the playful man he had come to love who seemed constantly ready to make every topic into a joke, even while speak- ing of them in serious and informed ways.

"Micah. You cannot know…." He swallowed hard and paused. "You cannot know how much I love that girl in there. I have loved her for longer than she's been alive. I loved her before I held her in my arms the first time. I loved her when I was there to catch her when she took her first steps right over there by the door. I made that little horse over there with big hopes that she'd be happy to have it, and her big eyes, the little kiss on my cheek were more payment for it than you could earn in a lifetime."

Micah looked at the little wooden rocking horse in the corner.

Mr. Stone continued. "I carried that little girl on my shoulders and didn't care they hurt as long as she was happy to be there. I baited her hook and took off the fish and fixed her that swing outside and taught her her letters and the names of the animals and how to catch a butterfly and how to think about what she reads in the papers and…and I've only had one clear plan in it all. That girl's happiness is more important to me than my own life. If you ever do anything to hurt my little.... I'm sorry. Micah, if you want to marry Anna Lee, and if Anna Lee wants to marry you, you have my blessing as long as that's what she wants. I reckon you've already had her say on it, and I guess that's proper. If she's settled on you and you've settled on her then I guess there's gonna be another wedding around here." His voice cracked. "You're a good man, Micah."

Mr. Stone pulled a handkerchief from his pants pocket and blew his nose hard. He wiped his eyes and his forehead. "I'm sorry Micah. Of course we'd be happy to have you in the family. I hope you two don't move too far from here. You're as fine a man as I know and I know you'll take good care of her. I guess it's just...it's just that I can't imagine that you could love her like I do. But that's not the same thing."

"Thank you, sir. Thank you. Truth is, I haven't asked Anna Lee yet. I told her I'd talk to you about it and she didn't tell me not to...so I figure we'll both know before I head home tonight."

CHAPTER 9

WISHING THEY HAD HEARD IT FROM HANEY

Captain McMorrow sat among the others around the fireplace in the old hospital building at Cumberland. The room was warm and well-lit with lanterns, so there was no discernible reason for the half-circle about the crackling flames. Perhaps habit and custom called for this focal point of flames during their nightly appointment.

Cumberland would stand apart in memory from all other encampments because of its differences. Someday these men would gather children and their grandchildren around and tell the tales they had heard around campfires without recalling where most of those fires had burned. The ring around one fire would seem about like the ring around another, whether in dense wooded places or on hillsides or beside stacks of hay in level fields. The fire gave all places a sameness that settled men amidst unsettling circumstances.

Cumberland would stand apart for the fireplace and the half-circle and men would remember that the stories told there had been told in that place. It would be where they ate soft bread, tasted soft drinks, and where some of the officers wore paper collars. Someday old men in comfortable homes with food and treasures more abundant than anything they had during the war would recall that Cumberland was a place of luxury and of good times. Time and distance would kindly extract from those memories of Cumberland the discomfort of drill, the misery of frigid nights on picket duty, sicknesss, the dread of attacks, back-breaking work on the fortifications, and other elements that were just like what they experienced at other places all through the war.

Talk in front of the fireplace turned to the possible disloyalty of some of the citizens of Cumberland. Statements published in Cumberland before the war had circulated and these suggested that the leading citizens of the city had been sympathetic to Southern grievances at first—even though they opposed secession generally—and no public retraction had corrected those statements after the commencement of hostilities. Some of the young officers avowed that they had seen no evidence of continued disloyalty and that the matter ought to be left alone. All agreed that private citizens at Cumberland had treated them well, finer than at any other place.

"I'd like to pronounce a blessing upon all of the fine citizens of this fine city," said an Irishman as he lifted his glass.

> May those who love us, love us,
> And those who don't love us,
> May God turn their hearts,
> And if He doesn't turn their hearts,
> May He turn their ankles
> So we'll know them by their limping.

Hearty approval expressed by foot-stomping, knee-slapping, and laughter met the blessing.

"Did you men hear about what Haney's been tellin' about the swindle some of the boys pulled over at the hotel?"

The question came from the same lieutenant who had told of "Nosey's" calf-rustling a long time ago, and of other adventures since. The others looked at one another as if seeking consensus. Then they looked at the floor except for the man who smiled and said on behalf of the rest, "I don't think I've heard that one."

The door was now open and the story commenced.

"Anyways, Private Haney over in company K tells it like this. If I miss some of it you might want to have him tell it to you himself. You might oughta have him tell it even after I do 'cause I'm just gonna give you the short version of it."

This brought a collective smile to the rest of the group.

"Anyways, some of the boys in company K were gettin' tired of the water they were drinkin'—it's the same water we've all been drinkin' so I don't see that there's anything really wrong with the water other than that they were gettin' tired of water in general—at least that's what I take it to be—but they got to thinkin' they wanted to have somethin' stronger than water and I think that's really the point of it. Haney says they got to talkin' about wantin' to taste some of the 'tangle foot' down at the hotel by the railroad station. I guess he's callin' it 'tangle foot' on account of the fact that men's feet get tangled if they drink too much of it—so Haney's callin' it 'tangle foot' when I think he's meanin' just any sort of whiskey they could get. I think 'tangle foot' is a word that some of the men use for whiskey and it seems kinda clever to me for them to come up with a name like that for plain old whiskey. It has a ring to it, I think. Anyways, they slipped down to the hotel in the morning when the owner—I think his name is Kelley, same as the general—when the owner was still in bed and the place—the hotel and the bar room—wasn't open yet 'cause he doesn't open in the early part of the morning when the men got there. I think he does more of his business at night when more people want to buy what he sells. That makes sense to me on account of the fact that most men have more money to spend for that sorta thing at night than in the mornin'. Anyways, the men decided not to wake him up and they weren't sure how to pay for it anyways if they did wake him up and he was still in bed."

"Okay. We know that the bar is open at night more than in the morning and that some of our boys went there in the morning. What did they do there?" One officer asked on behalf of the others by silent consensus.

"That's what I'm tellin' right now. Anyways, whiles they waited for him—Kelley—to get out of bed and open the place one of the boys reconnoitered to the rear of the hotel and found a string of fish on the porch there. Mackerel is what Haney says but I think it might have been something else because mackerel doesn't keep all that long after its been caught—I don't think—like bass or some other fish. But let's say it was mackerel. Anyways, when the landlord—Kelley—got up and opened the door without them bein' the ones to wake him up—he got up on his own without anybody knocking or anything like that—when he got up and the place was open the boys went and got the fish—probably not mackerel—and took it in the front door—not the back door where the fish was. They said that—they told this to the man who opened the bar after getting out of bed—they said that the army had been serving them this fish—they said mackerel—for days and that they were getting tired of it and they wondered if he could trade them a few drinks for this string of fish. The landlord, Kelley—I think he's an Irishman—he says, 'sure, boys,' and he pulled out a bottle and some glasses and left them with the bottle while he put the fish out the back door on the porch where it had already been before."

The men laughed at the story and felt a sense of relief that it was over, but the lieutenant continued.

"That's not the end of it. After these boys did that they saw some more boys through the window from their company—that's Company K—Haney's from that company—Company K—they saw some more boys and one of the boys in the bar went out and told what they'd done. These boys—the new ones from Company K who weren't in on the first trick—these boys went around back and got the fish and brought 'em around front and told that there sure was a lot of mackerel—or whatever kind of fish it really was—back in camp and they wondered if they could make a trade. They said that the mess back in camp had more fish than the men could eat. Kelley made the same trade with these boys—for the same fish. Then they saw some more boys through the window from their company—K—and they went and told them and they did the same thing. Well, they figured three times was enough and they thanked the man—Kelley, like the general, Irish, I think—they thanked him and headed out the door. They didn't get far before they heard Kelley yellin' after 'em, 'Hello, boys.' Well, they were thinkin' 'we're in for it now—we're in for a real blessing from the Irishman.' That's what made me think of this when we heard the blessing about limping. But the blessing was not what they expected. It turns out that the landlord—who'd sold them 'tangle foot' for fish—knew all along what was goin' on. He yelled, 'Come back, boys. Any man that's darned fool enough to buy his own fish three times ought to stand treat.' So the men went back in and got a fourth drink for their fish. This all happened before we got paid. After the boys got paid they went back and paid for the 'tangle foot' and the Irishman—Kelley—said that these are 'the broth of boys.' I don't think the boys told the story until after they went back and paid—after they got paid—by the army I mean."

The half circle paused and someone asked it that was the end of it. Learning that it was, the group thanked him for the story while silently—but collectively—wishing they had heard it from Haney of Company K.

At Cumberland new recruits came into the regiment. Veterans of the battle at Winchester and other hardships made clear distinctions between themselves and these "conscripts" in fresh uniforms. Colonel Curtis moved the regiment to a hill west of the city. Amidst the light picket duty, guard duty, and working on the fortifications, Curtis found time to drill the regiment thoroughly in battalion drill, the manual of arms, and dress parade.

*   *   *   *

HE RESIGNED

The smallish general looked Captain McMorrow straight in the eye as the inspection of John's company commenced on March 12, 1864. The new commander did the same to every soldier in the ranks as John assisted in this most thorough inspection. Privates would later say that Major General Franz Sigel was looking into their eyes to see if there was fire in them to fight. McMorrow would always hold to his own interpretation: Sigel was trying to transmit some impression of himself more than to read what he might see. Maybe the sense that Sigel was trying to find fire in their eyes was precisely the impression he had hoped for.

This new general was different. He had agood deal of history packed into his thirty-nine years. When that exotic, romantic history circulated and enlarged among the men, it inspired them. Sigel had graduated from some German military academy and had served as minister of war under some Grand Duke—Leopold, they said—before the Prussians revolutionary forces defeated his. Sigel had spent time in Switzerland, then England, before moving to New York in 1852, where the government had given him the rank of major in the 5th New York Militia. He had moved to St. Louis where he rose to director of schools in that city with a large minority of German-born American citizens. Sigel's reputation among the German population nudged government to commission him a brigadier general in 1861, and then a major general in March 1862. Germans in the North turned out in droves, flocking to recruiters exclaiming, "We fights mit Sigel!"

Sigel had been in on the capture of the Confederate Camp Jackson in St. Louis under Nathaniel Lyon and he had been engaged in the skirmish at Carthage, Missouri, with honor. These were minor skirmishes but they had been successful. The German-Americans who read of them in the papers were proud to see one of their own serving with distinction in the Union army. Sigel's name was connected with the Union victory at Pea Ridge in Arkansas.

Now, as he took command of the Department of West Virginia, and as he took the time to look every man of every company in the eye, the men formed a favorable impression of the man as he formed his impression of them. He watched the men drill and commented favorably on the efficiency and celerity with which soldiers executed orders and moved as a unit. Although many regiments were part of his command, Sigel specifically complimented the colonel of the 12th West Virginia and declared that he had no idea that there was so well-drilled a regiment in that department. This compliment circulated among the men and they stood taller because of it.

Lieutenant Colonel Northcott rejoined the regiment after his long and dreary incarceration in Confederate prisons, where he had been since Winchester. After dress parade on March 27, Northcott appeared before the men, in apparent good health and spirits, and gave a brief speech.

Their former major, Francis P. Pierpoint, now Adjutant General of West Virginia, visited the camp on April 2 and paid respects to his late comrades. Spirits remained high. Things were happening. Rested men were ready to proceed with the war and finish it. As fine as duty at Cumberland had been, these men had homes waiting for them and a war to end before they could return. Trains carried them to Webster, West Virginia, where they were to join forces with General George Crook's men and prepare to launch a fresh campaign in the Shenandoah Valley.

In preparation for great things, yet unclear to the men in the ranks, the 12th West Virginia took charge of a herd of 250 cattle on April 3 and herded them out ahead of the main force, where the other regiments were to meet them. War taught West Virginia soldiers to be cowboys. A whole regiment to herd this small number of cattle gave them odds that required no refined herding ability, but with the enthusiasm that comes with trying new things, the men did their part.

After moving the cattle all the way to Beverly, forty-two miles out, they received word that Sigel had changed his mind. He decided that he could not get his artillery over that route. The cowboys were to stay put, guard the cattle, and await orders.

Two days later they received orders to return with their charges. Heavy rains and 250 head of cattle did more to churn mud than any regiment of men. Boot-sucking mud, deep and well-mixed, made every step a miserable attempt to keep up the march. Since the whole regiment was not needed to move the cattle, four companies stayed at Philippi for a few days while the rest delivered cattle back to where they had begun.

As he trudged with the herdsmen-soldiers approaching Belington, a little town between Beverly and Philippi, John McMorrow saw Colonel Curtis up ahead talking with some junior officer from another unit who was pointing at a field lined with new fence rails. John hoped this meant they might be stopping here for the night, that those rails might soon be stacked and set afire.

"That's exactly where you should go into camp, sir. You can't punish these people half enough. These are all Rebels around here. Mean 'uns. They had to have helped the Rebel raiders who came through here. Some of 'em are likely bushwhackers themselves. I'd say it'd be fair if you used the place up before you leave it."

Curtis merely nodded and thanked the young officer, then prepared to move his men into camp for the night.

As the regiment was setting up camp a young man from the farmhouse came toward them. Colonel Curtis spoke civilly to him. "My men have no shelter and the ground is wet and cold. I wonder if you might help us procure some straw for them to sleep on."

The response was equally polite. "I'm sorry, sir. We'v nothing of the sort on the farm. We've been pretty well cleaned out by the Union army. We have to cut limbs from the trees to browse our cattle and keep 'em from starving to death."

John expected more of an argument from Curtis but the colonel just nodded and thanked the man for his consideration.

As the two walked toward the main body of men, Curtis smiled and said, "You know the men of this regiment as well as I do. They can take care of themselves. Do you suppose that any will sleep on wet ground tonight?"

"I think not, sir." Soon men carried large bundles of straw to their unfinished rail pens.

Curtis took quarters in the farmhouse along with the regimental surgeon. He soon learned that the elderly lady who lived there was clearly in charge and he asked if he might purchase some meat to supplement what he was authorized to give his men for food.

"No, sir. We have not a bit of meat on the place." He thanked her and went to his quarters.

Soon after the chickens should have gone to roost, those in the house heard them. Fluttering wings and squawking sounded like some animal was disturbing the chickens. Colonel Curtis heard it. Then he heard the shouting of the old lady's daughter.

"Ma, them Yankees is stealin' all our chickens."

A loud knock on his door was followed by, "Colonel! You need to git out there and stop them men from stealin' 'em chickens. Colonel. Do you hear me?"

"Give me time to get my boots on, Ma'am. I'll check on it for you." Leisurely, he went out to inspect the henhouse, only to report that he had seen no one anywhere near the coop.

An hour later the racket recommenced. The girl ran out and then returned with her own update: "Mam, them infernal soldiers have stole every chicken we had except fer old speck."

The colonel sat calmly while the old woman cursed him and called his men all manner of foul names. When she finished, Curtis politely wished her a good night and went to bed.

At daybreak all was still and quiet. The colonel had just opened his eyes, surprised that he had been able to have a full night's rest in this household. The door flew open and banged against the wall. A figure rushed in. Curtis had no time to go for his side arm before someone had him by the shoulders. He supposed that he was now a prisoner of some band of Rebel partisans. But no. This was the foul-mouthed elderly lady and she was shaking him wildly. "Git up. Yer men have stolen all my meat!"

Sitting up, taking a deep breath, and collecting his thoughts, Curtis politely said, "But Madam, you informed me yourself, just last night, that you have no meat."

"Well I said it, but I did have some and yer men has dug down under the smokehouse and took ever last bit of it."

"Ma'am, if you'd have asked for a guard to protect your smokehouse I'd have been happy to have supplied one. As it now stands it appears that someone, certainly not my men, has had the benefit of your deception."

"Just the same, Colonel, I know mah rights. You need to git on out thar and search fer that meat and git it back."

Dressing, while kindly listening to the lady's instructions, Curtis finally agreed to fulfill his obligation to search the camp.

An hour later he reported to the woman, honestly, that he had found no meat in the camp after a careful search. When he joined his mess for dinner that day, Curtis was not surprised to have a delicious roast ham. He would ask no questions now, for conscience' sake.

On April 20, the whole command reunited at Webster and on the next day the 12th West Virginia Infantry marched to Grafton where it took cars to Martinsburg. The trains arrived on Friday evening, April 22, and camped near the 1st West Virginia Infantry. It pained Captain McMorrow to be so near Anna Lee while passing through Grafton and yet unable to pause for even a short while. *The war will soon be over,* he thought. *We'll all be going home soon.*

At Martinsburg, Sigel's command underwent organizational changes and the 12th West Virginia became a part of the 2nd Brigade along with the 34th Massachusetts, the 54th Pennsylvania, and the 1st West Virginia. Colonel Joseph Thoburn took charge of the 2nd Brigade. The changes had little effect upon the men in the ranks. Some could not have told an outsider just what brigade they belonged to.

On the 28th of April Sigel ordered five days' rations issued to every soldier. According to plan they set out at daybreak on the Winchester pike and marched to Bunker Hill, ten easy miles. They camped there until May 1, when they marched to a position two miles beyond Winchester and made camp.

Signs of war were all along the route between Martinsburg and Winchester. Shallow graves, torn fences, splintered trees, farms of high grass devoid of livestock, and empty homes all spoke of past conflict and future danger. This fourth visit to Winchester gave the sense that the war was progressing—or degenerating. At least it seemed that it must be moving toward some conclusion or destined to turn this once-beautiful valley into a desolate wasteland. The veterans of the battle that they had fought here visited the scenes of conflict once again and felt the respect of the newcomers who had not participated.

General Sigel continued to enjoy the esteem of the men. Strong picket forces and other precautions told the men that Sigel was a vigilant commander and that there was cause for vigilance. They trusted Sigel's judgement even when they could not see the importance of dress parades and the kinds of inspections that might normally be expected with men in garrison rather than men in the field.

On the 9th of May the Second Brigade, under Colonel Thoburn, was proud to take the advance up the Valley as they marched thirteen miles to the south and made camp at Cedar Creek. Here they rebuilt a bridge that would allow the command to continue, and on the 11th they marched through Strasburg and made camp about a mile short of Woodstock, Virginia. Along the way the men halted and loaded muskets. Veterans of battle ripped the paper from their cartridges with bared teeth while scanning the horizon with furrowed brows and grave expressions. Raw recruits—who would remain raw recruits until they tasted battle, no matter how long they had been in service—examined the veteran's faces. Minie-balls rammed just then would not fire until later, but their presence in the barrels of those muskets gave veterans a sense of both comfort and dread. It gave hope of battle to new recruits who were spoiling for a fight, but would say so only among themselves.

Nothing much happened during the one day spent at the camp near Woodstock. Next day the 12th West Virginia was ordered seven miles up the valley to about one mile south of Edinburg with two pieces of artillery. This advance picket observed Confederate cavalry in the distance. Two men from the 12th West Virginia were captured when they left the lines to try to get some bread from a house nearby and, at the suggestion of the inhabitants and contrary to orders, went to some other house when they found no bread at the first.

On the morning of the 14th the regiment came off picket duty and marched down the valley to the camp near Edinburg in mud and rain, passing two other regiments going back up the valley.

Movement back and forth was about to come to a temporary end. On the morning of May 15, the regiment pushed on to Mount Jackson in clearing weather, where it camped. Within minutes they were ordered six miles up the valley, toward New Market where cannon blasts marked the place of fighting. The rains resumed and mud deepened, but the men of the 12th West Virginia joined in singing with German volunteers: "We fights mit Sigel."

"Hurry it up men. Double quick!" Stumbling over one another and struggling to cover miles of muck at the double quick, they reached the scene of fighting at about 2:00 in the afternoon. Still in the rear of the forward body of troops, on the safe side of a rise in the ground to the right of the pike, they formed in line of battle while the unmistakable whistle of Minie balls passed overhead. The men of the 12th remained in reserve, where they could not fire at the enemy without firing through the ranks of other Union regiments to their front. New Market was at the narrow bottle-neck formed by Massanutten Mountain filling the center of the otherwise wide Shenandoah Valley.

The 12th West Virginia could not take position to the right of those in front because of a cliff that dropped to the South Fork of the Shenandoah River. Positions in their front were taken by other regiments. Rebel lead thudded into blue uniforms worn by men who could not return fire. They were in a battle in which they served only as targets. This was not what the veterans had experienced before. It was no fulfillment of recruit fantasies. Lieutenant James W. Dunington bolted and ran to the rear.

The Rebel yell sounded to the front as soldiers in gray charged. Sigel ordered the regiment to resist the charge with the others. Terrified and willing, they formed into a column and met the charge, successfully repulsing it. Brief minutes passed before they withdrew from the conflict and went into line again in the rear, with orders to keep their heads down.

"Keep yourselves ready, boys!" Captain McMorrow had his sword in this hand. He hoped to soon be leading his company to chase the Rebels from the field. He was primed for action. John's heart sent hot blood coursing through his body as he looked for some order to press the charge. He sensed the common will to charge. He looked to his left and saw General Sigel ride by the men and shout something that John could not hear above the roar. No one responded. He shouted, "My men are ready to go into action, sir!" But even those nearby could not hear. To the front he saw the backs of men in blue. He watched as men fell, but his orders were to stay where he was until further orders. He could see a farm-house through the driving rain and billowing smoke when he dared raise his head. A flag come around the house at the bottom of the hill to the left and moved between the house and the barn toward the Union front. The flag disap-peared, through the smoke and driving rain, below John's line of sight.

The next order John was able to understand was *"retreat in line of battle."* He could hardly take it in. There were more men in blue than in gray on the field. If properly handled they could whip these Rebels and finish this ugly business of war, or at least press the matter in the direction of ultimate victory by defeating these Rebels at this place. Maybe Winchester had been a necessary retreat, but not this.

Now in the front, leading the retreat, the regiment slogged through mud to get away. Rebels did not vigorously pursue them as John expected. The retreating troops met two Ohio regiments at Rude's Hill, a few miles from the battlefield, who had been in reserve, not engaged in the fight. These covered the retreat back to Mount Jackson, where the regiment formed line of battle. Rebels failed to come within musket range, but close enough to lob a few artillery shells.

After dark the retreat continued until they reached Cedar Creek on the 16th of May. Now the men sang a revised tune: "We fights no more mit Sigel." It was an orderly retreat made under control and according to orders, but it riled sol-diers who felt badly used. The wounded had been left on the field. It was a dis-grace to men who outnumbered a foe and then retreated without making full use of men ready to fight. Excuses and explanations abounded. But the naked facts spelled shame and humiliation.

Next day, back in camp, a far-from-timid Captain—John McMorrow—stood before the tent of Colonel Curtis even though he had not been called. Knocking on the pole but not pulling back the flaps until invited, John stepped into the tent with a presence bolder than that of a captain standing before a colonel. He saluted but did not wait to be asked about his business.

"Sir. I demand—on behalf of the men—to have the name of the officer of the 12th West Virginia who received this order from General Sigel!"

One of Sigel's explanations for the failure at New Market had involved some vague reference to orders given to some portion of the 12th West Virginia that the 12th had not carried out. The colonel knew John's point.

"The general didn't give a name, John. Just that he gave an order to go for-ward and that those so ordered 'would not go.'"

"Then the General owes a retraction. If he shouted at some privates with no officer in sight then the general, himself, was out of line. If he shouted some order generally with no man to hear it then no one is at fault other than the General himself. For the sake of the men this assertion that they disobeyed an order to advance must be challenged. I was prepared to lead my men in. My men were ready to go. To have gone without orders would have been a punishable offense. It might have endangered the whole command if I'd ordered them forward on my own authority and contrary to some greater plan. My men are not cowards, sir!"

"First of all, captain, you will lower your voice. I can hear you very well and there is no value in letting the men hear what you feel you must say."

"But, Sir, I—".

The colonel interrupted: "Listen. I understand your point and I share it completely. The regiment performed its duties well. They formed up under fire. They watched comrades fall. WE watched men fall around us—and couldn't return fire. The General claims to have given an order that no one recalls having received. There was confusion on the field. Both could be telling the truth." Curtis paused, looked at the canvas wall, sorted through his thoughts, and edited them before speaking. "Captain, for my part our men behaved exactly as they should have behaved and just as we want them to behave in any future engagements. There will be no discipline for failure."

"But, sir, there's more—"

Raising a hand to acknowledge the point half-made, the colonel continued: "I know, John. It is more a matter of honor than a question of who'll be punished. Perhaps the honor of every last soldier in this unit has been insulted by the General's method of saving his own—" he paused again and then continued with the edited version, "by the ill-considered and possibly inaccurate comments of the General made under pressure." Looking John in the eye, Curtis said, "I will put in my report that I received no order to advance and this will be the truth. You will put in your report that you received no such order. Every one of my officers will make the same report. The General will possibly include some reference to some order given to nameless men. We can't change what General Sigel might say. Have the men heard of the General's comments?" Curtis looked at the desk on which his hands rested.

"Yes, sir. The men have heard it and they need some correction or we might be faced with…with…I don't know what all. Desertion maybe. Shame. You call these brave men cowards, even in oblique terms, and you can't expect them to stand there and take it and then wait for the next time they're misused and expect them to fight with a will."

"Agreed. And I'm grateful for your thoughts on this. Let's find ways to agree with these men and let them know that we feel the injustice with them without suggesting that our General has falsely accused them. He has, at least in a sense, but we must watch our own tongues. My official reports will be clean, sanitized for all to read—including the General. What I pass along to Washington by other means might be clearer and less guarded. Truth is, there were more of us at New Market than there were of them. We had troops that were not put into action. We retreated in the face of the enemy while we had a superior force yet in the field. That says more than anything we might say. Let's tell the men that we are proud of them for their work at New Market. Let's get them looking for their next chance to show that the 12th West Virginia Infantry is not made of cowards. Let's get them looking to the future."

John returned to his campfire and noted that the disheartened mood had infected the others in the circle who were quiet and subdued. The mood had dampened everyone in the circle except the lieutenant who seemed always unaware of the general sense of others about him.

"Did you hear about what one of the boys in the 34th yelled out when the battle was just starting?"

For a long moment no one responded at all. The hearers did not search for consensus in the faces of their fellow officers. John McMorrow, on his own authority and with designs that made sense to him—if to no one else there—said, "No. I don't believe I've heard that one. Why don't you tell it?" Several search John's face for explanation, but he gave none.

"Well, anyways, you all know that Colonel Wells is strict. You know. The colonel of the 34th Massachusetts. Well, the 34th was up closer to the front. And you know that the colonel—Colonel Wells would have a fit when the boys in his Regiment—the 34th—fired off their muskets in camp for no good reason. Course, our colonel wouldn't like it much either, but that's not the point here. Anyways, some of the boys in the 34th would fire off a charge, in camp, without any musket balls just to raise up some interest when they were in camp. Whenever they'd do that the colonel—Colonel Wells of the 34th—he'd yell out the same thing every time. He'd yell out and say, 'Orderly, orderly, go and ascertain who fired that gun and report him to me immediately!' Course, the orderly could never find the one that did it so it just got to be fun for the boys—the boys in the 34th Massachusetts—to fire off their muskets to see if he'd say that again. Well, anyways, when the first guns were fired down at New Market, right there in front of everybody some private yelled out and said, 'Orderly, orderly, go and ascertain who fired that gun and report him to me immediately!'"

This one bought a few laughs. John felt satisfied that consensus is sometimes a poor measure of whether or not a thing ought to be done.

On the 18th of May the regiment left camp at Cedar Creek for picket duty up the Valley at Fisher's Hill. Captain McMorrow did not share the enthusiasm generated in some by the brief visit from General Sigel at the picket line. John marveled at the blind approval that men in the ranks gave to their general. Mainly, Captain John McMorrow was tired. The disheartened officer walked among his men speaking encouraging words that did not generally match his own thoughts. The weary man who repeated the words, "Look alert, men." after every twenty dreary paces or so was commanding his own will as much as issuing orders. John was in earnest and completely consistent with his own mood when he said, "Men, let's look for every chance to go in and end this war and then go home."

The next day they moved back to Strasburg, to the old fort "built by General Banks." That is what the colonel had said when they went in. "This old fort was built by General Banks." John restrained his tongue. *This fort was not built by General Banks*, he thought. *It is an injustice to the men who built it to say it. Not a drop of sweat fell from the general's face from lifting logs or hacking down thick trees or hauling rocks or turning shovels of dirt. His soft hands were not blistered and torn by labor.* New Market had robbed John, for the time, of the respect he had uncritically given to senior officers.

"Mail call!" Eager men gathered around the voice. The man with the mail was the man of the hour and the hero of the moment. His voice was the sweetest ever heard in camp, shouting soldier's names scribbled on envelopes by mothers, wives, lovers, sons, fathers, and daughters. The absence of one's own name was the most revolting silence for those who gathered around the man with the mail.

"Captain John McMorrow!"

"Here! Pass it on back, men, thank you." Hands hoping to soon touch words penned by other hands sent the letter to the rear and John's grateful hands received it. It was from Anna Lee Stone, Grafton, West Virginia.

Soldiers scattered when the man with the mail called the final name. John strolled out of the fort to the edge of the woods, where he sat on a broad table of a stump. His hand caressed the name of Anna Lee Stone, whose very hand had put the ink there and whose fingers had touched this paper. He smelled it and even though it smelled of damp paper and nothing more, John imagined that he caught a faint scent of Anna Lee. Not of perfume, but of Anna Lee. The blade of his pocket knife slit the end and the fingertips of his left hand slid the two sheaves from the envelope. The folded pages drew themselves to his lips as he sucked in the air with his nostrils, kissed the paper, and formed pictures of Anna Lee as he had seen her in the balcony at the debate so long passed; as he had seen her in the lobby after she had tugged at his sleeve; as he had seen her in the parlor of her home with the searching, revealing look in her eye; and as he had imagined her many times before, wearing a pure white wedding dress and walking beside her father, coming to meet John at the front of the church building. The latter remained the ultimate landmark toward which John was marching one step after another until this war would end and he would go home to claim Anna Lee.

He laid the envelope to his right on the stump, unfolded the pages, and began to taste the sweet words of Anna Lee and the sweeter words that he could find between the lines.

The first paragraph told of news from around home. Anna Lee had seen John's father at church on Sunday and he had looked well. She had finished reading all the books John had loaned her. She had not forgotten who owned them, and she would be holding them for the day when John would come for them, after the war. This little promise for the future pleased him.

The next paragraph spoke of her awareness of the war and its progress. She seemed more aware than he, himself, of the progress of arms in other places. There had been talk of how General Grant had taken charge of all the Union armies and this, to Anna Lee, seemed like a good thing since he had a history of getting results according to the papers. Upon reading this part John had a little mental conversation with Anna Lee in which he explained to her that generals do not win battles; they give orders and take credit and give blame. He sensed that Anna Lee would think her way to the same conclusions if given the same premises from which to reason. He accounted that Anna Lee was still quite wise, even if she did not have proper conceptions of military matters

John finished the first page and shuffled it behind the second. He continued reading.

As he read once again of Anna Lee's "enduring fondness," the words warmed him. How could she continue to show such restraint when he knew that she loved him as much as he loved her? John had seen it in her eyes and felt it in Anna Lee's touch, even if her tongue and pen could not yet confess it. On this second page he read that she "would always count" him as "a dear and precious friend who had brought light" into her world. John spoke to the page and told Anna Lee that he had long known that they would "always" be "dear and precious" to one another and that she might as well yield to the greater implications of that now and speak her heart openly. Micah would get over it soon. There was no virtue in prolonging his brief agony.

Just as John was finishing this part of his apostrophic discussion with Anna Lee, his eye was drawn to a word farther down the page: "marriage." Interpretations fell on top of one another as John tried to put it in its true context. At first he was surprised that Anna Lee would be the first to suggest it after such prolonged restraint. Then he supposed that it must be some reference to someone else known to both of them.

Then the truth sucked his heart like cold mud on a soldier's boot. The context was clear. The sentences leading up to it were designed to prepare him for it, if words could do that. Anna Lee had accepted a "proposal of marriage" from Micah Johnson.

Captain John McMorrow stood up, walked into the cover of the woods, and threw up. He walked farther as he spit out the burning acid that he had coughed from the back of his throat, and cleared his nose of caustic obstructions. When John was sure that he was out of sight he sat down, pulled his knees to his chest, and cried.

How can this be? His chest heaved against his thighs. *How can a thing be heading in one direction like a locomotive and then turned in another direction without warning?* Doubt seeped into his jumbled stream of thought. *Did she EVER love me? Was it all just an illusion? How can what feels so much like the shared love of a lifetime be so one-sided? Did my own need for her to love me force me to conclude—irrationally—that she loved me as I loved her? No. She loved me. I saw it in her eyes and felt it flow from her fingers. No. That's not reasonable. I can't make a syllogism out of the look of an eye and the touch of a hand. What then? How can I know? I'll ask her to tell me. No. I don't need to know. No. I DO need to know. I'll tell her that I love her and ask her to tell me her feelings. NO. It's too late. She is to be the wife of another man.*

Then his disorganized thoughts turned toward Micah Johnson. *Who is he anyway? Is he as good a man as they say he is? Will he make her happy? Will he treat her right?*

The questions evolved into halting demands and retractions. *He'd better be a good man. He'd better treat her right. He'd better make her happy. He can't begin to know how much his prize has cost me. If he ever causes her a moment's pain and I find out about it I'll…No. I have no right to follow the progress of their marriage. They're sure to struggle along at times—and even to fight—like everyone else. I figure that I'd have caused her at least a certain amount of pain if she'd married me. It's just not rational for me to expect him to be perfect. I've seen the fire in her eyes a time or two, so I figure she can provoke a fight and then hold her own anyway. I won't try to follow them and guard her. She's as strong as anyone I know without me standing picket around her. I can't be some knight in shining armor waiting around for her to need rescuing. Then I'll MAKE him a good man. I'll find some way to see that someone helps him in whatever way he needs help. I'll send business his way. I'll send a letter to whoever buys his rifles and tell them its the best rifle I ever saw. I'll pretend I don't know who makes it. I'll spread the word to everyone I meet in the Army that this is a straight-shooting rifle, and I'll hope that there's some truth in it. No. I don't know. If he's not a good man, then I guess I'm powerless to make him into one. If he's a good man then he'll hold his own and make his way without me playing like a crooked quartermaster handing out favors. If he's bad…If he's bad…If he mistreats her more than average…I'll…I think I'll…just let her know that I want to help and ask her to tell me how. That's where I'll settle this for now. Maybe that's where it'll stay settled.*

Not able to blame Micah for doing what he himself had expected to do, and not able to blame Anna Lee because Anna Lee had made no promises or been unkind, John McMorrow laid the blame for his life's greatest loss at the feet of the Rebels, and Jefferson Davis, and the war. He had long held a strong sense of loyalty to the Union and a sense of the rightness of its preservation. John had come to think that slavery needed to end and that the war should accomplish that. But now he would look at men in gray and see those who had robbed him of life while he yet lived. Every day endured without hope of Anna Lee's hand would be due to these treacherous savages who had disrupted the country and torn lives apart. *They say that the shots fired at Sumter didn't kill anything but maybe some horse. That's not so. It killed men who are now in their graves and it killed me while I must endure life.*

John wiped his eyes on the knees of his britches and sat on a hard rock. The sweet smell of the leaves and disturbed soil where he had been kicking at it slowly entered his awareness. Through the trees he saw the blue sky with wisps of white. His surroundings started to take shape. The bark on the trees and the surface of the rock had textures John had not noticed. Distant voices from the fort reached his hearing ears. John realized that he was warm. He took off his coat. He was now aware of being thirsty and thought how good it would be to have a cup of cool water. The bees, the birds nesting in the tree with fledglings ready to try their wings and face the world, and the dirty white cocoon on the leaf, seemed to emerge from the mists. As he stood on his feet John McMorrow found strength in reminding himself aloud, "I'm not dead. Let's see where things go from here."

When he finished, he felt a vague sense of relief that his eyes were now open and that he was no longer one of the parties tugging on Anna Lee. He determined that he would do nothing to hamper the happiness of the two, and that he would do all within his power to help them if they were to ever need help. John felt no sense of betrayal. He felt profound loss. There was no sense of bitterness, not really, but there was a lump in his throat and a bittersweet ache in his chest as John tried to re-map his own life and to organize it around new plans somewhere other than Clarksburg, and possibly with someone yet to be found.

That evening the band from the 34th Massachusetts played in the fort and Colonel Curtis, along with two others, made speeches. Curtis expressed profound respect for the men of the 12th West Virginia and all the others who had fought bravely at New Market. Without naming names, Curtis apologized to the men for the "failure of leadership," and he promised to do his best to see that matters in the future would be "much improved."

On May 20, General David Hunter arrived to take command of the Department of West Virginia. Major General Franz Sigel was relieved of command.

CHAPTER 10

CLARIFIED THE PAST AND ALTERED THE FUTURE

"Things are changing in the Army of the Potomac. U. S. Grant is now in command of all the armies. We will press this war to its conclusion. Get ready, men. You are about to enter on an explosion of hardships in which we will move forward whether or not our supply wagons can keep up. We will live off the enemy's bounty and use up what they have as we go along. We will eat mule meat after we've eaten that last piece of Confederate bread if that's what we have to do. This is a new kind of war, men. There'll be no dancing around with the Rebels from here on out until this thing is ended!"

John McMorrow was not alone in hoping that these were not the empty words of a new strutting peacock echoing the words of some other windbag called General Grant. The army had long talked about what it would do to the enemy. Few put the talk into action on the field of battle. McClellan was going to take Richmond, way back then, and Richmond still stood. Sigel looked for fire in the eyes of men but when he had the chance to send fire upon the enemy he had led them in disgraceful retreat. Fire does not come from eyes or words. It comes from muskets, up close and dangerous. *Are we actually going to do something or are we going to listen to fancy speeches?*

"You are all to draw ten days' rations of coffee and sugar and three days' rations of hardtack. You in the infantry will draw 80 rounds of ammunition instead of the usual 40 rounds. Those who can find a place to put it and can stand to carry it can draw 100 rounds."

This was all new and different. Maybe the new generals meant business?

In the early afternoon on May 25, 1864, Hunter launched his raid. Camping near Woodstock on the first night out, the cavalry burned a house and barn to the ground. The general said the owner was a bushwacker. They marched on.

On the 29th they camped near New Market and had chance to visit the battlefield without Confederates in sight. Rebels had buried the Union dead in a mass grave where stone had been quarried. They had buried their own in the cemetery. John took note. He accumulated arguments to justify wrath against these Rebels. He was strangely disappointed to find out that they had taken thirty-one of the Union wounded to private homes, where they had been treated well. John was grateful for the welfare of the men. He was confused by the kindness of the enemy and attributed it to the selfish desire of local citizens to avoid Union wrath.

Foraging became the rule rather than the exception for necessity. Its purpose was not only to feed Union soldiers, but also to deprive the Rebels and their supporters who harbored them and supplied them from the fertile fields of the Shenandoah Valley.

On June 2 the regiment pressed on to Harrisonburg, where it drove Imboden's men from the town and discovered that sixty Union wounded from New Market had been deposited and cared for there.

On the 4th they marched toward Staunton, but turned to the left toward Cross Keys when they learned of a force of Imboden's men waiting in the path of their planned march. At Port Republic they put up a pontoon bridge and continued toward Staunton.

On the morning of the 5th they did not travel far before their cavalry began skirmishing with Rebels. Union troops captured a few and drove the rest up the road. The whole command marched on. John passed an Irish woman, standing over the fresh grave of boys from the 1st New York Cavalry.

Seven miles out from Port Republic they met a force of eight or nine thousand Rebels, Imboden's and General John C. Vaughn's men under General William E. Jones. John McMorrow learned that he was now one of 8,500 men who were ready to fight and that Confederates were to their front. *What will the new general do now that we have the chance to press this war?*

Ahead, the enemy line spread on both sides of the road. Breastworks of fence rails, soil, and rock stretched from the road a few hundred yards to the left. The two Union brigades of 8,500 men faced them from a wooded area across a broad and empty field.

Hunter called his men into line of battle. Colonel Thoburn and his 2nd Brigade formed on the left of the pike while Colonel Moor put the 1st Brigade into line on the right. Artillery opened from both sides. The 12th West Virginia and the 34th Massachusetts were ordered forward to charge enemy artillery, but they were pulled back when the artillery opened on them. The rest of the brigade was coming forward to the new line of battle on ground purchased by this advance when Colonel Thoburn, Colonel Curtis, and Adjutant General B. Caldwell rode onto open ground to direct Union artillery. A well-placed Confederate shell covered them with dirt and took a leg off the adjutant's horse. No men were seriously injured. It was a thrilling sight. *Leaders in danger. Standing up to it.*

The other regiments came up and Thoburn rushed his brigade to a slight depression about 200 yards from the enemy, planning to work around to flank the Confederates. As Thoburn's men were moving forward with fixed bayonets, Union artillery opened fire to cover the advance and the Confederate guns answered. The earth shook. A Confederate band played "Dixie" while a Union band struck up "Yankee Doodle."

Captain John R. Meigs rode across the front of the line. "Make this charge good, men! Do your duty. We cannot be defeated here. We're a hundred miles from any help from others. Don't hesitate. Don't falter. Go right through 'em when we make this charge. Make it good, men. Make it good!"

The men rushed forward to within 100 yards of the fence-rail works. Men fell during the rush. They drew fire and returned fire.

"Follow me, men!" Captain McMorrow led his company as other captains led other companies forward. John's sword pointed to the front. Men faced bayonets in the same direction and cheered as they rushed toward, and then over the parapet. Color bearers planted flags amidst smoke and fire and roaring guns. The flag of the 12th West Virginia took the lead into the woods beyond the breastworks that were now vacant of Rebels except for those who had chosen the bayonet or surrender. "Come on, men. This is where we need you. Keep it going!"

Corporal Joseph S. Halstead, who bore the flag beyond the works, fell at last. He fell upon the cloth as if it had been spread on the ground for the purpose. His blood thoroughly stained it. Other hands carried forward the banner of the 12th West Virginia Infantry.

Hundreds of prisoners stumbled to the rear under guard as more regiments poured to the front. As the 12th West Virginia pushed forward, Union soldiers tore Rebel flags to rags and threw them to the ground. Some were so wild in their enthusiasm that they rushed into small bands of Confederates who captured them, for brief moments, before the main force surrounded them and captured the captors. This was to be a victory. Here the officers fought. Here there was no retreat.

Maybe. Maybe this Hunter will prove a fighter. Maybe this Grant is leading the whole Federal army so as to finish this awful business. The Rebel dead, too many to bury until morning, bore silent testimony to the fact that the Department of West Virginia and the 12th West Virginia Infantry in particular, had fire in their eyes that could be unleashed with effect.

Talk around the campfires that night was animated. Every man had a story to tell—and to tell again when he could find at least one listener who had not heard his story. When distant men try to describe battles, recounting the overall movement of troops, they miss the thousands of individual fights that raged man-to-man all along the clashing lines. When a soldier recalls a battle he sees scenes measurable in square inches with blood and smoke and fire, and he remembers personal desperation and local acts of heroism. He does not recall maps and broad landscapes. He sees again the bark that exploded on the oak beside him and the bayonet that gouged the specific man and the severed limb that fell to his feet after the cannon roared.

Thousands of men told their tales to thousands of other men who had tales to tell around the campfires after the Battle of Piedmont.

Private Isaac Cullen, seventeen years old, had met a gray-haired Rebel at the breastworks who put a musket to his chest and demand his surrender. He grabbed the musket and twisted it from the old man's hands and kicked him over the works and said, "Old man, you're too old to bayonet. Git to the rear. You're a prisoner." When another who saw it told the tale, Cullen said, "I can't believe that really happened."

Some boy from an Ohio regiment reached the top of the works and yelled, "Look out Johnnies, we're comin' down on you like a thousand of brick!" At the retelling around the fire the men laughed.

There were tales of barbarism on the part of Rebels, but no one confessed to having seen Union troops behave so dishonorably. The theory ran through the camps that this was due to slavery and that Rebels must be accustomed to treating human life not their own as if it were a low thing. "I tell you now more than ever," declared one, "slavery devalues humanity and must be eradicated from the earth."

First Sergeant Hartley Marks of Company K captured a Confederate lieutenant who surrendered fair and square. The men saw it happen. "Just when Marks turned his back, that Rebel drew a gun he'd hid in his coat and shot Marks in the back. We grabbed that prisoner and do you know what we did with him? No. We didn't shoot him. We spared 'im and sent him under guard to the rear as a prisoner. That's the way we treat our prisoners. We're not like them Rebels down at Fort Pillow who just killed 'em all with their hands in the air and a white flag."

"We did the same when Barney Wiles was a prisoner of the Rebels for a few minutes before we took him back. After he surrendered one of them Rebs shot at him and missed—but cut his pants with the ball—and after we rushed in and took them prisoners we didn't do nothin' to that Reb but send him back to the rear as a prisoner."

A loud moan came from out in the woods. It was some wounded Confederate soldier but no one seemed to hear it just then. They had already agreed that they would see to them in the morning.

"And another thing that went on all the rest of the day. Our men was feedin' their wounded men and givin' 'em water from their own canteens all through them woods. I tell ya. Even after the war's over we're goin' to have a time gettin' the South up to bein' civilized people. Slavery's turned all them people into nothin' but savages and it's easy to see that the North ain't like that!"

Another predicted, "And after we git our own boys buried proper in the mornin' what do you figger we'll do with theirs? I figger we'll give 'em all a Christian burial and put up some proper markers and send their names over to the other side—if we can find their names on 'em."

A more subdued voice responded, "Maybe."

Private Shinn, from Harrison County, had a story that seemed not to fit the general theme regarding the barbarity of all Rebels. "I had the drop on a colonel from Virginia. I told him to surrender or I'd shoot 'im an' he up and told me that he was a colonel and wasn't goin' to surrender to no private. Well, I wasn't sure what to do. He didn't have no gun that I could see an' I didn't want to shoot 'im just standin' there like that an' he wasn't tryin' to get away or nothin' but he just said he wouldn't surrender to no private. Just then Colonel Curtis come along on 'is horse and that Rebel colonel just throwed up 'is hands and waved at Curtis an' yelled out, 'Ah surrender to you.' So I guess you could say that he surrendered to the colonel because I had my gun on 'im but it didn't make no sense to me. Well, Colonel Curtis took 'is sword an' turned 'im over to me and the boys to take to the rear an' as we was takin' 'im back there he pulled out a real shiny revolver an' just handed it over to me and told me to give it to the colonel. Well, I give it to the colonel just a little bit ago but it seems to me that I oughta be the one to have it on account of I'm the one that got 'im to surrender even if he did git the colonel to take 'is surrender official."

Another theme ran through the talk around the fires that night. This had been the third battle in which the 12th West Virginia Infantry had been engaged and it was its first victory. This called for analysis.

At Winchester the loss could not have been helped. They were outnumbered and outgunned and it was only reasonable to get out when they did.

New Market was different. They left the field too soon and later reports from both sides made it seem that they would have won if they had just used what they had on the field to advantaged and pressed the matter on.

The Battle of Piedmont proved it. They pushed hard with what they had and the men were well-used and they won.

There were no raw recruits in the 12th West Virginia that night and none wore the disgraceful moniker of "conscript" any longer. These veterans had common experiences that would shape future battles. "Goin' in fast and hard and not turnin' back is what will end this war. Stoppin' too soon and quitting before a battle is won is what'll keep it goin'."

Word spread through the ranks that the Rebel army was being used up and no reinforcements would be filling the ranks vacated by dead and wounded. The Union could replenish its own ranks at will. The math made sense to all who considered it. Every Rebel killed, captured, or wounded moved this war closer to an end even if equal numbers of men in blue were to be lost. Grant knew what he was about.

Captain John McMorrow spent that restless night on the verge of sleep as horrific spectacles played out again and again. They were scenes of blood, death, smoke, victory, flags waving, men falling, and of two sheets of paper drawn from an envelope from Grafton while he sat on a stump. All had clarified the past and altered the future of this former professor from Clarksburg.

*   *   *   *

IT ALL SEEMED SO REAL

Anna Lee dropped the newspaper to the floor. Captain John McMorrow had been killed in action at a place called Piedmont. She felt intense guilt for the relief that came with her release from having to make a choice. Now she could spare him the pain. Anna Lee's sense of loss was genuine and awful. Tears streamed down her face.

Somewhere out there on the field of battle, she thought, *lies the body of a man I loved. A part of me is now beneath the sod in a place called Piedmont. I will go there someday and visit the site of my greatest loss. I know that John loved me. I cherish the thought. I cherish the memory of his embrace, of his kisses, of his loving words, of his reasoned words, of his simple hopes. I treasure this last letter from him expressing his love for me. I wish that I had told him. I still love him. If he were here I'd tell him in the clearest terms that I love him. I love Micah. I must tell him so. To lose him as I have John without telling would be an outrage. If Micah and John McMorrow had known one another well in life I think they'd have been friends. I don't suppose it'd be proper to tell Micah of my love for John. I don't think Micah'd understand. I wonder if John would've understood if it were the other way around. I think I could have told John and that he'd have understood. He always seemed to. But he is gone.*

Somehow the last letter from John McMorrow appeared in Anna Lee's hand and it made her suspicious. Her stream of experience continued.

Someday they'll build a monument here in Clarksburg with some gallant officer with his sword drawn leading men into battle. Captain John McMorrow's name will be engraved on it, along with other names, but the officer with the sword will be John McMorrow no matter what the plaque says.

Now Anna Lee stood beside the monument that she had just supposed might one day be built. Her children were gathered around her and their presence confused her. Anna Lee did not know their names, but these were certainly her children. Micah was her husband now and these were their children.

"Children, we must learn to honor the brave men who fought for the right."

Anna Lee bowed her head in silent tribute. The fingers of her right hand tenderly caressed the name of Captain John McMorrow, while her left hand rested on the shoulder of her son and magically transferred the good spirit of John McMorrow to this much-loved son whose name she could not recall. She transmitted the love of learning and the ability to think and the poetic words from the plaque on the monument through her fingers and arms down into the soul of this fine son with bowed head. She felt it happening.

I know there's no magic like that, but I'll guide my son to think while he also learns to use his hands. Then it struck her hard. *Will I ever have a son?* And then, in anguish, *Will Micah be his father?—Am I presuming too much?* Looking up from the letter in her hand and drying her tears with her apron that had not been there moments before she resolved with a firmness and certainty that shocked her: *I will break the dam that holds back my love from Micah and pour the now-undivided torrent upon him as no woman ever loved a man.* Even as Anna Lee thought the thought she felt release from all the indecision. The dam had burst and the gushing waters were finding the channel to flood Micah.

But I do have a son and Micah is his father and these other children are ours and we love them and all these things happened a long time ago. What are the names of my children?

Just then the son under her magic hand looked up. He had John's mouth even though he was only a child and he had John's mustache and he kissed Anna Lee on the finger where the wedding band had suddenly appeared before he opened his mouth and bit off her arm all the way to the elbow.

Anna Lee screamed as she sat up and opened her eyes. Moonlight showed the dim outline of her room.

Mr. and Mrs. Stone came through the door as it flew open. Mr. Stone's rifle trained on the window as Anna Lee's mother rushed to the bedside. "What's happened, dear?"

Not quite sure yet, Anna Lee stared blankly at her mother hoping to hear an explanation instead of expecting to give one. "It…it…it was only a dream, Mother. A terrible, awful dream."

Her mother held her as her father sat on the bed and stood the rifle between his legs and as Anna Lee wept and silently sorted out the facts. *John is not dead. Those are not my children. My arm is not missing. Micah is not my husband. I am to marry Micah. John is in the army and fighting.*

"I'm so sorry. It all seemed so real. It still seems like a thing that just now happened."

"What was it, dear?"

"Some…something bit my arm off. But I'm okay now."

"Can I get you anything?" Her father was always ready to look for some way to fix broken things more than he was interested in hearing the details.

"No. Thank you. I'm fine. I'm just sorry I woke you."

"That's all right, dear." Mrs. Stone rubbed Anna Lee's back and held her hand as she spoke. "We need to get you good and comfortable and rested. This is a big day and I'm sure it has you worked up. A girl doesn't get married every day you know."

Anna Lee had forgotten.

✳   ✳   ✳   ✳

LEAVING LIBERTY

On June 6, 1864, the day following the Battle of Piedmont, the 2nd Brigade and the 12th West Virginia Infantry marched eleven miles to Staunton. Cheers went up some miles from town when word spread through the ranks that the Rebels had fled. A sense of power gripped them. They passed houses on the outskirts with white rags flapping from door posts—submission. Terrified women in the town, unlike the brash, saucy ladies of Winchester, begged for mercy as if they expected otherwise.

As the 12th West Virginia Infantry established camp on the hillside east of town it did so with a sense of satisfaction that the war was going to end. Grant was planting men in front of Petersburg in ever-increasing numbers. Sherman's forces moved across the South teaching other lessons in submission. Hunter's men were now farther up the Shenandoah Valley than Union forces had yet gone. Their movements drew the thinning ranks of Confederate soldiers away from Richmond.

On June 9 the 12th West Virginia did its part to choke off supplies from the Shenandoah Valley to Richmond and other points south where the dwindling Rebel army might use them. They burned railroad bridges and made massive piles of rails and ties and placed lengths of iron track atop the piles. The great fires bent the tracks beyond repair, like hair pins, and the men enjoyed the novel work. They saw, in these acts, progress in the effort to finish the war, proud to be a part of it.

The morning of June 10 the whole Union force left Staunton with pockets, haversacks, and other nooks and crannies stuffed with surplus Rebel tobacco, courtesy of the retreating Johnnies. Those who did not consume it knew that it made good trading stock. The roads to Lexington were soon littered with tobacco plugs as men lightened loads.

Seven miles down the road the men cheered when a courier brought news that a large wagon train was on the way with coffee and sugar. They cheered again when he reported that Grant's men had forced Robert E. Lee and his forces into their entrenchments around Richmond. Events now answered the oft-asked question: *"What'll happen when Grant goes up against Bobby Lee?"* They camped for the night at Midway, about eighteen miles from Staunton.

The force entered the outskirts of Lexington, joined by Crook's division. They saw the smoldering remains of the bridge destroyed by Rebels yet in the town. After skirmishing with Rebels, and throwing a few shells, they paused by the river without crossing that day.

Next day they crossed the river on the new bridge constructed by their own Pioneer Corps and camped near the town.

Captain John McMorrow walked among the vacant, impressive buildings of the renowned Virginia Military Institute. Normally these buildings were home to about 200 cadets who had pledged loyalty to the treasonous government of the so-called Confederacy. The school had produced officers loyal to the South. The flag John had seen coming from around the house at New Market had been carried by cadets—young boys, *children*, he thought—from this place. The boys had charged at the stars and stripes. He counted this—that the Rebels would send children to their deaths—an indication of Confederate desperation and low estimate of human life rather than some high and honorable feat of bravery.

Near the institute was the traitor governor's house—Governor Letcher. Houses belonging to Rebel officers stood arrogantly. After John surveyed these impressive buildings he found the grave of Thomas Jackson—"Stonewall," they had called him—from Clarksburg. John had never met him. Jackson had left Clarksburg long before the war. A Rebel flag had flown over Jackson's grave when they entered the town. It was gone now.

"Torch the place!" Captain McMorrow was in full accord with General Hunter's order. He felt no shame when the imposing structures and the nearby ironworks became one roaring inferno at the hand of the men. These were symbols of that which had robbed John McMorrow of life itself. Blazing buildings crumbled to restore the Union, to end slavery, and to punish Jefferson Davis and all his Rebel horde for stealing from Captain McMorrow a lifetime of happiness. The fires warmed him on a hot afternoon in June. His dreams reproached him that night.

Next day the supply wagons arrived in the camp. The rationing of coffee and sugar recalled memories of John's childhood. After he and his brothers had made a regular habit of complaining about inequities whenever a fresh pie was divided between them, his mother devised a plan that settled all disputes. She would select one to cut the pie into equal slices. Then she would let the others take turns selecting their slices. The cutter of the pie would have the last pick.

John smiled as he saw the men of his company collecting rations. On a rubber blanket spread on the ground were approximately equal piles of coffee. The men stood in a group. A corporal with his back to the group faced the blanket. A sergeant with his back to the corporal faced the men. The corporal pointed at a pile and asked, "And who shall get this one?" The sergeant pointed at a man in the ranks who came forward with a container to receive his ration.

Walking away with a fading smile, John thought of all the disputes that might be settled if only his mother's methods could be applied to all human conflict. Then his thoughts took a serious turn. *Some things are best left to struggle, to fair defeat or victory, rather than random chance.* He pictured heavenly beings—*angels maybe*—standing back to back like the sergeant and corporal and one of the beings pointing at Anna Lee saying, "And who shall get this one?" with the other unknowingly pointing at Micah Johnson. Then he pictured these creatures back to back pointing at soldiers in battle and asking, "And who shall die next?" And then pointing at nations and men with the same randomness: "And which shall fall now?" *No. That's not the way of it. If things are not always equal and fair, they are also not entirely random. If life and death and everything in between is nothing more than getting the next thing randomly allotted, then life's without meaning. Somewhere there must be purpose. Our choices and decisions must count for something.*

In the dark hours of the morning of June 14 the column marched toward Buchanan. It arrived there after dark. This was a long, hard march in the heat of June with each man loaded down with eighty to 100 rounds of ammunition and other equipment.

Next day they marched eleven miles to the Peaks of Otter. John saw a dead man in civilian clothing at the side of the road. He would later learn, around the campfire, that the civilian had been shot in the act of attempting to fell a tree across the road in front of the advancing column.

They marched about nine miles to Liberty, a small town on the Virginia and Tennessee railroad in the morning. John led his men in burning the depot. Others made hairpins of iron rails atop pyres of railroad ties. They marched on five more miles toward Lynchburg and camped.

Early the next morning they pushed on toward Lynchburg. As they marched John thought he heard a shot fired up ahead. The column pressed on. A fine-looking home with neat rows of trees was just starting to blaze. They passed through New London. At about 4:00 in the afternoon they came to within three miles of Lynchburg and camped. Word filtered back from the front. Crook's division had engaged the enemy, taken prisoners, and captured a few artillery pieces before the Rebels retreated into the inner line of defense in the town.

On June 18, they moved forward to within about five hundred yards of the enemy's fortifications. Union skirmishers engaged Rebels. Artillery threw shells from both sides, but most of the troops were not engaged until afternoon. The 12th West Virginia lined up along the Bedford road. At about 2:00 in the afternoon heavy firing opened to the left of the regiment. Then the Rebels charged out of their works toward the position of the 12th West Virginia on the road, across the open ground, while Rebel artillery aimed to scatter the men on the road. Shells overshot, hitting mainly treetops. Five rows of Union troops opened fire and kept up a steady stream of lead. Men all along the line fired, reloaded, and fired again, driving the attack back into the fortifications.

Not all on the Bedford road held their ground. A good many scrambled for the cover of one particular big tree. These left a gap in the line under fire. An equal number went immediately forward to fill the gap. Sergeant Thomas J. Ormsby of Company C ran through the gap and about thirty feet in advance of the line, trusting the rest not to shoot him. Ormsby, all alone in front of a line of thousands of massed troops and shouting while laughing, "They're runnin', boys. They're runnin'!" Sergeant Ormsby regularly demonstrated such courage and often gave rousing and encouraging "talks" when battle was imminent. They called him "the preacher."

The day ended with little more than skirmishing after the repulsed attack from the works. That night Union soldiers heard cheering and drums from inside the Rebel works. Next morning, after learning that Jubal Early's corps had reinforced the Confederates in the night, Hunter made plans to retreat. He withdrew the troops that night. Opinions, which were never consulted anyway, varied among men in the ranks. Many felt they should have stormed the Rebel works and risked the loss of Union lives before the Confederate reinforcements arrived. A few figured that the officers must know what they are doing. "We must have accomplished something important—drawing Confederate soldiers away from other actions to sit in those fortifications and beat on drums." A good many were of the firm opinion that this slow and orderly retreat was a fine thing, no matter how it fit into bigger plans. Drinking coffee and crunching hardtack at leisure was a good bit better than dodging lead and hard marching.

Leaving Liberty at about 2:00 in the morning on the 20th of June, the regiment marched hard. Rebels threatened the rear as the troops passed through Thoxton's Station and then continued on to Buford's Station. In spite of rapid marching they destroyed bridges, stations, and water tanks. Then they went on to Buford's Gap in the Blue Ridge, where they paused to rest and eat. The infantry resumed the march a little after dark. The cavalry soon followed after capturing some Rebel cavalry who had been harassing their rear. They marched all night, reaching Salem in the morning. The Rebels attacked the rear again, but were repulsed. From Salem, the wagon train, some artillery, and cavalry went ahead of the main body.

Rebels under General John McCausland attacked the wagons, captured and killed some horses, cut down the carriages of five guns—grounding them—and captured thee guns. The infantry rushed forward and drove off McCausland's men, losing thirty of their own in the fight.

The whole force marched another ten miles—hard and fast—and camped for the night. Exhausted men yet in danger of attack slept well. To guard the rear they placed two artillery pieces at the top of the mountain they had just crossed to guard the rear. These sent Rebel cavalry, who approached in the night, back down the mountain.

Rations of solid food were depleted by consumption, capture, and necessary abandonment. The men continued the retreat on the 22nd. The next days became a blur of exhausting, hard, continuous marching, with little to eat and meager rest. General Hunter ordered those who could not keep up to form themselves into squads for protection against bushwhackers. They trudged on through New Castle, over Middle Mountain, then over Peter's Mountain, through Sweet Springer, then over the Allegheny Mountains, through White Sulphur Springs. There the men found a potato patch. They sifted soil to find old tubers to eat. They crossed the Greenbrier River, passed through Lewisburg, and crossed over Little Sewell Mountain. At Big Sewell Mountain dead horses, used up—starved for want of feed, and then shot to keep them from Rebels—lined the route. They camped on the western base of Big Sewell Mountain.

At Big Sewell, supply wagons met hungry men. John McMorrow, like all the rest, was now more interested in getting something into his pleading stomach than he was in fighting Rebels, teaching students, torching buildings, preserving the Union or ending slavery. The rush for the wagons would have seen John fighting with privates for food if reason had not taken hold. He saw his own yearning in the eyes of his men. He addressed his company: "Men, we're all hungry. Powerfully hungry. Within a short while we will have more than enough to eat. There's plenty. As we approach the wagon, no corporal is to receive his portion until every private has received his. No sergeant is to have his food until every corporal has his. No lieutenant is to get his food until every sergeant has been supplied with his allotment. I will not touch my rations until our lieutenants have gotten theirs, and I intend to have mine within ten minutes of our reaching the wagons. Are there any questions?" There were none. The distribution to the company was efficient and swift.

The next day they pushed on. They passed Hawks Nest on the New River on the 29th. The junction of the Gauley River and New River was the site of their next camp. They rested for two days and mustered for pay. On July 2 they marched to Camp Piatt on the Kanawha River, ten miles from Charleston and about 230 miles from Lynchburg—from which they had retreated.

Measures of success in an unfinished war are difficult to gauge. Soldiers cannot compare cost with what has been purchased with precision. And yet men take the measure and make the comparison without really knowing how much value to place upon personal anguish multiplied by the number of men who share it. No scale accurately measures hunger. No yardstick can be laid across searing pain to yield a number. Yet men want to know the score when there is a pause.

They had destroyed about fifty miles of the Virginia Central Railroad in this expedition. They had torn up the Virginia and Tennessee Railroad "to some extent." They had wrecked "large amounts" of public property—canal boats, railroad cars loaded with ordnance and commissary stores, "numerous" and "extensive" iron works, saltpeter factories, musket stock factories, shoe factories, saddle and harness-making works, wool mills and grain mills. They had captured about 300 muskets, 20 artillery pieces, "quantities" of shells and gunpowder, and other quantifiable physical things. Union troops had killed or wounded about 1000 Rebels. They had taken at least that many more as prisoners. The command had kept thousands of Rebel troops busy in the Shenandoah Valley who would have been giving Sherman or Grant greater trouble elsewhere.

Hunter's command lost "only" about 1,500 men to death, wounds, and capture. It lost "a great many" horses, mules, and wagons. Hunter sent a dispatch from Lomp Creek near the Gauley Bridge on June 28: "...the expedition had been extremely successful inflicting great injury upon the enemy.... The command is in excellent heart and health." When Captain John McMorrow read the dispatch he recalled that the general had somehow managed to eat fairly well along the way. Hunter had covered the miles and crossed the mountains on horseback. *The general,* John thought, *can speak with certainty of the status of his own heart and health, but maybe Hunter ought to ask these weary, footsore, soldiers in the ranks before he writes about the excellence of their heart and health.*

On July 3 the 12th West Virginia, along with other infantry regiments under Hunter, took steamboats to Parkersburg, where they boarded railroad cars for the Shenandoah Valley. After all of the hard miles of marching to the west they were now on their way back to the northern end of the valley. The trains stopped at Hedgesville to await repairs. Rebels had burned bridges. Rumors of Rebel activity nearby ran through the camps, but nothing certain or official reached the men in the ranks.

*   *   *   *

JUST STARTING TO LEARN

Anna Lee Johnson lay stiffly on her side of the bed, facing the wall. Moonlight from the window sent pale gray through the rising curls of smoke from the extinguished candle. The smell of the suffocated candle still filled the room. Smother-ing doubts filled her head. Micah slept soundly on his side of the bed, snoring.

How can he place so much importance on a flickering candle? If he says he can't sleep with such a slight thing as that, then I suppose I ought not feel put out by his request that I put it out. But what is reasonable about his complaining about the little noise made by my turning a few pages and reading for just a little while by candle light and then snoring like that while I suffer through it? If all were equal I guess I'd wake him up and ask him to either stop snoring or go sleep elsewhere. But, no, I just accept it and go on.

And what was that about this morning? I can accept the fact that he likes to have his eggs left with a softer yolk, but isn't there room for some gratitude mixed in with the correction? During all those months when I helped in the shop he was never like this. Back then he was always thoughtful, grateful for every little thing.

Was I so blind all that time? Did I look at all the wrong things when I measured this man? Did I strain out the trifling gnats and then swallow the whole obnoxious camel?

His pants are just slung over the back of the chair. Didn't his mother teach him to put away his things? Will he ever learn? Will I ever learn to ignore such things? Am I supposed to put them away for him? Does he think he just slings them down and that I'll just pick them up and thank him for the opportunity?

If he really cared how I feel he wouldn't be sound asleep and snoring. He'd be as wide awake as I am. It means nothing to him. He stomps right on me with, "Please put out the candle and go to sleep. I can't sleep with a flickering light and all that rat-tling of paper." Then he turns right over and goes to snoring like a contented hog.

After a restless night of troubled sleep, Anna Lee arose, gathered fresh eggs from the henhouse and bacon from the smokehouse. She cooked an ample break-fast as near perfection—as defined by Micah's preferences—as possible. When Micah thanked her profusely for such a perfect meal Anna Lee felt a twinge of guilt for the unpleasant things she had covertly rehearsed for his hearing, if he were to complain. She was grateful for her own restraint and glad that she had not done as she had thought to do and spoil the meal just to make a point.

"The eggs were good yesterday. I hope you don't mind that I told you I like 'em better like this, but on a scale of good, better, and best—these rate best."

Anna Lee melted. The candle incident suddenly seemed a small matter. She wrapped her arms around him, kissed his cheek, and said, "I love you, Micah." He was surprised that complimenting an egg could have such effect.

The day went well. They worked together in the shop. Anna Lee had learned to do a good many things beyond keeping accounts straight. She had watched

Micah work with men to find just the right size stock that would fit them. Now Anna Lee took care of this while Micah kept at work on the barrels. She had learned to smooth the stocks and to work in the linseed oil by hand. Apart from the boring of barrels, Anna Lee helped with just about every phase of the work. She teased about wanting to have her own name stamped on the stocks.

When the two closed up shop and started for the wagon Anna Lee asked if Micah would mind stopping off at the general store for a few minutes. "Sure," he said as he hitched the team and headed for town. It was a beautiful late afternoon in June. As they rode along and made small talk Micah counted the hours he would have before dark. He thought of chores he would like to finish. He would repair the chicken pen before some fox or possum found the gaps and caused trouble. He would get a load of fresh hay for the milk cow and look over the field to see if it might be nearly ready for the second cutting. These were all pleasant tasks for Micah, as long as he did not have to rush. He pulled the watch from his vest pocket and wound it a few twists.

"I'll be back in a minute, I hope you don't mind." Micah watched his beautiful Anna Lee hop down from the wagon and enter the store. He did not mind sitting in the wagon for a few minutes. He appreciated that Anna Lee was frugal and that she kept a close eye on expenses. The horses jostled a bit as a wagon passed close by, using the limited space left by Micah's wagon as he waited. Ten minutes later, by Micah's watch, he had to back up to allow a small buggy to pull away from the side where he would have liked to put the wagon if it would only fit—and it would not. As Micah backed the wagon, it got started to the right and he could not get it straightened. He hated backing it and had never gotten the hang of it. The mistake embarrassed him. The back of Micah's wagon touched the wheel of another before the other buggy had enough room to get out. He took a deep breath and pulled forward to his original position in front of the door from which Anna Lee would soon be coming—surely. Thirteen minutes later, by the watch, another small buggy approached. The driver asked politely if Micah would mind moving on to allow him into the space vacated by the first.

"Certainly," Micah said, and this time he pulled forward to the end of town, turned the wagon around at the wide spot near the stables, and returned to a position opposite the store from which Anna Lee would be exiting at any moment.

If only I'd known that it was going to be this long, he thought, *I'd have left the wagon over at the stables and walked.* He wanted to go in and check on Anna Lee, but knew his neighbors would frown on seeing the team in the street unattended.

Micah was not willing to shout to find out what was keeping her. So he sat. He waited. The glare on the window obscured his view inside.

Twelve minutes later he moved for yet another buggy. This time he went to the end of the street and found a place to leave the wagon and team. Walking toward the store he saw Anna Lee standing in front with nothing more than a small package wrapped in brown paper and tied with a string.

She spoke first, "Where have you been? You've left me waiting for minutes."

"I've kept you waiting?" He spoke quietly but with force. "Anna Lee, you were going to step in there for 'just a minute' and you left me out here waiting for…" he checked his watch, "forty seven minutes. I have better things to do than sit in a public street blocking the way and wasting time while I have chores waiting and plans for the evening."

"Nonsense, Micah. It won't hurt you to wait just a few minutes while I…."

"Nonsense? I can't believe you're not even ready to say you're sorry or something. I could understand if some emergency kept you in there, but I didn't see anybody running for a doctor. Don't get me wrong, Anna Lee. If you want to go socializing I have no objection to that as long as you work it out with me and I agree to my part in it before you do it, but I am not some steam engine that you can just cool down and poke in some corner until you're ready to put it to use again. In the future, I expect to be treated with just a little more respect! I'm sure you'd see this better if the shoe was on the other foot."

"Well, I'm sorry." This started to make him regret his anger until she continued. "I just didn't know that you were so impatient."

Micah's face flushed red. He edited the words that came to mind. He took her by the arm and said, "The wagon's down this way." As they walked he finally settled on what to say. "Well, I'm glad you now know just how impatient I am. Please put that knowledge to good use in the future."

Micah found little pleasure in chores that evening, even though he was quite pleased to have them to do. As he forked hay, stretched wire, and hammered nails he wondered what he had gotten himself into. *I never thought it would be anything like this! She never seemed so spoiled before we were married. Now she seems to think that the whole world turns for her alone.*

Slipping reluctantly into the house at dark, Micah found Anna Lee sitting in a chair in the front room reading by candlelight. "Where'd you get that?" He asked, pointing to the unfamiliar candle.

"I got it at the store today. I plan to read out here until I'm ready to go to bed. I hope you have no objection."

"No objection, sweetheart, I just hope it burns for at least as long as it took you to buy it!"

Inexplicably, to both, they laughed. They laughed hard, and when they finished Micah knelt beside her, held her hand, and kissed it gently. "Honey, I love you. I figure we both have a few things to get used to. I appreciate you for thinking of this plan for reading out here. It means something to me that you're willing to make adjustments. I'll do the same. I figure we're just starting to learn about what it's like to be married."

Anna Lee put her hand on his shoulder, patted it, and said, "Thanks, Micah. I love you too."

CHAPTER 11

I WOKE UP FIRST

On July 11, 1864, the 12th West Virginia Infantry returned to Martinsburg. The last time they had been here there were at least 800 men in the ranks. Now death, wounds, sickness, and straggling had reduced the regiment to about 250. The Lynchburg campaign had taken a toll on the health of the men. The majority of those absent were sick—in spite of Hunter's dispatch proclaiming them to be "in excellent health." At least Hunter had told the truth on the day he had taken command, when he declared that they were "about to enter on an explosion of hardships." The future would answer further questions about the purchasing power of those hardships.

While the 12th West Virginia was marching into Martinsburg, the Rebel General Early was attempting to capture Washington with a large force. He might have come nearer to succeeding if the 6th Corps had not arrived in time to reinforce those protecting the nation's capitol. The next day Early withdrew his forces.

To meet Early's men the regiment left Martinsburg on July 13 and marched toward Harpers Ferry. They went beyond Harpers Ferry on the next day, crossed into Maryland, and camped near Knoxville. The whole of Hunter's force was about 9,000 men, including the 12th West Virginia. On July 15, they waded the Potomac and moved toward Leesburg. They camped at Hillsborough, expecting that Early would lead his men in their general direction, vigorously pursued by the 6th Corps—about 15,000 men.

One July 16, the regiment marched through Hamilton and Purcellville to positions near Snicker's Gap and Ashby's Gap where they hoped to delay the

Rebel retreat. The gaps in the mountains provided opportunities for Early's men to escape—and reason to expect them to try. After movement back to Purcellville, and then back again, the regiment attempted to cross the Shenandoah River along with the rest of Thoburn's men. Rebel pickets started blasting from concealed positions behind bushes with a brisk fire. Wells' brigade found a place to ford the river below them some distance. His men captured the pickets and the captain commanding them. Thoburn's force moved across the river without interference, but received orders to stay in place until reinforced by a brigade from the 6th Corps.

"Stand fast, men!" Captain McMorrow saw the brigade from the 6th Corps arrive atop the hill. He wondered why the the new troops did not come down to reinforce them. His orders were to keep his men in place until reinforced—and then to await further orders. His small company was part of a much larger force, yet that force was small by all the measures of this war. At the beginning of John's war experience a regiment seemed an invincible force. Now, that notion was laughable. The regiment had a good position in a road parallel to the river and actually a part of the river bank, which made a fair natural breastwork.

"Keep your eyes sharp!" John shouted at the men, knowing that they needed no such command, but feeling the need to say something to show himself in command. Then muskets sounded in front of his company—and then off to the right. They faced the hazard of being flanked.

"Those are Rebels. Shoot 'em!" Men in the ranks hesitated for a reason. The Rebels here wore a blue-gray uniform that looked a good deal like Union uniforms from a distance. The Confederate soldiers would fire at the Union position and then turn their backs to reload, looking like Union troops advancing forward.

Some Union officers were fooled. They ordered men to cease fire.

"It's a trick!" John shouted. "If they want a bullet in the back then that's where you will put it. Fire, men. Fire! Reload and fire as fast as you can. There are no Union soldiers in our front. Shoot!" Although these Rebels in the 12th West Virginia's immediate front were actually being driven back and kept in check, that was not the case all down the line.

Cannon belched shells from the mountaintop. Thoburn ordered his men to reform—to deal with the problem developing on the right. The men kept up a heavy fire while many fell. Then the colonel ordered them back across the river.

"Quickly, men. Quickly!" Captain McMorrow was at the rear of his company and sending them across in front of him. "Keep them moving, sergeant! Artillery's keeping Rebel heads down, but they can't keep it up for long. Move, men.

Move!" The regiment crossed in fairly good order, considering that they forded under fire, but some were drowned and others shot and killed by the enemy. The 12th West Virginia Infantry was the last regiment to retreat across the river in the dusk..

That night the men remained in line of battle. They got little sleep. Rebels lurked in line of battle across the river. Sharpshooters from each side took advantage of whatever target might show itself on the other. They remained in this face-off throughout the next day.

A number of boys who were killed in that brief, but fierce, struggle below Snicker's Gap were not officially soldiers. One regiment's time had expired and they fought in spite of discharge papers in their pockets. They had every right to walk away and go home, but these were loyal men who could not leave their last chance to get into action in defense of the United States of America. To leave at such a time would have seemed disloyal.

When day dawned on July 20 the Rebels were gone. A division of the 19th Corps had moved up the Valley from Martinsburg and would soon have been in position to the enemy's rear. The Rebels escaped the trap, but they were not yet prepared to leave the valley.

On July 22, the regiment, along with others under General Crook, marched through Berryville to Winchester once again. They camped about two miles from town on the Strasburg road. On the 23rd, the Rebels drove the Union pickets back to the main body of troops, but after brief skirmishing the troops drove the attackers back.

On Sunday morning, July 24, Captain McMorrow rose early to worship with the few men of the regiment who shared his religious convictions. They had kept this up whenever possible on every Lord's day, even when chaplains held religious services for others. Rising early increased their chances of worshiping without interruption. They started with the Lord's Supper and concluded with simple prayers, singing of psalms, hymns, and spiritual songs, and Scripture readings. Hardtack, they had concluded, was acceptable to use as unleavened bread, but they sometimes lacked grape juice. Sometimes they found wild grapes and used small quantities of its sour juice. Sometimes they could find no grapes. In such cases they did not substitute, but skipped that portion of the worship hoping that God would understand.

John made a few remarks following the reading of Scripture, from the forth chapter of Ephesians. "As we meet this morning we can be assured that on this day our brethren everywhere join us in expressing worship to Almighty. May we find some measure of comfort in knowing that our fellowship with the saints is unbroken except by geography. There is one Lord, one faith, one baptism, and one God. Let's keep the faith no matter how far we must go from our homes and loved ones."

"It's hard to know what to think of our brethren in the South," commented one of the men as they parted to return to their companies.

John had tried to sort through his thoughts at other times concerning his "brethren in the South." *Do I really have brethren in the South? Are they not in error if they support taking up arms against the Union? Surely, I am at least out of fellowship with such brethren.*

He remembered reading of early Christians who had renounced the faith under Roman persecution. When the persecution ended, many of them wanted to return to the church. A controversy had arisen over whether or not they could return. Some who had endured the persecution concluded that the backsliders could not be accepted back. Others held that they certainly could return and that the church had a duty to receive them, after they gave clear evidence of repentance. John held that the latter view had been the correct one, according to Biblical principles, and that this would likely be the principle on which "Southern brethren" and "Northern brethren" would be reunited after the war.

"Form up for inspection, men!"

The command demonstrated the wisdom of meeting early for worship. No one could predict when these spur-of-the-moment inspections would come. John rushed to his company while men flowed out of tents in various stages of preparation, tucking shirts, pulling on boots, buttoning pants, and dragging haversacks, rifles, and accoutrements.

Just as he reached his company the order changed. Distant shots echoed from the direction of Kernstown. "Form up to march, men. Form up! Load at will. Get your rifles loaded and prepare to march!" Within the half hour the whole brigade marched toward the sounds of battle. They marched past fields in which blackberries were hanging, juicy and ripe. Men stepped out of ranks and picked blackberries.

Captain McMorrow laughed. Here before his eyes was one of the most incongruous sights he had ever seen, or would ever see. Up ahead waited fire, smoke, flying lead, death, and unspeakable danger. These men were not failing in their duty as they picked berries. They continued to march to the front. Before he laughed, John started to order his men back onto the road. While he laughed he thought of what this simple action spoke of the character of these men. After he laughed he felt the hair on his neck prickle, and he wanted to salute each man and shake every berry-stained hand. These men inspired him by the childlike act of picking berries on the road to battle. The question of whether or not these men would live to see nightfall was unanswerable. In this moment, however, they picked and ate sweet berries provided by the hand of God as they marched without slowing into the face of unnatural warfare. John thought of the many times that he himself had ruined present moments by filling them with worry about an uncertain things. *Berry-eating is a fine thing,* he thought.

Just then Colonel William G. Ely of the 18th Connecticut, who commanded the brigade, rode up. He shouted, "Get those men back in the ranks. This is no time to be gathering berries!"

John wanted to protest, but he had no quick argument that would make any sense or any difference. So he waded into the berry patches as if to retrieve the men who were already returning to the road. He shouted, "Back to the road, men!" as he picked a handful of sweet, juicy, blackberries and stuffed them into his mouth, where he held them for as long as they lasted.

Nearing the fight, the whole brigade shuffled from one position to another until officers formed them in line of battle to the right of the road. General Early's Rebel troops attacked in full force, hitting both the center of the line and the left flank. Keeping his men firing and reloading at will, Captain McMorrow saw the center of the Union line give away as men in both blue and gray fell. Then the left flank seemed to fold as more men in the 12th West Virginia fell. "Make them count, men. Reload and fire at will. Targets are plentiful now!"

Colonel Ely ordered the retreat. This one was reasonable. No one still standing objected. John heard the order given to Colonel Curtis, "Move your men off the field by right flank!"

The Rebels followed and for six or so miles the question of whether or not the whole brigade might be captured was debated by halts and skirmishes. They passed Winchester. No one seemed to know just where the brigade was headed, but they were together. The retreat was in good order. Just before dark, Rebel cavalry appeared to the right. Union men sent them flying toward Winchester. The brigade continued toward North Mountain. Men stumbled over rocky ground and one another in the dark of night until they halted and camped at Gerardtown at the base of the mountain. Somehow both Colonel Thoburn and Colonel Curtis were separated from the command. In the confusion John found himself wishing that the mysterious mountain maid who had helped them near this place before would suddenly appear and put things in order.

Before dawn they set out on the march for Martinsburg where the force was reunited after having taken different roads in the night. Guarding the wagon trains, the brigade marched to Williamsport, Maryland, and made camp.

Beginning on the morning of the 26th, they marched through Sharpsburg, Sandy Hook, and Harpers Ferry to Halltown, where they arrived on the 28th. Colonel Thoburn and Colonel Curtis rode into camp smiling and the boys cheered. They had abandoned their horses when Rebels fired on them and hidden in a corn field for the night. In the morning they found the whole Rebel force between themselves and their commands. They made their way toward North Mountain, traveling by night, living off blackberries, assisted by some blacks and loyal whites along the way. Sometimes the enemy was so close to their hiding places that they could hear them speak.

On the 29th of July it became evident that the struggle for the Shenandoah Valley was becoming a serious matter. The 6th Corps and one division of the 19th Corps joined the forces at Halltown and the whole force was ordered to deal with Early's men, who were still present. General Hunter commanded the now larger army at Halltown.

They started for Frederick, Maryland in response to reports that Early was about to make another attempt to attack Washington. After uncertain marching in one direction and then another for a few days, they camped near Frederick where Hunter made headquarters. General Grant left his forces at Petersburg to confer with Hunter concerning future operations in the Shenandoah Valley. A large force of cavalry from the Army of the Potomac would soon join Hunter's already enlarged force. Hunter was to make full use of his men to drive the Rebels south.

More shuffling soon superseded all this. Hunter was relieved of command. After General Grant returned to Washington on August 6, the War Department created a new division made up of the Departments of Pennsylvania, Washington, Maryland, and West Virginia, and placed Philip H. Sheridan in command of these 30,000 men.

On August 10, Sheridan moved his division from Halltown up the Shenandoah Valley in search of Rebels to fight. Confederate troops retreated from Winchester as this massive body of men under Sheridan moved through Berryville, on to Winchester, and then to Cedar Creek, where they made camp on August 12. Here the Rebels made a stand and here the 12th West Virginia participated in driving Rebel skirmishers east of the road and across the creek where two corps, the 6th and the 19th, drove them a mile or so farther up the valley. For the next few days little more than skirmishing went on between the opposing armies. These were sometimes hot contests, but neither side charged the other or seemed to have advantages in position.

On the 14th of August Sheridan learned from Grant that fresh Rebel troops were about to reinforce. Consequently, Union forces began an orderly retreat during which Generals George A. Custer and Thomas C. Devin used cavalry to drive back pursuing Rebels. The 12th West Virginia, along with the great mass of the division, pushed on to Winchester and then to a position near Berryville.

General Early kept his men harassing the Union lines but he intensified his efforts on August 17 when he attacked the forces in Winchester. The line there held but lost about 350 men to death and capture. Grant wanted Sheridan to use his forces cautiously, to refrain from giving battle until they ascertained the strength of the enemy. Sheridan massed his troops near Charles Town and waited.

Early attacked the 6th Corps the next day on the right of the Union lines. About 260 Union men were killed or wounded when the line briefly gave way. An anticipated attack on the left did not materialize. Early pulled back for the time being. Sheridan kept his men in a defensive mode and moved back to Hall-town, where he formed a line of breastworks stretching from the Shenandoah River on the left to the Potomac on the right. Skirmishing and cannonading continued.

The hot sun beat upon weary men waiting behind makeshift fortifications of fence rails, railroad ties, rock and soil. Whistling lead flying above them kept heads below the top of the parapet most of the time, but the sound was common now and filled no one with either dread or questions. Squirrels were not dropping acorns in the opinion of any of these men.

Captain McMorrow walked along behind the lines, seeing the men and being seen by them. A cluster of privates laughed heartily at some joke and a sergeant shouted at them, "This is no time for playing, men. Keep your eyes sharp and your mouths shut!"

John invited the sergeant to come a distance to the rear with him, out of the hearing of the men. Captain McMorrow did not pull rank or interfer with affairs involving those under his command except when some principle called upon him to do so. This was one of those times. After a muffled conference with his captain the sergeant walked back to the men and shouted, "Get back to whatever you men were about. I guess there's no harm in exchangin' a little joke as long as nothin's happenin'. Just keep it down so you can hear orders and keep your eyes sharp."

On the 26th of August, three brigades of infantry and one of cavalry struck the Rebel line, scattered the men, burned some stacks of hay that had given the

Rebels cover, and damaged some of the Rebel breastworks. This cost only 141 Union casualties. The men on the Union skirmish line cheered the bargain.

On the 28th of August Sheridan moved his army to Charles Town. While the men ate, slept, wrote letters home, and lived normal lives for soldiers in camp they heard an almost seamless firing of cannon and musket in the distance to the west where Rebel infantry was driving Union cavalry out of Smithfield. Paymasters distributed six months pay. The sutler was on hand to take their money. The fall harvest gave him much to sell to hungry men who enjoyed choosing, for a change, what they would eat for a short while.

On September 3, the 8th Corps, which now included the 12th West Virginia, marched to Berryville. They arrived in the evening, set up camp, and made coffee. A few musket shots came from the direction of Winchester. Some thought that the butchers were killing beef for the evening's meal.

"Fall in. Fall in!" Colonel Ely gave the order and officers and non-commissioned officers repeated it all through the camp. Lines formed along the Berryville road to meet the enemy, who came out of nowhere and in great force. John's division held the ground into the night, until another division drove the Rebels off and captured about sixty prisoners. The real estate to which they held title, for the time, cost 166 Union casualties. While they held it they could hear wagons moving rapidly down the valley. The Rebels threw shells over their heads in the direction of the wagons. In the morning they drew back toward Charles Town, without finishing their coffee, and there the whole force began to entrench. Word spread to the infantry, as they were digging and piling, that they had saved the wagon train from capture. The fight, they would later learn, had been a surprise to generals on both sides. Neither had anticipated being in the way of the other at that place and time.

On September 13, a division of Union cavalry claimed to have captured an entire regiment of South Carolina infantry. This had a great morale-building effect on the men of the 12th West Virginia. How many of them knew that the captured regiment consisted of only about 100 Rebels is uncertain, but the capture of an entire regiment of Rebel infantry just down the Berryville road had such a ring to it, and spoke so of a hopeful Union victory, that it made for frequent retelling. When Captain McMorrow, who had always been meticulous regarding facts, spoke of it he made no mention of the number captured. It was a whole regiment of Rebels. That was enough and it was a fact.

The Baltimore and Ohio Railroad needed to be protected. The citizens north of the Potomac needed to have assurances that Early's army would not harass them. On Friday, September 16, General Grant paid a visit to General Sheridan to see what might be done. A part of Early's troops were known to have left the area and the time seemed right to attack. When Grant asked Sheridan if he could attack on Tuesday, Sheridan replied that he could be ready by Monday. These two generals were of one mind in many ways. Early's troops were scattered out now, but by Tuesday they might be concentrated once again. Action was needed now, more than talk or concern about how to excuse failure if it were to be their lot to fail.

Sheridan sent trains and equipment to the rear on Sunday. Before dawn on Monday, Sheridan moved his men out of their fortifications and on the attack. The brigade of which the 12th West Virginia was a part marched under the command of their own Lieutenant Colonel Northcott. They were well to the rear of the main body of troops. They were so far to the rear, in fact, that they did not even begin the march until afternoon. All had the sense that a fierce battle was before them. It had a sobering effect as they marched forward. As they neared the Berryville ford of the Opequon, they heard heavy skirmishing ahead. The battle was beginning.

The men were disappointed upon reaching the ford. They had been marching into battle. They had prepared themselves for fighting. Now they were told that their brigade was detached—to guard the wagon train and the field hospital to be established here at the ford.

John McMorrow heard the exchange between Lieutenant Colonel Northcott and Colonel Thoburn, who commanded the division.

"How can you have me tell these men that they are not to be in on this fight? They are ready for it!"

"I have no choice in the matter, believe me. My orders are explicit. I am to detach the smallest brigade for this service. That's yours."

"Well, sir, if you count the numbers, maybe some other brigade will soon be smaller. When that happens, you can switch us!" This was not a joke. At that moment it seemed perfectly reasonable to the officer who wanted his men to share in the honor of fighting Rebels in a great battle. The brigade remained at the ford while battle raged in front. The sounds of battle told nothing of how it was going. Smoke and the roar of cannon bear the same signature of sound when they float through the trees whether they signal Union victory or defeat. By evening the enemy was routed. News of the Union victory reached the ford where men who felt they had been cheated cheered.

The Union lost more than 5,000 men in this bloody battle, about 4,300 of them killed and wounded. The Rebels lost about 4,000, nearly 2,000 of them taken as prisoners. Sheridan's men captured five pieces of artillery and seven battle flags. No matter what the numbers confessed, the Rebels ran and the Union won. A dispatch came for General Sheridan. It read: "Have just heard of your great victory. God bless you all, officers and men. Strongly inclined to come up and see you. A. Lincoln." Sheridan had purchased, with the blood of his men, the confidence, respect, and profound admiration of those still on their feet. Future victory seemed certain with Sheridan in command.

On the 22nd of September the brigade left the ford and followed the rest of the army up the Shenandoah Valley. After hard marching to Winchester they continued on the march with a wagon train of supplies to Cedar Creek. Just as they arrived at Cedar Creek, at dusk, a large portion of Sheridan's men were driving Early's men from Fisher's Hill. The 12th West Virginia had just missed another battle in which the Union had lost only about 400 men, while the Rebels lost more than 1,300. Sheridan captured 16 cannons at Fisher's Hill.

Although the 12th West Virginia had missed the battle, its men were to be in on the pursuit of fleeing Rebel forces into the night, even though they had been marching all day. It was a rare thing for one army to pursue another after dark and on the same road, but Sheridan was determined to capitalize on his victory and capture all who could yet be captured before they could consolidate—and come back.

Captain McMorrow was exhausted as he stumbled through the dark woods with the rest of the men of the 12th West Virginia in pursuit of the Rebels. In sentiment, he was in complete agreement with this action. If belief alone could energize men, then this Rebel chase would have been perfectly executed. But a body can only go so far and at such speed as they were moving. In the darkness, John could not use his method of picking out distant landmarks. In the moonlight he saw men who had fallen out of the ranks ahead of him. His will to go on could not override his physical inability to continue. So when he tripped over a rock and landed face-first on the ground, he decided that he, too, would take a few minutes to rest. He did not make a sound when someone stepped on his hand and the pain called upon him to shout something. Instead he crawled to the side, into the woods beside another soldier and closed his eyes without anything like shame. At that moment he would have gladly accepted all the scorn and ridicule of all the men and officers in the army in exchange for ten minutes of rest.

Birds were singing. There was nothing strange about that. He had heard birds singing all his life. Then why did this seem so strange? He could not name the kind of bird that it was, but it was a common song. *That can't be the point of its seeming so important or different from what ought to be expected. A whippoorwill would be different, because they only sing at night, but this one is normal. And that's the problem!* He opened his eyes and saw the first faint rays of dawn. He thought of the many autumn mornings he had spent with his father squirrel hunting at just this hour in the middle of the woods. He mentally retraced the events that had put him here this time. It took him a moment to catch up to the present. John turned to the left and saw the figure of the man who had been there first. He would wake him in a minute and they would catch up with the rest who must be up ahead at Woodstock by now. He started to sit up when something else dawned on him. *This is a Rebel!* It jolted him awake. John grabbed for his pistol. Then he slowly looked around. No one else was in sight. The gray-clad figure was breathing steadily. John tapped the Rebel on the shoulder, gently. "Good morning, Johnny." No movement responded and John was glad. He had not thought to disarm him before waking him. He picked up the musket from beside the Confederate and then, without touching him, looked for evidence of some other weapon. Then he poked the sleeping figure hard and said, "Good morning, Johnny." A startled Rebel opened his eyes. His hands made for the place where his musket had been before he looked back at John with a resigned expression.

"Ah reckon ah'm yer prisoner, captain."

"You are that, Johnny Reb. And do you know why you are my prisoner?"

"Ah reckon on account of you caught me here sleepin'."

"That's part of it. The main point is that I woke up first."

John laid the musket aside. He was too tired to carry it. With his pistol trained on his prisoner he started on the road toward Woodstock.

*　　*　　*　　*

THE POINT MOST IN QUESTION

Anna Lee sat in her customary place between her father and Micah as the minister stood to preach. She took notes. It had come as a surprise to her that Micah seldom seemed to recall even the most basic points of the sermon afterward. Her own family had always taken time to review and evaluate the main points as they rode home after church, to see if they could discern the connections between the passages cited and the points drawn from them.

Her mother had warned her, or at least informed her correctly, that Anna Lee would discover many things after wedding vows. Adjustments had to be made and Anna Lee understood this. Just how to make those adjustments was the point most in question. At least she could take notes on the sermon and see if she could interest Micah. She would try to keep the tradition with her own children. *Micah is a good man*, she thought, *but he seems to make little effort to see the fine distinctions. Or maybe it really is more a matter of inability?*

The preacher read:

> For as many as are led by the Spirit of God, they are the sons of God. For ye have not received the spirit of bondage again to fear: but ye have received the Spirit of adoption, whereby we cry, Abba, Father. The Spirit itself beareth witness with our spirit, that we are the children of God: and if children, then heirs, heirs of God and joint-heirs with Christ, if so be that we suffer with him, that we may also be glorified together (Romans 8).

"Friends and brethren, we have read this Scripture to draw our minds to those influences wrought by the Holy Spirit on our spirits. This subject is often discussed, seldom understood, and frequently misunderstood. Yet it is basic and important. A misconception here will most certainly lead to confusion about a thousand other Bible subjects."

Anna Lee felt she knew where this was headed. She was glad to have such an involved subject to use in her experiments in drawing Micah into subjects involving fine distinctions.

"Why this subject is shrouded in mystery—at least in the minds of many—is itself a mystery. The ambiguity isn't in the Bible. The Scriptures are clear enough. The fault must, therefore, be placed at the feet of those who preach their own thoughts without going first to the Holy Scriptures to discover the mind of God. These men may be kind and honest and sincere, but I must kindly say that they are honestly mistaken. We must learn to have a healthy distrust for all that men formulate and teach. Differences in religious belief are the result of man's failure to 'hear what the Spirit saith unto the churches.'"

Anna Lee took no notes up to this point in the sermon. These were settled principles in the minds of all those around her and this might have been the introduction to almost any sermon that she had heard from this pulpit.

"We are accused of believing that there are no spiritual influences today; that God doesn't act so as to touch the minds and hearts of men and women. This is unfair. Lost souls are converted to Jesus Christ only when there is a Divine influence to bring about that conversion. Those who have been 'born again' by obedience to the Gospel of Christ can only grow in sanctification by Holy influences. We read—just this past week—of a man who claims that the disciples do not believe that the Holy Spirit takes an active part in our lives today. He is most badly mistaken."

Anna Lee scribbled notes, anticipating what was coming. She drew a crude sword and beside it wrote, "the Word of God." Then she drew a stick figure with a hand grasping the sword's handle. She labeled the figure, "the Holy Spirit." Out at the end of the sword she drew a heart and wrote the word "mind." She wanted to nudge Micah and show him her predictions, but she feared she might disrupt the flow of his thoughts and cause him to miss the points as they unfolded. Even so, she held her notes so as to make them visible if he happened to look.

"The point at issue—the matter that seems to be so often overlooked—is the question of the means by which God exerts His influence upon human minds. Is that influence direct? Does He directly put thoughts into our heads and feelings into our hearts? No. If He were to do so then there would be no need of preaching or teaching or reading the Bible. Man would know no duty. We are not puppets. We are active creatures created in the image of God with the ability to choose what we will believe and what we will do. The Holy Spirit is active today, but He acts by means of an instrument and that instrument is the Word of God. According to Paul, in Ephesians chapter six and verse seventeen, 'the sword of the Spirit is the word of God.' He wrote to the church in Rome and told them in the first chapter of that letter, in verse 16, that he was not ashamed of the gospel of Christ and then he added, 'for it is the power of God unto salvation to every one that believeth.' He wrote a letter to the Hebrews, and in the fourth chapter and verse twelve he wrote that 'the word of God is quick'—that means living—and powerful, and sharper than any two edged sword, piercing even to the dividing asunder of soul and spirit, and of the joints and marrow, and is a discerner of the thoughts and intents of the heart.' Over in Romans again, this time in chapter twelve and verse two, he wrote that we are transformed by the 'renewing of the mind.' Just follow the apostles through the book of Acts and see how often it is said of them that they 'reasoned' with the people 'out of the scriptures' and it was the response to this preaching that brought about conversion. That means that Paul and the others reasoned about things taught in the Bible. Some preachers get what they say out of the Bible in another sense, because it is clear that they didn't find what they say in the Bible!"

Anna Lee was satisfied with her predictions and hopeful that Micah was taking in the import of these words.

"Does the Holy Spirit enlighten the mind? He certainly does, but the Psalmist tells us how He does it. 'The entrance of they word gives light' and 'thy word is a lamp unto my feet and a light unto my pathway'—and so many other statements of Scripture make the point over and over again. So it is a profound mistake to sit passively with your Bible closed and expect God to poke His thoughts into your head. It's an error to expect Him to answer your prayers for wisdom if you are not searching His word for the wisdom He has already provided. I don't have one bit of wisdom to share with you that I didn't get from God's word. That's not a statement of humility, because I'll also tell you that no other preacher has any wisdom for you and you don't have any wisdom from God that you did not find recorded in this final and complete revelation of the mind of God."

As Anna Lee and Micah walked to the wagon after more than an hour of standing about and visiting with others in the church yard, Anna Lee chose her words carefully. She had accepted the truth that she was now discovering many of her husband's qualities for the first time. She had not, however, given up the goal of working toward bringing about some changes in Micah. She would not demand changes, but she could encourage them. This distinction made her approach more gentle and caused less internal frustration. She would chose her methods carefully and apply them to only those issues worthy of taking risks, without demanding success of herself.

"What did you think of the sermon today?"

"It was fine, I guess. I noticed you were drawing pictures."

"I was really taking notes on the sermon and the pictures worked better than words. You want to go over it?"

"I suppose that'd be fine."

"Let's see. It had to do with the Holy Spirit. I wonder if there would be a way to summarize the main idea in just a few sentences?" Anna Lee paused, hoping that Micah would propose some sort of beginning place. As the pause grew longer she silently measured time and wondered how long she could remain silent. She could endure it no longer.

"I suppose it might also be good to think about how the main ideas really affect what we do or believe in practical ways."

Then Micah offered his summary. "Seems to me that the main point would be that people in the other churches think that the Holy Spirit is still teaching them things and that we don't think that way."

Anna Lee wanted to say, "No. It has to do with the manner in which the Holy Spirit teaches people." That would have been reasonable and inoffensive in her original family, but Anna Lee was probing the boundaries with Micah.

"I wonder if we could alter that just a little and make it clearer by saying that the Holy Spirit is not teaching us new things, things that are not already in the Bible, but that He is teaching us whenever we read the words that He inspired the writers of the Bible to write? Seems to me that the preacher made quite a point of that and wanted to make sure we saw the difference."

Micah's face showed no signs that he felt corrected or rebuked. "Many think the Holy Spirit just directly pokes ideas and feelings into people, but He uses a tool, a sword, that's able to get right down into our core and change the way we think."

It was important to Anna Lee that Micah had a clear conception of the sermon, but the greater personal victory for her was that she had drawn him out, and helped him to clarify thoughts without making demands or causing offense. She followed it up with questions and clarifications about the importance of being sure that what "we believe" is also "what the Bible teaches" and how it might be wise to make sure that one is always the same as the other.

It dawned on her that John McMorrow had really taught Anna Lee the skill that now shaped a marriage. John had loaned her a copy of Benjamin Franklin's autobiography and pointed out Franklin's methods for convincing—or attempting to convince—others without offense. John had spoken to her of his own difficulty in applying some of Franklin's methods without feeling that he was being dishonest, expressing uncertainty when he really had no doubt—and of his own modifications that allowed him to soften the blow of direct disagreement. Anna Lee thought she would like to write and thank John—and explain just how he had helped her, but she decided to leave that for some future time when the war would be behind them and she could tell him.

The newspaper terrified Anna Lee whenever reports came in listing the dead, wounded, and captured from the 12th West Virginia. It comforted her whenever John's name was not listed. She prayed for the end of the war and the future happiness of John McMorrow.

CHAPTER 12

IN HONOR OF ANOTHER

The 12th West Virginia remained at Woodstock for only a day before pushing on to Harrisonburg, where it arrived on September 25. Along the way they saw smoke rising from all directions as the cavalry complied with Grant's orders to burn all mills, barns, stacks of hay, and granaries. They marched on a road torn by the hooves of thousands of cattle taken from civilians and driven before them to Harrisonburg. When they arrived, John McMorrow expressed uncertainty around the fire about the moral rightness of the treatment shown to the citizens who might or might not be Rebel supporters in every case. Someone told of great explosions and of other evidences of hidden firearms and powder when some of the barns, hay stacks, and granaries were burned.

"Well," he allowed, "if they can't make distinctions between civilian and military operations then I don't suppose we can either." He wanted to believe the stories of Rebel gunpowder and arms hidden in the mounds of grain and hay, therefore, he believed them. He was glad to have justification for the extreme measures in which he was a participant. Such measures would have crushed his will to fight only a year ago. Now, the reported presence of hidden Rebel military stores in grain and hay gave him greater resolve to put down this rebellion by all reasonable means. He filed away the stories for possible use back home, when the war would end and when neighbors or children might question the burning of civilian barns and food.

On October 6 the 12th West Virginia marched with the whole force in the direction of Strasburg where they made camp on the 8th. Smoke yet filled the air and Rebels followed close. Sheridan figured that the aggressive Rebel cavalry—

especially General Thomas L. Rosser's men who called themselves "the Saviors of the Valley"—needed to be taught a lesson. Word spread that he had directed Union cavalry on the morning of the 9th to get out there and "whip the Rebel cavalry or get whipped yourself." The attack made in response to this directive lasted about two hours and routed these "Saviors of the Valley," sending them about 26 miles up the valley. The attack captured about 330 prisoners and 11 guns—all the Rebels had except for one—and 47 wagons. When the smoke cleared and the news reached camp it was said among the men that these "Saviors of the Valley" were now only interested in saving their bacon. Sheridan offered $50 for the last remaining piece of artillery.

Two days later the 12th West Virginia marched with its brigade toward Martinsburg guarding a wagon train. As they neared the little town of Newtown they met a few Union cavalrymen galloping toward them. These had been guarding an ambulance just ahead that had just been attacked by Mosby's raiders, who had captured their ambulances and killed or wounded half their men. Lieutenant Colonel Northcott sent troops, too late, to see if the matter might be reversed. The wounded who could not travel were left at the side of road. They had taken the ambulances, and all they contained, including the mail. The brigade camped at Winchester that night. Now Colonel Curtis took command of the brigade. Next morning they set out for Martinsburg where they arrived after dark that evening. Two days later, on October 15, they camped at Winchester.

While they moved back and forth, the Union leaders did not know the location of Early's men. Although Early's cavalry were badly wounded, his infantry troops were still active. Thoburn lost more than 100 men in an unexpected encounter with Early's men on October 13. Colonel Wells of the 34th Massachusetts, the stern disciplinarian who had often called upon his orderly to "go and ascertain who fired that gun and report him to me immediately," was killed in the fight. The crude mountaineers from West Virginia and the uppity New Englanders who spoke with strange accents had long since come to appreciate their solidarity. They mourned the shared loss of Colonel Wells with a common sorrow. Grant had called for the 6th Corps to join him to the south, thinking that Early would not be making much more trouble in the valley for awhile. When Grant found his premise mistaken, he canceled the plan. He ordered the 6th Corps back to the Shenandoah Valley.

On October 15, Grant ordered Sheridan to make efforts to destroy and disrupt the Virginia Central Railroad. That night he sent a division of cavalry as far as Front Royal, intending to reinforce it with another division and cross the Blue Ridge en route to tearing up the railroad. At about that time he received a dispatch detailing a message that they had intercepted from the Rebel signal flags atop Massanutten Mountain. It read: "To Lieutenant General Early: Be ready to move as soon as my forces join you, and we will crush Sheridan. Longstreet, Lieutenant General."

Sheridan suspected a trick, but being uncertain he ordered his cavalry back to Cedar Creek while he went to Washington for a conference with leaders there. Along the way he received a telegraph suggesting that Longstreet had not recently moved away from Richmond.

The 12th West Virginia was ordered to Cedar Creek along with the rest of the brigade. On the night of October 18, they sat about the fires and talked of the obvious progress of the war.

"I figure the hard fighting in this valley is just about over," said one. "Early has just about had it and we've hobbled his cavalry."

"We've figured about like that before," said Captain McMorrow, "and he keeps coming back at us. His numbers have to be shrinking, but somehow he puts them back into action. But I figure you're right. Sooner or later he's going to have to see—and his men are going to have to come to terms with the fact—that the Union army is in the valley to stay and can't be driven out. I figure it'll be sooner than later."

Content with this interpretation of their world, the 12th West Virginia went to sleep that night at Winchester, surmising that the hardest days were now behind them—that better days were ahead. They shared the sentiments of many in the Shenandoah Valley who wore the blue and slept in relative comfort that night.

In the morning, as they formed up for the march to Cedar Creek, they heard cannon blasts to their front. By 9:00 they were well on their way. Retreating Union troops met them going back in the direction from which they had just come. Even wagon trains were on the retreat toward Winchester. The 12th West Virginia guarded a wagon train going toward the battle while other such trains were retreating from the battle. It made no sense to continue under such conditions and risk the loss of stores until the direction of things could be clarified, so the colonel halted his men and parked the wagons awaiting word from the front.

A steady stream of retreating soldiers came past them. These were not really running or in extreme disorder. Some even stopped to boil coffee in the fields while on the retreat, but it was clear that all were moving away from the conflict. Stragglers from different units mingled on the retreat. No one tried to rally them or turn them around. Hundreds of men, wandering far from their allotted places, filled the road now in front of the 12th West Virginia. Curtis ordered men into line to keep retiring soldiers from retreating further. Off to the sides hundreds more made for Winchester.

Then an extraordinary thing happened. Loud cheers rang out from the direction of Winchester. The mass of men on the road moved to the sides. Cheering moved like a massive wave toward the position of the 12th West Virginia. A smallish man on a black horse at a brisk trot rushed toward them. Staff officers trailed him, stuggling to keep up. As the rider approached, John recognized first the battle flag and then the man who waved his strange little hat in the air. It was Sheridan. Men along the route shouted in unison, "Sheridan! Sheridan! Sheridan!" as Sheridan yelled, "This way, men! This way. Follow me." Men turnedaround, checking their ammunition and rushing toward Cedar Creek. When Sheridan came to the stragglers detained by Curtis he rode right up to them, stood straight up in his stirrups and shouted through gritted teeth, "Boys, if you don't want to fight yourselves, come back and look at others fighting. We will whip them out their boots before 4 o'clock!"

Turning to Colonel Curtis, Sheridan shouted again, "Organize these men. Don't worry about what unit they're with. Make them into a battalion and put officers over them and move the whole force to the front." Sheridan rode on. The frenzied cheering continued to build and then grew faint as he rode toward Cedar Creek with enlivened men following.

Colonel Curtis organized the makeshift battalion and sent it to the front. Then he moved forward with the wagons. Before he had led his own men more than a mile, orders came back from Sheridan to return with the wagons to Winchester and prepare to protect them from a possible attack from Rebel cavalry. As they turned about Captain McMorrow wanted to ask—but did not, "What cavalry? I thought they were only interested in saving their bacon."

No Rebel cavalry attacked at Winchester that night. The 12th West Virginia once again felt cheated. After heavy losses in the morning at Cedar Creek, inflicted by a surprise attack at dawn, the troops to the front rallied and won a complete victory. Of course the men of the 12th West Virginia were happy to hear of the great victory. They felt at least remotely a part of it, but they shared collective pain in the knowledge that all of these events had transpired while they guarded wagons in the rear and prepared for a cavalry attack that never came.

When the tally was made, 4,335 Union soldiers were listed as killed or wounded. The number of those captured was put at 1,429. A few men from the 12th West Virginia, separated from the regiment, actually went into battle and some lost their lives there. Colonel Thoburn was killed. Captain Philip G. Bier, who had enlisted as a private in Company D of the 12th West Virginia and risen in the ranks, was killed. To show their regard for Captain Bier, the officers of the regiment paid to have his body embalmed and returned to Wheeling, where Bier's family gave him a proper burial. Once again, the Union lost more lives than the Rebels in this battle in which the Union had won a complete victory.

Rebel General Early gave 1,860 as the number of killed and wounded among Rebel forces at Cedar Creek. The Union had captured about 1,200. Perhaps because of the element of surprise, the Union lost twice as many men as the Rebels. But there were still young men at home in the North who could fill the Union army. Those lost to the South would not be so easily replaced.

The morning after the battle, October 20, the 12th West Virginia accompanied the wagon train to Cedar Creek. Some Rebel dead remained unburied. The next day they marched with the brigade to Newtown, where they guarded the temporary hospital set up there.

On October 25, 1864, the soldiers who were citizens of West Virginia were permitted to cast their vote for President of the United States. These who had endured so long—fighting what many called "Lincoln's war"—cast their votes, almost to the man, for Abraham Lincoln.

While stationed at the hospital at Newtown, the 12th West Virginia moved out a time or two in pursuit of Mosby and his men, who had captured a forage train a few miles out of town. They, of course, could not find him. They felt useless marching out on foot in search of mounted men, but they were in the war on these pursuits instead of doing guard duty.

Sheridan was promoted to major general a few weeks after the battle of Cedar Creek. In giving this commission President Abraham Lincoln said that it was "for a brilliant victory achieved over the Rebels for the third time in pitched battle within thirty days."

With winter approaching it seemed reasonable to position men close to their base of supplies. On the 9th of November the infantry moved to Kernstown. The other units soon followed. They pitched camp there. Men went to work building fortifications.

The ever-threatening Rebel General Early interpreted this movement to mean that Union forces were withdrawing from the Shenandoah Valley to join General Grant to the south. Early moved his forces from New Market to Middletown. Sheridan responded by sending two cavalry divisions, General Wesley Merritt's and Custer's, to drive them back. They captured two Rebel artillery pieces and 245 officers and enlisted men. Sheridan, assuming that Early might well attempt an attack upon the main body after Sheridan learned that Early had received reinforcements after the battle of Cedar Creek, ordered his troops to have sufficient ammunition and to prepare for an attack. The anticipated attack did not come. Early returned his troops to New Market.

On November 19, Sheridan's army was officially named The Army of the Shenandoah. The camp at Kernstown was named Camp Russell. On the 23rd the men dined on the most sumptuous meal of chicken that any had eaten in a very long time. Someone—they knew not who—had sent a wonderful Thanksgiving dinner. Some came into possession of strong drink at about that time. Men who watched a young Irishman of the 19th Corps sauntering along making up a little song would later recall it. His corps had suffered heavy losses at the battle of the Opequon and his song was simply, "The 19th of September, in 1864, is long to be remembered by the 19th Army Corps."

Resting in his tent after Thanksgiving dinner, Captain McMorrow was startled at first to hear men outside chanting "Mosby! Mosby!" Just when John was about to rise, a harried man rushed into his tent wearing a plug hat like that worn by the Rebel partisan whose name was still being shouted outside the tent. John was terrified for a moment, thinking that the Rebels had somehow infiltrated the camp. But the shouting outside sounded more like a jest than anything else and this man was certainly not Mosby. He looked frightened more than he appeared threatening.

"What can I do for you, sir?" John was still sizing him up and trying to make sense of it all.

"The men outside seem to think I'm Mosby—or at least one of his men."

"I think it's your hat. What are you doing in camp anyway?"

"I'm a tailor. I've come all the way from Wheeling to see about getting these men some new uniforms. I've brought samples and all. What about my hat?"

"It's the kind Mosby and his men wear."

The trembling tailor took off the hat.

"Here. Wear this one," John said as he handed him a slouch hat. "I'd appreciate it if you'd return it before you leave camp, but I figure you'll fit in around here a little better with that on your head."

Thanking him for the use of the hat, the tailor went out to wherever he was going.

The 12th West Virginia left Camp Russell on the 24th of November and marched to Stephenson's Depot where they unloaded cars and performed picket duty for a few weeks. On the 16th of December, heavy cannon fire from the direction of Camp Russell disturbed the men. It appeared that the Rebels must have attacked—until a dispatch came in revealing that the guns at Camp Russell had been fired as a salute in honor of General Thomas' victory the day before at

Nashville. The next day the guns were fired again in honor of another victory at Nashville and the fall of Savannah before Sherman.

* * * *

ANNA LEE GOT IT ALL STARTED

Mr. Stone knocked so as to be heard and then whispered to Mrs. Stone: "You know, it seems like a strange thing to be knocking on my own daughter's door. Do you reckon we could just go on in?"

"If you want my opinion, dear, I think we ought to wait here. She shares her home with Micah, you know, and we can observe common custom until we're invited to do otherwise. These little questions are tricky, but to be on the safe…."

Just then the door opened and Micah said, "Come on in. You two don't need to wait for an invitation to come in. You're family." They smiled and entered the warmth of the front room. Micah smiled too.

Micah hung their coats in the pantry. They sat and waited. It seemed strange to both that Micah was the only one in sight. Without commenting, both took note that Micah was at home and it was still early in the evening. An aroma from the kitchen told them that a meal was being prepared, but Anna Lee had not shown herself.

"I'll tell Anna Lee you're here." Micah was still smiling in a way that caused both of them to wonder what might be the cause of it. "She's been resting, but I'm sure she's ready to get up now. I've been tending to supper—after she got me started."

"I hope she's not ill." Mrs. Stone was asking more than she was stating her hope. Micah's smile ruled out the likelihood.

Anna Lee's father did not reason that way. He supposed that maybe Micah was just so proud of himself for helping out in the kitchen with Anna Lee being sick, that he had allowed that pleasure to take precedence over genuine concern for Anna Lee, to produce a smile of self-satisfaction where a look of concern really belonged. He had not seen this sort of self-centeredness in Micah before, but he had worried that it might be there. It concerned him that he now saw evidence of it.

"No. She's not sick or anything," Micah said casually, "she just wanted to rest up before you all got here." He left the room.

Anna Lee's father was not convinced just yet. As much as he had thought about it, and as thoroughly as he was determined to stay out of the affairs of his married daughters, he could not keep himself from worrying. He had not raised these girls to become the wives of thoughtless men who would fail to appreciate them. Any sign of mistreatment, no matter how slight, concerned him.

Mrs. Stone scanned the room. She took pleasure in its neatness. She credited Anna Lee for keeping her house in order. It pleased her to see that, even though Micah's business had been doing very well, there was no ostentatious display in the room. The furnishings were useful. Everything was in its place. The basket beside the chair with the candle stand behind it seemed vaguely out of place, but not for any reason that she could name, or that she tried to name. The ball of yarn in the basket with the knitting needles stuck through it was just another vague confirmation of Anna Lee's industriousness.

"She'll be right in," Micah said as he passed through, smiling, on his way to the kitchen.

Mrs. Stone got up and followed him into the kitchen, saying, "Let me help in here."

Micah surprised Mr. Stone by saying, "Thanks. I don't mind doing it, but you can help me make sure I'm getting it right. This is not usually my job. Anna Lee got it all started."

When Anna Lee appeared Micah left the kitchen to join her in the front room. Anna Lee's father was puzzled. His daughter looked perfectly healthy, almost like she was suppressing a smile. Her eyes seemed unusually bright. Inwardly, he rebuked himself for having misjudged Micah's smile. He stood to embrace her and to tell her how beautiful she was.

Turning toward the kitchen, Anna Lee invited her mother to set the things off the stove and to come join the rest in the front room. "It should be ready now. Let's give it a few minutes to cool." Although it felt strange, once again, to be ordered out of her daughter's kitchen, Mrs. Stone complied. She was being careful to keep herself on the safe side of any semblance of trespass in this new home. She went right into the front room, hugged her daughter, and sat down.

Micah and Anna Lee stood in awkward silence. There was a sense of awkwardness in the room. Mr. Stone picked up the poker and poked the fire for no particular reason.

"So what's new in the Johnson household?" Mrs. Stone asked.

"Well, Mother, there is something new but you mustn't tell anyone."

Mr. Stone replaced the poker and prepared himself. The possibility that they might be moving away ran through his mind. He prepared to discipline his tongue.

"It appears that you are going to be grandparents!"

They were stunned. Both rose at the same instant. Mr. Stone shook Micah's hand while he waited his turn to hug his daughter. The tears came to Mr. Stone's eyes first and Micah was the first to notice. He patted his father-in-law's back and then picked up the poker and poked the fire while the other three shared an embrace. When he turned back to the little group Mrs. Stone pulled him into it and said, "We're so proud of both of you. You'll be fine parents."

As the four sat down to eat, Micah offered a prayer of thanks for the food that was before them and for the good fortune to be a part of a wonderful family. He petitioned God for His continued blessing upon "this growing family."

The talk around the table turned to the progress of the war—especially in the Shenandoah Valley. The papers hinted that things had settled down in recent weeks. Mr. McMorrow, John's father, had received a letter from John and had told them all at church that John was still well and wanting to come home.

"Did you hear about the fellow from the 12th West Virginia who came home on furlough?" Mr. Stone asked. No one had heard so he continued his report. "His wife wasn't expecting him. He was goin' to surprise her. Well, he came home and found his wife with one of Sheridan's cavalry officers, the one that got promoted straight from lieutenant to general last year."

"Custer?" Anna Lee asked.

"You bet he cussed 'er! He called her every foul name he could think of."

*   *   *   *

CONSEQUENCES THAT MIGHT FOLLOW

John McMorrow was cold as he rode along in the cattle car that still smelled of manure. He was more concerned for the men riding on top of the car. It was the 19th of December and freezing. The brigade had just left Stephenson's Depot, outside of Winchester, on its way to Washington, D.C. Early's Rebel forces had all but abandoned the Shenandoah Valley and the bulk of the Union forces from there were being reassigned to other areas. The 12th West Virginia was to go over to the Army of the James, where they would become a part of what was most directly "Grant's army."

At Washington they boarded boats and floated down the Potomac to the Chesapeake Bay, then up the James River to City Point, and then finally to where they made camp near the Dutch Gap canal. No one had been allowed to visit Washington. They saw Mount Vernon from the boats. They ran out of rations and endured severe weather along the way. There was a general sense that they were moving into the most dangerous place on earth, joining Grant's army. Along the way they passed a vessel moving North and Major Brown remarked, so as to be heard, "Well, I notice that some fellows at least are getting back from Richmond alive."

They landed the day after Christmas, marched four miles, and camped in quarters temporarily vacated by General Butler's troops. It was a blessing, in such severe weather, to have these shanties waiting for them. On the 30th, however, the original inhabitants of the quarters returned, so they marched a few miles away and had to build their own after all.

In the Army of the James, the 12th West Virginia became a part of the 2nd Division—sometimes called the Independent Division—of the 24th Corps. The regiment was now in the 2nd Brigade, which included the 54th Pennsylvania and the 23rd Illinois. Colonel Curtis commanded the brigade. General John W. Turner led the division. General John Gibbon headed the corps. General Edward Otho Cresap Ord commanded the Army of the James now that General Benjamin F. Butler had been relieved.

The Army of the James consisted of two corps, the 24th and the 25th. The 25th Corps was composed of blacks—except for its officers. The 25th Corps went to work on the Dutch Gap canal project begun by General Butler. The object was to dig a channel across a narrow neck of land to bypass a long horseshoe bend in the James River, and thereby avoid obstructions in the bend while floating supplies to the area around Richmond. As the black soldiers worked at digging this channel the Rebels threw artillery shells at them from time to time. The diggers dug holes in the sides of the canal. They would jump into these whenever a shell landed. A lookout kept watch to warn the workers in the canal whenever a shell was fired in their direction. The lookout would shout, "Gopher hole!" and then watch men diving into the protective holes. If the Rebel shelling inadvertently helped in the digging of the canal, at least it can be said that the canal helped only those who used it following the war. Water only tricked when these men finished.

The state of affairs in the Army of the James around Petersburg differed from anything the 12th West Virginia had seen. The Union breastworks stretched on for miles, parallel with Confederate works. In places they were within shouting distance of one another, yet they seldom fired their muskets. The ranks, on both sides, called an unofficial truce not recognized by generals. In the area occupied by the regiment, in front of Fort Harrison, pickets from each side walked their beats in plain sight of the other without fear. Men ordered to fire obeyed, but only after courteous warnings of "Down, Billy Yank!" and "Down, Johnny Reb!"

There were few reported cases of men being killed or wounded—and sincere protests and genuine apologies followed these. Generally, the two opposing armies outside of Petersburg conspired for mutual comfort. Pressing the conflict under such conditions could result in a meaningless blood bath.

The 12th West Virginia kept busy making corduroy roads of logs over the soft and muddy ground, cutting and hauling firewood, practicing drill, preparing for and standing inspections, picket duty, and standing in line of battle for an hour or so each morning. The hard marching had ended for the time. They were now part of an entrenched army, with the enemy near.

On January 7 the highly regarded Lieutenant Colonel Northcott, whose resignation had been accepted, made a farewell speech and left the command. Major Brown was promoted to lieutenant colonel. Captain Burley accepted promotion to major.

At noon on the 17th, guns fired a salute in honor of the capture of Fort Fisher. Land forces under General Alfred H. Terry and naval forces commanded by Admiral David D. Porter had combined their efforts to take this fortification on the coast of North Carolina. Their success bottled up the South's major point of entry for blockade runners. It was a considerable blow to Confederate hopes.

"Get your things in order, men. We're to be inspected tomorrow." It was January 21. Captain McMorrow grew restless. The war had surged forward and that drive now stalled before Petersburg. John had grown into his role without really knowing how to trace the transition from civilian professor to useful soldier. His men recognized him as an officer who would carry his load and lead men without lording it over them or abusing his position. Troops in the ranks did not recognize some of John's fellow officers who had begun the war thinking they already knew all that could be known about leading men. Men in the ranks obeyed officers who gave needless orders, but they knew how to execute such orders slowly, technically, and imperfectly. They knew how to sabotage their own efforts so as to be able to say, at the end of the day, that they had done what they had been ordered to do.

John looked on without intervening while a second lieutenant "supervised" log hauling for the fortifications. The lieutenant stood with hands behind his back and reminded them of his authority. "You privates don't need nine men to a log. Six of you can carry a log of that size. I wasn't born yesterday. I know sloth when I see it. You, you, and you. Break off. The rest of you spread out along the sides. Three to a side is enough. You other three beats—get back over to the pile and come back with no more than six men to a log."

After the lieutenant left, Captain McMorrow approached the men and spoke as though he knew nothing of what had just transpired. "You men look tired," he said. "Why don't you take a break?" They remained sitting on the log and said, almost together, "Thank you, sir."

The captain looked at the log and then at the men and said, "Now, I don't want to interfere with your work here, men. I'm sure that you know your own business well enough to not require my opinion, but I wonder if it might be better to have a few more men to each log? Anyway, you men do what you think is best."

The lieutenant later made his report and got his coveted credit for efficient use of soldiers. John knew that such men were often promoted far above their abilities, both in civilian and military service. He saw it in the management of colleges, churches, and armies. Some rise on self-promoted reputations and then get in the way when work is to be done. Crises, like war, sorted them out eventually, but the rule held.

"Tomorrow's inspection is important. You know how to clean your equipment and how many rounds you should have. Your sergeants will be checking some, but the responsibility is on you. You can do the minimum and pass. You know that and so do I. You can give it your best effort and show these other regiments what West Virginia boys can do. These other regiments are still saying that you boys are crude—and even lazy—but I don't believe it. Get things in order. If the fellow beside you doesn't care what these others are saying about West Virginians, then maybe he needs a little lesson that only his tent mates can teach. I am going out now to brag to the officers in the other companies of the regiment about how this company is going to come out in the inspection tomorrow. I hope you'll not make my boasting vain. I know that a lot of you think of inspections as little more than window dressing, but there's talk of light duty for the regiment that comes out on top in this inspection. So if you like hauling logs and walking the picket line, I suggest that you just give it little effort. Now, the fellow beside you may not share your love of such duty, so be prepared if he decides to punish you some for imposing your preference for hard duty on him. I know if it were me, and if the fellow next to me was not giving it much effort, I think I'd be instructing him in the way of preparation for inspection more perfectly. He'd either have his things in order or he'd be falling out for sick call in the morning with a mysterious black eye. That's just me."

When the brigade was inspected on Sunday, January 22, the 12th West Virginia came out ahead and was excused from duty for one week. This did not mean that they could go home. It just gave them a week's relief from normal duties around camp. On the 24th, however, an anticipated attack had them under orders to be ready to form ranks at a moment's notice.

Rations were plentiful for the Union soldiers. A steady supply poured into City Point daily. Conditions among the Rebels were different. On February 4, a lieutenant colonel and a captain deserted from the Rebel ranks in front of the 12th West Virginia. It looked like the beginning of the end of the war. The next week Rebel pickets passed along Richmond newspapers telling of the recent "Peace Commission" and its failure. Even at that stage of the war the Confederacy was not willing to consider any proposition that did not grant independence from the Union.

Men in blue also deserted the Union lines. The Rebels had issued a statement saying that all deserters would be sent through the lines to their homes in the North. Homesick boys sometimes deserted in the hope of being sent home. On February 10, while some of the boys from the 12th West Virginia were on picket duty, three boys from the 10th Connecticut got through the lines and deserted to the enemy.

During this time Union cannons were often fired in celebration. On the 21st of February they fired in honor of the capture of Charleston and Columbia, South Carolina. On the 22nd they fired in honor of Washington's birthday. On March 7, they blasted to celebrate Sheridan's victory at Waynesboro in which he captured nearly all of Jubal Early's remaining forces.

On March 17 General Grant and his staff reviewed the entire corps. Large numbers of prominent citizens attended. Secretary of War Edwin M. Stanton was there. Mrs. Grant was there. Around the fires that evening, men spouted theories explaining the attention.

"Something big's about to happen," said one. "It's clear that the Rebels can't hold out much longer. The government's pouring everything into this thing and it can't hold still like this much longer."

Another picked up the theme. "They're going to expect us to take those works. We can't just wait until the Rebels all give up. They're stubborn. The grand review today wasn't just for nothing. It means that something's about to happen. We might as well expect to charge those Rebel defenses."

"Remember after New Market?" Captain McMorrow asked the group. "It stuck in the craw of the men when Sigel claimed he'd ordered some men of the 12th West Virginia to move. If we're ever ordered to take those works over there," he pointed in the direction of the Rebel fortifications, "I figure there'll be no time for hesitation. They have all those little forts over there and if we go after one we'll be exposed to fire from the others. Once we start in, if that's what we're going to do, we'd better keep going fast and hard until the job is done. If we pause, they'll cut us down. I don't know about the rest of you men, but if my men are ordered forward I'm not going to wait around." Officers nodded.

This moment around the campfire was the first time in his military career that he got the sense that his opinion carried weight. The idea scared him just a bit. He would have some responsibility for the consequences.

CHAPTER 13

NEW LEVELS OF UNCERTAINTY

As Micah sat idle in his shop waiting for the clock to suggest closing time he, knew the war was drawing to a close. Everyone seemed to know it. Grant was positioned in such a way that he could, according to reports, crush the Army of Northern Virginia at any time now. Orders for sharpshooter rifles dwindled. Micah was awkwardly pleased to have this bit of reliable intelligence when so much so-called information that came otherwise proved unreliable.

Anna Lee no longer worked with him in the shop. He doted on her, making her condition a constant excuse to bring gifts and defer to her. At her insistence he continued to bring the books to her at home—to let her suggest ways to continue the operation. It was Anna Lee who had planted the thought of making future plans in light of the coming end of conflict.

"I wonder if the end of the war might bring about a sudden drop in the demand for rifles of all sorts?" She had asked. Micah thought of all the arms that had been produced all over the country that would suddenly be on the market. He sensed that he had no right to complain, that he had profited from the war at a time when so many others had lost so much. Mothers and fathers had lost sons. Young ladies had lost husbands. Many had lost farms, livestock, and revenues that would have come from normal commerce if not for the war. Thousands had given their lives and thousands more had lost limbs. All who served in the armed forces had endured hardship and lost years of life.

He felt shame for having stayed out of uniform. All of the logical arguments that led to the conclusion that he should have been where he had been, doing exactly as he had done, were good arguments. But Micah felt he would spend the rest of his life under the cloud. He would have no rousing stories to tell when brave men stripped sleeves and showed scars or when children, and grandchildren, would ask. He had worked hard and he knew it. He had labored from motives akin to those of soldiers. The appearance of things, however, would not measure up to their substance in the minds of observers.

Character is more important than reputation. He imagined the playful banter that friends might one day pour upon him, and the hateful scorn that might come from ignorant men. He determined that he would make no public effort to justify himself and offer no answers. He would avoid all semblance of boasting for his part in the war. He would bear the insults.

These musings during the closing months of the war led Micah to redirect himself in ways that went beyond coming to terms with having remained out of uniform. They led him to define a larger course that would steer him through the years ahead. He would henceforth look toward doing things that were right and good, while making a deliberate effort to look away from those things that might serve only to enhance reputation and standing. This decision was for self-protection, although he did not understand it that way. It was a completely liberating choice that freed him from concerns about public opinion and insulated him at once from indignities fostered by the ill-considered words of others. At least in that moment when he made this choice, it narrowed his focus and shortened the list of things to be considered when future decisions were to be made.

This choice cleared the slate of his future. His conscious eschewing of ostentation fit into Anna Lee's ways. It pleased him to think that it would avoid the impression that he was boasting or gloating about his success during the war years. Then he reminded himself that his new goal involved being unconcerned about making or avoiding impressions, but he allowed that there was no harm in recognizing advantages as long as they were only to be incidental benefits of his plan.

This level of introspection was new to Micah. He was unaware that subtle questions and veiled suggestions from Anna Lee had goaded him. He felt that he was simply taking steps that were called for by the circumstances—the end of the war and the coming of a child.

The blank slate of Micah's future also created something like a crisis. How would he determine those things that were right and good? It struck him that he needed a map for the course he was plotting. It occurred to him that he must be feeling a good deal like recently freed slaves might feel. His liberation produced new levels of uncertainty and risk.

He determined that he would not discuss his new directions with Anna Lee—at least not yet. For one thing, he knew that she would approve and he wanted to assure himself that this was not his purpose. Micah wanted to give himself. He did not want to seem to promise what he might not be able to deliver. He thought that Anna Lee would rather see results without promises than hear pledges amounting to nothing. He started to correct himself again, but he paused long enough to settle on the truth that it was right and good to please Anna Lee and to have that as a goal, as long as false impressions were not to be the means.

On Sunday, March 19, Micah took his own Bible to church and took notes. Anna Lee would not know that he would be taking his notes with him to the shop and working to reconstruct the whole sermon, but it heartened her when he took the lead in the discussion in such a way that caused her to think that he had listened and made the fine distinctions.

*   *   *   *

COLLECTIVELY TOUCHED BY DEATH

Dark humor is not easily understood by those who think of death, when they think of it at all, as a distant reality. When men fall in battle never to rise again, those who stood beside them know that they might well have died and that only the random selection of flying lead had killed others instead of themselves. Diseases that killed one soldier could just as easily take another. For the men of the 12th West Virginia, death was near. Men had died recently. Men would die soon. Men known by name were now gone. Tent mates would shortly sleep beneath the sod.

One who might predict profound depression as the result of this state of affairs would be badly mistaken. Often, that life becomes more precious when its future and duration are uncertain. Present moments can have profound significance when they might be the last.

This differs from the normal course of things among civilians. When civilians die they generally die one at a time. The one who is "dying" does not share that condition with friends. The living direct sympathy toward the dying. For civilians there is often time to sort through feelings. Loved ones who are not dying offer comfort to civilians who are dying.

The Civil War soldier often had only seconds, if any time at all, to deal with the fact that he was certainly dying. Some wrote their names on paper and pinned the note to their backs before going into battle, to ensure that their remains could be properly identified and loved-ones informed. Dead soldiers could be seen after a battle with their jackets torn off by their own hands. They had learned to identify fatal wounds, and many had time to make the fateful self-diagnosis just before the terminal moment.

Soldiers going into battle, who have been in battle before, share a mutual sense of the high risk of death. There is certainty that death will come to some and uncertainty as to who is about to die. Comfort cannot be directed toward anyone in particular. Sympathy cannot be expected from others who share the experience.

To leave the subject of death alone is to deny the most pressing reality of soldiers at war. Some few prefer silence and denial. The majority find other outlets. Songs around the campfires were of death. Some dealt with the honor of dying for the cause and of being buried beneath the flag where brave deeds were done. Others mocked death and shook a fist in its face. Songs expressed parting words to mothers.

Soldiers told jokes about death that no civilian would think of telling to a dying man in a hospital bed, but they served a purpose for soldiers. In any other circumstance they would be grotesque and crude and thoughtless. But dying men had the right to share dark humor with dying men as they, together, faced harsh reality.

Captain McMorrow had only a vague awareness of the changes in his thinking as a result of his experiences in the war. Some of what he had studied academically had only been confirmed by what he had seen. As he listened to the songs and laughed at macabre jokes, he thought of how he might have reacted to them a few years before if he had heard them. Although he could only guess, now, about how he might have felt about them at an earlier time, he could place his finger on facts that might have prepared him for the change.

He recalled a nursery rhyme from the middle ages when the Bubonic Plague decimated Europe. The plague produced rose-colored blisters, ringed by pink, on the skin. During epidemics people carried posies in their pockets, possibly to ward off the disease or to cover the stench. Bodies were cremated. Clothing and personal belongings of the dead were burned, he thought, to prevent the spread of the disease. In that context and then from that circumstance children would sing for generations:

> Ring around the Roses,
> A pocket full of Posies,

Ashes, Ashes,
We all fall down.

John thought of this cheery little child's song and supposed that few in his day would be able to guess or comprehend that it had come from people collectively—and daily—touched by death. It came to mind when Assistant Surgeon Alexander Neil did a most extraordinary thing on March 24 while the men tramped through a field near the Chickahominy River.

The 12th West Virginia was sent out to intercept and possibly aid Sheridan and his men on their return from the Shenandoah Valley. The movement came to nothing. They did not meet with Sheridan, so they returned to camp in the evening. While they were out, however, they moved slowly and cautiously over the ground where McClellan had been soundly defeated nearly four years before in what had come to be called the "Seven Day's Fight." Bones from shallow graves had washed to the surface. The men passed these at intervals along the way. The bones produced an eerie, undefined sense among the men.

John McMorrow walked alongside Surgeon Neil and passed the time by asking Neil's opinion of phrenology. John had learned of the curious discipline at Bethany, where opinions were divided. The science had become popular in the decades before the war, but John remained skeptical. The notion that character could be discerned by measuring the dimensions of a man's head, the distance between his eyes, the shape of his nose, and the placement of his cheek bones was too simplistic. He had seen the books with the sample drawings of various "types" and he had noticed that many seemed to fit his own observations. A line drawing of Alexander Campbell, the founder of Bethany College and a man John admired, illustrated the features of a man with the nearly perfect qualities of intelligence and industriousness. Men were too immediately impressed with seemingly scientific tests that yielded numbers and conclusions supported by graphs and diagrams. *These might be valuable tools*, he thought, *but they are not sound measures. John* had known men whose heads were shaped in ways that would not fit the predictions of phrenologists. *If the relationships do not exist in fact, then it's a dangerous science*, he thought.

As he walked along with Neil, listening to him explain the claims of phrenology, John noticed that Neil made no defense of the claims. Then he noticed that Neil's head was unusually round. He could not recall just what that should signify to a phrenologist. He was not willing to ask. It occured to him that most of those who had argued in favor of phrenology were men whose own heads made favorable statements about them according to it. As much as he appreciated careful investigation and the advancement of science, he could not shake the thought that errors accepted quickly and completely could have devastating consequences. John's father had accepted unscientific theories about slavery and its place in the scheme of things so as to make it acceptable—even beneficial—to the black race. Others might use unproved scientific systems like phrenology and Darwin's ideas to subjugate whole new categories of men. He concluded that untested principles are even more dangerous in the hands of men in high places than they are in the mouths of common men like his father. He had just about dismissed phrenology after seeing bravery in men classified "weak;" weakness in men labeled "courageous;" and stupidity in men stamped "intelligent" by the system.

Alexander Neil had graduated from the Cincinnati College of Medicine and Surgery in 1863. Although he had lived in Ohio, his roots were Virginian. He had graduated from Ohio Wesleyan University in 1858 before enrolling in the College of Medicine. As John walked with him in the fields near the Chickahominy he felt something like kinship with this newcomer to the regiment. If the intellectual grounds they occupied were not identical, at least John could understand his thoughts and gain a sense of him. Neil was practical and spoke most of ideas that were useful. John was logical and spoke most of ideas that were true. Alexander Neil tended to deflect tension with humor and sarcasm. John was more inclined to pursue troublesome subjects to some sort of rational conclusion. There was a balance between the two. John had, over time, grown tolerant of different modes in men.

Other than to point them out, no one among the men commented much about the sun-bleached bones of dead comrades and enemies strewn about the field. These were sure reminders of shared transience. Rebel bones looked exactly like loyal bones. It troubled some that bones were neither blue nor gray. Each knew from experience that the crack of a sniper's rifle could deposit his own bones in this soil at any moment.

The whole command halted on the field. No one seemed to know why. Neil reached down and picked up a skull. Men gathered densely around as he held it in his left hand and inspected it, while the thumb and forefinger of his right hand held his rounded chin and stroked his whiskers. The white skull had a round hole, obviously made by a musket ball, situated in the center of the forehead. The back had been shattered. As Neil examined the skull he turned it slowly around so as to show observers its condition. Tension grew. He spoke as though giving a lecture. Soldiers listened intently.

"Gentlemen," he began, "examining the bumps upon this cranium hastily, yet as carefully as circumstances will at present permit, assisted by the light of past and passing events, I think that I may say, with a confidence amounting to conviction, and that you will be justified in accepting my statement as an assured fact, that the original possessor of this poll was evidently of a more or less combative disposition."

Men laughed.

"And gentlemen, judging from the light of current history, and the apparent time that this skull has lain where it was picked up, and the patent, convincing, ocular evidence sustaining me in the assertion, I have no doubt that the wearer of this cranium died of a gun shot wound."

He mounded up soil and placed the skull atop it, facing the rear of the column. The men once again began to move forward. John did not know how to take a measure of what had just transpired. He would not have thought it proper to do what Neil had just done if anyone had asked his opinion in advance. He sensed that he would someday meet with disapproving looks if he were to attempt to explain and justify it after the war. Even so, men who had been tense and unsettled a few moments before while stiffly marching through this field of bones, were now smiling and striding with a renewed spring in their steps. Their burdens were lightened. The lecture was repeated by others, imperfectly and with a fading resemblance to the original, as the column moved past the bleached skull on the mound of soil.

No rule of logic could account for the evident truth that men had been powerfully touched by outlandish remarks in ways that no studied philosopher could approximate with refined syllogisms. A space opened up in John, allowing him to embrace other modes even when he could not be completely understand them. Whether or not he could learn to use them and identify those moments when such humor might be used with good effect, John would from this time forward allow that it belonged in the mix of meaningful human interactions.

*   *   *   *

SHE FELT CLEANSED

Her hand moved uncertainly across the page as she tried to put into words the truths of her heart in ways that would not create needless pain for John McMorrow. Anna Lee had already discarded three attempts and watched them burn to ash in the fireplace. If all were as it should be, she thought, she would have no need to hide her thoughts or words from Micah. It would be safe to tell him openly and he would understand. Some truths, she felt, were only dishonorable in their false translation. She trusted John and his sense of honor and his ability to keep her words from eyes that might misjudge them. When she had thought of waiting to speak them with her lips, instead of expressing them with paper and ink out of fear that her printed words might be less safe, she felt guilty for mistrusting John. After winning the protracted debate with herself, Anna Lee had concluded that she could trust him with written words as much as she could trust him with spoken thoughts—and she could think about and choose written words.

Maybe the prospect of the war's end pressed her to complete this matter, she thought. Maybe Anna Lee could clarify and tie up loose ends before she would see John face-to-face. She did not want to end her relationship with him as much as she felt a need to define it—or help define it—for both of them. Her sense of honesty required her to tell him of her enduring affection for him, while her sense of propriety demanded caution. Wedding vows had not worked some sort of magic that erased John. Conceiving a child had cemented the vows and somehow finalized the commitments, making it possible to encounter John McMorrow with simple honesty and perfect trust. As Anna Lee wrote she realized that lack of self-trust had held her back in the past and that she was now certain enough of her fidelity to Micah that she could safely share feelings, carefully, with John.

Somehow, she could now use words that she had felt less free to use when circumstances would have allowed them in the minds of others. She told John that she loved him and that she sensed that she would always love him. In using the word that she had held back before she sensed the need to talk about it. She wrote of her love for her mother and of its dimensions and qualities; of her love for her father and of its elements; and of her love for Micah and of its commitments. All of these, she said, were real and deep and meaningful. Her love for Micah had obligations attached and a mutual loyalty that would allow them to build a family and endure whatever hardships that might await them. Her affection for her parents differed from her affection for her sister. Her warmth for Micah was real and her hopes for their future together were genuine and wonderful. As she explained these things to John she found her confidence growing and sensed that he would understand and appreciate knowing her heart.

She carefully chose words to describe her affection for John that she hoped would strengthen him and further their friendship, without threatening Micah or the home that she had made with him. At the same time she felt that she owed enough honesty to keep him from being cheated of love that was completely his. She pledged a lifetime of committed friendship to him. "Friendship" seemed too weak a word, but she stumbled over the alternatives. She confessed to having a physical attraction for John and asked him to help her to cope with this in honorable ways when he would see her again. She admitted to an ongoing yearning for his well-being and a deep interest in his future happiness. She apologized for not writing often and telling him of her horror every time she read of battles in which the 12th West Virginia had taken part, and of her tears of relief when she learned that he had made it through. She poured out heartfelt pain, spawned by fear that harm might yet befall him before the war would close. She declared that she had never prayed more fervently for anything or anyone as passionately as she had daily begged heaven for John's safety.

In concluding the letter, she asked him to hold her thoughts in complete confidence. She winced when she asked him not to reply directly—by sending a letter to her home address. She suggested that he might want to wait until his return to talk with her about what she had said, or that he might want to send a reply through someone who could be completely trusted. She paused after penning the latter, and then added that she would trust his judgment completely as to how he would reply as long as he was aware that it was her wish to keep their correspondence between the two of them alone.

When she finished the letter and sealed the envelope Anna Lee felt uneasy about its presence in the bottom of her drawer. After she passed it on to her sister to mail on her way through Clarksburg, she felt relieved to have it out of the house. After Katie reported with a wry smile that she had mailed it, and was on its way to John, she felt cleansed. She had a sense that her life had been brought up to date, even if the matter did not seem to be completely finished.

CHAPTER 14

A GREAT CHEER ROLLED UP

The rain drummed a monotonous cadence on the stiff canvas of John's shelter. On March 29, after days of expecting momentous events to transpire, life had reverted to the mundane. Tedium is more obvious when soldiers expect something else.

John had been preparing himself and his men for some final movement that would be their last and end the war. He had regained a measure of respect for generals. If he and his men would trust the judgment and orders from current leaders; if they would charge with a united will and hold back nothing; then they might be glorious participants in the last actions of the war. John reminded his comrades of New Market and of Sigel's claims that they had not done their duty. His little speeches roused the men and stimulated John himself, but such a state is difficult to maintain for stretches of time without some beginning of fulfillment.

The movement that had planted the regiment near Humphrey's Station stopped there. On the 17th they had crossed the James and the Appomattox rivers and marched toward the left and in the rear of the Union lines southwest of Petersburg. Their blood had warmed that day as they heard heavy firing along the lines to their right, at no great distance, as they marched. The musketry combined with rumors of great action to lead them to think that the moment was near when the final assault would end the war. Farther down the Union lines to the left they heard cannons roar. But now they were camped and cold water drummed dreary sounds that connected this night with uncounted nights in the past stretching all the way back to the day they had mustered into the army. All of those nights had terminated in dawns betokening more days and more nights of discomfort, danger, and death. Experience made it impossible to hold onto an expectation that this night, or the next day, would be different.

At daybreak on March 30 the division moved on as the rain soaked men and soil and as thousands of feet churned mud. A wagon train of ambulances filled with wounded men from the 5th Corps passed them on its way to the rear. Then wagons loaded with Rebel prisoners went by. Something was happening. The sense of inaction gave way to the pain of being cheated once again—of the chance to take part in the action evidenced by wounded men and prisoners. Trudging through muck so far in the rear, John wanted desperately to turn his men to the front. The 12th West Virginia spent that night, like the last, listening to the interminable drumming of raindrops on canvas.

In the morning the rain stopped. The division continued its movement in the rear of the line and farther down to the left. Heavy firing broke out in the front. "Get your heads down, men." John shouted with a sense of satisfaction. "Something's brewing up ahead, but we can't get into it from here!" After a pause the column moved on. Evening shadows fell and pickets ringed the camp. Drummers beating *Tattoo* put them to bed while continuous musket fire and the intermittent blasts of siege-guns kept restless men waiting for the opportunity to finish the war.

Captain McMorrow flew from his tent and called his company into line to await orders. It was still dark but nearing morning. Loud and heavy musketry had broken out among the pickets very near the camp. He had his men load their muskets and fix bayonets as they waited. Soon reports filtered back that the Rebels had charged the skirmish line of the division, but had been sent flying.

After an uneasy breakfast and an uncertain morning, matters became clearer when orders came from General Grant. The 6th Corps was to attack the Rebel lines to their front as early as possible on April 2. All the other troops present, including the 12th West Virginia, were to be ready to attack.

The attack by the 6th Corps broke the enemy lines and the Rebels evacuated their entrenchments. The brigade marched now to the right and toward Petersburg. They arrived near the city just before noon. All the Rebel works were now under Union control with the exception of three small forts. As the 12th West Virginia neared its position in sight of the forts some soldiers from some other unit standing alongside the route surveyed the relative newcomers to the Army of the Potomac and seemed to have reason to believe that hard-fighting was yet ahead. One shouted to the others, "I wonder if these fellows will stand up to it?"

John McMorrow liked the question. "Did you hear that, men? They want to know if the men of the 12th West Virginia Infantry will be able to stand up to it. Tell them to tag along and watch!"

The brigade marched up and halted on the high ground facing Fort Gregg. From their position they saw open ground between them and the fort, maybe 500 yards distant. The field sloped down and then rose again to the trenches around Fort Gregg. Below and to the right were men from the 1st Division, taking fire from the fort but making no forward movement toward it. As they watched, Captain McMorrow commented to those near him that it seemed more dangerous to stay on the open ground than to rush toward the fort.

An aide rode up to Colonel Curtis and spoke to him rapidly in words that John could not hear. The Colonel's face went white. Unflinching, Curtis rode forward and announced the order: "Attention! 2nd Brigade. Shoulder arms. Right shoulder shift, arms. Forward. Double quick, march!"

The line surged forward with a yell approximating the famous "Rebel yell" they had heard coming at them so many times before. At first the line held together at the double quick, and then it cut into a broken line going forward at speeds never tried by these men before. The rate of movement now depended upon each man's individual ability to run, and his inclination to be ahead of the others. "Forward, men. Forward!" Captain McMorrow had his sword pointed to the fort with his left hand and his pistol in his right. His commands were only to encourage what the men were already doing. John had to run at his own top speed to keep up with the general center of his company. Only those nearest could hear him anyway because of the incessant yelling.

They had not yet begun to fire when they reached the bottom of the hill where low swamp brush and mud slowed them enough to force them into something more like a line of battle. Here the Rebels opened with canister that thudded into the mud and tore at the swamp brush. No one really stopped here. John was shocked to see that few of the men had been hit as the line gushed like a wave up the hill toward the fort. John took in what was happening as the men of the 1st Division poured fire at the parapet and subdued the Rebel fire.

Private James W. Caldwell of Company D took off his hat and swung it over his head as he shouted, "That's our fort! That's our fort!" just before a lead ball tore through his chest and laid him on the field. The color-bearer, Sergeant Emanuel Adams from the same company fell within 50 yards of the wall. Private Joseph R. Logsdon of Company C recovered the flag as he charged over the dead and wounded men of the 1st Division who had gone before him.

The 12th West Virginia rushed on with the others into the deep ditch surrounding the fort. Rebels who risked moving to the parapet and firing down on them were soon cut down, but rocks, and dirt, and metal rained down on them from inside the fort. The men paused in the ditch, knowing that death awaited the first to try to go over the parapet above them.

Private Logsdon climbed the loose dirt, mounted the parapet and tried to plant the flag of the 12th West Virginia before he was cut to pieces by shots fired within the fort. His lifeless body tumbled into the ditch as Lieutenant Joseph Caldwell from Company A scrambled up the wall—his hands bloodied from clawing at soil and rock—and leaped upon the parapet, took up the flag and tried to plant it. His bloody and torn body tumbled back into the ditch as the flag fell into the fort. As if on command, the whole regiment rushed to the parapet to recover the flag. Captain McMorrow sheathed his sword and holstered his pistol as he shouted for his men, most already ahead of him, to follow him up the banked soil. Reaching the top, he saw that others had planted the colors of the 12th West Virginia firmly on the parapet. He drew sword and pistol and waded through his own men trying to find a target. No white flags showed. No Rebel soldiers had hands raised in surrender.

Good men were falling around him, but John could not see far through the acrid smoke and biting dust. Men poured in behind him, pushing him forward while he looked for gaps through which to move as he stumbled over writhing men, some grabbing at his legs. He lunged through an opening and found himself facing Rebel soldiers still in the fight. Off to his left he heard someone shout, "Drop that lanyard or I'll shoot!" And then he heard the deadly reply, "Shoot and be damned!" and the blast of a cannon and the continuous roar of muskets. A Rebel soldier with fire in his eyes lunged at him with a bayonet—he instinctively slashed at the arm behind the left hand at the forward part of the musket and regarded the resulting gash as though he were a spectator rather than the man who had made it. When the man cradled the musket in his torn arm and came at him again, John fired his pistol into the chest at point blank range and turned for another target without watching the result. He pointed his pistol and sword in response to rapid movement, but no men in gray were on their feet and near, only Union soldiers rushing forward through the gaps.

And then the fighting was over. The hot blood coursing through veins had not cooled or slowed, but the motion—furious and intense—suddenly ceased like a storm that gives no warning or shows evidence of slowing before abruptly stopping. Emotions have momentum that is sometimes inconsistent with changed realities. It took Captain McMorrow's gorged senses a stretch of time to begin to digest what they had consumed. The business of collecting involuntary prisoners who had been overpowered and captured without surrendering seemed a serene thing, unworthy of the careful focus he knew he must give to it.

The capture of Fort Gregg had cost the Union 715 in dead and wounded. Dancing joined the spirited songs around the fires that night. Some men, however, were as somber as they had ever been in their lives. The singers and dancers had shared the same events with the others, but human responses to horrific events cannot be predicted, anticipated, or explained with accuracy like things purely physical. What drives one man to his knees might well compel another to leap for joy. What propels one into the company of his fellows might send the other looking for solitude.

John McMorrow was both an observer and a participant in the variations of response to death and destruction and loss and victory—seen up close. His laughter and rapid speech around the fire were somewhat controlled by his observation of them. He supposed that these were all common consequences to uncommon events. He learned from fellow officers that Colonel Curtis had not fully intended to order a charge just yet—at the time he had ordered the men to go forward at the double quick—and that the general had actually issued orders, unheard by the men charging forward, calling off the assault after it had begun. This struck John McMorrow at that moment as certainly the funniest thing that he had ever heard in his entire life. He laughed uncontrollably and literally could not master himself to stop even when a few of his fellow-officers got up and walked away at the news. Others shared the irony of the joke and recalled the assertions of another general who claimed to have issued orders that had been unheeded by the 12th West Virginia at New Market.

After Fort Gregg, these men would be pleased—thrilled—if the commanding general wanted to issue public statements to the four winds that the men of the 12th West Virginia had disobeyed orders to retreat in the face of danger—that they had made this assault contrary to orders. John thought it would be a wonderful thing to spread such truths—to remove the credit from the hands of the generals and to deposit it in the accounts of men who earned it for a change.

The taking of Fort Gregg was over, but the war was not. On the morning of April 3 the regiment awakened to learn that Lee's forces had evacuated Richmond and Petersburg. The Union forces went off in pursuit. No one in the ranks really seemed to know just what they were supposed to be accomplishing as they covered mile after mile of exhausting marching. Some segments of the army still encountered Rebel soldiers—and prisoners were still brought in here and there, but the men were, for the most part, marching for days in response to orders without much sense of mission. Questions arose in the ranks concerning the likelihood of catching the Rebels—and of engaging in another battle soon and about the outcome if such were to happen.

The regiment was no longer spoiling for a fight. Some had no desire to find the fleeing Rebels. As they marched on, John heard a private declare, "I've seen enough of the Rebels. If they are fleeing I hope we never catch them. I hope they run until they come to the Gulf of Mexico." Another put in: "If I have to fight Rebels at all I'm willing to do it right now. No sense followin' them for weeks at this pace and then having to fight them after all."

Of course, no one in authority listened to these opinions. The men of the regiment who held them would likely have considered them more carefully if they had power to put them into play. Powerless men are free and quick in their interpretations and opinions. Responsible men cannot afford to be.

On April 9, before the dawn, the regiment marched from its camp and soon started on the double-quick. As they clanked along at this rapid pace some Union cavalry appeared out of the woods to the right. One of the horsemen exclaimed loudly, "Here come the Doe boys!" He rode up and reported to no one in particular that the Rebels had up the black flag.

The regiment halted, and then formed into line across the roads. They were, according to the horsemen, a short distance west of a place called Appomattox Court House. In conjunction with all the other regiments in the two divisions they moved cautiously and slowly forward. Shells crashed through the tree tops, but none seemed to be causing much harm.

Then they halted. Grim-faced and tired men looked ahead, expecting battle. "It'll be good to meet 'em on open ground instead of storming breastworks." said one. "I say we push ahead and find them and finish this thing once and for all," said another. Two hours or so passed as men gave advice that would have no effect whatever.

At about 9:00 that morning the order passed down the line: "Cease fire. Cease fire! Until further orders no one is to fire his musket." This was not just some rumor spreading through the ranks. It came through the officers—who would not issue orders based upon hearsay. But what could it mean?

John McMorrow listened to the theories and formulated his own. He recalled the first time these men had been under fire, when they had interpreted the flying of lead to be raindrops and acorns. He listened. Someone suggested that this cease fire must be a Rebel trick to buy time. Finally, John announced his own conclusion. "Men, surely this must mean that the Rebels are either surrendering or discussing the possibility under a flag of truce." This interpretation seemed to become generally, if cautiously, accepted by men who feared to allow themselves to believe such a lie more than they feared the prospect of further bloodshed. So the possibility of a surrender did nothing more than to put the men in a condition of confusion. The pain of being taken in by a glorious lie can be cured in advance with a healthy dose of skepticism.

As the regiment remained halted and waiting, rumors gave way to reliable reports from men who claimed to have seen the white flag. Men who had heard directly from men who had seen Union officers conferring with Rebels began to accept it as the truth. The officers spoke of surrender now as a reality. A little after noon the divisions moved forward toward the Rebels, until they came upon open ground that allowed them to see the Rebel camp. Far to the right a great cheer rolled up from the Union lines, and then a general pause, and then another cheer, and then a pause…. it seemed to move down the line in a wave that grew stronger and stronger. Finally Colonel Curtis rode in front of the regiment and officially announced that the Army of Northern Virginia had surrendered. Some fell silent while others acted out their delirium of joy in physical acts, trying to match the sentiments of their spirits. Shouting was general. Men climbed trees. Frantic men threw hats into the air and then jumped up and down on them where they landed. Some of the silent ones had not yet accepted the truth that the surrender of the Army of Northern Virginia meant final victory and the end of hard marching, constant danger, gnawing hunger, bitter cold without relief, burning heat, close and frequent death, and longing for home.

A short while later they heard their own cheers mirrored in the Rebel camp. As men often do, they assumed that Rebel motives were similar to their own. The sense among the Union soldiers was that the Rebels were just as elated that the end had come and that they were no less exhilarated in defeat than the conquerors were in victory. Union soldiers marveled from a short distance away at the cheering of Rebel soldiers, and assumed that the cheers were their delight at the news of defeat and of having been paroled rather than imprisoned. They were wrong. Rebel soldiers cheered their gallant leader—Robert E. Lee—and expressed gratitude for all that he had done. They were offering to make a final charge upon the Union lines. Presuming to know other's motives is dangerous.

For the rest of the day guards kept the two armies apart. Many had seen a Union officer meeting with Robert E. Lee under an apple tree at Appomattox Court House, so it was generally held that the surrender had taken place there. This was mistaken. There had been a meeting between Union General Orville Babcock, one of Grant's staff officers, and General Lee under the tree, but the actual surrender took place elsewhere. Men from both armies scrambled to get mementos of wood from the tree. They literally tore the tree to the ground. Souvenir seekers were not satisfied until they had taken the last fragment of the roots.

On the day after the surrender the armies mingled freely. No one seemed disposed to fight. It was as though they had never been at war. There was even playful banter. Former Rebels insisted that they would have won if only they had had as many men as the Union could put in the field. Paroled Confederate soldiers were happy to trade their Confederate money for greenbacks and to spend the greenbacks at the Union sutlers.

Captain John McMorrow was elated and disoriented as he strolled the grounds around Appomattox Court House. He came upon another Union officer who was talking with a local citizen. John introduced himself and learned the name of the citizen—Wilmer McLean. With a wry smile and a shaking of his head, McLean said, "I own the ground where the first battle of the war was fought over at Manassas. I got myself and my family away from there to get away from the war. I own this ground where the war ended."

John was already aware of the answer, but it pleased him to hear it said again. "So you men regard the war as being certainly over?"

"Yes." said McLean. "I spoke with General Lee, one of the greatest generals ever to walk on God's green earth, and he regards it as over."

John held his peace, but he had a vague sense that such praise for the Rebel general was not proper at such a time. If McLean was now prepared to pledge loyalty to the Union and submit to the government, how could he call the Rebel general responsible for leading many thousands against that government and its soldiers "one of the greatest generals ever to walk on God's green earth?" Lee, who had been an instrument of treason who had gone so far to attempt to help found a government upon barbarism—slavery—, and who had imprisoned John's comrades at Andersonville and Libby and elsewhere,—killed so many others—could not be, in John's thinking, a great man. John walked away, grateful for the confirmation that the war was now over but muddled by the sentiments of the late Rebel citizen.

In a camp without pickets or enemy threats the men sat around fires and pieced together events that fused to become that single event—the war—and to pose theories about the future of the blended Union. The South would have adjustments to make. The North would have decisions. Would the North follow the lead of Lincoln and Grant in showing gentle leniency? Would hotter heads find ways to pour out punishing wrath? Would the South follow the lead of Lee and set aside the Southern cause for the sake of peace at the close of the settled matter? Or would many count that the South had not yet reached the last ditch, and search for ways to press on? Some answered these questions with clear opinions about what would happen and about what ought to happen.

As the discussions, which would have no effect upon policy, continued, John McMorrow resigned himself to the fact that he was both ignorant and powerless with regard to the greater scheme of things. His thoughts were drawn more immediately to his own future. He planned to return home but he was only remotely aware that home was less a point on the map than a condition, and that he could not really return there, even if he were to go back to Clarksburg. If a home was to be made in Clarksburg, it would be a new one rather than the condition that he had left behind. The thought of returning, or of going to the new circumstances in the place where he had long lived, to find Anna Lee married to Micah Johnson and carrying a child was sharp. Like the fear of battle, it seemed that the entrance would be more difficult than what might follow, but the entrance into that world still lay ahead. So he resigned himself to uncertainty and ignorance, and to pick berries in the fields that lay between him and that event.

While the 12th West Virginia camped at Appomattox one of many released slaves wandered into camp. "Where will you go now that you are free?" John was probing for some sense of how the outcome of the war touched this man.

The black man seemed unaware that matters had changed. "North with the ahmy seems da only way fa me. If ah goes home massa'll be hot to whip me. Ah run off when da soldiers come."

John explained to him that he was now free, really free, to go wherever he wished to go and to do whatever he chose to do. When he explained the Emancipation Proclamation and the surrender of Lee's army the man just looked straight ahead and rubbed his hands together. John sensed that realities were not sinking in for this man any more than they were sinking in for himself. The man explained that his wife and children had been sold off to some place that he could not name—that was his reason for running off. John offered genuine sympathy for the injustice of it all, but as he tried to put it in the perspective of a righted injustice the man seemed to take more pleasure in sympathy than in the prospect of now being in a position to reclaim his family and to attempt some new beginning.

"Do you plan to go find them?"

"Maybe."

John felt incredibly like this man who had known only slavery. The responsibility of making decisions when one has been accustomed to obeying orders weighs on the mind. John had obeyed orders for a matter of a few short years that seemed a lifetime. This visitor to the camp had known nothing else and now faced the horror of freedom for the first time. It was as though they had met on the road coming from opposite directions, taken a turn together, and found themselves facing the same frightening issue.

The Confederate soldiers were all paroled and sent home in peace. On April 12 the division marched for Lynchburg. It arrived there on the 14th. The streets were lined with cheering blacks who were wild with joy as they hooked arms together and danced and shouted, "Glory be to God! Da Yanks am come and we's free!" The meaning would come to them later.

By the 24th the command marched to Richmond. They were paid to the first of January 1865, and remained near the city until they were finally mustered out of the army on June 16. Strangely, John was in no great hurry to receive his discharge papers. He had no difficulty waiting, until the letter came from Anna Lee.

The letter somehow completed a circle for him while leaving an empty void at the center. It revealed that he had not lost her love, that he yet held a precious connection with her. John's sense of loss began to heal. His trust in his own sense of what had passed between them was somewhat restored by Anna Lee's words. In fact, he felt more trusted by her now than he had felt before. For an honorably married woman expecting her first child to risk such words only for his benefit seemed generous. His love for her took on new shapes and larger dimensions. Once again, he felt that Anna Lee—Johnson—was his closest friend. The reciprocal aspect of it all gave him a sense of warmth like nothing had in a very long time.

John accepted the likelihood that he could not have Anna Lee as his lover and wife and that she would not be the mother of his children. He at least accepted the reality that dramatic and painful events would have to occur before that could be possible—and he rebuked himself for entertaining the transient hope that Micah would die. But with all the rules and limitations and restraints where they now stood, he was warmed by the certain knowledge that he and Anna Lee could love one another and speak quietly of it without shame.

Virginia and West Virginia would soon be rejoined. Virginia would be readmitted to the Union. They would remain two states and separate, but a new unity would exist between them. Anna Lee would be separated in a sense that John could not have imagined a year earlier, but he now sensed the possibility of a new unity that would have a chance of working—and lasting. *Maybe.*

While the 12th West Virginia waited on one beautiful June afternoon, they were marched close to Richmond as the shadows of another unguarded night fell. A solemn ceremony helped to conclude the long episode of the Civil War. The 12th West Virginia won its eagle, Colonel Curtis won his general's stars, and

Captain Bristor won his promotion to major for gallant conduct at Fort Gregg. Lieutenant Josiah M. Curtis, Private Andrew O. Apple, and Private Joseph McCauslin won medals of honor. Some of the boys from Company I grumbled a bit because they felt that their own Private George H. Bird should have been recognized with a medal of honor for having been among the first to climb the parapet. The regiment marched away feeling that it had been rightly honored for its role, and for the price it paid in putting down the late rebellion. No one mentioned unheard orders or failures to obey.

On the 20th of June civilian John McMorrow set out with his regiment, still in uniform, for home. By water they floated to Baltimore. By rail they rattled to Wheeling, where they arrived on the 24th. There they were paid for the remainder of their time in service and received official discharge certificates. Each gave final farewells to comrades at a fine dinner provided by the grateful citizens of Wheeling. The next day John sat on a crowded train with a mixed assortment of familiar faces on the way to Clarksburg. He chatted amiably and animatedly with all, but he felt especially gratified when the big man across the aisle looked him in the eye and spoke to him as an equal. It was Edmund Jasper Smith who had shared his first trip out of Wheeling—so long ago.

John tried to sleep, but issues loomed at Clarksburg that struck him as bigger than the possibility of battle. His mouth was dry as the train slowed and he saw folks waiting at the station. John scanned the crowd until he saw Anna Lee, her face aglow and her eyes locked on his. Anna Lee stepped forward and when they embraced John felt the bulge at about the same time he noticed his father, Mr. and Mrs. Stone, and Micah coming through the crowd.

Chapter 15

"I Only Wish You'd Put Your Foot Down Sooner."

John McMorrow's marriage to the former Alice Stout began sixteen years and three months after their wedding and five months after he had completely given up hope. When his marriage began he was the father of two boys in their early teens whom he loved deeply. No observer, not even the boys, knew of the long delay between the wedding and the marriage. Everyone assumed that all was nearly perfect between John and Alice from the start.

After the war John had relocated to Clarksburg, where he returned to teaching at the small college and caring for his father. His brothers had died as prisoners of war. He kept up the farm and dabbled in carpentry after his father died of consumption in March of 1869. He found renewed pleasure in impressing principles of thought upon young minds, who had as yet experienced so little of life. Cocky young students, who seemed so certain of things far beyond them, amused him. His challenges to them were gentle but firm. Political questions once again served as fodder for illustrating classroom discussions, more than as matters requiring his direct involvement. He learned again to love the smells of the farm—hay, manure, and animal sweat. Roaming the hills on cool and colorful fall days in search of game connected him with his childhood and his father and his brothers. It mattered little to him if he left the woods empty handed. Before his wedding he ate most of his meals alone. Hunting was sport. Food from other sources was always plentiful and available. His closest ties were with comrades from the 12th West Virginia, but their chance meetings were infrequent after the war. He attended most of the reunions.

John had met Alice at church. Anna Lee had introduced them and encouraged the courtship. During their courting days, John had so badly wanted to find love and begin a family that he allowed himself to see what was not there. On a picnic he leaned against a tree, looked at the passing clouds of white in the pure blue sky through the green canopy of leaves, and spoke of his hopes and dreams as easily as if he were talking to Anna Lee. Alice said that she shared them all. His hopes of having a fine family, she said, were her hopes. His detailed principles of parenting, she agreed, matched the very principles that she had always believed in. His desire to lead a simple life on the farm while teaching at the college, she said, agreed perfectly with her own long-held wishes. As he looked into the clouds and spoke of his deep longings, he neglected to notice that Alice never spoke first.

On the evening of their wedding Alice announced that she hoped they could move into town soon. "I could never be happy living on a dreary old farm," she said, as though she had just considered the question for the first time. Within weeks she expressed the desire that John study law and begin exploring a career in politics. "Teaching in a college is good, for a beginning," she declared, "but there are bigger colleges and bigger opportunities away from here. We will make a much better living in greater style when we finally get you started looking at what you can do. College professors make good senators and such, but they don't go straight from Clarksburg to Washington without some other steps." John would only say that he had not considered these things before, but that he might give them some thought if it would please her.

Alice soon made it clear that she disapproved of most things in John. He dressed to simply. His ambitions were too low. His salary was small. His manners embarrassed her. While they were courting, she had never ceased to smile when they were together. Now that they had exchanged wedding vows, she frowned at all that he did. When he brought her flowers she complained that she would rather have had the money he used to purchase them. When he built the cupboard exactly as she had described it and precisely as he had sketched it out for her, she insisted that they throw it away and buy one elsewhere.

The newlyweds had spent their first Thanksgiving together with Alice's parents. Her mother smiled constantly and chatted amiably as she and Alice laid out the finest china in the house. John felt completely bewildered when Alice boasted about him to her parents and smiled fondly at him when she spoke.

As mother and daughter talked about days gone by, the conversation turned to one of Alice's friends. "What has become of Margaret?" her mother asked. "The girl who laughed so loud in public places and drew so much attention to herself?" Alice responded, "She's still living at home with her parents. She doesn't have many men chasing her right now." Her mother grimaced and said, "It's a shame about her weight. If she could just lose those extra pounds until she could latch onto a man, she could put it back on and not worry about it anymore after the wedding." Alice agreed. They continued setting the table—perfectly.

John felt the personal force of what the two had said. This mother and daughter shared the value that it was reasonable, and normal, to do whatever needed to be done to "latch onto a man," and then to quit whatever the strategy had been as soon as he had been caught. He felt insulted rather than complimented when Alice's mother spoke of how pleased she was with the man Alice had caught. He excused himself and took a walk in the woods.

It had been some time since John had allowed himself to think of the stark honesty of Anna Lee and the evident genuineness of her affection. Now, as he walked beneath the multicolored leaves and the dark evening clouds, he envied Micah and cursed his own fortune. John could not speak of these things to Anna Lee across the distance that weddings and births had placed between them, but he imagined that she would understand. Although they had seen one another a great many times over the past several years, they had not talked of their relationship since he first spoke to her upon returning from the war. Then he had thanked her for the honesty of her letter and pledged to her his enduring friendship within the limits imposed by circumstances. He still felt that he held a signed contract, and that Anna Lee knew that her title to that pledged portion of him remained good. The pact bore no date, but he wondered if it might be reasonable to renew it from time to time with fresh words. He sensed that the pleasure of such repeated words—both spoken and heard—might be less important than the safety of leaving them unspoken. At least he could imagine that the contract was still in force without any harm. The belief was a mountain of strength for him.

After his passions had cooled on the autumn breeze, John returned to the home of his in-laws in time for the meal. He was pleasant enough for one enduring a distance produced by deception. He formulated a new way of viewing his entrapment that allowed him to work for a slow escape, and permit him to take Alice with him. He determined that he would work to lead her toward better thinking by gentle example and kind, reasoned, prodding. As he ate his meal with a counterfeit smile and listened to the superficial talk around the table, he felt that he finally understood how this family had produced Alice. He thought of the challenges ahead of him. Divorce was out of the question. The Scriptures were clear enough on that. Patience would be required and the Scriptures had much to say on that too. Children would be coming—at least that was a likelihood since

Alice would occasionally reward his attempts to please her with brief moments of physical intimacy. John would school them in every virtue, even if he had to contradict the shallow traditions that might compete at home. Guiding his children was one goal that he would not turn loose. As he pondered his disappointment in the discoveries he had made since the wedding he heard the faint echo of his father's voice: "You'll have 'at."

For years John tried to use opportunities that presented themselves naturally to explain principles to Alice that she seemed not to understand. When she left him sitting in the street in the wagon while she shopped, he waited patiently and then explained to her that he would "much prefer" working out some other plan that took both of their needs and wishes into account. She told him that this was nonsense and that he would be happy to wait if he really loved her. He sometimes expressed his anger forcefully, but he waited in the wagon in the street the next time, and the next, and at every similar time in the future for years. When John bought Alice gifts and when she disliked them after getting them, he attempted to express his frustration calmly and to try to help her to see the pain of a man who yearned to please her. But he continued to pursue her with more gifts that she rejected. When he took her to places that he thought she would enjoy, and when she despised them, he worked to find amusements that might please her. He wore himself out in the effort. When she demanded that he go to bed at whatever hour she wanted, because she could not stand the noise of his coming later, he protested; but he complied in the hopes that he could win her over with reason while pursuing the goal of pleasing her. Sometimes he won permission to stay up later, as long as she approved of his explanations. Through those years she complained about the money he failed to bring home, the things she could not possess, the status that she could have enjoyed if only she had married someone else, and his inability to measure up to what her mother and father had hoped she would find in a husband.

In public Alice was another woman. She would smile and stand close to him—and engender the good-will of all their friends. He realized that her public image enhanced his own standing. Folks at church warmed to her. Among their closest friends, Alice talked as if she and John were deeply in love when this seemed a thing that would impress them. At times she would hint, in ways that seemed to John subtly risque, that their private love life was marvelous. Even as their children grew old enough to notice, Alice would hug him at times when they were present. At times she would even kiss him, just when one of the children was about to enter the room. She would say to him after such orchestrated episodes: "I think its good for them to catch us in affectionate moments." But when Alice was alone with John, she turned to ice. John had come to feel like nothing more than one of the props decorating Alice's carefully scripted show. He enjoyed the public pretense even less than the private disdain. She interfered little in the training of the children—seemed pleased to have little to do in that regard. She basked in the public approval of her intelligent and well-behaved offspring except when they spoke their own minds in ways that threatened to diminish her standing.

Finally after fifteen years and ten months of concentrated effort, John McMorrow gave up. He had no energy left to pursue her. Alice had sucked all of his emotional strength. John felt drained of all reserves of potential passion. He did not choose to wear out, but he recognized that he had no more vitality with which to continue the struggle. Then, when Alice spoke to their teen-aged sons at the supper table of her hopes that their father would be finding a better position at a more respectable institution he interrupted her. "No, Alice. There is nothing of the sort in the works. If they'll keep me on here, I'll likely die here of old age." She glared at him and he did absolutely nothing to lessen the glare. Instead, he looked her in the eye and said, "Now I hope you can find some way to learn to live with that."

For days she did not speak to him. Before, he would have pressed flowers into her hands and endured her displeasure at the money spent; he would have offered gifts of things and of words and weathered the insults they would have produced. Now, he left her alone and she spoke to him only in the presence of those who might be impressed with their close relationship.

When she finally spoke to him she suggested that maybe it would be best if she just went back to her parents to live. He was not sure if this was some new manipulative bluff or an honest intention, but neither moved him. "The boys and I will be fine. You go and do what you must do." She flew into a rage and told him that if he really loved her he would correct whatever was bothering her rather than send her off. "Think of what people will say when I leave you. It'll set the whole town to talking." John knew that she spoke of her own concerns more than of his. He did not like the prospect of people thinking less of him on account of his wife leaving him for a few days, or longer, but he knew the effect would be devastating to her. "I can live with it Alice. I will not try to stop you if you want to go home—or anywhere else you decide."

And then Alice tripped the one trigger that could yet touch John. "You hate your own children. Otherwise you'd keep us happy." The boys had just entered the next room. Footsteps told of their nearness. She had said such things before when she wanted to set John to proving his love, but he was no longer prepared to do that. As calmly as he could manage, John asked the boys to step outside. Then he turned to Alice with eyes she had never seen.

"Alice. I am finished trying to please you." She tried to interrupt but John raised his hand and his voice. "Alice. Alice., I've devoted most of my life— years—trying to please you, trying to be a man who can please you, trying to help you to grow up by words that have not been consistent with my actions. Those days are over. They are gone! Now you have some adjustments to make. I have no demands to make of you. I have never had any demands to make of you. My only request—no—my firm position is that I no longer care to know of your opinions of me, of my work, of my income, of my talents, of my dress, of my bedtime, or of my plans for the future. I refuse to be enslaved by your self-centered and shallow ways. I'm worn out. I have no more such efforts to offer, even if I could find the will. You have sucked the joy out of my life, and I will pursue life in the future without reference to you. You must learn to adjust. I don't care what you think and don't want to know what you think. Let that sink in. Pursue whatever course you want. I'll not get in your way. Go home to your parents if you want. I mean that. Leave me if you want. Stay if you will, under conditions as they now stand, but leave me alone. You have the same freedoms that you've had since the wedding. I am just asserting that I'll claim for the rest of my life those freedoms as well. I'll say only this about your freedom to speak to my children or in the presence of my children. If you ever again use my children for your own ends in ways that might harm them I will not remain passive. That's a promise. I've no way to know in advance what steps I might take to protect them, but I want you to understand clearly that I will not stand by while you harm them. Do you have any questions?"

Alice glared at him for a full minute. Then she turned and walked out the door, slamming it. John did not know whether or not she had understood a word of what he had finally found the courage to say. He had no way to know the effect. But he felt wonderfully alive for the first time in his own home.

Alice withheld all signs of affection and attention for weeks. She said nothing about going to bed in the evening. She just went. John ignored it, and rather enjoyed his newly asserted freedom. Alice did not leave. John did not ask her opinions about his clothing or things that he made of wood—or of anything else that he might have asked about before. During those weeks of silence he supposed that she was possibly working for a reversal of John's resolve, that she was possibly feeling some pain in the changes he had made. He felt good about bursting shackles that he now knew he should have never accepted. Whatever Alice would do about the changes, for John they were final.

The line that marked the end of the silence arose when John's oldest son suggested that he would like to have a new sled for Christmas, and added: "But Mother says we can't afford it because you're not willing to get a better job." John felt the pain again and assured his son that he had told his mother no such thing.

The only thing to be done was to confront Alice immediately. He did. "Is it true that you told your sons that they can't have things because I refuse to get a better job?" Alice literally had not spoken to John for weeks when he asked without warning.

She did not raise her eyes. "Yes. I said that but—"

John interrupted her, "I will not stand for that. I don't know what you need to do to correct yourself with your son, but I have already corrected the notion as far as I am concerned! If you continue to use my sons to further your childish ends I will deal with them honestly. At the very least you are going to lose all respect from your own children." She tried to speak but John would not give an opening. She hung her head and listened. John continued, "I'm not finished yet. You can respond when I've had my say! Do you hear me? I will not stand for it! Leave if you must, but you will refrain from putting your selfish ways into my boys. Do you hear me?"

And then she looked up. "Yes, John. I hear you." Her voice was calm and her eyes were soft. Tears flowed. "Can I answer you now?" John was taken aback. This was a new mode for Alice, and for him when he was with her.

"What would you like to say, Alice? What possible defense are you going to try to make?" His voice softened, but it was firm and in earnest.

She answered calmly. "John, you're right. I said what I said about your refusal to get a better job and now I'm ashamed that I said it. I said it before you laid things out for me a few weeks ago. I'll never say anything like it again. I promise."

She tried to hug him, but he pulled back. "I'm not interested in that from you. Just see that you watch what you do to my sons. You're not going to pull me back into your web again."

Alice walked away and gently closed the door behind her.

Over the next few weeks John felt energized. The very presence of his sons filled him with pleasure. He felt renewed interest in the growth of his students. He found more pleasure in working with his hands than he had years. As he worked the soil he experienced the earthy smells and textures that he had not noticed for some time. The sun soaked into his pores. Breezes touched grateful flesh.

Alice tried to approach him as never before. For months this became the greatest annoyance in John's life since the war. She insisted that she had learned from him that life is not all appearance. Alice now agreed that she had mistreated him for a long time, and said that she wanted to make it all up to him. He would not hear it at first. His life had been renewed by escaping her grasp and he was not about to return to it. "No one," he said to her, "can change overnight in the ways that you say you have changed. Please understand, Alice, that I was not demanding changes in you. I only meant to inform you of my own. When I entrusted my heart to you, you ripped it out and stomped it. I took it back. I can't easily give you that chance again."

Alice did not become angry at such clear restatements of John's grievances. "I understand, John. I only wish you'd put your foot down sooner."

Such responses confused and angered him. Years of careful and wearisome effort could not buy his freedom to be himself or to order his life or to have the love of a wife. *Wearing out and demanding that I no longer care should not be the answer*, he thought. So Alice's assurances appeared to John as nothing more than new ways for her to try to accomplish old goals.

Gradually, almost imperceptibly, John began to accept a changed Alice into his life in new ways. The marriage began. It grew. When she now complimented his efforts and gifts he did not really believe her, but he was grateful anyway. John was elated when Alice took it upon herself to gather eggs for sale to others and to save the money. He would not think of suggesting that such things were beneath the dignity of the wife of a college professor. Alice volunteered for benevolent activities and put herself before others in her own light rather than trying to fashion her husband so as to define herself by his light. John watched her grow with a sense of satisfaction. Alice seemed to find meaning and happiness. She belonged to committees and took pleasure in new friendships. In demanding his own freedom, John thought, he had released Alice. He had not planned for that. His plan, his attempts to convince and bring about change through careful reasoning, had stalled the marriage for fifteen years and ten months after their wedding. It would be many years before he would recognize that the painful years were worth the beautiful end.

Conflicts continued, as in all marriages. But John and Alice McMorrow developed a workable relationship that allowed for reasonable dispute. Neither enjoyed conflict. John still struggled to resolve issues through reasoning to some sort of conclusion. Alice still sought to end them by—just ending them. His efforts to reason and her efforts to end them unsolved still did not blend, but mutual effort made marriage manageable.

John had pursued her, at first, too vigorously. When he stopped, Alice pursued him to his own exasperation. They found marriage on the middle ground only when both let go of past grievances.

Still prone to state principles in the ways of life, John vaguely saw parallels involving the beginnings of his marriage and the late war. The war and reconstruction had been a painful process in the South. The government had stepped in and said that slavery would not be tolerated. Decades of compromise accomplished nothing. The South rebelled and there had been a battle of wills in which the government held its ground. Men who had violated the rights of others for their own benefit had been forced to look to their own resources now that slavery had ended and former ways had passed. The slaves were now free and would continue to struggle with freedom's responsibilities, but former plantation owners also struggled with adjustments that would eventually bring on new prosperity. If the changes had come against their will, they were not against their best interests. *Someday,* John thought, *when the nation is completely reunited and mutual agreements have been reached to the benefit of all sections—when the North is finished shouting about past errors and the South no longer hangs its head—maybe the South will look at the North and say, "I only wish you'd put your foot down sooner."*

*   *   *   *

THE INCIDENT AT THE BEE TREE

Andrew McMorrow played in the woods with his brother Aaron. They had been playing at war using sticks for muskets and root balls for artillery shells until something moved in the brush. "It's a snake!" Andrew's stick was then a snake probe instead of a musket. Aaron came up beside him and jiggled the leaves at Andrew's feet with his stick, "There it is!" Andrew jumped back while Aaron laughed and said, "Just kiddin'!"

"What kind is it?" Aaron wanted to know.

"I think it's just a black snake."

Both were disappointed because it's more exciting to go home with tales of having killed a copperhead than to have found and handled a black snake. Their father had taught them the difference between the varieties of snakes. He had taught them to identify all sorts of things. They had learned to distinguish between edible plants and those best left alone. From John's casual instruction his boys could name the trees by their leaves and bark and the uses of each variety. They knew the insects around Harrison County, the constellations—at least most of them—and the sound that a squirrel makes when it skitters on the far side of a tree. They could recite the names of flowers and trace the paths of rivers and mountain ridges on a map of West Virginia. Dates and kings and world events seemed things that everyone likely knew as a matter of course. They had been surprised to learn, as they rapidly made their way through the grades, that other youngsters knew little of these things.

Although Andrew and Aaron were aware that some would consider it childish of them to be playing at war at their ages, fifteen and seventeen, they did not particularly care as long as no one was on hand to draw attention to it. Both boys possessed a sense of self that allowed them let go of inhibitions while exercising a healthy measure of self-control. They felt loved and accepted by both of their parents. If their father loved them more because of who they were and their mother loved them for how they raised her in the eyes of those who admired them, the boys had not mapped out the differences. They felt loved and accepted at home.

"There he goes!" Andrew had seen it first as the snake slithered to the edge of the brush and into a hole in the dirt. Both tried to capture it, but gave up the chase when the tail disappeared before either could reach it.

A squirrel darted from behind a nearby oak and they saw it scurry up a hickory and sit on a limb facing away from the trunk. Then the game of trying to knock it down began. Aaron threw first. The rock struck leaves above the target. The squirrel chattered, waved its gray tail, and faced the trunk. A second chance was a rarity, so Andrew threw his stick like a spear and it skimmed the limb beside the squirrel and the squirrel shot up the tree and out of sight.

Beyond the hickory limb the makeshift spear created another commotion that was even more exciting. A gnarled old oak, dead for years but still standing, had taken a whack beside the entrance to a cavity about 20 feet from the ground. Bees responded—swarming out in great numbers, a moving, buzzing dark cloud at the entrance.

When what they had found became apparent, Andrew shouted, "I claim it."

"You claim what?"

"I claim the bee tree. The rule is that the person who finds the bee tree gets to claim the honey."

"Is that true? What if it's on somebody else's land?"

"Well, I don't know what the actual law about it is, but I've always heard that the finder who claims it first gets the honey. Besides, this is our land." Facing the tree and pointing at the settling bees he made a solemn ceremony of it. "I hereby claim possession of all the honey that rests within this mighty old oak." Even if it was all in fun, the boys were competitive. The bee tree allowed Andrew to claim a win at something. The family would enjoy the honey and he figured that his father would know how to get it out without being stung too badly.

At the supper table the boys told the story. John made a great deal of it. "Tell you what, boys. This is something like squirrel hunting. The one who kills it skins it. Andrew, you'll have to do the chopping. First thing Saturday morning we'll go over and chop the tree down. After things settle down a little we'll dress up and smoke 'em until they settle down some more. Then we'll carry away buckets of honey."

"It'll be my honey." Andrew was playfully asserting his win more than he was really demanding to have it all to himself.

"That's all right," John added to the banter. "You can just plan to get it all by yourself too."

"I'll accept all the help I can get, Daddy, and I'll share with all who dare to battle the bees." Everyone agreed to take part. Alice agreed to do her part in the kitchen after the honey was safely away from the bees and in need of someone to put it in jars.

No one rose particularly early on Saturday morning. At the breakfast table they reviewed the list of items they would need to complete the task. John would gather the straw and the billows for making smoke. Aaron would gather the pails and clean them to his mother's satisfaction. Andrew would collect the bow saw that had belonged to his grandfather. He would leave the axe behind because he had negotiated with Aaron to man the other side. His argument was that chopping would stir up the bees and that sawing would be faster anyway.

As the three McMorrows walked together up the path toward the hollow where the boys had found the bees, they crunched through the autumn leaves with string dangling from their pockets. They would tie off the ends of their pant legs and long sleeves to keep bees from entering at unguarded places. The approaching danger was exciting, if not intense. John had often told the boys that life without risk is not worth much and he had regularly added, "but it is always best to be careful." Secretly, John enjoyed seeing his sons show courage in the face of small potential consequences. It pleased him to know that they would risk a few stings to provide the family with honey that they could well afford to purchase from someone else who had taken the risks. For John, money was not the point. It seldom was.

Then they heard the unmistakable ring of an axe against wood and the dull echo of a thudding axe on a hollow tree. At first no one spoke. Each tried to locate the sound filling fill the woods generally and bouncing off the hillside so that each blow sounded twice. John understood it first.

"Did you boys tell anyone about finding the honey?"

When Andrew and Aaron paused to look at each other John continued, "I'm not saying that you shouldn't have told it. I'm just wondering if you did."

Aaron quit editing how he would answer the question that he had already determined to answer honestly. "I did. I told some fellows at school. None of them would try to beat us out of our honey, but I guess I should have told them to keep it quiet."

"It's nothing to worry about, son. You did nothing wrong. We'll just see what's going on."

As they rounded the hillside they saw a figure swinging an axe at the base of the big tree. They drew closer. Aaron said, "That's John Hawkins. I didn't tell him about it." John McMorrow cringed for reasons the boys could not know. The boy could not be more than 15 years old, but John recalled his own painful experiences with Samuel Hawkins, this boy's father, many years before.

Although he surely could hear the noise of steps in brittle leaves, Hawkins did not look up. He continued chopping while bees swarmed above.

"Hello, young man! How are you this fine morning?" John had no desire to appear threatening.

"Not bad." Hawkins still did not turn to look. Neither of the McMorrow boys spoke. They would leave whatever was about to transpire in the capable hands of their father.

"Would you mind telling me what you're doing?" If the question was abrupt it was at least consistent with the mood produced by the insolence of the silent axe-wielder.

Turning to look at the trio he said, "What does it look like I'm doing, mister? I'm claiming my honey. The rule says that the one who finds it gets to claim it."

Andrew and Aaron were not surprised by John's calm response, but they could sense the firm resolve that held it up. "Well, son, maybe if you would stop what you're doing there for just a few minutes we could have a little talk. There may be some mistake."

"No need for that. I got here first and I have the right to claim the honey and there's nothing you can do about it! I know my rights. You people strut around like peacocks and think you're better than everyone else around here, but you can't cheat me outa my honey. I know my rights."

"Well…," John's voice was even and calm and his sons could hardly believe the generous offer their father made: "I don't know if you are aware that this honey has already been claimed and the claim has been registered with the land-owner—that's me—but I might be willing to talk with the man who has already claimed it—see if he'll be willing to share the honey with you if you settle down and help us get it out." He looked at a wide-eyed Andrew whose brow furrowed before nodding confused approval. "What do you say young man?"

John was stretching beyond the likely to win young Hawkins over by kindness and help him end what seemed a Hawkins family tradition. It amazed him that generations could operate under the same obnoxious habits without gaining a foot forward. When he looked at this steely-eyed, tough-talking, bitter young boy John saw a victim to rescue. His sons saw a tyrant to defeat.

John sensed that he would nurture great evils by walking away and allowing the boy to keep the honey. Doing that would reward behavior that would continue to victimize others. It would empower young Hawkins. It would show John's boys a level of unreasonable passivity that would either handicap them for life if imitated, or cost him their treasured respect—or both.

Hawkins just smiled and said, "Nope."

"Then I'll just ask you to leave."

"Not until I've gotten my honey."

"You'll leave now. If you go without more trouble I'll have no cause to call for the sheriff. If you threaten no harm you'll not be hurt."

Hawkins turned, holding the axe in his right hand with the handle clenched just below the axe head, "Come on. I dare you!"

John looked at his sons. He was uncomfortable, on the one hand, that this thing was playing out as it was. He was pleased on the other that they were gaining another experience together that might prepare them for life beyond their settled home. "Aaron. Andrew and I will stay here with our young friend. I'd appreciate it if you'd run to town and fetch the sheriff. We'll be here when you get back. Don't tell your mother what you're doing. If it's late when you get back, we'll still be here. If you see the doctor you might want to tell him to stand by."

Aaron started trotting down the path.

"Keep yer honey!" Hawkins shouted loud enough for Aaron to hear and turn back. "But I'll tell you what. You are in for a lot of trouble. Big trouble! We have friends. Big friends."

"We'll keep our eyes open," John said to the back of the young boy as he walked away.

To his sons he said softly, "Why don't we go ahead and harvest a little honey."

The McMorrow family sat together in its usual pew at church the next morning. John listened with a discriminating ear to the sermon, which had to do with turning the other cheek and refraining from vengeance. He had been annoyed by the failure of some preachers he had heard in the past to make the fine distinctions that were crucial to a true understanding of the matter. *Jesus*, he thought, *had not required His followers to be entirely passive. He had, Himself, driven the money-changers from the temple and stood up to the hypocritical Pharisees with strong words. In teaching men to refrain from reviling the revilers, He had not taught the kind of placid acquiescence that some seemed to preach about without noticing their own violations of the supposed principle.* The events of the preceding day still forcefully played in the minds of the three McMorrow men as they sat with Alice and listened to a sermon that seemed related. *No,* John thought, *there comes a time when a man must stand up and respond to threatening men. If some preachers can't see the difference between revenge and reasonable resistance to injustice; if small men can preach that it is always wrong to challenge others' claims and then proceed to challenge those who differ with their pronouncements; if they can preach on the one hand that no one ever has the right to defend his life, family, and property, and then turn around and teach that men have an obligation to protect and care for their wives and children, then I will leave them to such fuzzy doctrines.*

This day's sermon did not press the matter into some of the extremes that John had heard before. In fact, it struck a balance that John had long held to be right. The mention of the verse that says, "If it be possible, as much as lieth in you, live peaceably with all men," struck him as timely and appropriate. It was only John's memory of other sermons heard at other times that seemed to rebuke him for what he had done the previous day. This one reminded him to refrain from vengeance, to leave law enforcement to agents of civil government, to live so as not to provoke conflict, and to seek peaceful solutions. He liked it, and was glad that his sons had heard it so soon after the incident at the bee tree.

As was their custom, the McMorrows visited with other families lingering on the lawn after services. Mr. and Mrs. Stone were as pleasant as always. John felt connected to them in ways that others no longer seemed to recall. Years tend to push things into the background at varying rates. John had come to notice that his memory was quite strong, especially for events that touched him profoundly. New Market might as well have been lost a week ago. He could still describe Snicker's Gap as if he had seen it this morning. Fort Gregg seemed so recent that it sometimes intruded into present moments. The smell of gunpowder, a shower of rain, the sound of sucking mud on a shoe, the crack of thunder, and other sensations would pull old events into the moment—whether or not John wished to relive them.

The sight of Mr. and Mrs. Stone often pulled Anna Lee out of John's past and placed her in the present moment. He listened for reports of her well-being without asking directly. Sometimes he casually asked how Micah and Anna Lee and their children were doing, then listened for evidence that she was happy. John felt that no report was full but that any was enough, because it had to be.

He still saw them from time to time. Micah still worked as a gunsmith, making repairs more than manufacturing new rifles. They still lived nearby. They were absent from the church in Clarksburg only because Micah had begun preaching for a small church out in the country. Mr. and Mrs. Stone seemed pleased with the homes their daughters had made with their sons-in-law and their grandchildren.

John McMorrow had developed a reserved, but friendly, relationship with Micah. Anna Lee and Alice remained friends and sometimes visited in town. The two families had visited, several times over the years, in one another's homes. John and Micah respected one another. Anna Lee and Alice liked one another. A general sense of trust enveloped the four of them. Propriety had muffled expression of what remained of the friendship that yet belonged to John and Anna Lee alone. The sentiment remained real, but surrounded by the general friendship of the two families. John had been tempted to probe it, at the time when he had put his foot down and before his own marriage had begun, but he sensed a danger for both himself and Anna Lee and the others and that had kept him silent. Now that he and Alice had stumbled upon a healthy, loving, trusting marriage, he sometimes wondered about the status of the old contract with Anna Lee.

Mr. and Mrs. Stone stood beneath the tree in front of the church building and spoke proudly of thriving grandchildren. John silently shared in their joy as though he were a participant.

CHAPTER 16

I ALMOST THOUGHT I WAS TOO LATE

Alice heard it first and woke John. "Wake up, Sweetheart. Wake up."

Still groggy—it was past midnight—John asked, "What? What's going on?"

"Something's going on outside!"

John heard the sounds. Chickens clucked from their roosts. Horses moved restlessly in the corral. Hogs grunted.

"I'll go check on it, darling. I figure it's just a fox or possum or something." He picked up the shotgun, put on his boots, and started down the stairs.

As he approached the front door he noticed a strange dancing glow on the glass. Still, he sensed no danger now that he was awake and oriented to the present with war in the past and men living in peace. He opened the door.

"Drop that gun!" a vaguely familiar voice commanded from atop a horse. John looked up to see five men sitting on horses holding blazing torches. They all wore white sheets with white hoods covering their faces and little holes cut for the eyes. Only gun belts and holsters stood out in contrast to the white cloth.

In his astonishment John cradled the shotgun and asked, "Who's talking?"

"Never mind. Drop that gun!" Then John recognized the voice. It was Samuel Hawkins.

"What's this all about?" John asked as he continued to cradle the shotgun with the muzzle pointed at the sky to his left.

"You insulted and stole from one of our number—or from one known to us— who had made rightful claim to the honey tree. We are not here to take back the stolen honey. We've come to warn you and to teach you a lesson." Hawkins' voice had a lordly air about it. He obviously felt powerful in his strange clothing in the middle of the night.

"Why don't you take off that mask and let's talk about it?" John asked. "I'm not used to talking about matters like this in the middle of the night. I'm sure not used to talking to bed sheets."

By now Andrew and Aaron had awakened and convinced their terrified mother to stay in her room. They quietly loaded their rifles, John had the only shotgun, and the boys moved to a window where Andrew watched and whispered his reports to Aaron. "If anything starts to happen, I'll open this window and we'll shoot whoever has a gun out. Okay?" His heart was beating fast and his chest heaved with labored breaths. He knew he would have a challenge holding a bead on anything, but he fully intended to shoot whoever might make a play for a gun. Andrew hoped his brother could do the same.

John kept up a brave front, but his own heart raced like those of his sons. The situation looked hopeless and he was about to conclude that death might take him on his own doorstep in peace time after missing him on the field of battle. He made no move to put down the shotgun. He would see what might be done with words.

"For all I know, the law might be on your side. This seems to me like a thing for the courts to decide. I don't think I've stolen any honey, but even if I have, this seems like pretty heavy artillery to bring out over such a small thing as this."

"This is not about honey!" thundered Hawkins. "You parade around town like you think you're better'n all the rest of us. You went off to school and came back here thinkin' you're some kind of big man in town. You betrayed your state and went off to fight against true Virginians and put on your fancy officer clothes until you had people thinkin' you're some great man. You trot out your little perfect boys an' set people to talkin' about what a great big man you are. You're nothing! Then you have the gall to steal honey from a boy who claimed it fair and square."

"Like I said," John started, "there's the law and…"

"Silence!"

John stopped while Hawkins held out his hand with the palm facing John and shouted the order with affected dignity. "You might as well get used to the fact that we—the Klan—are still a force in this country. We have eyes everywhere and we'll enforce the laws that need enforcin'!"

The boys sat by the window, terrified. They feared to move lest they provoke some danger. They feared to remain still lest they lose the chance to avert it. The whispers helped them feel they were doing all they could. Andrew's breath and heart had slowed—just as they had after he had learned to steady himself to shoot a buck. He was now fairly sure he could get off a clean shot if needed. He hoped that he could get it off in time to save rather than to avenge his father's life. At that moment he did not worry about the fine distinctions. Neither did Aaron.

Horses shuffled as Hawkins launched into a loud and disconnected harangue about states rights, self-rule, Yankee law, and John McMorrow's long history of persecuting common folks by parading his highfalutin' ways all over town and acting uppity. He concluded with what sounded like the passing of a judge's sentence: "And since you have been duly warned and you have shown no signs of altering your ways or of humbling yourself before the Klan, we shall teach you a lesson you'll not soon forget!"

As Hawkins reached for his revolver a shot rang out and a window flew open behind John. "Nobody move!" Someone shouted. No one seemed to know who had been ordered to remain still or by whom the order had been shouted. John could not tell where the shot had come from. He was relieved that he had not been hit. From the window the boys were just as puzzled—and still terrified.

John's eyes followed the muzzle of the shotgun in his hands as he cocked it and pointed it at Hawkins. Hawkins dropped his torch to the ground from his left hand to grab his right hand. Other sheeted horsemen started to reach for guns when several voices shouted in unison, "Don't move!" They stopped. Two rifle barrels trained on them from the window. They could not detect that one of them was wobbling horribly. A loaded shotgun covered them from the porch. Hawkins held his hands to his chest. Flickering torch light revealed a growing stream of red down the front of his garment.

Within seconds it was clear to John that, incredibly, their midnight visitors had been subdued. "Who fired that shot?" John wanted to know, grateful that it had been fired but amazed that it had picked off a moving hand in nothing but flickering torch light. "Not me," said Andrew. "Not me," squeaked Aaron. A shaking feminine voice came from the slight opening in the other window from John's bedroom and said, "Not me either," as John noticed a quivering derringer that he had forgotten he owned in the tender hand of his good wife.

The henhouse door thumped open. Micah Johnson stepped out. "Sorry, John. I didn't make it in time to warn you. I got here just seconds before they did."

John could hardly believe it or understand. It made no sense. Micah walked to the porch, keeping his muzzle on the night riders. He explained that he had just heard the rumor that John was to receive this visit. "One thing about these fellows," Micah said, "they love to talk. Two of 'em were talking in front of the shop just a few hours ago. I got here just as soon as I could. I alerted the sheriff but didn't wait around. He told me to wait for him to get help, but that didn't seem like the thing to do. I was going to warn you and see if I could help out. I almost thought I was too late."

Stunned and numb, John smiled and said, "No, Micah. I'd say you made it just in time." In that moment two manly hearts were joined by chains that can only be forged by shared danger. Micah shed the last vestige of shame for not having served as a soldier. John looked at Micah. He saw a man who had charged to the front in spite of orders to the contrary. In John's eyes, Micah was the 12th West Virginia at Fort Gregg—not at New Market.

Looking at the riders, John said: "Boys. While we wait for the sheriff I think it might be a good idea for you to drop those gun belts and take off those masks. I'd appreciate your removing them slowly, if you don't mind."

✳   ✳   ✳   ✳

SETTLED SENSE OF ENDURING WARMTH

"That was an absolutely perfect dinner," Anna Lee said to Alice as she pulled her napkin from her lap and placed it alongside her plate. "I don't know how you did it after all you went through last night."

"The truth is," Alice said, "I had to keep my hands busy today or I'd have gone mad."

Everyone around the table was having a wonderful time and all were glad that the Johnsons had come to dine with the McMorrows on the day following the encounter with the Klan out front. Extinguished torches still lay in the dirt. No one seem inclined to pick them up just yet. Andrew made eyes at—and stammered when he tried to talk to—Anna Lee's second daughter. The young lady seemed perfectly confident and composed. From all appearances she enjoyed the attention. In fact she was deciding whether or not to reciprocate. She kept herself pleasantly indifferent in the process.

Anna Lee detected that things had changed in this household since the last time she had been here a few years ago. Things were less perfect, but better because of it. The house was well-kept, but generally less immaculate than before. Maybe it was due to the events of the night before, but Anna Lee doubted that this was the only cause for the sense of relaxed happiness that now filled this home. She wanted to speak of it, but she knew the rules prevented such talk. John's smile seemed incredibly genuine. Alice smiled less often than before, but with sincere intensity.

Micah seemed more relaxed too. A place had opened in this otherwise bewildering circle. He had stepped in to fill it. It had always been there but he had not seen it until now. He looked John in the eye now when he spoke and saw his equal. He saw no threat. He felt no distrust. He saw no competition, even though he could sense the enduring bond between this upright man and his trusted Anna Lee. Somehow it all seemed proper when he sat at this table as an peer and watched John's eyes meet Alice's gaze and speak of committed devotion. Even Micah could see that this was different and better than what he had seen here before.

As they shuffled into the front room, John poked at the fire and sat down beside Alice on the couch. They talked of the events they had shared here the night before. John could recall every episode as though it had just happened. Alice detailed everything she could remember and raised quite a laugh when she told of pointing the empty derringer out the window in the hope that it would scare the Klansmen. Andrew had his version and Aaron corrected some of the small details along the way. Micah traced his part from the moment he heard the hooligans talking just a few feet away from his workbench on the other side of the boarded wall. Anna Lee openly spoke of the anger she had first felt when Micah did not come home for supper, and then of the concern that grew into fear—and then of the cycle of relief and then renewed fear after he returned home so late when he recounted the events that had kept him away. She was proud of him, proud of John, and proud of the conduct of all the McMorrows. She regretted, jokingly—now that it was safe—that she had not been there with an empty derringer to frighten away the night raiders.

It warmed John to see Alice enjoying the joke that might have humiliated her only a year before. It amazed him that Anna Lee instinctively knew she could pull it off without damage. As he looked around at his guests sitting before the fire he thought of the countless times he had shared such post-battle reviews around fires with animated men working to make sense of senseless conflict.

He excused himself to go check on the animals before dark and to make sure the barn door was closed. On his way back to the house he paused at the rail fence and looked at the vast spread of orange clouds to the west. The sun hung over the ridge, a ball of orange half exposed but uncommonly bright. Trees stood starkly silhouetted against it in one of those rare and fleeting landscapes that only God can paint. *No canvas could capture that,* John thought. *No word could describe it.* He put his right foot on the lower rail and leaned against the top on folded arms. The sweet smells of autumn leaves and farm blended with the textures of rough wood and warm breezes and the distant sounds of young laughter. *When we wait and attune ourselves, when we hold on and look ahead,* he thought, *moments like this, when heaven smiles, come to us unforeseen.*

He felt the warmth of a tender hand on his shoulder. He was not startled to hear Anna Lee's voice softly say, "That's the most beautiful sunset I've seen." Before turning he expanded his thought: *and just when we think that God's canvas is full—that nothing could make it more complete—we are granted the privilege of yet greater beauty.* Anna Lee leaned against the rough rail to his right with folded arms. Her right hand rested on John's arm. She spoke.

"When Micah came home in the middle of the night and started explaining what had happened, I felt that we were back to the days when you were in the war. I was horrified to think of the dangers to you and Alice and the boys. It was just like I was scanning the papers for your name when Micah was telling the story, and I got him to tell me the end before filling in the details. The relief I felt when he told me you'd made it through was just exactly like what I felt when I learned, back then, that you were still well. I remember that I tried to write to you about my feelings just before the end of the war. Do you remember the letter?"

"I still have that letter, Anna Lee. It meant, it means, more to me that you may ever know."

She squeezed his arm. "I remember it well, John. I meant every word of it. It's still good."

Alice and Micah and the children all came to the fence, drawn by the sunset and the loved ones waiting to share it. Alice stood to John's left. She put her arm around his shoulder. Micah was at Anna Lee's right with his arm about her waist. Anna Lee's hand stayed. John's left hand patted it gently. He caressed Alice's left hand with his right. The young ones came alongside on both sides of the line and leaned against the rails—a pure symmetry of size, sound, and spirit.

As the sun tucked itself behind the magnificent, rugged mountains of West Virginia, this company of friends took in its fading orange glow. Faces reflected the sun's waning light while hearts held onto a more settled sense of enduring warmth. In that moment, always thereafter present in his memory, John McMorrow, like the bubble in his father's old level, found his center.

The End

Note to the Reader

This story explores the experience of the Civil War from the perspective of those who endured it. It is reasonable to suppose that thousands of real men and women dealt with issues much like those of our fictional characters. The challenges confronting John McMorrow, Anna Lee Stone, and Micah Johnson certainly tested many of those who braced themselves against the winds of the Civil War, regardless of how the real actors resolved those trials.

War is much more than hard marching and battles. It is countless separations, losses, and moral dilemmas. War is disrupted life and redirected goals for those who fight and for those who go on with life at home. Other works give close details of battles and troop movements. I have not attempted to compete with such works or to resolve perennial debates about doubtful aspects of specific engagements.

I have made choices regarding discrepancies in historical accounts, but the broad outline of events is accurate. The 12th West Virginia Infantry pressed one of its own, William Hewitt, to compile a history of the unit. Hewitt invited all former comrades to submit material for the work, which was published in 1892. This is my chief source for the history of the regiment. Events recalled by soldiers in the unit seemed worthy of inclusion, even when they have been impossible to authenticate elsewhere. If one discredits Hewitt's account and suggests that there is no evidence that some specific event actually transpired, another might reasonably respond by saying that Hewitt's account is evidence that it happened. Hewitt wrote with full awareness that his fellow soldiers, who were present for those events, would read his work closely. While an individual might enlarge upon his own war experiences when retelling them to children at home, I have assumed that the discriminating eyes of the surviving regiment gave Hewitt strong incentive to attempt to be accurate. On the other hand, it is likely that fading memory caused some of the events to become confused with others, and that apocryphal tales found their way into his history. I approached Hewitt's regimental history with the belief that there was at least a grain of truth in reports unique to his material.

When official records appear to conflict with the regimental history, I have sometimes given preference to official records. In some cases I have combined the accounts or omitted one account or the other. I sometimes included what seemed most likely, and often what was most colorful.

I deliberately refrained from placing thoughts in the minds and words in the mouths of authenitic historical characters. With few exceptions the words in the mouths of such characters are drawn from credible sources.

Micah Johnson and his evolution from private gunsmith to government contractor are fictions. While it is true that sharpshooter rifles, much more accurate than the standard weapons carried by the common soldier, were produced by such men, there is no reason to believe that such rifles were produced in Grafton during the war. The methods of production and descriptions of hardware are accurate.

Portrayals of the attitudes and issues of the day through John's classroom lecture, the debate, diary entries, campfire discussions, and internal musings are offered as interpretations. Surviving literature from the period will show that living men and women had views similar to those of our fictional players.

Foraging, and other crimes against Confederate citizens, were widespread during the war. I have presented the moral quandaries of soldiers without endorsing or condemning their behavior through the fictional narrative. Real men foraged and destroyed the property of private citizens during the war. John's anger, which he turned toward Rebels after experiencing the loss of Anna Lee, might well reflect one of the many mental mechanisms that rationalized such behavior. Men committed atrocities on both sides. Therefore, men struggled with conscience. That Union soldiers chose to believe that Rebel citizens hid munitions in haystacks, and other such things, does not mean that Confederate civilians did such things. Men in the 12th believed those rumors, according to Hewitt.

The tendency to attribute high moral principles to ones own behavior, and to regard the enemy as ugly, badly motivated, and dishonorable is nearly universal. Depictions, in *The Reunion*, of Union soldiers attempting to substantiate that view should not influence the reader to assume that those soldiers were correct.

The references to tensions in the church at Grafton reflect actual controversies of the time. There is no clear basis in fact for placing those conflicts, specifically, among the churches at Grafton or Clarksburg. The general objection to the

American Christian Missionary Society's War Resolutions, and the basis for it, is accurate.

There are some, apparently irreconcilable, discrepancies in the record of the capture and eventual hanging of Confederate Captain Andrew T. Leopold. Hewitt's regimental history calls him "Lapole" and refers to him as a "guerrilla" leader (suggesting that he was not a part of the regular Confederate forces). The official record has (for April 29, 1863):

> Lieutenant Wyckoff, First New York Cavalry, Lieutenants Powell and Means, and 40 men of the Twelfth [West] Virginia Infantry, crossed the Shenandoah by twos, in a skiff at midnight, and captured the chief "Leopold" and 6 of his confederates.

General Milroy sent a dispatch to General Robert C. Schenck on April 26, 1863 saying: "I think it would be best to turn Leopold over to the civil authorities of Maryland. Shall I do so?"

The Confederate Compiled Service Record for Andrew T. Leopold suggests that he was private soldier in the 12th Virginia Cavalry, captured at Shepherdstown on November 28, 1862, and hanged at Fort McHenry on May 25, 1863. It seems possible that he was captured more than once, that Union reports of his April, 1863 capture are mistaken regarding the actual date, and that Union officials did not consider him to be a regular Confederate soldier. "Guerrillas" were not afforded the same rights as regulars, so this would possibly account for the hanging.

The account of the 12th's retreat from Winchester, separated from the larger force, is given in Hewitt's account but not otherwise documented. The account of Confederate Cavalry blocking their route into the mountains, and the struggle to break out of the Rebel ring is likely exaggerated. There were no reported losses to the 12th at that place and time. The story of the mountain maid coming to the aid of the regiment comes from Hewitt's account.

John McMorrow's defense of Milroy is not to suggest that the general had, in fact, demonstrated qualities worthy of such. Historians do not give Milroy credit for outstanding generalship, and this work of fiction is not intended to do so. But John, in this story, exhibits a fairly common phenomenon among soldiers. Unless a man in the ranks has personal reasons for thinking otherwise, he gives preference his own officers and his own unit. The opinions of officials in Washington seem distant and removed. John was present and held to his own, eye-witness, point of view about Milroy.

The quotation marks around "the Honorable" in the reference to Charles James Faulkner, while the 12th was camped on his property near Martinsburg, are not to suggest that Mr. Faulkner was, in fact, a dishonorable man. The quotation marks merely suggest that the men then camping on his lawn might have been cynical in their use of the title for him at that point in time. In fact, the people of western Virginia had elected Mr. Faulkner to the U.S. House of Representatives four times before the war. After the war, the citizens of West Virginia would elect him to the U.S. Congress. This speaks well of the man, and this work of fiction should take nothing away from the man's true honor.

The capture of the regiment of South Carolinians cannot be documented apart from Hewitt's account of it. We might reasonably assume that it was a story current among the men at the time. Its mention in this work of fiction should not be taken as an argument in favor of its historicity. South Carolina troops in the Valley, at the time of this alleged event, reported no action of any kind on the date cited.

Robert E. Lee was not responsible for what became of prisoners after his forces turned them over to authorities. Many, on both sides, seem to have believed that he was. In a letter to Mrs. Jefferson Davis, dated February 23, 1866, Lee wrote:

> As regards the treatment of the Andersonville prisoners, to which you allude, I know nothing and can say nothing of my own knowledge. I never had anything to do with any prisoners, except to send those taken on the fields, where I was engaged, to the Provost Marshal General at Richmond.[1]

That John McMorrow entertained unpleasant thoughts of Lee while still at Appomatox Court House should not influence the reader to adopt John's views. In fact, John McMorrow's opinion was not shared by all members of the regiment at the time. Alexander Neil, surgeon for the regiment, wrote home from Appomattox Court House, on April 10, 1865:

> I was at the House in Appomattox when Genl. Lee & our Generals had the conference. I saw the great Lee. His head as white as snow, about 60 yrs of age & dressed in fine grey with a white hat & feather, rides an iron grey horse. He is a handsome man and looks like a Statesman. Poor Robert, had to be humiliated; still we recognize him as a great general.[2]

---

1. Captain Robert E. Lee, comp., Recollections and Letters of General Robert E. Lee (NY: Konecky & Konecky, n.d.), p. 224.

The original Ku Klux Klan had disbanded prior to the time of the events portraying their activities in this story. The Klan would revive in the early twentieth century and become active in central West Virginia. Fictional license allows a group of local thugs (former and prospective Klansmen) to don old bed sheets and terrorize John's family during the interim. In fact, there is little reason to believe the Klan was active in central West Virginia, or elsewhere, during the period. The story is based upon an anecdote shared by a relative who heard it from an elderly lady. The incident regarding the bee tree and the Klan visit allegedly involved my great-grandfather, Edmund Jasper Smith.

---

2. Richard R. Duncan, ed., <u>Alexander Neil and the Last Shenandoah Valley Campaign</u> (Shippensburg, PA: White Mane Publishing Company, Inc., 1996), p. 98.

Tim Nichols

Route 1, Box 206A

Burlington, West Virginia 26710

(304) 289-5011

978-0-595-34948-7
0-595-34948-X